DISCARD

Jayce 4/95
Bob/95
29-10/95
AⅡ 11/99

Binding Glued 02/00 MP

LM 10/13
A1-1/14
A-3/14

MAR -- 1995

THE LAST HEIRESS

Portway Large Print

Published by us ~
chosen by you

She waited. Perhaps he would say that he had always loved her secretly, but never spoke of it so that she would be free if she fell really in love with someone else. If he would only say he loved her, everything could still be all right. She would be grateful, and out of that gratitude real affection would grow.

He took the case with the ring from his inner pocket. He opened it, took out the ring. He advanced a little so as to take her hand, which hung limply at her side. He raised it, and waited for her to separate her third finger to receive the ring, which he guided towards it.

She snatched her hand away.

'No! No, I can't! I can't'

Utter astonishment struck him speechless. The ring was knocked from his hand to lie sparkling in the Turkey-red carpet.

He stared at Nora. Tears were pouring down her cheeks. She shook her head vehemently. 'I'm sorry, Edmond. I know I'm . . . I just *can't*!'

THE LAST HEIRESS

TESSA BARCLAY

A Portway Large Print Book

PUBLISHED BY

Remploy Press, Halifax

First published in 1987
by
W. H. Allen & Co. (p.l.c.)

© Tessa Barclay 1987

Published in large print 1993
by arrangement with
Darley Anderson Books

ISBN 0 7066 1020 2

Typeset and Printed by
Page Bros, Norwich
Bound by Remploy Ltd
Halifax

ONE

There wasn't the slightest doubt, something was dreadfully wrong. Madame Presle didn't even bother to say 'Good morning' before she was urging Nora to drink up her coffee like a good girl and be ready to start for school.

'But I'm not late, Madame Presle—'

'I know that, but just be quick about breakfast. Jacques is waiting to drive you at once. I'll pack a few things while you eat.'

'Pack? What for?'

The housekeeper hesitated at the door of the breakfast room. She'd expected Monsieur Auduron-Tramont to be here to explain to the child. But of course, he'd wanted to stay at the hospital. It was only natural, while Madame was in such danger.

She looked back at the thin, pale face peering at her over the porcelain coffee-cup. Best to make light of it, pretend the whole thing was a treat. 'You're going to board at school for a day or two—isn't that nice?' she coaxed in her light, Parisian voice.

'Board? But Cousin Gaby always says no when I suggest—'

'Well, things are different for the moment, dear. Quick now, eat up your roll, put plenty of

1

honey on it, honey is good for you. I'll bring down your overnight bag—'

'I need my gym shoes today,' Nora put in, her eleven-year-old brain ticking over with the precision of a watch. Staying overnight at school . . . And Cousin Gaby not down to breakfast, and not even Cousin Marc to explain what it all meant. 'Madame Presle!'

The housekeeper intended to hurry on through the hall, but there was enough command in that young voice—the voice of the future mistress of the estates—to bring her reluctantly back. 'Yes, Mademoiselle?'

'What's the matter? Where are my Relatives?'

The term was the one they had decided they must use of themselves, her two grown-up cousins who were all she had in the world by way of family. It saved trouble when explaining themselves to new acquaintances: 'Monsieur and Madame Auduron-Tramont are relatives of the late Madame de la Sebiq-Tramont, Nora's mother.' They were her guardians, her friends, her only bulwark against the great loneliness that sometimes threatened to engulf her.

Everyone else had gone in the War. Mama . . . She could scarcely remember her now, lost somewhere on the road from Epernay in the first big push of the German invasion of 1914. Lost . . . Yes, lost for ever. One moment with her, the next vanished in a maelstrom of movement and smoke and noise and terror.

Then there had been the bewilderment of being alone on the great highway. Sometimes in dreams she felt again the shuddering sobs that had engulfed her then. She'd wake up, threshing about in bed, terrified, shaking. Then relief would flood through her as the nightmare faded. That was all in the past. Mama was gone, but she had the Relatives.

The kindness of a small family heading for the south had saved her from being lost without trace in the retreat from the Marne. They had taken her aboard their laden farm cart, tried to get her to eat a morsel of food, tried to find out through the barrier of her stricken bewilderment who she was, where her parents were. 'Clearly well-brought-up,' the wife had murmured. 'Look at her clothes, that's real silk, Pierre.'

Weeks went by, she was told—to her it had seemed like an eternity. Then she was traced through the protracted routines of the Red Cross and sent to a distant connection of her dead Papa's, in Touraine. The well-meaning officials had nodded their heads over her. 'Tours is safe, surely it'll remain safe, the Boches will never get that far . . .' Safety, that was what they wanted to give her. But it wasn't what she wanted, what she needed.

She'd asked—begged—to be allowed to go back to Mama or Grandmama, but was always put off. 'It's not a good time, dear. There's a war on.' At last, one dreadful day, the truth came out. Cousin Cecile, unaccustomed to handling a little girl, had thought she would get peace and quiet if she told her the facts. Mama and Grandmama were dead. The great house near Rheims had been in the hands of the enemy for a time. Great-Uncle Robert was back there now, however, struggling to make champagne under the very guns of the German front line.

'So you see you must be a good child, Nora, because France is at war, and we must all do our duty.'

News of the family was sparse. Only later did Nora understand that things had been kept from her, 'for her own good'. She lived for a long time in secret fear and confusion but trying to 'do her duty' as it was laid out for her by her aged guardian—be quiet and obedient, do her school work and the household tasks thought suitable, never understanding how her life could be so changed without warning.

It dawned on her that she was expected to wait—to do nothing, simply endure and wait. That was her duty in the long war that was draining away the life-blood of France.

Birthday presents came, and occasional short letters. Uncle Robert sent his love and hoped she was being a good girl. Cousin Gaby made her a present of a pretty party dress, but it was a size too big. In her round schoolgirl hand, Nora wrote back to these strangers, these voices speaking from so far away of home and family and the precious things that were gone.

One day, one day, someone would reclaim her. Oh, Cousin Cecile wasn't unkind, but she was old, she liked tranquillity and order in her little house, she had no point of contact with a six-year-old child. Nora learned to be quiet and tidy, to play games with her doll in a far corner of the little garden, not to invite noisy schoolfellows to tea. She went to the local school, worked hard at her lessons, wore the dowdy little frocks that the old lady chose for her, and waited.

One day her patience was rewarded. A gentleman and a lady came to Tours. They said they were her cousins, her Relatives, all that remained of the great family of the Tramonts, and one of the pair, as he smilingly pointed out, was only a Tramont by adoption.

Nora loved them with a fierce but concealed love. It wasn't that she wanted to seem cool towards them—it was simply that she didn't know how to express her feelings. With Mama and the grandparents, she seemed to remember, there had been kisses and hugs and little endearments. But they had disappeared, those people to whom she'd been so open and trusting. And then there had been old Cousin Cecile, who seemed not to know any warmer term than 'my dear', a phrase she used to her elderly friends and the maidservant. So something in Nora had dried up, and that was good, because it kept her

5

safe from the hazard, the *mistake*, of showing her feelings too much. People you loved went away, and left you lonely.

The housekeeper, looking now at that quietly perplexed face, was debating with herself what to tell Mademoiselle. The master had said the child wasn't to be upset, which was understandable, for she was so quiet and self-controlled that you felt the slightest knock might break her in pieces.

'Madame isn't quite well this morning,' she said after a hesitation. 'Monsieur feels—'

'Is the doctor here?'

'He's been.' My God, yes. Two in the morning, while the child was as deeply asleep as only children can be. Servants flying up and downstairs in an attempt to save Madame's baby, the ambulance creeping in under the *porte-cochère*, the attendants carrying her with infinite care down the wide staircase.

'Don't make a noise, we mustn't wake Nora,' Madame had muttered through teeth clenched against the pain of the baby's desperate attempt to come too early into the world. Typical, that was, thought Madame Presle. Madame would do anything to save the little girl from anxiety.

Mademoiselle Nora was so wrapped up in the thought of having a 'little brother' to play with. It was one of the few things that would bring a bright smile to that pale face.

'It's nothing, Mademoiselle,' lied Madame

Presle. 'You know, when ladies are expecting babies, they have days when they don't feel well.'

'Oh yes, Cousin Gaby explained that. But I still don't see why I have to—'

'It's just for a day or two,' said Madame Presle. 'Just to let Madame have a good rest.' Just to hide from you, in fact, that she's been rushed to hospital and is fighting for her life.

'But I wouldn't be a nuisance to her,' begged Nora, putting her coffee cup down with unusual carelessness. She almost put her hands together to plead her case. She didn't want to go as a boarder, not now, when something serious seemed to be wrong. Normally, to be allowed to stay overnight at school with her fellow-pupils would have pleased her, but Cousin Gaby had always refused. And now suddenly it was all right for her to stay at school, and she felt, she *knew* it meant crisis in the Tramont household.

'Of course you're not, Mademoiselle,' agreed the housekeeper. 'You're never a nuisance.' No, on the contrary. Unnaturally quiet and obedient—quite unlike the two rascals Madame Presle had raised and launched into the world. 'But it's nothing to do with you,' she went on. 'It's just that Monsieur feels . . . He thought that . . . Well, Monsieur's decided you'd be better off at school for a day or two, while Madame has a really good rest.'

Impossible to argue against the wishes of Cousin Marc. Whatever he commanded must be

7

right. Nora sat back in her chair and nodded. She didn't even sigh in protest. Madame Presle, hurrying out to pack her night-dress and tooth-brush, sighed for her. Poor little chick, poor motherless child . . . Madame Tramont loved her like her own daughter, more, perhaps. And Monsieur worshipped the ground the child trod upon. But who understood her?

When Nora went out to the courtyard, the old Delage was waiting under the patched-up *porte-cochère*. The door to the passenger seat besides Jacques was open—she and Jacques had an agreement that he would always let her ride beside him when they were alone together.

Usually he was full of quips and absurd riddles that he made up himself. 'Whose socks have the largest holes in them?' 'I don't know, whose socks have the largest holes?' 'The man whose wife hates him most.' Ha ha. 'What's the dif-ferences between champagne and licorice?' 'I don't know, Jacques.' 'Good heavens, if you don't know that, what good are you to one of the greatest champagne families in France?' Ha ha.

Today there were no jokes. 'All right, eh, minnow?'

She shrugged. 'I'm to stay over at school, Jacques. They won't tell me why.'

'Nothing much, I shouldn't think.' He had been warned to say nothing. Mademoiselle mustn't be upset.

But it was something serious. She could feel it in her bones. Why wouldn't they tell her? It was as she thought—you couldn't be too careful over people you loved. Something was sure to go wrong.

The school was in Rheims, about fifteen minutes' drive away. Jacques had told her that his grandmother remembered the day when it took four hours for common people to get to market in the city, on the great lumbering carrier's wagon, and that was on good days. On bad days, when the weather had wrecked the country roads yet again, it might take twice as long if the wagon got bogged down in the heavy chalk.

But since the end of the Great War, money had been poured out by the government to restore the devastation in this front line region. Two years of work had done much to give the population the means to earn its living again. Of course there was still a huge task ahead. The vines of Champagne had been blasted by the howitzers, ground into the soil by army lorries and later by tanks, uprooted by trench-digging, and as if that weren't enough, ravaged by that old and dreaded enemy phylloxera. Houses, whole villages, wine bottling plant, presses, every-thing—all wrecked, and the country folk either forced to shelter in the great old chalk cellars or evacuated so that the army could manoeuvre.

Now the roads had been not only repaired but

greatly improved. The railway lines had been restored, riverbank quays had been rebuilt, money had been made available for house building.

When Gaby and Marc Auduron-Tarmont first brought Nora to Calmady, the Villa Tramont had been almost a ruin. Only one wing still had a roof but even in that, all the windows were gone and the rooms had been used for temporary billets in the lulls between attacks, for snipers' posts and look-outs. The lawns and flowerbeds were a sea of chalky mud, the buildings in which the business of making champagne were carried on were a shambles.

Money poured in from the government but Monsieur and Madame Tramont had preferred to use it for rebuilding the works. The house took second place. Even now, two years after the end of hostilities, only that one wing was liveable.

At first Nora had been frightened by it—the grey shards of what had once been a great house in the midst of the wreckage of a great industry. The vines here lay about untended, quite unlike those she'd seen in Touraine. The contrast was terrifying.

She had clutched Marc's hand. 'Oh . . . Cousin Marc . . . When you said we had to rebuild, I thought . . . I thought . . .'

She'd seen it in something like the terms of a child using building blocks to erect a series of

10

houses, a village, placing little wooden animals to make a farm, toy bushes to make a garden. This was something quite different. The task of clearing up before they could even start again was enormous—it had seemed to her, insuperable.

Yet after two years the Delage was rolling smoothly along well-made roads. On either side, the vines were once more in tidy rows. The tiny grapes hung on the horizontally-wired branches, with the glow of the June sun upon them, making their skins look almost white because of the waxy coating they were developing. Workers were moving gently between the rows tying up the shoots so that they would bear the weight when the bunches grew heavy in August. There were about a score of shoots on each plant. The work was back-breaking, but the grapes shone among the carefully-trained leaves, pale yet somehow strong and vibrant.

'Looks pretty good, eh?' remarked Jacques, seeing her eyes rest on the vines. 'The pest doesn't seem to have done too much damage.'

'The pest' was phylloxera, that wickedly damaging disease brought by the aphid which ate the roots of the vines. Slowly it had spread all over Europe, and slowly the wine-makers had learned how to combat it. There was only one way—the precious grape must be grafted on to rough, wild stock which was immune to the predations of the insect.

Just before 1914 the great wine-makers had

begun to replace native stock with grafted vines. They had done all they could to make the grafted plants available to the small growers too. But the process was slow and the cost was high.

Then came four years of war, when the vineyards had had to be neglected as the male workers were called to the colours. The women and old men had done their best, and to their eternal credit some wine at least was made every year in the face of enormous difficulties. Even in Champagne, with the front line ranging through the actual vineyards, with shells going overhead and snipers ready to take aim from clock towers and belfries, the workers had crept out to tend the grapes.

But phylloxera had gained a hold again. This was an added expense. Conferences had had to be held to decide in what order to begin on the restoration of the wine-making, and the replacing of the European roots had taken precedence. Now, at last, for this first time, the vineyards belonging to the House of Tramont were completely replanted. This was the first full harvest from undamaged vines, and all looked well—the fragrant Pinot grapes growing well on the American roots. It might be a good vintage, one of those that would help to put money back into the coffers but, more important, would give prestige to the name of Tramont.

To be known to be at work again, and making good champagne—that was the prime target of

Cousin Gaby. In her hands lay the fortunes of the House of Tramont. Or at least, in hers and in Nora's. It always made Nora shiver a little when Cousin Gaby reminded her of that. She and Gaby . . . They were all that remained of the family. To Nora would come all the shares in the firm that had belonged to Mama and Grandmama and Uncle Robert and Pierre and David . . .

For they were all gone, all swept away in the tide of the Great War, lost even more completely than the house and the winefields. For the house could be rebuilt, the winefields replanted and reanimated, but the dead were gone for ever.

'Here, what's this?' cried Jacques. 'Tears? What's wrong, minnow?'

'I don't know,' she whispered, her throat closing up under the emotion that was overwhelming her. 'I just feel . . . sad.'

'Nothing to be sad about,' Jacques insisted, though he knew it wasn't true. 'What? With a lovely little holiday ahead of you, a few days with all your schoolfriends, little confabs after lights out, all that sort of stuff? You'll enjoy yourself a treat.'

'Yes, of course.' She blinked back the tears, sat up straighter in the seat. They were approaching the outskirts of Rheims. Jacques slowed for the policeman directing traffic, for people were coming away from market with produce for the outlying villages and there was a muddle of lorries and trucks and horsedrawn vans. 'Jacques,' she ventured.

'Yes?' He frowned. His attention was on the traffic.

'Cousin Gaby isn't going to die, is she?'

He was startled. He turned his head, his eyes shadowed by his chauffeur's cap but his mouth parted in a gasp of dismay.

'Of course not! What put such a thing in your mind?'

'Then why are they sending me away?'

He gave a little jerk of the head, to tell her he had to attend to the policeman and his waving baton. While he manoeuvred past the intersection, while his main attention was on his driving, the secondary thread was what to say to the little 'un. He could see she was scared to the roots of her boots. Damn nonsense, keeping her in the dark. She was no fool, she knew things were bad.

By the time he had been waved past into the avenue, he had made up his mind. 'Listen, sparrow, I'll tell you, but you've got to promise not to say I told you.'

'I promise.'

'Cross your heart?'

'Cross my heart with a silver dagger.' She made the motions of crossing her heart over the fine grey cotton of her summer school dress.

'Well, then, what I hear is, the baby's in danger.'

'Oh, no!'

'They don't say much to me—a mere man, you know.' He brushed his knuckles against his thick moustache to draw attention to his maleness. 'But Louise said Madame woke in the early morning in pain, and there was some trouble, and they sent for the doctor to put things right but it's a bit tricky, so she's had to go into hospital.'

He couldn't say more. There had been brief, vivid hints about bleeding and miscarriage, but those weren't suitable to tell an eleven year old who knew nothing of the facts of life.

Hospital . . . That was bad. It meant everything was very serious. Yet it was good too, because the hospital had mended Lucie Duchene's broken leg. 'He'll be all right?' she begged.

It always amused him to hear the little 'un talk about the coming baby. She took it for granted it would be a boy. 'My little brother,' she would say, although of course the kid would be second cousin to her really. Please God they'd be able to save the poor little blighter. Still, these dramas did tend to crop up in anything to do with childbirth, he supposed, especially when the expectant mother wasn't young any longer. 'He'll be fine,' he promised.

They drove in through the gates of the house which contained the Private Modern School run by Mademoiselle Hermilot. The directrice was

15

on the look-out, came out of the door before he'd put the brakes on. 'Nora! What a pleasure to have you come as a boarder for a change!'

Nora gave the little curtsey which was obligatory during school hours. Jacques handed her overnight bag to the maid who came out behind the headmistress. 'Look after her,' he said in a low voice. 'She's all shaken up.'

Elvire Hermilot heard the whisper. She didn't need to be told the child was upset. She knew Nora well—or as well as anyone could. She was a reticent little girl with her emotions seldom on display.

'Come along, you're a little early for classes. Armandine shall show you where to put your things.'

The little girls of the school were grouped about in the entrance hall. Mademoiselle Hermilot beckoned to one of them, a boarder whom she knew to be a friend of Nora's. She commanded the child to show Nora upstairs, explaining that she'd be staying a day or two.

'I *say!*' Armandine exclaimed. 'Are you in disgrace then?'

'Disgrace? No, why?'

'Well, that's why I got sent as a boarder.' She was a step or two ahead on the stairs, glancing back impatiently. 'Do hurry, Nora, or we'll be late for class.'

Instead, Nora suddenly turned back and ran downstairs. She went through the groups of girls to the headmistress's room. Mademoiselle Hermilot was just sitting down to her desk when she rushed in. 'Madame, Madame, I must speak to you!'

'Nora! What's wrong—'

'Is it a punishment? Am I sent away because—'

'A punishment?' Elvire Hermilot went quickly round her desk to put an arm about the child. 'Of course not, dear. What made you think—'

'Didi said she was sent away—'

'Oh, Didi . . . she likes to make herself the heroine of a drama. She was sent to board because it was thought she might work harder, that's all. Nora dear, you mustn't let yourself get in a state about it. Cousin Marc just thought you'd like a few nights in school while Cousin Gaby—'

'What's really wrong with Cousin Gaby?' Nora interrupted. 'I don't really understand—it's something about the baby, but . . .'

Mademoiselle Hermilot disagreed with the fashion of keeping young girls ignorant. In a year or so, Nora would be asking questions about her body that would have to be answered, so why not tell her the rest, instead of these fables about babies being found among the vine rows or brought in the doctor's little black bag.

She knew, in fact, that all sorts of stories about sex circulated among the older girls. If she had had her way, she would have had them all into

17

her office in small groups, for a short sensible lecture giving them the truth. But she knew most of the parents would object violently. They wanted their daughters given enough education to hold their own in polite society, to do the household accounts and supervise the staff. Once that was done, they would go to finishing school to be taught how to be attractive to young men.

Somewhere between that and marriage, a girl was expected to learn all she needed to know about the physical side of sex. Hints from her mother which gradually grew more detailed, or conversations with an experienced older woman . . . Or sometimes direct experiment, greatly frowned upon by the more rigid families but known to be more and more common these days.

Somehow the system worked. Yet Mademmoiselle Hermilot wished that in cases such as this, she could take a more direct line. Little Nora Tramont was in a state of extreme distress heightened by the secrecy that convention demanded.

Elvire Hermilot was an old friend of the Tramonts, bound to them by suffering they had shared at the time of the Dreyfus Case. They had kept in touch intermittently, and it was due to their financial backing that she had been able to open this little school in Rheims.

She suddenly decided to take matters into her own hands. Friendship gave her the right. 'Close the door, Nora,' she said.

When the child had done so she beckoned her to a chair in front of her desk. She herself took up a position half-seated on it, so that her linen coat-dress showed rather more leg than she would have approved of had she been aware of it.

'Nora, I'm going to tell you what I was told on the telephone this morning. Your cousin is in danger of losing her baby.'

'But how can she lose the baby? She hasn't gone to fetch it yet.'

'Ladies don't really go to hospital to fetch babies, Nora. Cousin Gaby has carried the child inside her for eight months now—'

'Ah,' breathed Nora. Now so much was explained—the change in her cousin, the unfashionable clothes she'd been wearing recently. She looked expectantly at the headmistress.

'Something's gone wrong. It happens sometimes. The doctor is trying to help your cousin keep the baby safe. So you see you've been sent to me just so that they don't have to worry about you for a few days. The house will be disorganized, I expect, and then everything will settle down again and you can go back. But I want you to understand that you've done nothing wrong, that you haven't been sent away because they're displeased with you. It's just . . . you know . . .' She sought in her mind for an everyday comparison. 'When we have the school repainted, we wait till the holidays, when all the girls have gone. That's because it wouldn't be very nice for them, would it, trying to do their lessons with dustsheets over the desks and the carpets taken up. That's a bit what it will be like at home for a day or two, everybody very busy and perhaps being very anxious and preoccupied. You understand?'

Nora nodded in thankfulness. The relief at having some certainty at last was like a tide of warmth. To Mademoiselle Hermilot's surprise, she jumped up and threw her arms around her. 'Thank you, Madame,' she whispered. 'I was so afraid it was something terrible . . .'

But in a day or two she learned that her relief had been mistaken, that in fact it *was* something terrible. Jacques came to take Nora to the hospital, looking very solemn. 'Your Cousin Marc is waiting for you. I'm afraid it's pretty bad, minnow.'

'She's not . . . she's not . . .?'

'Touch and go,' said Jacques. He'd heard that a priest had been called, the premature baby had been baptized at once because its chances were almost nil, and Madame herself had received the seventh sacrament. And this poor kid—banished from home, looking lost and scared, white as a sheet. 'Trust in God, little finch,' he said, he who since the war had no faith himself. 'Trust in God, He's watching over them.'

When she reached the hospital she was taken by a tall nursing sister in a long white apron to a

20

little ante-room on the first floor. Cousin Marc rose to his feet as she came in. She rushed to him. One look at his face was enough to tell her there was bad news.

'What is it?' she cried, her voice coming out in a stifled gasp.

'I'm afraid there will be no little brother, Nora. He's left us already.'

'Oh, Cousin Marc! And Gaby? Is she—?'

'She's still fighting back. She asked for you a while ago but . . .'

But the doctors had decided it wasn't yet time to give up and allow relations to come to a deathbed. They had lost the baby, yes, but the mother could perhaps still be saved. There had been a tremendous loss of blood. Luckily, since the War, there was this new possibility of blood transfusion. A suitable donor had been found among the nursing staff, arrangements were now being made to collect her blood in the prescribed bottle containing 3.8 per cent of sodium nitrate solution to prevent coagulation. This would be administered at once, while further supplies were obtained from the Central Surgical Stores in the city's main hospital.

The doctors didn't want to raise unjustified hopes. Madame Tramont was a very sick woman, with surgical repair work recently carried out and suffering from extreme shock. But she was strong-willed and determined to live. She'd murmured to her husband, only an hour or so ago: 'Never mind, dear heart. Better luck next time.'

Better luck next time—when she had just lost a longed-for baby. 'Such a woman must be saved,' growled Dr Saumuche, and began the grim battle.

All that day there was no good news to give to the grey-faced husband and the little girl who clung to his hand. When the June daylight began to fade, Saumuche suggested the child should be sent home to bed.

'Oh no! No, let me stay! I'm not tired, not the least bit tired.' This although her eyelids were so heavy they drooped like grey curtains over her eyes, and her whole body sagged with fatigue.

'You need your bed, Mademoiselle,' said the doctor, shaking his head at her.

'No, I don't. I shouldn't sleep even if I went to bed!' She clutched at her cousin, staring up at him.

'Let her stay,' he said, finding some small comfort in having her there with him. 'She can nap in the armchair—'

Saumuche sighed. 'Sister, fetch a pillow and a blanket. How about you, Monsieur Tramont? Would you like us to give you a bed—'

'I'm all right, thanks.'

'Some coffee? A bite to eat?'

'No, thank you. But Nora should have some milk.'

Nora drifted off to sleep in the leather

armchair, her head pillowed on one arm and the blanket tucked about her. She woke with a start in the early morning to hear a blackbird singing with June-time vigour on the cherry tree outside.

For a moment she couldn't think where she was. Then she saw her cousin coming through the inner door of the ante-room. She untangled herself from the blanket, tumbled forward to greet him.

'Marc! What's happened? Is she—is she all right?'

'Yes, thank God. Very weak, and scarcely able to move a muscle. But she wants to see you, Nora.'

All at once the great dark clouds rolled away. The sun came out for Nora. She pulled down the creased skirt of her grey cotton dress, made tidying gestures at her mousy hair. 'Can we go at once?'

'Yes, dear, but I want you to be very quiet and good. She's—you'll see, she doesn't look like the Cousin Gaby you know—you mustn't cry or be upset.'

'No, no, of course not. No, I understand.'

'Very well.'

He took her hand. He went to the door and tapped. It was opened by a sister holding her rosary in one hand. She put a finger to her lips as she let them pass.

Cousin Gaby was lying in a bed around which stood Dr Saumuche, a junior doctor, and another nursing sister. By the bed a strange gantry rose, holding a bottle from which a tube went down to Cousin Gaby's arm.

The figure in the bed looked very small and, to Nora's childlike memory, very flat after the plumpness of the last few months. That was because, she told herself quickly on remembering what Mademoiselle Hermilot had said, the baby was gone. She felt tears well up at the thought, but clenched her teeth to hold them back. She had promised Cousin Marc.

'Only a moment,' Dr Saumuche murmured.

Marc nodded. He made a little movement with the hand Nora was holding, so that she was urged forward towards the bed on the side not occupied by the blood transfusion.

'Gaby . . .'

Her cousin opened her eyes. For a moment it seemed that she didn't know who had spoken, then her gaze focused, the great dark eyes held recognition.

'My little girl,' she said, the words like the whisper of wind over grass.

'Everything's going to be all right,' Nora said, trying not to let her voice tremble. 'You'll be home soon.'

The faintest of smiles curved the pale lips.

'It'll be school holidays in a week or two. I'll be at home all the time. I'll do everything—I'll tell the gardeners what you want done and take messages to Monsieur Coubet and—'

'Ssh . . .' cautioned Saumuche.

'No, let her,' said Marc. 'Gaby understands—don't you, Gaby?'

Gaby smiled again. Nora arranged her mouth so that she smiled back. She didn't know if she had the strength to keep this up much longer. Gaby looked so different—so ill, so fragile, so defeated. It was impossible to believe life had treated her like this. Gaby was the mistress of the House of Tramont, the moving spirit, the will that caused everything to have its being. How could she be lying here in a hospital bed at the mercy of strange doctors and a piece of equipment that dripped red liquid into her?

'Go now,' Gaby whispered. 'Be good.'

'Yes, Gaby.' She hesitated. 'Can I go home instead of school, so I can look after Cousin Marc?'

Something that might almost have been a laugh came from Gaby Tramont. 'Of course,' she said.

The nursing sister came to take Nora out of the room. Marc Auduron-Tramont remained for a moment longer at the very faintest of movements from his wife. He leaned over to hear what she had to say.

'She's all we have now,' Gaby murmured, 'all we ever shall have.'

For that was the final verdict. Gaby was going to live, but there would be no more children.

Marc took her thin hand. 'We'll give her all

the love we would have given Robert,' he said. For the child had been a boy, named after Gaby's father.

'She's the House of Tramont. It will all belong to her, Marc.'

All the love, all the possessions . . .

TWO

Cousin Gaby's recovery took a long time. Nora's school holidays had already begun when at last her cousin was brought home in a private ambulance on a drizzly day of July. Two nurses became part of the household, a day nurse and a night nurse, with a third who acted as relief. Unlike those at the hospital, they were not nuns, but brisk businesslike young women in white uniforms, who required almost as much attention from the servants as the invalid herself.

Each day Nora was called for to spend some time in Gaby's room. She read to her at first, then played foolish card games. When the patient was allowed downstairs and finally outdoors to the sheltered terrace, they spent the time talking.

Gaby had always taken a keen interest in all that Nora did, particularly her school activities. Now it seemed that her cousin wanted to know every little thing in her life—who her friends were, what they did together, how she felt about her future.

'My future?' Nora echoed in astonishment the first time this was raised.

'Of course, my love. One day you'll inherit all this.' Gaby's little gesture took in the vine-sheltered terrace, the view before it of the shrubbery and beyond that, the fields and buildings where the wine was made.

'Ye-es . . .'

'It's a great responsibility, you know. That's why I'm glad to hear your good subjects at school are botany and biology. You see, growing the vines is a difficult business, and making the wine even more complex.'

'Oh, I know that.' Nora had heard the conversations between Marc and Gaby and between them and Monsieur Coubet, about the health of the plants, the degree of sugar forming in the grapes, the probable alcohol content, the analysis of the yeasts. Recently she'd begun to understand some of it, as her grasp of her science subjects grew firmer. At first she'd sat in awe when they talked, thinking how enormously clever they were to understand such things.

Now she knew that they only partly understood. There was a mystery to the making of wine, so many variables that luck or fate or providence came into it too. But, as Marc was fond of saying, 'Luck goes away again if you don't give it a welcome.' So as to see good points in the growing season as they arose, constant vigilance was necessary. Likewise when the pressing was done. And, most importantly of all, when at last the blending took place, in the winter, when the wine had rested and 'chosen its role', as Gaby said.

'I'd like you to begin going round the winefield with Cousin Marc—'

'Oh, but I do that already!' Yes, on every occasion she could persuade him to it. She loved to ride beside him on the little pony they had given her for her tenth birthday, Butterpat, so called because of his blond mane. But to go riding it was *de rigueur* to change into her riding outfit—hacking jacket, cotton shirt and tie, well-cut little jodhpurs in the English style. Sometimes when she asked to go with Marc he'd say, 'Sorry, kitten, I can't wait while you change into all that fallal, I'm in a hurry this morning.'

'No, my love, from now on it won't be a little outing when it can be fitted in,' Gaby explained, 'but a regular part of your routine. After all, you'll be twelve next birthday. It's time you began to take an interest in the way the business runs.'

'I see.'

'Don't you want to?'

'Of course! I was only thinking, though . . .'

'What? Tell me.' Gaby's eyes were upon her, anxiously taking in every mood or thought that was shown in her face.

'Well, you see, I've got Mademoiselle Lacier

28

for music and Herr Bruckner for German, and the dancing lessons in Rheims . . .'

She meant that the summer was going to be full of tasks, with no time for picnics and boating and tennis.

At Cousin Cecile's the summers had always been very quiet and dull yet there had been gentle festivities—outings to the woods or the riverbank, the town fête.

When she spent her first summer at the Villa Tramont it was a revelation to her. Despite the wreckage of the main part of the house, the Tramonts entertained. In their turn they were invited everywhere. The neighbourhood was determined to celebrate the peace, to get back to normal and something more than normal. There were country fairs, open air concerts, regattas, outdoor dances, garden parties for charity.

True, many of the rich vineyardists had followed the English fashion and gone to the Riviera for the hottest month. Some took their children with them. But there had been enough left in the neighbourhood of Calmady for Nora to spend long happy days swimming, gathering wild flowers to identify, watching butterflies.

She wanted of course to do everything that the Relatives commanded. She studied under her holiday tutors, she spent hours of practice at the piano because Cousin Marc liked to hear her play simple pieces in the evening.

But if she were to go round the estate for a couple of hours each day with Marc, it meant she would almost never have time to see her friends. Perhaps that didn't matter, ought not to matter. But she had been uprooted and lost friends before. She never found it easy making them anew. And if she drifted away from her school friends during the long vacation, she might never be able to put the friendships back on their former footing.

'Of course you'll have plenty of time to enjoy yourself,' Gaby soothed. 'You can invite your friends here. I'm going to have the tennis courts repaired while the men are doing the entrance yard and the porte-cochère.'

This was an enlivening thought. Nora had discovered to her surprise that she was quite good at tennis although she'd only had her first lessons a year ago—Cousin Cecile had never even thought of such a thing.

'Could I have a proper coach?' she asked.

'A tennis coach? Oh . . .' Gaby had to bear the thought of expense in mind. As much income as possible had to be ploughed back into making the business efficient again. A small part was set aside for restoration of the house; this summer, for instance, the entrance court, the *porte-cochère*, and part of the central building would be repaired. This would bring back the ballroom, so that during the winter they could give dances

30

again and also use it, as it had always been used, for receptions for the wine shippers.

The cost of her own illness had not been small. The three nurses were paid well, and the hospital bill had been high. There was also the disappointment that during the week or so when Marc had been out of his mind with worry, he had cancelled meetings with important buyers so that they had gone elsewhere. They had lost some business, although they would regain it.

It was odd that, in the years immediately after a devastating war, the whole world seemed to be in the mood to buy and drink champagne. Luckily, there were some fine vintages available. The vintage of 1914, made in the face of all kinds of difficulties, was particularly good. It was now being sold and doing well. The years 1915 and 1916 were also good though, in the case of Champagne Tramont, rather scarce. After that there was nothing ready to sell as yet, but the 1917 and 1918 were passable. The 1919, by the grace of God and whatever spirit guarded the land, had seemed superb and when it was ready to sell might go down in history as one of the great vintages.

But taste seemed to be changing. It wasn't the same people now who bought champagne. The great owners of estates, particularly in England, were poorer now because of having to pay for the war. The champagne industry too might have to change, aiming its sales at a different public.

31

All this, Gaby felt, had to be learned by Nora. And the sooner the better, for Gaby's close brush with death had taught her how vulnerable she was. The family of Tramont was too small to let any of its members have a long, carefree childhood. Nora must begin her apprenticeship now, harsh though it might seem.

To compensate her, Gaby vowed, she would be loved and cherished. Everything that could please her would be offered—but within the strict confines of her world here at Calmady, where she was being trained to inherit the House of Tramont.

These facts, thought of a thousand times already as she lay weak and almost helpless in bed, flashed through Gaby's mind yet again. The child was asking for a tennis coach. Very well—a tennis coach. Tennis was becoming a fashionable game, it would bring useful contacts, opportunities for parties and gatherings. Yes, tennis was a useful tool in the task of shaping the future heiress.

As time passed Nora asked very little. She wasn't much interested in the things that enthralled her schoolfellows. When she looked in the mirror she saw that she was going to grow up plain and colourless, so fashion scarcely drew her attention. At dances and social events she found herself, as always, shy and too silent, so parties had no attraction.

On the other hand she was good fun when it

came to sports. There, she was easy with the gangling youths who were invited to the house or to share their villa on the Côte d'Azur. She played good tennis and grew better as she was taken more seriously by her coach. She rode well, and progressed from Butterpat to a strong young mare—but at that point Cousin Gaby grew anxious and forbade hunting. 'You might be thrown, darling—'

'Well, that's part of the fun, Gaby—'

'No, no, it's too dangerous. I forbid it.'

In this as in all things, Nora obeyed. She swam well, but gave up learning to dive because it scared the Relatives. As she advanced towards her mid-teens she asked for driving lessons, because it was all the rage now to drive a neat little sports car with a silk scarf flying in the breeze.

'It's too dangerous—'

'But all the senior girls are taking lessons, Gaby!'

Her cousin was about to give a firm refusal, but Cousin Marc intervened. 'I think, my love,' he murmured, 'we ought to allow it so long as she learns on the estate roads.'

'But Marc—'

'It's becoming so necessary to drive, Gaby, so commonplace. I think she would be at a dis-advantage if she didn't learn.'

That of course settled it. Nothing would be refused if it would seem a disadvantage. The heiress to Tramont must be seen to be equal and more than equal with others. As the years had brought increased good fortune money had flowed into the Tramont coffers so that on the grounds of economy it was never necessary now to say no.

At sixteen Nora was taken to Paris to attend finishing school. She would now be groomed and dressed for the début which must come the following year. She was escorted to the great houses of *haute couture* to see who would be her designer, had her hair cut by a famous coiffeur, was instructed in the use of a light application of cosmetics—the very faintest of lipsticks for her pale lips and rice powder for any occasion when a slight perspiration might make her nose shine.

She found it a dreadful bore. 'What's it all *for*?' she groaned to Émilie, who shared her room.

'To find a husband, silly. What else?'

Émilie was a pretty, plump girl who had no problems on that score. Her family had already arranged her marriage, with a young man she had known since she was a baby. She was inclined to be lordly towards those who would be thrown into the marriage market in a year or so.

'Well, I know that,' said Nora. 'What I meant was, why do they try to dress us up like puppets? I'm pretty sure that once I'm married I'll spend half my time helping to run the business, so why do they try to give the impression I'm something I'm not?'

'Oh, Nora, you *are* a card!' laughed Émilie. 'Just imagine the face of a fellow you said that to! Do you think anybody wants to marry a girl whose chief interest is going to the office? Of course you won't really run the business, that's all nonsense. Your husband will do that—'

Nora shook her head. 'My cousin runs the business—'

'Your Cousin Marc—yes, I know that—'

'No, Gaby runs it. Marc helps, certainly—he runs the legal side, and knows all about contracts and so forth. But Gaby is the brains.'

Émilie threw down the lipstick with which she was experimenting, to turn from the mirror with great amusement. 'And is that how you see yourself? The brains of the business?'

Nora blushed and was silent. No one understood. It was useless to try to explain it to outsiders. Somehow in the Tramont family there had grown up the tradition that the women were the mainstay of the firm. She had known this from the moment Gaby had brought her home from Tours, and to her it was like the air she breathed. She was the heiress to the House of Tramont, on her shoulders would rest all the responsibility of decisions for its welfare.

And her husband . . . Well, she must marry. She understood that.

But sometimes, when she talked with a girl

like Émilie, she wondered what her husband would actually do. Émilie was looking forward to a life in Paris as the dutiful wife of a young stockbroker. She would entertain for him, run his house, bear his children, and make sure nothing distracted him from the important matter of making money. He would always be the superior, Émilie took that for granted.

Nora couldn't imagine how things would be between herself and a husband who had notions like that.

She had no idea who might eventually offer for her hand. She felt sure she wouldn't be as lucky as Émilie, unofficially engaged already to someone she'd known all her life. The boys Nora knew were quite unattracted to her. 'That skinny kid,' they called her, or 'the mousy one'.

None of that had been changed by expensive clothes and short hair. If anything, those had made her more noticeable without improving her. When her hair was long and in pigtails, it at least had had a shape that suited her face. Now, cut to eight inches and pressed into what were called 'Marcel waves' invented by Monsieur Grateau, it no longer seemed to clothe her head but belong to some helmet she was wearing.

The current dress styles would have suited Nora's flat-chested figure well, if only Cousin Gaby had not taken her away from Patou. But Monsieur and Madame Delormeuil, who ran the finishing school, had recommended a designer with a liking for ornament. They felt that Patou's severe frocks looked too much like a uniform on Nora. The result was, she wore dresses that had 'a touch of sparkle', as Monsieur Tenet put it. This was produced by motifs of sequins or beading near the neckline. Consequently people always seemed to be looking just below her chin, their eyes attracted by the little bouquet of flowers or Chinese dragon that Monsieur Tenet had placed there.

Alone in their room now, just the two girls, Nora surveyed herself in the cheval-glass. She was wearing a straight dress of moss-green crepe, fluted at the knees by a shaped flounce which was repeated at the cuffs. The neckline was severe, cut in a flat V. But to one side of it was an iris in two shades of blue, beautifully and eye-catchingly embroidered in silks and beads.

Above it rose a thin neck which was adorned with a choker necklace of false grey pearls, all the rage this season. Her face, pale and sharp-boned, wore the permitted cosmetics—pale pink lipstick, a faint dusting of powder. The eyes were a strange grey, the irises mingling amber brown and slate so that they changed in differing lights. Her brows were good, she thought—well defined, darker than her mousey hair.

What a verdict—'My brows are good.'

'Émilie,' she said, 'is there any way I could make myself attractive?'

Her room-mate was too honest, or too tactless,

to say, 'But you are attractive already.' She replied, 'It's a pity you don't have poor eyesight. Then you could wear the new style glasses, you know, horn-rimmed, and then you'd look intellectual.'

'Nobody's ever going to fall in love with me,' mourned Nora.

'Well, that doesn't matter too much, because I heard Mama saying that your Relatives would see to it. They want you married young.'

'Really?' Nora asked. She wasn't arguing against the news—that had always been implicit in the talk at home. But she wanted to encourage Émilie to go on.

'Mama was saying to Papa that they'll keep you under stricter surveillance than your mama. No running off and causing a scandal.'

'My mama did that?' Nora asked in astonishment.

'You didn't know that? Well, I suppose they wouldn't tell you—it's such a bad example. I don't know the ins and outs of it. It seems your mother ran away from home. She came back, though, or at least was brought back. In disgrace, I suppose.'

Nora was enthralled. No whisper of this had ever reached her before. Mama, running away? She tried to call to mind that shadowy figure dressed in dark clothes, putting a valise into a carriage while other people jostled and pushed around her. The smell of carnations, Mama's scent. The swaying of the carriage, the terrible sound of explosions. The horses neighing in terror, then a rushing along too fast and going over with everything crashing about them. Where was Mama in that scene? Picking herself up from the road, a pretty, shaking voice urging the coachman to get up . . .

Then the troops coming by, gun carriages— Nora remembered those, a long train of them. And shells coming over, the railway line attracting the enemy gunners, she heard some-one say. The crossroads too, a target. Army traffic marshals pushing everyone this way and that, kind hands taking her up when she fell almost under a wagon. Kind hands, but not Mama's.

Émilie was still talking. 'When that old teacher of yours dropped in to see how you were getting on here—'

'Mademoiselle Hermilot?'

'Is that her name? Funny little old thing, isn't she? I heard her arguing with Madame Delor-meuil about you.'

'You seem to have a great talent for over-hearing things, Émilie!'

'Well, if you don't listen, you don't get to know, do you?' The other girl sat on the side of her bed to try on her new flesh-pink silk stock-ings. 'Parents and people like that never tell you anything—or at least, they tell you what they want you to know and that's all. But if you think it's wrong to listen at doors, I won't go on.'

'Oh, Émilie, don't be a beast! Tell me!'

Émilie giggled, turned one foot this way and that to admire the sheen of the silk over her ankle, and adjusted the garter of ruched silk just above her knee. 'Mademoiselle Hermilot was saying she was sorry to hear they'd cut down on your swimming, and Madame Delormeuil said after all you weren't training to swim the Channel and Mademoiselle Hermilot said that if you did something well, it was a pity not to let you go on further, even if not Channel-swimming. Then Madame Delormeuil said that it was a lucky thing you had no particular talent that was likely to lead you away from family life and try to please yourself, like the other champagne girls.'

'The other champagne girls' were the daughters of the other champagne families. 'It's all right for them,' Nora sighed. 'Most of them have brothers and sisters or young cousins and things. I'm the only one in our family.'

'I don't know why you don't make the most of it,' Émilie said. 'You could have a great time if you wanted to—all you have to do is blackmail them.'

'Blackmail! Blackmail Cousin Gaby and Cousin Marc?'

'Don't see why not. I'm jolly sure I'd get my own way a lot more if I were in your position.'

'But I owe them everything, Émilie. They've been like mother and father to me—'

'Yes, yes, and so they should. For heaven's sake, Nora, why are you so meek about it? It's different for me, I know Alphonse and I'm quite pleased with my engagement. But you'll end up being married off to someone you scarcely know.'

'How can you say such a thing! The Relatives would never do that!'

'All I know is I heard the Delormeuil say that she knew your family would like to see you engaged in your first season and starting a family as soon as possible. But it won't be too bad, Nora. With money like yours, you'll have plenty of choice. You can pick someone you like.'

Nora went cold with horror. Pick someone out of a group of strangers, go to bed with him, and make a baby just so that the Tramont family could have an heir?

She fell silent. Émilie, with both stockings on, was now trying shoes to see if her ankles would really look slimmer in the new Cuban heels. Her attention wandered, as it was apt to do. Nora was left to think about her prospects and realize, perhaps for the first time, what was really entailed. Until now she'd always allowed herself to think that by the time she made her début she'd somehow become more attractive. She would thereupon meet young men on a different footing—no longer 'one of the boys', as quick on a horse or on the tennis court as they, but a young lady to be reckoned with. After getting to know them, romance would follow.

What 'romance' actually was, she wasn't quite sure. She knew now the basic facts about being a married woman, because Mademoiselle Hermilot had explained it all and Gaby had confirmed the information.

But 'romance' . . . That was different. It was how you had to feel about someone. Nora had never experienced this. She'd seen her friends almost swooning over a handsome tutor or one of the new stars of the cinema—Rudolf Valentino or Douglas Fairbanks. She'd never felt any of that. It was a mystery to her.

But the time was upon her. In a few months her first season would commence, the White Ball and then the stream of invitations to parties and a ball of her own, which Gaby would arrange with the help of a social secretary.

Somewhere in the host of young men that would gather around the débutantes must be the man Nora was expected to marry. She hadn't even met him yet, but nevertheless by the time the season ended she would be engaged.

She thrust the thought away, but it kept coming back to haunt her. At night in bed, this nameless figure tipped over the beginnings of sleep and gave her nightmares. Anxiety made her feel sick and restless. She couldn't eat, grew even thinner. Madame Delormeuil eyed her and diagnosed anaemia. She was dosed with iron tonic.

The Christmas break followed quite soon. The Relatives came to Paris to take her to the various family gatherings and to the theatre. They had a big apartment now not far from the Rue St Honoré. It was quite fashionable these days not to have a house but instead to have an establishment close to the shops and the opera. Here, from time to time, Marc would stay while he conducted business at their offices in the Rue Lelong. Here Gaby would pay off arrears of hospitality during the winter season.

And here, one afternoon while Gaby shopped for presents for the house staff at Calmady, Marc settled down to some business papers in the study. Nora gravitated there, on the pretext of looking for something to read until it was time to change for dinner.

She liked to be in the same room with Marc, even if they said little to each other. He was a comforting presence to her, easier to be with than Gaby, who always seemed to expect too much.

Presently he put down his fountain pen, to watch her riffling through an English magazine. 'Why aren't you out with your friends, princess?' he enquired.

She shrugged. 'Most of them have gone home to their families.'

'Oh, come, Nora, you have plenty of Parisian friends.'

'I suppose so.'

'Wasn't there a party going to the circus this afternoon?'

'Yes.'

'Why didn't you go?'

'I don't like to see elephants wearing funny hats and balancing on stools.'

'Oh,' he said, with a laugh, 'so it's a matter of principle. I thought perhaps you'd quarrelled with them all.'

She coloured a little. 'Well, as a matter of fact . . .'

'What, my dear?'

'Oh, they can be so *tiresome!*' she blurted. 'The girls only talk about clothes and flirting.'

'And the boys?'

'They creep off by themselves to smoke and tell silly jokes.'

'My goodness, it sounds terrible. My dear girl, surely there are some of your friends with whom you feel at ease—'

She shook her head. 'Scarcely anyone. It was better at Mademoiselle Hermilot's, but at the finishing school . . . And then when we have the dances at which the boys are invited, it's so . . . so . . .'

'What, Nora?' he asked, getting up from his chair to come and stand over her. He took the magazine from her hands. 'What's the matter? What's really troubling you?'

She gazed up at him. His eyes were full of kind concern. He didn't say, as Cousin Gaby might have done, 'Come along now, Nora, what's all this nonsense?'

'Is it really true you and Gaby want me married off as soon as possible?' she blurted out.

'Nora!' He was shocked. He took hold of her hand and pulled her to her feet, tilted her chin so that he could study her face. 'Who on earth told you such a thing?'

'If only I liked the boys I meet, it wouldn't worry me so much. But they all seem such idiots, Marc . . .' Tears welled up and tipped over onto her cheekbones. She drooped against her cousin's shoulder. He patted her gently on the back.

'There, there, don't cry about it, sweetheart. Of course no one's going to make you marry someone you don't like—you couldn't seriously have imagined that?'

She nodded then shook her head. She didn't really know what she imagined. All she knew was that she was miserable. While all the other girls she knew were full of pleasurable anticipation of the coming year and its festivities, she dreaded them.

'Dearest child, don't be silly. Is that what you think your bad old Relatives are plotting? Of course not! We want you to be happy, Nora.

Your cousin and I know what it's like to be unhappy. We wouldn't inflict it on anyone else.'

Nora snuffled against his lapel, sought for her handkerchief in the cuff of her bishop sleeve, and dabbed her eyes. 'Then it's all right if I don't get a husband first time out?'

'Nora! What a way to speak!' He gave her a little shake. 'What's got into you? We don't want you to "get a husband". We want you to settle down with someone you love.'

'Yes, but everybody says you want me to be quick about it, to start a family as soon as possible—'

'No, no—'

'But it sounds so logical,' she interrupted, her voice shaking with unhappy determination. 'I do see the point, Marc. I'm the last of the Tramonts, after all. I quite understand it's my duty—'

'Nonsense, little girl, it's your duty to be happy and make a success of your life. What do you take us for? A pair of ogres?'

She blew her nose. He let her go but only so far as to draw her down on the leather chesterfield beside him. 'Nora, I do wish you wouldn't listen to other people's nonsense. If you want to know our plans, come to us and talk about it.'

There was some censure in his tone. She nodded, looking down.

'But I will be quite frank with you. As you say, you are the last of the Tramonts. When it became clear Gaby couldn't have any children we pinned our hopes on you, I don't deny it. But that doesn't mean you have to go out like an army scout, looking for a young man to bring back prisoner—'

She laughed, a little unsteadily. 'I'm not up to that kind of thing, Marc. I'd have thought you knew that. And as for it happening the other way round . . . You see, nobody seems to take the slightest interest in me.'

'Oh, don't be absurd. A pretty little thing like you?'

'But I'm not pretty, Marc.'

'Of course you are.' He spoke with utter conviction, and she knew that to him it was true. He thought her the most delightful girl in France, and she loved him for it. But she saw herself more honestly. She knew that even with all the help arranged for her by the Delormeuils, she was not going to be the rage of the season.

'You see, that's what scares me, Marc. Nobody's going to fall head over heels in love with me and so it looks as if you and Gaby are going to have to take a hand. I just feel that I . . . I . . .'

Marc wanted to comfort her but didn't know how. He was sure this was just débutante's nerves, the kind of thing every girl went through at some time before her first season. How many little ducklings must have cowered in the nest, unaware that they would turn into swans when the moment came?

'You're being silly,' he said. 'Probably the minute you get out into the world next year you'll find you like half a dozen of the young men, and I bet they'll be after you in droves. And in any case . . .'

'What?'

'Well, since we're talking about it, I may as well say . . .' Naturally, like all right-minded guardians, he and Gaby had put out feelers about a match for Nora. One couldn't leave it all entirely to chance. There were two or three families taking an interest, but there was one that Gaby liked particularly—only son of a fine family with a decent financial base. They had been property owners in the Alpes Maritimes for a couple of centuries, were now making surprisingly large amounts of money out of setting up facilities for this new sport of skiing.

'You realize of course that we'll be arranging escorts for you—'

'Yes, Marc, Gaby showed me the provisional list a few days ago.'

'They're decent boys, all of them, though I think Roger Benoile is a bit dull. But I feel Edmond du Ceddres is rather nice. What did you think?' They had been introduced informally about a week ago, at a charity concert.

'Yes, very nice, Marc.'

'Good,' he said, with too much casualness. 'Well, then, you've nothing to worry about, have you? There are these good young men already getting to know you and then when you're launched they'll squire you around, and it's to be hoped that you'll get to like them quite a lot.'

'But Marc—!'

'What, princess?'

She shook her head and gave up. She could not seem to get it clear enough to explain it to anyone else. She shrank almost physically from the knowledge that she would be expected to get one of these young men to like her enough to make an offer and, if not, suffer the shame of having him pushed into doing so by family pressure.

Marc recounted some of this conversation to his wife. The finer points eluded him—he didn't quite know why his little girl was so upset: 'So far as I could gather, she's afraid she isn't pretty enough to make a man fall in love with her.' He chuckled as he said it, and was surprised when Gaby didn't laugh too.

Gaby was frowning. 'The trouble is, you see . . . Paris is full of pretty young girls.'

'But besides being pretty, Nora is a Tramont.'

'Yes, I don't forget that. And neither does Nora, I suppose. She feels it's quite likely that anyone paying her special attentions is after the cash.'

'What nonsense! You and I would take damned good care no fortune hunters—'

'It goes without saying that she'll be properly looked after, so far as that goes. But Marc . . .

I made some terrible mistakes when I was a girl. You know that Lucas was completely approved of by my family.'

Marc knew all about that disastrous love affair. At the time he had been a very junior partner in the law firm which handled the Tramont business. He had been negotiating the marriage settlement when the Vourvilles broke off. He had seen how heartbroken Gaby was in those days, and since then she had told him the whole story. Lucas Vourville had been, plainly and simply, a cad.

'Edmond's not like that,' he protested. 'He's a thoroughly nice lad. If they take to each other, I for one would have absolutely no qualms for the happiness of our little princess.'

'I agree with you.' Yet Gaby understood more of Nora's feelings than could ever be explained to Marc. The unwillingness to take a man who regarded you as part of a business transaction no matter how good his manners were . . . The sense of being inferior . . .

'Let's just wait and see what the season brings forth,' she sighed.

The answer was, nothing. As usual, three of four girls dominated the Parisian scene. They were photographed wearing a new ball gown every week or so, their hairdressers were sought after, they were quoted and gossiped about.

Nora was quite unnoticed except as a name in

the guest list. Even at her own ball, she was eclipsed by Mai D'Agran.

No swarm of young men buzzed about her like bees around the queen. Marc saw it with astonishment. What was wrong with these young fellows? Couldn't they see that Nora, with her great hazel eyes and fine bones and quiet ways, was far more lovable than those gorgeous butterflies?

'I don't understand it,' he mourned to Gaby. 'I was so sure everything would be fine once she got out there into the swim of things. A little assurance, that was all she lacked.'

Gaby shook her head. She herself had been a great beauty but at the time of her coming-out lack of money had restricted her activities. All the same, she'd had young men flocking to her until she fell headlong for Lucas Vourville. She remembered clearly the shallowness of judgement at that time others valued you for being sought after, and you were sought after if you had looks and spirit and money.

Nora had the last, true enough. But as the season progressed she grew more and more quiet. She had to be urged to wear a new dress, to write thank-you letters. Gaby had to make desperate efforts to get her to take part in conversation.

In August they went to the villa they had hired near Cannes. Gaby arranged beach parties, poolside parties. She hoped that Nora in a bathing suit flashing through the blue waters would arouse more interest than Nora in a party dress looking drained of colour. Besides, there was the little red sports car, an enticement to any young man who thought of himself as something of a racing driver.

Alas for such hopes. Nora took to driving off by herself in the early morning. She did this for almost a week, until Cousin Gaby verbally prohibited it.

'What is the point of being here, Nora, if you go away by yourself and sulk?'

'I'm not sulking.'

'No, of course, I didn't mean that, dear.' Gaby controlled herself. She didn't really want to be here. She wanted to be at Calmady, where the grapes were ripening and the last spraying would have been done. She wanted to be chatting with Coubet about estimates of the harvest, with the other local vineyardists about prices.

Instead she was at this fashionable resort, trying to make a recalcitrant girl take some part in finding herself a husband.

She quite saw that the young mashers weren't going to take an interest in Nora. She'd thought perhaps the less witty types—the tennis fans, the golfers, the riding enthusiasts—would have been attracted by Nora's prowess at sports. Or perhaps even a nice quiet lad, shy himself, might have understood Nora's shyness.

But no spark seemed to be lighted, no friendship was formed. Only the faithful group recruited at the beginning of the season kept turning up to escort the child. And their families were beginning to murmur that it would be nice to know what the Tramonts' choice might be, because you see if Roger or Louis or Edmond were not to be selected, then there were other young ladies in their circle to whom they could turn.

'It had better be Edmond,' Gaby sighed one Sunday afternoon to Marc, when packing was already in hand for the return to Calmady and the vintage.

'Has she said she likes him specially?' He rubbed his knuckles hard against his cheek, a habit he had when he was anxious.

'She likes him—I don't think anyone could dislike Edmond.'

'What are his feelings on the matter?'

'His mother says he thinks Nora is sweet—'

'Oh, now, that's good, he obviously sees her qualities—'

'Marc, dearest, Madame du Ceddres says Edmond thinks Nora is sweet and would do quite well. He's been brought up to understand he must marry young—their case is the same as ours, there's only the one son left.'

'That damned war,' sighed Marc. 'A lot of family names are going to die out . . .'

'Well, Madame du Ceddres shares our views, we should help each other survive. I think you know, Edmond will go into the Civil Service when he leaves university. The family has a tradition of public service.'

'Yes, yes, but will he make Nora happy?'

She held out a hand to her husband, and he took it. 'We could leave it another year,' she said. 'She's only seventeen, after all. But . . . she shows no signs of changing in any significant way. And another year of being a nobody would be very bad for her.'

'Being engaged would be good for morale, you mean.'

'That's it.'

'And she could break it off if she found she didn't take to him a bit more.'

Gaby made no reply to that. She didn't want the engagement broken if it was entered into. It never did a girl any good, to be known as changeable or capricious.

'We'll ask her,' she said after a moment. 'See what she thinks.'

Nora had seen it coming. Four months had gone by in which she'd made no new friends, only acquaintances. Always slow to get to know people, she'd found it even worse in the hectic activity of the Paris season. People came and went like trains in a station. There was hardly time to say, 'Do you prefer black coffee or white?' before they whisked away to some other gathering.

There were four young men in the group who

had been detailed to offer themselves as escorts to her: Roger Benoile, Aristide Parradou, Gilles Sez, and Edmond du Ceddres. It had become noticeable that Gilles was being drawn away by Liliane Tratanne, a pretty dark girl who laughed a lot. Roger was too dull to take seriously, and she had discovered that Aristide was vain to the point of being silly.

That left Edmond. He was tall, calm, polite. He had a pale skin and darkish hair. He played good tennis but didn't disguise the fact he found it rather boring after the first hour or so. He rode well, liked horses, gave her some good tips at Longchamp so that she actually won some money.

She couldn't say she loved him. But she could at least say she liked him. If she had to get engaged, Edmond would do. She knew, however, that once she said yes, she would have to go through with it. Cousin Gaby expected that.

The Relatives explained to her that there was no hurry. The legal business would take some weeks, perhaps months. She and Edmond could spend more time together, unchaperoned—that was quite usual these days, since the war young women somehow seemed much more independent. By the time the engagement was announced it was to be hoped the two young people would be really fond of one another.

'And, if not—if Nora finds she really can't bear

55

him —we can break off,' Marc murmured to his wife.

'Certainly.' But Gaby was inwardly praying no such disaster would occur. Families weren't going to line up for a girl who rebuffed a perfectly nice young man.

Certainly it was more agreeable for Nora once matters were in train. Edmond was a pleasant escort. He took her to the cinema in Paris to see Cecil B. de Mille's epic, *King of Kings* and didn't laugh when she gasped as H. B. Warner's extraordinarily Christ-like features were first faded in on screen. He came regularly at weekends to Calmady so they could go riding together. He even waited patiently while she poked about among some old wrecked houses trying to identify a lichen growing on the stones.

The day came when the formalities were completed. The Tramonts went to their Paris apartment. Edmond was to take Nora to choose an engagement ring.

'Don't get carried away,' warned Cousin Gaby as Nora came into the drawing-room in a sable coat against the February cold. 'You have small hands so choose a small ring—sapphires are good, you can wear them with anything but avoid anything showy, my love.'

'Yes, Gaby.'

'If you don't see anything you like, you can have something specially made—but that will mean you won't have it for another week or so.'

'Does that matter, dear?' Marc enquired, putting aside his newspaper.

'No, no, but it would be nice if she could wear it for the engagement party.'

'I suppose so.'

Nora came to drop a kiss first on Gaby and then on Marc. He rose as she approached, so that she had a sudden impulse to throw her arms around him and say, 'Don't let it happen! Don't make me do it!'

But he was grinning conspiratorially and saying, 'A great day for you, eh? Choosing the ring!'

'Lovely,' she murmured, and went on tiptoe to kiss his cheek.

The ring she chose was a small cluster of diamonds set in platinum. It needed alteration, would be ready for the day of the official engagement in three days' time. 'Shall we send it, sir?' the salesman at Cartier enquired.

'No, I'll collect it.'

Only the immediate families and a few friends were aware of the arrangements. Among the friends Nora had to number Émilie, who had taken some pains to keep in touch with her after they left finishing school.

'So it's the engagement party on the 17th and the wedding in May? That's rather nice, it puts you almost alongside me, Nora.' Émilie's wedding was scheduled for just after Easter, which was in April that year.

The two girls were in the Viennese Café in the Boulevard de Sebastopol, a favourite rendezvous with Émilie because they had a good pastrycook.

'Who's going to design your wedding dress?' she asked, her hand hovering over the cake tray.

'I . . . we . . . haven't thought about that yet.'

'I should take a firm line on that, Nora. Don't let Tenet do it—he'll swathe you with tulle and diamanté.'

'I suppose we could go to someone else . . .'

'It's rather good, isn't it,' Émilie said, choosing a millefeuille. 'Both of us getting married within a year of our coming-out. We've done pretty well. I'd hate to have been hanging around for another season, wouldn't you?'

'It wouldn't have been much fun, I suppose—'

'Oh, it would have been *fun*—I mean, the season's marvellous, there's never a dull moment. But it would be embarrassing to be left on the shelf for another year, wouldn't it?'

Nora stirred her coffee.

'Joelle Lerrier didn't land anybody. She was really too absurd, imagining Georges Brochet was serious. *He* got his nose put out of joint—he wanted Liliane, but she's settled on Gilles. Gilles was one of yours, wasn't he?'

Nora shrugged.

'Well, I think you've done rather well, considering,' said the other girl. She meant, but didn't say, considering you're not all that attractive and made absolutely no effort. 'Edmond strikes me as being a really nice man.' She sighed. 'I wouldn't have minded him myself.'

A scream seemed to be rising in Nora. She wanted to lean across and shout in Émilie's face, Then take him, take him! I don't want him!

'Still, it wouldn't be fair on Alphonse.' She giggled. 'He's really keen on me, you know. It's rather flattering. And of course it'll be a great advantage once we're married.'

Nora shivered. She understood what Émilie meant. It would make the going to bed easier.

No matter how she tried, she couldn't imagine herself going to bed with Edmond. She couldn't picture any passion between them, any overwhelming need for each other. They were too polite. Even when Edmond kissed her—and he had kissed her on three occasions—his arm had rested lightly around her waist and his lips had pressed gently against hers.

Émilie was still talking, speculating about her trousseau. 'Mama and the lingiste say I should have white crêpe de Chine but I'm insisting on flesh pink—'

'Flesh pink?'

'My night-dress, silly! Haven't you been listening? I think flesh pink is far more exciting than white.'

'I don't know . . . Exciting?'

'Well, after all, darling, it'll be the first time

59

he sees me without a top layer, won't it? I want him to like what he sees.'

'Don't, Émilie!'

'Don't what? Talk about underwear? Why on earth not?' Émilie swallowed the last of her cake in a gulp that made her cough. When she recovered she said in a stern tone, 'You're not scared of it, are you? You've gone as white as a sheet.'

'I. . . I. . .'

'It's quite natural, after all. And the men know all about it, so you can be sure Edmond won't let you down.'

'Oh, Émilie! Don't! I *can't*—'

'Can't what? Of course you can!' Émilie, who wasn't a bad-natured girl, was assailed by a sudden concern for her friend. 'Look, Nora, if you're still bothered about it when it comes to the wedding day, all you have to do is drink champagne until you're giddy. That way, you'll probably go through the whole thing in a golden daze.'

Nora said nothing to this, which Émilie took to be acceptance of her good advice. She felt kindly towards poor Nora. Even with all the help of *haute couture* and sheaves of flowers, she wasn't going to be much of a blessing to her husband on their wedding day.

This conversation haunted Nora for the next two days. She longed to talk to someone, but who was there to turn to? Cousin Gaby? But she would only be kind and soothing. Marc? No, no—she could never talk about it to Marc! Mademoiselle Hermilot? Yes, perhaps Mademoiselle Hermilot could help her.

In her desperation she had to dial twice before she got it right. The phone was answered promptly at the old school in Rheims. 'May I speak to Mademoiselle Hermilot, please? This is Nora de la Sebiq-Tramont, one of her old pupils.'

'Oh, yes, Mademoiselle, I recognize your voice. This is Celeste, her secretary—'

'Of course. How are you, Celeste?'

'Mustn't grumble, despite this flu that's running around the city. And you, Mademoiselle? How are you? I believe Mademoiselle Hermilot had an invitation to a party at your Paris address—'

'Yes, tomorrow. I wonder . . . Could I speak to Madame? It's rather urgent.' Mademoiselle Hermilot was known as Madame in her role of headmistress: it conferrred more dignity.

'Oh, I'm so sorry, I'm afraid she's in bed with this terrible flu. I've just posted a note to your parents to say she will unfortunately not be able to attend the party.'

'Oh no!'

Even across the faulty telephone connection the dismay in her tone was clear. 'Is anything wrong, Mademoiselle?' asked Celeste.

'No . . . Thank you . . . I'm just disappointed. I was looking forward to seeing her.'

'I'll tell her that. I'm sure it will cheer her up.'

'Yes . . . Tell her . . . And give her my warm regards.'

'I'll certainly do that.'

Next day the florists arrived early to do the flowers for the party. Marc went to the office on business but promised to be back for lunch, at which Edmond was expected. He was to give Nora the ring beforehand so that they could have a private little celebration before the party in the evening.

Gaby came into Nora's room about noon. Nora was already wearing the frock that had been delivered the previous day, a special dress of hyacinth blue crêpe, but not so special as the evening dress that hung still in its light wrappings of tissue paper in her wardrobe—shell pink, embroidered with dark red roses formed in sequins, sleeveless, costing a fortune, and to Nora's eyes quite overpowering.

'You're very pale, dear. Are you feeling all right?'

'Yes, thank you, Gaby.'

Nerves, thought Gaby. It was only natural. This was a big day for the child.

'I thought we'd have a bottle of the 1920 at lunch. But don't drink too much of it, my pet, because you want to keep a clear head for this evening.'

'All right.'

'The announcement will be in the papers tomorrow. It's possible we may have the social

62

columnists ringing up in the morning about the wedding plans, but Annette will attend to that.'

'Yes, Gaby.'

'Naturally this evening, if people ask, you can say that we've tentatively settled on the 14th May. It's quite a good date because the first spray and the hoeing will be done by then, and our minds will be at rest about the growth of the vines. The only drawback is, Monsieur du Ceddres has business that may take him abroad about that date. However, so long as you say that it's a provisional date, we'll be quite safe.'

'I'll remember.'

'Are you sure you're all right, my love?'

'Yes, I'm fine.'

The maid came in search of Gaby. 'Monsieur du Ceddres has arrived, Madame.'

'Right on time. Good, Lucie. You've shown him into the drawing-room?'

'Yes, Madame.'

'Very well.' She waited for Lucie to withdraw, then turned to Nora. 'I've arranged you won't be disturbed in the drawing-room. I think the best thing will be for you to come and show me the ring in my boudoir, and when you do that I'll order lunch to be served. All right?'

'Yes, Gaby.'

'Very well, off you go. And Nora—' as her young cousin made for the door—

'What?'

'Smile!'

She tried to obey this injunction as she went across the hall to the drawing-room. Edmond was sitting in a tapestry armchair looking at a newspaper. He rose as she came in.

'Nora! How pretty you look in that dress.'

It was quite untrue, but she appreciated the lie. He was a nice young man. She ought to consider herself lucky to have been paired with someone so considerate.

He for his part was thinking something the same. He liked Nora a lot. Occasionally, when she was deeply engrossed in something that interested her—looking at plants through a spy-glass, for instance—he would catch a glimpse of someone remarkable, someone he hadn't yet got to know.

He had had the usual escapades with girls but they didn't occupy too much of his attention. He had accepted early in life that the family name must be preserved and, since he hadn't found anyone with whom to fall desperately in love, the alliance with the Tramonts had seemed suitable. His own family were keen on it. The girl herself was 'sweet'—she'd make a good, loyal wife. The financial side was all that could be desired. Really, it was a good match.

All the same, it had its problems. One of them was what to say at this moment. Both of them had known that on a given day they would become 'officially engaged'. This was a state into which they would enter.

But what did one say?

He had rehearsed a few words to himself the previous evening. And since she didn't turn to him with glowing eyes, inviting him to take her in his arms and thus do away with conversation, he began.

'I'm very honoured that you chose me, Nora, out of all the men you know. I'll do everything I can to make you happy.'

He paused. In a muffled voice Nora said, 'Thank you.'

He waited. Perhaps she would say something about wishing to make him a good wife. But no . . . she was standing about three feet away, looking at her shoes.

She waited. Perhaps he would say that he had always loved her secretly, but never spoke of it so that she would be free if she fell really in love with someone else. If he would only say he loved her, everything could still be all right. She would be grateful, and out of that gratitude real affection would grow.

He took the case with the ring from his inner pocket. He opened it, took out the ring. He advanced a little so as to take her hand, which hung limply at her side. He raised it, and waited for her to separate her third finger to receive the ring, which he guided towards it.

She snatched hand away.

'No! No, I can't! I can't!'

Utter astonishment struck him speechless. The

ring was knocked from his hand to lie sparkling in the Turkey-red carpet.

He stared at Nora. Tears were pouring down her cheeks. She shook her head vehemently. 'I'm sorry, Edmond. I know I'm . . . I just *can't!*'

Her hands held up to shield her face, she ran to the door, wrenched it open, and ran out into the hall.

There she cannoned straight into her cousin Marc, who had just divested himself of his overcoat.

'Good God, child, what's the matter?'

'Marc—oh, Marc!' She was sobbing wildly.

'What's wrong? Has Edmond—'

'Nothing—nothing to do with Edmond—no—it's me—I can't go through with it!'

'With what? Dear child, what's happened?'

Edmond had come out of the drawing-room. He stood, tall and offended, just outside its door. 'Nora has refused my ring,' he said.

'Oh, good Lord, you mean she doesn't like it after all—?'

'No, no—Marc—help me!' begged Nora. 'Don't make me! Please, please! I can't marry Edmond!'

'But Nora . . .' He had put his hands on her shoulders now, trying to hold her steady so he could see her face. 'Nora, it's all arranged.'

'I know, but . . . You must help me! I can't! I feel trapped, I can't!'

'I think I'd better go, sir,' Edmond said, glancing about for his coat.

Marc pulled the bell-pull. The maid, who had been told to stay out of the way until summoned to serve lunch, appeared from the far end of the hall.

'Give Monsieur du Ceddres his coat, Lucie,' said Marc.

'His coat? But what about lunch, M'sieu?' she gasped.

'His coat, damn it!'

Gaby came hurrying from her room. She had heard the first sounds of distress while her maid was doing up the tiny buttons of her afternoon dress, and couldn't come out until she was decent. She stopped in amazement at the scene— her prospective cousin-in-law shrugging on his outdoor coat, Nora sobbing against Marc's chest, and the maid hovering with the main door half open.

'What's going on?' she cried.

'Good day to you, Madame,' Edmond said. 'Perhaps you'll telephone to let me know your wishes.'

'Edmond! Wait—what—?'

'Nora will explain,' he said, and went out. The maid shut the door quietly behind him, then stood aghast.

'You may go, Lucie,' Gaby said. She took hold of Nora's shoulder. 'Nora!'

Nora huddled closer to Marc.

'Nora, look at me! What has happened?'

Nora was crying too hard to be able to reply. Marc, over her head, said, 'She says she can't marry Edmond.'

'Can't marry—? What on earth do you mean?'

'Edmond says she wouldn't put on the ring.'

'Nora, turn round this moment and explain yourself,' Gaby commanded.

Nora did no such thing. She clung to Marc in desperation.

'Now come on, Gaby,' he said. 'She's in no state to explain anything. Come along, princess. Come and sit down. Come along, precious.'

He led her into the drawing-room and made her sit with him on the sofa. He jerked his head at Gaby, who poured brandy into a glass to bring to him. He took it, and little by little coaxed Nora to sip it. It went down the wrong way because she was sobbing still. She coughed and choked, and was ready to die of shame at her own ineptitude and stupidity and cowardice.

'What happened, exactly?' Gaby asked.

'God knows. I came in at the door and she hurled herself on me in a flood of tears. I wonder if Edmond said or did anything—'

Nora shook her head. With a great effort she got out a few words. 'No, not Edmond—I was the one.'

'What did you do? Did you have a quarrel?'

'No.'

'Nora, please. Please try to make sense. What's wrong?'

'I just suddenly . . . I knew . . . suddenly I couldn't go through with it.'

'Couldn't go through with it? You mean—the engagement?'

'The engagement, the marriage—everything. I can't, Gaby. I can't. Don't make me!'

'Make you? What are you saying. No one is forcing you! Nora, you're being absurd.'

Marc gave her a sharp glance. 'Don't speak to her like that, my dear. Can't you see she's very upset?'

'I can see that. I don't want to be unkind but I really must get to the bottom of this. We have people coming this evening—Edmond's parents, all the way from Digne—I must know what to do.'

Nora was rocking backward and forward with her handkerchief to her eyes. 'I can't face them. I couldn't!'

'But why not? Tell me what's happened?'

'Don't ask the impossible, Gaby. You can see she's not capable of explaining. We'll have to put everybody off.'

'At *this* hour? With the party due to start at eight this evening?'

'We'll have to do the best we can.'

'But the du Ceddres—they're on a train—'

'We can leave it to Edmond to tell them. As

69

to the others, you'd better get Annette to sit down to the phone and get in touch with them.'

'And what's she to say, in God's name?'

'Tell them Nora's been taken ill.' He glanced at the girl. It was true enough, in all conscience. 'There's flu about at the moment. Tell them it's flu.'

It seemed Gaby would object, but a long look at Nora convinced her of the good sense of his plan. Whatever had happened or was going to happen, her little cousin was in no state to be the star of an engagement party that evening.

Marc pulled Nora to her feet. 'Come along, you must lie down and get some rest. We'll talk about it all when you're feeling more yourself.'

She got up falteringly. He put an arm about her to lead her to her room. Lucie, hovering in the hall to be of use when needed, darted ahead, opened the room door, turned down the bedspread.

Thankfully Nora fell on her bed, face first. She hid her sobs in her pillow. For perhaps half an hour she wept, until she had cried herself out. Then she fell asleep. All kinds of weird dreams visited her, she thrashed about as she slept.

Then suddenly sat up, wide awake.

She knew why she couldn't fall in love with Edmond and marry him. It had suddenly become clear.

She was already in love, and had been since she was about eleven years old.

And the man she loved was her cousin Marc . . .

THREE

When Gaby came in about half an hour later to see how she was, she pleaded a blinding headache, which was true enough. By this means she avoided more conversation that evening and for the same reason she was excused sitting at table for the light evening meal the cook provided in place of the lavish buffet.

She slept badly, partly because of the headache and partly because of nightmares which woke her, gasping and whimpering, several times.

She was oppressed by a terrible sense of wickedness, of actual sin in the sense so often used in church sermons. She was in love with Marc. Marc, who was like a father to her.

There was a word for the unnatural love between father and daughter, a word so terrible that she could hardly allow it to form in her brain. She must be depraved beyond belief to have allowed such a thing to happen.

She tossed and turned, sometimes burying her head in her pillow and holding her arms over it to shut out the thought. She was evil, degenerate. There was no hope for her.

The only good thing was that she had refused Edmond. How wrong, how utterly wicked, it would have been to accept him with this buried secret waiting to wreck their marriage. Poor Edmond. He deserved better.

In the morning she looked so ill that Gaby summoned a doctor. He recommended rest and gentle treatment, prescribed a sedative.

'We'd better let everything lie as it is for a day or two, my dear,' Gaby told her, obeying the doctor's instructions. 'You needn't get up if you don't feel like it. Take your time.'

Nora mumbled her thanks. As Gaby pottered about twitching the flowers in the vase and setting books upright on the bureau, she made herself ask: 'What about the du Ceddres?'

'Don't think about that. Edmond is handling it. I don't know what's he's told them.'

'He . . . Is he very angry?'

'I think he's perplexed, Nora.' She was about to go on to say, 'So are we all—what's at the back of it?' But she checked herself, kissed her young cousin lightly, and turned to go.

'Oh, by the way—'

'Yes?'

'Marc sends his love.'

She was outside the door before Nora let the tears spill over again.

Two days went by. Nora was treated like an invalid. She stayed in her room, had delicate meals on a tray, rested on her bed in the afternoon in a slight daze brought on by the sedatives. She felt disconnected from the real world.

But her thoughts kept returning to Marc, what he meant to her, how impossible life seemed without him. She loved him so much . . . And it was so *wrong*.

But after a couple of days a thought even more wicked began to whisper somewhere inside her head. What was so wrong with it? Marc was not, after all, her father. He wasn't her cousin, really. He was no blood kin. He was only her cousin by marriage.

So what was so wicked about being in love with him? There was no traditional tribal curse on that. He was handsome, kind, decent—he was just the kind of man whom she might have fallen in love with if he had turned up among her acquaintanceship.

That is, if she hadn't already been bound by a long affection to Marc.

She told herself she wasn't to blame. It had all begun when she was too young to be aware of it, and had grown so innocently that she ought not to feel in the wrong.

Ha! said the censor inside her head. Playing the innocent, are we? *The man you're thinking about is your cousin's husband. Your Cousin Gaby, who has been a mother to you.*

How could she be so ungrateful, so self-centred and greedy? Marc belonged to Gaby. They had shared great sufferings, proved their love by hardships and dangers—something to do with the war.

She had never heard the whole story but once when she had come across the medal of the Légion d'honneur in Gaby's jewel case she'd understood they had done something wonderful together, something so important that it had been rewarded by the French government.

And she—who was she to dare to think she had any claim on Gaby's man? She who had never done anything important in her life, who was so shy and uncertain she couldn't even make interesting conversation in strange company.

Besides, it was all useless. Marc had no eyes for anyone except Gaby. She was almost sure he was totally faithful—unlike so many husbands of whom she heard gossip.

He looked on Nora as if she were a daughter. He certainly saw no other love but daughterly affection when she looked at him. And, truth to tell, that was all it had been until the blinding revelation of the engagement day.

It had been hidden until now. It could be hidden still. Not easy—not now that she was aware of her own feelings. But that was part of her punishment.

The time came when she had to make an attempt to take up the threads of daily life. She left her room at midmorning after a late breakfast in bed. The maid helped her dress although no special pains were to be taken today—after all, there was no engagement party ahead now, no eager young suitor to please.

Marc had gone to the Rue Lelong. Gaby was in the study, giving instructions by telephone to the chief of cellar at Calmady. She gestured to her cousin to sit down, quickly concluded her conversation.

'Well, darling? Are you feeling better?'

'Yes, thank you.'

She didn't look better. In fact, she looked quite ill—thin and haggard. Oh, God, thought Gaby, please don't say there's anything really wrong with her. She'd always been a thin and wiry child, seldom ill.

'Do you feel able to talk about Edmond?' she said gently.

'I don't really want to. But of course I know I must.' She gathered herself for the question. 'What did he say about . . . about the other day?'

'He's completely at a loss. He told his parents you'd been taken ill suddenly and they accepted that. His father had to go back to Digne, for business reasons. His mother is still in their Paris apartment waiting to meet the family. As far as she's concerned, the engagement is still going ahead.'

She stopped, Nora was shaking her head with vehemence.

'Nora, for God's sake explain yourself!' She caught herself back. She mustn't become peremptory. 'Look, my love, we're terribly worried

75

and upset. We do need to know what caused this upset.'

Nora swallowed. She had made up her mind what to say. 'I can't marry Edmond. I'm sorry.'

'Why not? What suddenly changed your mind?'

'I can't explain.'

'Don't you like him?'

'Yes, he's very nice.'

'Then why have you turned against the idea?'

'I'm not ready to get married. I suddenly realized . . . I'm too young, I can't take the responsibility.'

Gaby caught back an exclamation of impatience. Responsibility! What nonsense! The child would have no responsibilities she didn't want. There was money enough to take care of every task in a married household.

But yet . . . The hope of both families had been that the young couple would soon have children. And children were a responsibility.

'Is it starting a family that worries you? Because, if so—well, darling, you know we want that, but if it really worries you it can be deferred for a year or two.'

Nora looked up. The strange grey eyes flashed with sudden spirit. 'Then if it isn't so urgent, why do I need to be married off so quickly?'

'Married off? What an expression—'

'All right, I withdraw it. But you just said it can all be deferred for a year or two.'

Gaby got to her feet, masking her impatient anxiety with movement. 'Nora, the du Ceddres aren't going to wait a year or two.'

Nora understood the dilemma. She had hurt and offended Edmond by her behaviour but he, out of goodwill, had hidden all that from his parents. However, the moment there was any suggestion that he should be put off for a year of two, family pride would be involved. Why should he hang about waiting for a girl who didn't seem to know her own mind? There were other girls, just as suitable, just as rich, and probably prettier.

'I'm sorry,' she mumbled.

'Being sorry doesn't help! Why did you let us get so far with the arrangements if you didn't really want to be married?'

'Because . . . because I didn't want to be disobedient.'

'Disobedient?' Gaby turned to her, shattered at her use of the word. 'My dear child!' She put her arms about her, held her close. 'Nora, Nora! This isn't a thing you have to do to please us! It's your whole life—we want you to be happy— don't you understand?'

'Yes,' whispered Nora, in tears again.

All the same, she didn't quite accept that. They had put pressure on her. They could say it was for her happiness—'for her own good'—but if she had really been allowed to say, honestly, what she wanted, she'd have said she wanted to be left as she was. She had been happy, in her own quiet way. But she had to have a coming-out and find a husband and start a family—not because it was her own wish, but because it was the next step in the preservation and furtherance of the Tramont kingdom. She was its crown princess: she had to have a consort.

Now that the discussions had begun, they were resumed throughout the next few days. She even managed to talk to Marc about it without giving herself away. But she said very little, and he in his turn was bewildered and hurt.

'I don't know what's gone wrong, Gaby,' he sighed to his wife. 'She and I used to have such a good relationship. But now she hardly says more than yes or no to me.'

'She feels she's in disgrace, I think.'

'We-ell . . . isn't she? I think we ought to be less reproachful to her, my love.'

'And what about the du Ceddres?'

He squared his shoulders. 'I'll speak to Edmond. It'll be a blow to him but he's a decent lad. If the thing's been wrecked beyond repair, he'll understand.'

What was said between her guardian and her prospective fiancé, Nora never knew. Marc came home looking drawn and tired.

'You must write to him, Nora. You owe him that. He's agreed to withdraw his claims on you and try to soothe his father out of feeling insulted.'

'I can't write to him!' Nora cried. 'What would I say?'

'Damned if I know, child. But he deserves an apology, at least, and if you can put down some words of explanation to show to his people, so much the better.'

Nora wasted many sheets of notepaper as she sat at the bureau in her bedroom. But in the end she concocted something she thought would do.

'Dear Edmond, My cousin Marc asked me to write in apology, and I do so in the sincere hope that you'll forgive me. I know I was wrong to let things get so far. I can only say I was confused and unhappy for a long time.

'Everything is my fault, not yours. I wish you every happiness. Yours, Nora de la Sebiq-Tramont.'

Nothing more was heard directly from the du Ceddres. The lawyers tidied up the debris. Polite letters were sent to all who had written in concern over Nora's illness. No explanations were needed about the engagement because there had been time to cancel the announcement in the newspapers. There was no public scandal, although there was some speculation.

Émilie telephoned Nora to ask what was going on. 'This is a long bout of flu! You haven't been out for days and days—weeks, in fact.'

'I'm all right now, Émilie.'

'But what about the wedding plans and everything? I'm waiting to hear about that. If the

79

wedding's going to be held in Calmady I want to—'

'There won't be a wedding, Émilie.'

There was a long pause. The wires sang with astonishment between them.

'It's off?'

'Yes.'

'You're joking!'

'No.'

'But why? What happened?'

'I changed my mind.'

'You . . .?' A gasp. 'Are you out of your wits?'

'Perhaps, Émilie.'

'But why? Good God, what on earth—?'

'I can't explain. It's just the way things are.'

'I think you're insane! You mean you've jilted Edmond du Ceddres?'

'No. I didn't do that.'

'He jilted you?' There was the sudden beginning of hidden glee in the voice of her friend. 'Is that it, Nora?'

'Believe what you like,' Nora said, and put back the receiver.

She was taken home to Calmady 'to convalesce'. The household staff knew that something had gone badly wrong, because there had been gossip about the betrothal and talk of a May wedding. Now it was all to be forgotten, it seemed.

They were all too well trained and too fond of the little cousin to stare or look contemptuous.

She'd been jilted, poor kid. Extraordinary, that it could happen to a girl with so much money. But life could be hard on anybody.

In the comforting round of the work of the winefields, Nora began to return to something like her normal self. She didn't go out with Marc so often to do the daily inspection, but she worked with Gaby in the office, and spent a lot of time in the caves with the chief of cellars.

The year went on its accustomed round. The new earth was placed round the vines, then it was time to prune them. In the cellars, the new vintage was fined and then racked. The wine for use in future years was taken to the coldest cave under the chalk.

As April progressed towards May, it was inevitable that thoughts of the intended wedding should arise. Gaby began gently to probe Nora's state of mind. Not this year, not this May, but perhaps next year. 'You might meet someone during the season—.'

'I'm not going to do the season, Gaby.'

'Oh, but—My angel!—How are you going to meet anyone—'

'I thought we'd agreed on all that, Gaby! I thought you understood—'

'Oh, of course! Not Edmond—I quite see that—but you know we could easily—'

'*No*, Gaby! Please don't go on about it!'

Nora rushed out of the house and, as a means to get out of the reach of her well-intentioned

Relative, threw herself into the little Lagonda she had been given on her seventeenth birthday and drove away.

There was scarcely anywhere to go. She had few friends to whom she wanted to confide her troubles—certainly not Émilie, who in any case was in the throes of last minute preparations. She turned the car towards Rheims and the only person she could think of, Mademoiselle Hermilot.

The school was already closed for Easter. The elderly maid looked surprised when she opened the door to her. 'Is Madame expecting you, Mademoiselle Tramont? She didn't mention any visitors . . .'

'Would you tell her I'm here? And it's important. I very much want to see her.'

Elvire Hermilot was at that moment on her hands and knees in the stockroom, with piles of textbooks around her. A visitor was the last thing she wanted. However, she was close enough to the Tramonts to know that there had been a match almost made and then inexplicably called off. No doubt the child was in distress about it. To be jilted was a terrible blow.

She rose somewhat stiffly, took off the brown holland apron which had been protecting her dress, went to wash her hands quickly in the pupils' cloakroom, then hurried to her office. She had to stifle a gasp when she saw Nora. The child looked really ill.

Heartbreak, no doubt, over this young man who had so cruelly turned her down.

'My dear!' she said with more warmth than she had ever allowed herself before. 'Come and sit down. Would you like anything? A glass of wine? Coffee?'

'A cup of coffee would be good, Madame. Thank you.'

Elvire nodded instructions to the maid, who went off grumbling inwardly about being expected to stop the clearing up to make unexpected pots of coffee. Nora took the seat that Elvire offered.

'Now, this is nice,' said Elvire. 'I haven't seen you for ages—I didn't get to the party—'

'The party was called off, Madame.'

'So it was, because you were taken ill. I had flu, you know, but I think I had it more lightly than you.'

'I haven't been ill,' Nora blurted out. 'That was just an excuse to get out of seeing people.' She hesitated. 'Did the Relatives tell you that . . . that . . .'

'Not in any detail. You mustn't take it so much to heart, Nora. If he didn't want the marriage, it was as well to say so before any public announcement had been—'

'It wasn't Edmond, it was me! I was the one who backed out.'

It was so unexpected that Elvire Hermilot wondered if perhaps the child was making it up.

Hurt pride . . . But Nora had never been one to fantasize about her life. Quite the reverse, she was apt to be too hard on herself.

'Do you want to talk about it?' asked Elvire in a quiet tone. No dramatics, no exclamations of surprise or reproach. Clearly the girl needed help and if she were to get it, she must have a sympathetic listener.

'I came to you . . . I came because . . . You and the Relatives have been friends a long time . . . Perhaps you can convince them . . . I mean, why can't they just take my word for it? I don't want to be married. I thought they accepted that when they agreed to call things off with Edmond.'

The maid tapped, then entered with a tray on which were a china coffee filter-pot, two large cups, cream and sugar. 'There's no cake,' she said crossly. 'You didn't say anything about catering for a guest.'

'That's all right, Bettine. We don't need anything else. If there are any calls, please answer them in the hall and say I can't come to the telephone at the moment.'

Grumbling, the maid went out. Elvire had had time to pull herself together. Complete openness was best, she felt. 'I'm right in thinking the party was to announce your engagement?'

Nora nodded.

'And you changed your mind at the last moment?'

84

'Yes.' She coloured. 'Cousin Gaby picked up Edmond's ring off the carpet that evening.'

'You didn't throw it down, for heaven's sake?'

'No, it just fell when I jerked my hand away. I suddenly realized I couldn't let him put it on.'

Elvire took off the lid of the filter. The water had still some way to go. 'You dislike him?'

'No, no—how could you think such a thing. He's quite nice. I've nothing against Edmond, nothing in the world. But I didn't feel about him the way I ought to feel for the man I'm going to marry.'

'Mmm . . .' said Elvire. How did it suddenly come about that young Nora Tramont, never a romantic, suddenly had notions about love? She turned the cups right way up on their saucers to employ her hands. Then she said, very gently, 'Is there someone else?'

She looked up as she spoke. She saw the colour rising in a scarlet tide from Nora's thin neck to her cheeks and then to her brow.

'Ah,' she said.

Nora sprang up and moved a little way off, one hand to her cheek. 'How could you possibly know that?' she whispered, her face averted.

'It was just a guess. Come now, dear, sit down. If we're going to talk, I don't want to address the back of your head.'

After a hesitation Nora obeyed. Madame's question had been a tremendous shock. She had been happy in at least that one point—that no one could possibly suspect the real reason for her change of heart.

'Nora,' said Madame in a matter-of-fact tone, pouring coffee with a steady hand, 'if you love someone else, there's no reason why the Relatives shouldn't approach his family—'

'No!'

'Why not?'

'I don't want them to know!'

'But I don't quite understand, Nora. The whole trouble arose because they wanted you to find someone to settle down with. It seems that you've done so. Perhaps it all happened after they'd started the negotiations with the du Ceddres?'

Nora shook her head, unwilling to say a word that would give Madame any further clues. She regretted now that she had come. She'd been so sure that all she had to do was appeal to her old teacher for help and it would be forth coming. If Mademoiselle Hermilot told the Relatives to leave her alone, they would do so.

'Well, the timetables don't matter, only that you should be frank with your cousins. They do most sincerely want your happiness, child. Just tell them about this young man and they'll understand.'

'No, no! I don't want to talk to them about that.'

Madame pushed one cup of coffee towards her, indicating the cream and sugar. Nora ignored the gesture. Madame said, 'He's unsuitable, then.' It wasn't a question.

Nora couldn't avoid a little movement—not quite assent, but it was enough.

'What's the problem with him? Is he poor? I don't think money is a factor, so long as he's not one of those penniless adventurers—and I feel sure you haven't been allowed to meet any of those.'

'Please, let's just forget about it—'

'We can't do that, Nora. Be sensible. Tell me why you don't want the Relatives to know about this man.'

There seemed no way out. As if it was being dragged out of her, Nora heard herself say: 'He's married.'

The headmistress bit back an exclamation of dismay. Married . . . That was a terrible blow. And yet, after all, it was only too likely to happen.

These young things were thrown together in an atmosphere of high excitement, spending almost every day or evening in each other's company. There was no denying that the young men were often handsome, charming . . . Some young rogue had clearly put himself out to win Nora's heart but had chosen another girl, perhaps for family reasons, perhaps because he simply didn't find Nora attractive enough to marry.

What mattered now was to find out how deep it went.

'Did you go to bed with him?' she asked.

Nora's whole body seemed to shudder with surprise. 'Of course not!' she said, aghast.

Quite clearly it was the truth. The horror and outrage in her grey-flecked eyes was completely genuine.

Mademoiselle Hermilot didn't smile at so much innocence. She said, 'I'm sorry I had to ask that, my dear. But I needed to find out how serious it was. You could hardly call it an affair, then?'

'Not at all! I don't want you to talk like that about it! He.. , He doesn't even know . . . Oh, why can't you just leave me alone? Why can't I just say, I don't want to be badgered about getting married, and have people believe me? I'm sick of the way everybody thinks they know better—how can they know better, *I'm* the one who has to live with the situation!'

'That's true. And quite clearly, your nerves are suffering because of it. I'll tell you what, Nora. How would you like to stay with me for a week or two? It would give you time to yourself, and perhaps that's what you need most at the moment.'

'Could I? Could I really? Oh, it would be such a blessing! I know they try not to show it, but the Relatives are so disappointed in me, and it makes me so . . . wretched . . .' Tears were brimming yet again. She was furious with herself. Every time she thought of her cousins and their bewildered kindness to her, she wanted to cry her heart out.

'Drink your coffee,' said Mademoiselle Hermilot. 'I'll ring your Cousin Gaby and ask if you can stay. I don't see why not—you've done it before.'

Gaby was at first surprised, but agreed. 'Perhaps it's a good thing,' she sighed. 'I don't seem to be able to communicate with her at all. She might talk to you, Elvi.'

'She has talked to me,' Mademoiselle Hermilot said. 'I'll tell you all about it, but this isn't the moment. Would you send on some clothes for her? I think she'll need enough for about a week.'

'I'll tell her maid. And, Elvi, come and see me tomorrow, If you can give me any clues about her behaviour, I'd be so grateful.'

The story, when Mademoiselle Hermilot told it, caused Gaby to go red then pale. 'In love with a married man? It's impossible!'

'It's not the least impossible. For all we know, it's that boy Gilles Sez, who fell head over heels for the Tratanne girl. They were married in the autumn, weren't they?'

'Ye-es. But I never saw her show the least interest in him, Elvi,'

'But then she's so quiet and reticent.'

'But he scarcely even looked at her, although he was supposed to be one of her escorts. I was on the verge of speaking to him about it.'

'You don't know what might have gone on when you weren't there, my dear. These days, you know, young people have so much more freedom—it's not like when you and I were young, Gaby.'

'No.' It was a sigh, but whether of regret or acceptance, Elvire couldn't tell. 'Well, thank you for letting me know. At least I have some idea of how to go on. Of course it's all nonsense about being in love—she's just in the grip of an infatuation, poor child. She'll grow out of it.'

'But meantime I think it would be a good idea not to try even to talk about marriage. And if you can leave her with me for a few weeks, that would help. She feels terribly guilty towards you and Marc—feels she's let you down.'

Gaby didn't make any rejoinder. Sometimes she felt she agreed with Nora's self-criticism: she'd put them in a terribly embarrassing situation, to speak only of the least of their troubles. And the fact remained that the girl must marry. This year, next year, the year after—either Nora must marry or they must try to find some distant relative, some young, intelligent male who could be adopted into the family and trained to take over.

But that needn't be thought of for some years yet. The child would come to her senses, would find a man she liked, and everything would be all right. The handsome young husband of the first season would be forgotten.

90

Gaby wasn't loath to have Nora out of the house for a while. She had other troubles. The law promulgated that year, establishing the boundaries of the Champagne region for the purpose of legitimizing champagne wine, had naturally been greeted with a storm of protest and abuse from those ruled out.

But more was being proposed. Severe restrictions were being considered, which would guarantee the absolute purity and consistency of the wine. The House of Tramont had absolutely no objections to any of this, for the processes of their establishment already met the requirements.

But the smaller *négociants* were very unhappy. They didn't have the money for changes to their cellars and bottling plants. It was all, they cried, due to the miserliness of the big firms, who refused to pay decent prices for the grapes.

So Gaby and the other big houses were trying to set up a conference for a time close to this year's harvest, at which a fair price would be set in the presence of a government official.

The negotiations seemed endless and were very time consuming. It would be a blessing to be able to relax at home at Calmady, without coming across that pale woebegone face to remind her of yet another problem.

'What would you do with her, Elvi? Wouldn't it interfere with your own plans?'

'Oh, I'm spending the Easter break reorganizing the stock of textbooks and refurbishing the school library. Nora can help me with that. And there's a charity event I'm involved with—she could do the last-minute arrangements for it.'

'Another charity show? What this time? A concert? A play by the local amateurs?'

Mademoiselle Hermilot was interested in educational matters, particularly to help the less fortunate pupils of the state schools extend their studies. This year she had brought off something of a coup. The great dressmaker Gabrielle Chanel had agreed to put on a show.

'Coco Chanel? How did you manage that?' cried Gaby. 'She's not noted for her interest in good works!'

'She did it to please that English milord she lives with—he's rather a soft-hearted type who let himself be talked into helping us by the Baron Belpacy. And of course she's only showing frocks that have already been shown.'

'Well, I'm sure Nora will be useful—anything practical like counting the takings, and she's in her element.'

Elvire Hermilot knew that very well. She'd had Nora as a pupil for eight years. She put her in charge of the final correspondence and telephone calls for the show, which was to be held in the ballroom of one of the great villas of Épernay, now completely restored after the depredations of war.

The tickets were fiendishly expensive but included an excellent buffet and as much champagne as you could drink. It should have surprised no one then, when the Baron Belpacy got hopelessly drunk. The organizing committee were in a panic. The Baron was supposed to make a speech of thanks at the end, but it would take at least an hour to sober him sufficiently and the programme had only forty-five minutes to run.

Nora was despatched with a message for Madame Chanel, who had been given quarters for her models, dressers and clothes in a suite of ante-rooms.

'Madame, the committee asks if you could extend the dress parade by about fifteen minutes?'

'What?' cried Coco Chanel, whirling on her.

Nora recoiled. She was a very frightening little lady. Everything about her seemed aggressive. Her mouth was full of pins, she was brandishing a pair of scissors, and around her lay fragments of hem from a frock she was savaging while its wearer stood rigid under her attack.

'Another fifteen minutes, Madame—we need time—'

'Indeed? And where am I supposed to get another ten dresses? Out of the air?'

'The committee thought perhaps you could ask your mannequins to walk more slowly—'

'Oh yes! And then all those business pirates

will have more time to sketch the line and the detail—'

'Excuse me, Madame, but they must have got all the sketches they wanted weeks ago. The dresses aren't exactly new.'

'Ha!' said Madame Chanel. She stared at Nora with small black eyes. 'And why, may one ask, does the committee want this alteration?'

'Because the Baron Belpacy, who's to make the speech at the end, is as soused as a herring.'

Madame Chanel didn't exactly laugh, but her ferocity relaxed a little. 'How like him . . . Well, I refuse to tell my girls to walk more slowly. My dresses aren't stately. They need briskness.'

'The alternative is to have the string quartet play an interlude . . . if you would allot a point where there could be an interlude.'

'I didn't come here to waste my time planning your programme, Mademoiselle.'

'I'm sorry, Madame. I'm just giving you the committee's message. And I thought . . . you'd rather the audience were looking at your models, instead of chatting and half-listening to a string quartet.'

Coco Chanel gave her her full attention for the first time. The girl had the perfect figure for today's fashion—slender, almost boyish, with a good carriage—'*sportif*' as Chanel liked to call it. But the dress—my God! Too much ornament calling attention away from the face—although the face wasn't all that marvellous. And the

94

hair—who on earth styled her hair? Attila the Hun?

'I'll tell you what I'll do,' Madame Chanel said, having thought it through on another level of her mind while her dressmaker's eye assessed Nora. 'I'll pick out a dozen or so of my dresses. Go out and recruit four or five of your young friends—pretty if possible, but they must be slim like you. They can go on after the beach clothes, and then again just before the wedding dress at the end of the show.'

'Go on!' gasped Nora.

'Yes, yes, go on—it will fill in the time and give the audience the chance to see for themselves that *anyone* can wear my frocks.'

'But Madame—surely it takes training—'

'Nonsense. You don't spend all your time sitting in a drawing-room, do you? What do you do to fill your days?'

'Well, I go riding . . . I help Mademoiselle Hermilot . . . I drive my car . . .'

'Exactly. That's what my dresses are for, the daily life of a modern woman. So go and fetch me four or five of your friends and we'll put the dresses to the test. Go away, I'm busy. Nanette, stand still.' The model wearing the dress, who hadn't moved a muscle, grew even more rigid.

Nora, understanding this was a take-it-or-leave-it decision, turned to go.

'Wait,' called Chanel. 'Who dresses you, Mademoiselle?' She snapped her fingers, 'Don't tell me, I know. It's Tenet, yes? What a disaster! But it's not my business—go, Mademoiselle, go!'

The committee were put in a panic by her message. 'Ask our young ladies to act as mannequins—?'

'I'm sure they'd love it,' said Elvire Hermilot, whose career as a teacher had given her much insight into the minds of young ladies. 'Besides, what else are we to do? Time's getting short—if we don't do something there will be a yawning gap at the end of the programme. Run, Nora—find some girls who'll take it on.'

In the end only three girls agreed out of the six she had time to approach. That made four amateur models to wear Madame's frocks. They went nervously into the makeshift dressing room.

'I asked for five or six, Mademoiselle.'

'I'm sorry, these are all I could get in the time.'

'Very well. Marie, give me the beige jersey. Where's the fawn costume? Oh, here it is.' She was flicking hangers along the rail that held the clothes, picking things out. 'You, the blonde—you can have the gunmetal. What are you all standing there for? Take your clothes off.'

Giggling and blushing, they obeyed. They were revealed clad in various shades of pale pink crêpe de Chine, all wearing the new camiknickers edged with fine lace and held up by shoe-string shoulder straps.

'Not bad, not bad. Hey, the brunette, hold your shoulders back. You can wear the beige jersey—it won't hang right if you stoop so stand *up*.' She thumped Lucille Lormet between the shoulder-blades to emphasize the command.

In a few minutes they were in the frocks, patting their hair back into order. 'Now, I want you to walk out when I tell you. You, the blonde, you lead them. Walk down to the far end of the catwalk. Take small steps, look at a point ahead at eye level. When you get to the end of the catwalk, you stop, of course, otherwise you fall off into someone's lap.'

There was a nervous laugh.

'When I clap my hands, all turn to the right. Smile at the audience. When I clap again, turn slowly so that the audience on the other side of the catwalk gets to see the front of the dress. Smile. When I clap the third time, the girl nearest me leads the way off. Understood?'

'Ye-es, Madame.'

'You'll go on after the beach clothes. You'll change while the tennis and golf frocks are being shown. Then you'll go back and do the same thing again in different dresses. Marie, I want them all in evening frocks, pick out four that won't look too bad with their shoes.'

She shooed them ahead of her to the area curtained off at the end of the ballroom. Her professional models were coming off, having shown the amazing bright beach pyjamas in silk that were to take the Riveria by storm that summer.

97

Nora was second in the row. She'd never been so scared in her life. She walked on, everything a blur in front of her. She scarcely heard the gasp of amazement, even of horror, as these young daughters of the *haute bourgeoisie* trooped on like paid mannequins. She stopped when Lucille Lormet stopped. She heard Madame clap her hands. She turned to the right. Another signal. She turned to the left. At the final summons she walked off.

As for smiling, it was beyond her. Yet she felt a rush of relief as the audience applauded when they left the stage. Mothers and aunts and sisters had recovered from the astonishment and had decided to approve.

In the changing room the senior *vendeuse* had the evening frocks ready. Nora found herself in a sleeveless sheath of black sequins that stopped just at her knees. It was heavy as it slipped over her head, and yet when it settled on her shoulders it ceased to weigh anything. She was pushed towards the mirror to tidy her hair. She saw herself in it—a figure slender as a wand, clad in a shining dress that hung easily, almost loose, yet somehow seemed to outline her figure with grace and charm.

Only the ugly hair-style spoiled the effect. She pulled her hair back from her temples, holding it down. Immediately it looked better. 'Ah?' said Marie, the assistant, behind her. 'You want to flatten it. Here, Mademoiselle.' She handed

Nora two big clasps of imitation tortoiseshell. Nora shoved them into her hair, anchoring it down.

It didn't look like a hair-style, but it made her head smaller so that it sat atop the shimmering dress in just the right proportions.

Chanel, coming to inspect them before she ushered them on stage, drew back for a moment at sight of Nora. 'Better!' she said. 'My God, what I could do with you!'

Next moment they were being driven ahead of her to the curtains. The catwalk stretched ahead. The girls walked on. But this time Nora was aware of herself—of herself in this dress—of moving with her head up, looking at a point at eye level, walking with small steps, and hearing the audience applaud as they came to a halt.

'Why,' she thought, 'I'm wearing a dress that actually looks good on me! I actually . . . don't look bad!'

In a moment it was all over. They were back in the dressing-room taking off the borrowed dresses. Nora donned the frock in which she'd come to the show, and suddenly felt almost ungainly. She frowned at her reflection in the mirror, made for the door, and then when the other girls had trooped out, laughing and joking with relief over their experience, she turned back.

'Madame!'

The *couturière* was supervising the packing of the clothes. 'What, what? I'm busy.'

'Did you mean what you said, that you could do something with me?'

Madame Chanel paused. She gave Nora a long, cold stare. 'Your clothes are cut wrong. They are wrongly decorated. They should be designed to make you look like a wand. You move well—like a little deer. Your clothes should enhance that.'

'Would you dress me, Madame?'

'And what about Tenet?'

'My Cousin Gaby took me to him. He's popular with . . . with . . .'

'Provincial ladies of a certain age. Yes, that's so. Your cousin would agree to a change?'

'Of course,' said Nora, perfectly sure of Gaby's falling in with any little alteration to her way of life. After all, she wasn't going to change her religion—only her dressmaker.

'Very well, come to me in the Rue St Honoré. But first—!' She held up a warning finger.

'What, Madame?'

'Have your hair properly cut!'

'Yes,' Nora agreed eagerly. She had seen what a difference it made, even to smoothe down the rich waves inflicted on her by her current hairdresser. 'To whom should I go?'

'Go to Lucien. Tell him I sent you.'

'Thank you, Madame Chanel.' She went to the door. 'Till later, then.'

'Till later,' said Madame Chanel, and forgot about her the moment the door closed behind her. She hadn't even bothered to ask her name.

Next day, when her chief *vendeuse* came to the office to say Mademoiselle de la Sebiq-Tramont was asking for her, Chanel had almost no idea who it could be. She remembered the name from the magazines of last year showing the débutantes, but there could have been nothing memorable about the girl because she'd taken no special notice.

She went to the salon to greet a total stranger. She was wearing a not very attractive coat and skirt in steel blue with matching long fur-trimmed stole. She stood by one of the little tables, on which lay her gloves and hat.

'Good afternoon, Mademoiselle,' Chanel said. Then she hesitated. 'My God! It's you!'

'Do you like it?' Nora said, putting her hands up to her temples. 'It feels strange—almost light-headed!'

'But what an improvement!' cried Coco Chanel. 'What a pretty shape now that one can see it! Oh, good heavens, you look like a charming boy!'

It was the greatest compliment she could pay. In Chanel's eyes, the *garçonne* was the ideal of today's woman—as free and active as a boy in clothes that suited her yet accentuated her femininity.

The hairdresser had cut Nora's hair very close

to her head at the back and over the ears. From about the crown, a longer tress was brushed forward in a soft curve that ended in a loose fringe on her forehead. The hair itself seemed to have changed colour, simply because the cut ends reflected light and made it look paler.

Now Nora's face was revealed as small and fragile. Her features were nothing extraordinary, but the bones were good and the eyes, no longer overshadowed by bunches of marcel waves, looked out in their strange mixed brown-and-grey.

Chanel studied her. 'Take off that dreadful coat,' she said. Nora obeyed, revealing herself in a plain skirt and matching blouse of silk.

'Hm . . .' said Chanel. 'The skirt isn't bad. The blouse . . . Hm . . . The colour is too strong for you. You should wear beige, fawn, black or white. Black . . . In black you should have lipstick and a little kohl on the eyes—'

'Make-up?'

'My God, why not? Nature gave us the canvas, we must work with it to make the picture. I will tell you what I see. You have a perfect figure, a good carriage, a pretty head with average colour hair—ideally, you should have a little peroxide—'

'No!' cried Nora.

'Very well, you're too young for that, perhaps. Well, then, you must keep your hair perfectly trimmed so that it stays as light as possible. Your eyes are good, you should accentuate them. As for the clothes, you must be dressed so that you look all-of-a-piece but nothing to distract the eye from the good points. No decoration except perhaps pearls or a string of plain beads. *No* gems, not even the family jewels. You must go to Elizabeth Arden and have a consultation about cosmetics. I think you should wear a dark lipstick but try several until you find one you like. But that can wait. Let us look at a few dresses.'

She snapped her fingers. The chief *vendeuse* came hurrying up. They held a muted consultation, after which Marie hurried away. Chanel occupied the slight interval that followed by walking round her new client with a tape measure.

When Nora left the salon in the Rue St Honoré she had given orders for four dresses and a suit. Before her went a *vendeuse* carrying a box in which lay a present from Madame Chanel'. She was put into a taxi and carried to the apartment in the Rue Berger.

When the maid opened the door to her, there was a moment when she was about to enquire her name. Then she gave a silent 'Oh!' and stood aside to let her enter.

'Good evening, Lucie, is anyone else here?'

'Monsieur Auduron-Tramont is in Paris, Mademoiselle. He'll be home soon from the Rue Lelong, I imagine.'

'Very well. Let me know when he comes in—I'll join him in the drawing-room for an aperitif.'

'Yes, Mademoiselle.' Lucie was taken aback. There was something different about Mademoiselle apart from the hair. She spoke with a kind of hidden delight. She . . . she even seemed to walk differently. There was a tilt to her head that was new.

Marc Auduron-Tramont came home some half-hour later. He saw Nora's gloves and bag, left on the hall table. 'Someone arrived?' he asked the maid as she took his raincoat.

'Mademoiselle Nora, sir. She said . . . she said she'd join you in the drawing-room for a drink.'

'I could certainly do with one,' he sighed. He'd spent almost all day on the telephone to Épernav and Rheims, talking with wine *négociants*.

He went into the drawing-room. The decanters were on the side table. He poured himself a large whisky, picked up the evening paper.

When Nora came in he turned to greet her. He wanted to let her know he was glad she'd come, that it was grand to see her after an absence of over two weeks.

He stopped with the welcome unuttered. He stared—he almost gaped.

An hour later he was in his study on the telephone again, this time to Calmady.

'Gaby!' he cried. 'Gaby, you'll never guess what's happened!'

'What? What?' his wife replied, immediately

anxious. Negotiations with the wine-makers were at a very delicate stage —almost anything could go wrong.

'Nora's here!'

'Nora?' That wasn't at all what she'd expected to hear, but after a second she said, 'Well, that's good—how is she?'

'Gaby, you're never going to believe this but . . . but . . . she's had her hair cut in the Eton crop and she's wearing yellow silk lounging pyjamas!'

FOUR

Next morning before breakfast, Cousin Marc was talking to his wife again on the telephone. 'I'm out of my mind with worry, Gaby! She hasn't come home all night!'

He heard the gasp on the other end of the line. 'I'm sorry,' he went on quickly. 'I handled it badly.'

'How? What happened?'

'Well . . . I got cross last night . . . I told her to go and take off those silly clothes and put on something decent.'

'Oh, Marc!'

'I said I'm sorry,' he groaned. 'I don't know why I got so angry.'

'So she refused and then—what?'

'She refused because she said she was going to

a party. I said, What party? and she said something about Madame Chanel and I said she wasn't going to any party, and told her to go to her room, and she did, but only to get a coat, and the next thing I knew she'd slammed out of the apartment.'

'Marc, Marc, how could you be so silly?'

'Darling, you can't say anything to me I haven't said to myself. I waited up for her but she didn't come home. In the end I fell asleep in my armchair. I woke up about an hour ago, took it for granted she'd come in meanwhile, but it turns out she didn't—her bed hasn't been slept in. What should we do?'

'Inform the police!'

'Gaby, we can't do that. She's stayed out all night—well, after all, there's nothing much in that—I mean, these young things, parties go on all night nowadays, they go to Les Halles to have coffee in the market cafés . . .'

'But it's so unlike her!'

'It's unlike her to have her hair cut like a boy and go out wearing outlandish clothes.'

'Yes. I understand a bit about that. After you rang last night, I got in touch with Elvi Hermilot. Apparently at the fashion show in Rheims a couple of days ago, Nora was chosen by Madame Chanel to model a couple of dresses.'

'*Nora* was?'

'Yes. And then yesterday she told Elvi she was going up to Paris at Chanel's invitation. Elvi

106

thought nothing of it, in fact was rather pleased—she felt it was nice that Chanel should take an interest in her.'

'Good God, I don't mind her taking an interest in her, Gaby! What I object to is changing her out of all recognition.' He sighed. 'She doesn't look like our little girl any more,' he mourned.

'No,' said his wife. 'Perhaps that's the message she's giving us.'

'Message?'

'Never mind, Marc. I'm catching the next train to Paris. I'll be there by noon.'

Before she could do so, she was called once more to the telephone. She trembled inwardly, fearing it was her husband again with bad news. But no—it was Nora herself.

'Cousin Gaby? I felt I ought to ring you in case you and Cousin Marc were worried.'

'Nora! Where are you? Are you at home?'

'No, I'm at the Hotel Erlanger—you know, the one Mademoiselle Hermilot uses when she's in town.'

'Nora, what on earth are you doing there? Why aren't you at home?'

'I felt I didn't want to just at present.' Nora paused. She didn't want to confess how hurt she had been by Cousin Marc's reaction to her new appearance.

She'd thought he would be astonished, charmed, delighted. She'd even perhaps hoped, at some deeper, more instinctive level, that he'd be attracted to her.

Instead he'd barked at her, like a sergeant-major: 'Go to your room! Change into something decent!'

'Sweetheart, we've been very, very worried. I'm coming to town. Please be at home when I get there.'

'No, Gaby.'

'What?' Gaby said, astonished. Never in her life had Nora disobeyed a direct instruction.

'I don't want to go home just yet.'

'But we have to talk, dear. I gather you've . . . you've taken a drastic step about your appearance—'

'Yes, and I don't know why I didn't do it ages ago!' Nora cried. 'Gaby, I went around for years looking a nobody—'

'That's not true, Nora, you always looked—'

'I looked like somebody's little-mouse daughter! It wasn't until Chanel let me try on—' She caught herself up. 'Well, never mind. Everything's different now. And disapproving isn't going to make me go back to what I used to be.'

'But Nora—'

'And I'm not coming home except on different terms—'

'Terms? Terms? Nora, you sound like one of the little *négociants* arguing about a contract—'

'All right,' Nora said almost angrily. 'Perhaps

I'm being small-minded. But I want it understood that . . .'

'What?'

'I don't know,' she confessed. She didn't know what she wanted. All she knew was that this was the time to make them understand she was a person in her own right. Not just the small cousin whom they'd rescued from the depths of Touraine, not the heiress to the Tramont estates who must be made to fit her role, not the girl who could be directed hither and thither, even into a loveless marriage.

Gaby had been thinking quickly. 'It's clear we have to talk,' she said, and as she often did, carried the attack into the enemy camp by appearing to give way. 'I'll come and see you, my dear. At the hotel. How about that?'

'Would you? Gaby? Would you? I'd like that.'

'And then we can go and have lunch somewhere pleasant—the Tour d'Argent, perhaps.'

'Oh, that doesn't matter—'

'I'll see you in a couple of hours, my love. Have you had breakfast?'

'Not yet,' said Nora, half-laughing at the way the conversation, from high drama, had turned to total domesticity.

'Well, make sure you have some coffee at once. I'll see you soon.'

A short report to Marc set his mind somewhat at ease. He said he would go to the office, and she must come to see him there after lunch, so that he could know what on earth had happened to their formerly docile ward. 'I can't think what's got into her,' he sighed.

'She's grown up all of a sudden, Marc—that's all.'

She gave her name at the Hotel Erlanger and was shown up to Nora's suite. She was interested to see these famous yellow satin pyjamas mentioned by her husband. But when Nora came from the bedroom to greet her, she was wearing a neat little fawn serge dress with a white collar. The only wrong note were the shoes, which were evening wear.

Nora saw her cousin taking in her appearance. She gestured to the shoes. 'I couldn't get anything quite right,' she said. 'I had some things sent in, to choose from. Do you like the frock?'

'Oh, yes, Nora. You look—really elegant.'

'It's not bad for ready-made, is it? I'd no idea, you know, that you could buy things that would fit well.'

Privately Gaby thought that, with her figure, she could go into any modiste and buy clothes off the rail. But that wouldn't be fitting for a young woman of her class. She must have her clothes made, and if they were to be made from now on by Coco Chanel, perhaps it would be a good thing. The change in her was startling, but she found she couldn't disapprove.

'Your hair, darling!' she said, studying her. 'It . . . it changes you totally!'

'Do you like it?'

There was no denying it. The new style was perfect for that small, neat skull. Gaby was interested enough in fashion to see that there had been a metamorphosis. From being a little provincial miss, Nora had blossomed into a fashion plate.

'You look charming, Nora.'

'Pretty?'

'Not pretty—intriguing.'

Nora nodded, satisfied. If her cousin had said she looked pretty she'd have known she was being humoured. But she'd had the truth. She was never going to be a pretty girl in the sense that Liliane Tratanne was pretty, or have Émilie's plump attractiveness. Instead she had something else—luck had come to her aid, she fitted into the 'look' of the times as if she had been created for the part.

'Did you come here last night after you left Rue Berger?' Gaby asked with careful casualness as she took a seat on the chintz-covered sofa.

'Why no. I told Marc—I was going to a party.'

'He said you'd been invited by Chanel?'

'That's so. It was at a house belonging to her English duke. I said I hadn't an escort to take me and she just laughed and said, "Turn up, you'll soon have escorts".'

'And did you?'

Nora smiled. 'It was very strange. I chose a place on the end of a sort of divan covered with

111

a Persian tapestry, and before I'd even sat down, there were four men there too.'

'Really?' said Gaby, worried. 'Anyone we know?'

'Oh no. They were mostly pretty old, really. Friends of Misia Sert—she's Coco's great friend, you know.'

'So I've heard.' Misia Sert was the Polish lady through whom Chanel had taken to stage-designing. She was a friend of Sergei Diaghilev, Jean Cocteau . . . God help us, thought Gaby, if Nora's going to get caught up in that set! Nora's mother had been attracted towards the theatre—and scant happiness it had brought her.

'But around midnight,' Nora was saying, 'some of the younger folk suggested we should go to a night-club so we—'

'Nora! You didn't go to a night-club without a proper escort!'

'Oh, don't get hot and bothered, Gaby, we were in a big group, and really, it was lovely . . .'

Lovely . . . It was the first time she'd been to a nightclub with a negro band. The music had been extraordinary, filling her blood with irresistible rhythms. She'd danced into the small hours, foxtrotting to 'Button Up Your Overcoat' and trying to do the blues to a wailing saxophone playing 'Along Came Bill'.

When it came time to go home, they'd piled into two taxis and been driven round Paris, dropping off passengers as they came to the right addresses. She couldn't picture herself arriving at the apartment in Rue Berger with two giggling girls and four rather drunk young men—Cousin Marc would wake up and there would be another scene. So, with quick practicality, she'd asked to be taken to the hotel in the Rue des Marronniers she'd visited when Mademoiselle Hermilot stayed there.

Once in the little suite on the first floor, she'd shed the satin pyjamas—not yellow, as Marc had reported, but a shade Chanel called antique gold—and crept between the sheets in her crêpe de Chine underwear. But she didn't sleep. She was too wound up to sleep.

From being almost an ugly duckling she'd been transformed into—well, not a swan, but perhaps a swift, a slim, elegant, sleek bird. The swifts, just returned to Calmady, wheeled and darted over the village, superb in their element. So far, she'd had no time to learn to fly. But she would, she would! She had just made her first attempt— she had tried her wings.

She explained to her cousin that she felt different about things now. 'I can't tell you exactly what I feel. I haven't worked it out yet. But I know that I've got to . . . to take my life into my own hands.'

She saw the sadness come into her cousin's beautiful dark eyes. 'Don't,' Nora said, taking her hand. 'Don't be sad about it. It's my fault, really. I haven't been able to come out of my shell until now. I see that. I've been held back by something, I'm not sure what. But I know now that it's time to change. And I want you to let me, Gaby.'

'Of course, dearest. I don't want to hold you back in any way . . . Only . . .'

'What?'

'Don't go away from us, Nora. You're all we have.' She heard her voice breaking and tried to bite back the words, but they had been said.

Nora leaned towards her, to kiss her on the cheek.'I couldn't really go away from you and Marc, Gaby. But from now on I think I'm going to be different. You're just going to have to get used to it.'

'Yes,' sighed Gaby, searching for a handkerchief to wipe the corners of her lashes. 'Yes, of course, we must, I see that.'

In the afternoon she went, as asked, to see her husband at the office.

'It's a *fait accompli*, my darling,' she told him. 'We just have to accept it. Our little Nora is gone, gone for ever.'

He grunted disapproval.

'You haven't got used to it yet,' she soothed. 'But really—she looks marvellous. And you know, when we walked into the restaurant this afternoon, you should have seen how the men's heads turned!'

'Anybody's head would turn at a girl in yellow satin—'

'Oh, now, Marc, don't be absurd. She'd bought herself a very elegant little frock. The men looked at her because there was something . . . remarkable about her.'

He scowled. 'Men must be stupid if they need to see her made to look like a little boy—'

'She doesn't look like a boy, darling. Not in any intrinsic way. And once she's been to Elizabeth Arden for a consultation—'

'Elizabeth Arden? The cosmetician? Good God, don't tell me she's going to put layers of muck on her face—'

'Darling, darling, calm down. Nobody in their senses would advise Nora to put on layers of cosmetics—not with her young pretty skin. But one thing's certain, by the time she's wearing lipstick and eye shadow, she won't look the least like a boy.'

He growled dissent but she persevered in seeing the best side of it. She ended with, 'And another thing, Marc. We're not going to have to go out looking for a husband for her. She'll be able to pick and choose from a whole crowd.'

'Huh! A crowd of idiots, if they're attracted to a girl just because she joins the latest fad!'

She sighed inwardly. It was no use telling him that though fathers and guardians might like old-fashioned girls, young men tended to prefer new-fashioned girls. Her main preoccupation now was to ensure that when Nora returned to the apartment, he wouldn't express loud disapproval at her appearance. 'If you do, you'll only drive her away, dear—'

'Drive her away? Where would she go? She only has us!'

'If that were true, it would be blackmail, wouldn't it? "Do as we tell you because we're the only people who love you"—is that fair on her?'

'We-ell . . .'

'In any case, she'll soon have plenty of friends—'

'Friends! People who'll take her up because she's a protégée of Coco Chanel!'

'That isn't a bad thing, Marc. Please try to see it her way. Please don't disapprove.'

He did his best, but he could never bring himself to express spontaneous pleasure at Nora's appearance or her activities in the ensuing months. She plunged into the Paris season, but on a new footing—a member of a group who praised and flattered her, able to pick and choose whom she would honour with her friendship.

At first she turned to her new friends because she was hurt by Marc's coolness. But there was also a heady pleasure in being wanted by others. It was totally new to her. She went everywhere, tried everything. She was taken to all the latest 'in' spots, learned all the latest dances, met all the most fashionable people, was invited aboard the most elegant yachts.

She was greatly influenced by Coco Chanel

who, at that time, was going through her 'English' period. Striped silk shirting for blouses, tweeds and worsteds, costumes that looked like hacking jackets with skirts—the outdoor British style, the style she learned through visiting the home of her English milord. And the activities that were taken for granted there—riding, shooting, walking in rough country . . .

Nothing could have been more in keeping with Nora's own outlook. As an antidote to the hectic pace of life in Paris or the Riviera it was wonderful to return to Calmady, to ride with an agreeable partner over the chalky slopes all morning before an easy picnic lunch by the river.

Chanel herself would be of the party sometimes. She was a splendid horsewoman, who loved the gallop. By and by it became a tradition that she and her friends would organize a race, with small bets on who would win.

Nora loved it—the speed of movement, the horse like a smooth splendid machine under her, the wind rushing through her short hair, the laughing admiration if she came in first.

From there it was a short step to riding in point-to-point races. This was much more fun than a mere short gallop but of course very dangerous, particularly in the rough country of the Ardennes or the Seine valley where she would go for weekend parties.

Gaby and Marc only learned of it through a

newspaper report. There had been a collision between horses at an event near Cluny.

'Cluny . . . Isn't that where Nora is staying?' Marc said, looking over his breakfast paper at his wife.

'Yes, dear, with the Verdessiers—why?'

'I believe . . . hasn't she mentioned Jacques Gerard to us? Wasn't he here . . . I seem to recall the name . . .'

'Yes, I think so. He brought her home from Cannes at the end of August, he and his sister . . . Helene, I believe.'

'Damnation!' roared Marc. 'The whole gang of them—they were taking part in a point-to-point at Cluny—that boy Gerard's got two broken legs from a fall!'

They were both seized by alarm. Gaby rushed to the telephone and after some searching found a telephone number. The butler at the other end brought Mademoiselle Tramont to the receiver.

'Cousin Gaby! Is something wrong?'

'Not with us!' Gaby cried. 'But how are *you*?'

'Me? I'm fine. Why do you ask?'

'But, Nora—the papers this morning—'

'Oh, you've read about the spill on Saturday. I'm all right, I was miles away at the back when it happened.'

'At the back? The back of what?' Gaby demanded in bewilderment.

'The back of the race, of course. Blue Boy wasn't really a good enough horse—'

'Nora! You're not saying you *took part* in this race?'

There was a little pause. Then the young voice said coolly, 'Yes, of course. I've been racing in point-to-point since the season began.'

Gaby heard the danger signal. These days it was no use giving orders to her young cousin, and particularly not when that note entered her voice.

'Are you coming home to Calmady when you leave?' she asked, making herself sound quite calm.

'No, I shall go to Paris. I've got two or three engagements there. Why do you ask?'

In other words, Gaby sighed to herself, mind your own business.

'I'd like to see you, dear. You've been off with your friends a long time now.'

'But I was home for the vintage' Gaby—that was only a few weeks ago.'

There was impatience in the words. Gaby shrugged inwardly. Soon she'd have to write for an appointment to see the girl who had once been as biddable as a mouse. She felt irritation but quenched it.

'We just like to stay in touch, that's all. I'm coming to Paris on business—I'll see you there.'

'All right.' No hint of eagerness for a meeting, when they'd been apart for over two months.

She couldn't tell whether Nora deliberately tried to avoid her or whether it was accidental.

119

She herself kept to a businesslike regime: breakfast at eight, out to the Rue Lelong or other appointments by nine, home about five for a pre-dinner drink and a bath, the evening meal at about eight. It seemed to happen that Nora was out late at night, slept late and took breakfast late, and came home only to change quickly for another late night.

But Gabrielle Tramont was equal to the situation. On the fourth morning she didn't go to the office. So when Nora emerged from the bathroom to sit down, in a towelling robe and with her hair gleaming wet from the shower, to a midmorning breakfast, she found her older cousin sitting at ease by the table.

'Gaby! I thought you had business?'

'So I have, but it can wait. I need to talk to you.'

'Oh?' Nora spread jam on her croissant. 'About what?'

'Point-to-point racing.'

Nora had known all along that a confrontation would come. She'd heard the horror and dismay in Gaby's voice when she confessed that she took part.

She made herself remain outwardly quite cool. She bit off a large piece of croissant, chewed, swallowed, then said, 'What about point-to-point racing?'

'I want you to stop taking part.'

'I see.'

'It's too dangerous, Nora. You could be seriously hurt.'

'I could be hurt crossing the street—'

'So you could, and if there were any way I could protect you from that, I would. But to take unnecessary risks is foolish. I want you to give up point-to-point.'

'No.'

'Nora you'll agree that since you began this season I haven't interfered with your activities. I haven't always approved—'

'No one asked you to approve or disapprove.'

'Quite so. I led my own life when I was your age, Nora. Don't think I have a closed mind about it. I may not like some of your friends, and I may think you're wasting too much of your time in stuffy night-clubs—but I comfort myself by thinking you'll grow out of it.'

Nora was furious. She couldn't control the spurt of bright colour that flew into her face. 'Grow out of it! Don't speak to me as if I were a child.'

'Eighteen years old is hardly middle age.' If Nora had but known it, Gaby was smiling inwardly. She'd done what she wanted—she'd stung her young cousin into open conflict. 'I will speak to you, though, as if you were a mature woman with a mind capable of thinking about something beyond the immediate enjoyment of thrills and excitement. You could injure yourself

121

very seriously in cross-country racing, Nora. You could even be killed. Marc and I—'

'Oh yes, you don't have to tell me! I'm the last of the Tramonts—'

'It seems we do have to tell you. But apart from that, think of yourself ten years from now. If you were to have a bad fall and be crippled—if you got internal injuries so that you couldn't have a child—ten years from now, would you think it worth while?'

'I'm not going to have a fall. Hundreds of people ride point-to-point—'

'I want you to give it up, Nora.'

'No, I won't.'

'On this one point, I must insist. I forbid you to go on with it.'

'How do you propose to stop me? Are you going to follow me around like a warder?'

Gaby hadn't wanted to come to hard words, but it seemed it was necessary.

'I shall sell the horses at the Villa Tramont.'

'Don't be silly, I can always borrow a horse. I've been riding on borrowed horses most of the last few weeks.'

'I understand that. But do you want me to sell the horses you grew up with? Do you want to see Butterpat go to a new owner?'

Nora stared at Gaby. She felt a shiver of distress. 'You wouldn't sell Butterpat?' Butterpat, going on fourteen years old now, too small for her since she grew up, Butterpat living up to his name these days, plump, round as a sausage, contentedly cropping grass in the paddock at Calmady . . .

Gaby didn't reply to the question. Nora looked at her, and for the first time saw what a formidable opponent her cousin might be. They had always been friends, good companions, though she had never been as close to Gaby as to Marc. But now for the first time she saw Gaby as another woman might see her—still beautiful in her mid-forties, a leader in her community, the controller of a business worth some millions of francs. She wasn't someone to be trifled with.

Yes, she would sell the horses. She would do anything she thought necessary.

'You're saying that if I don't fall in with your wishes, you'd actually get rid of the horses?'

'To the knackers, if I have to.'

Nora met the cold glance of the beautiful black eyes. She knew she was beaten. Gaby had read her aright. She couldn't bear to have anything happen to that fat old pony.

'I never thought you'd stoop to blackmail, Cousin Gabrielle,' she said with contempt.

'I never thought I should have to,' Gaby returned. She gave a grim smile. 'I don't want to fight you, Nora, but always remember—I fought the Germans, I learned a few tricks. So—you agree to give up dangerous horse races?'

'Yes.'

Her cousin nodded, rose, picked up her bag

123

and gloves. 'I have business waiting for me. I'm sorry to have spoiled your breakfast. I hope the rest of the day will be more pleasant, my dear.'

'I was going riding in the Bois with Buddy. I suppose,' Nora said scathingly, 'I have permission to do that?'

'Buddy Garrenstein?' He was the son of the American ambassador, a young man of lanky good looks but so lazy he wouldn't even learn to speak good French. The thought of him brought a faint frown to Gaby's brow.

'Don't tell me you disapprove of him too!'

'Is he a particular friend of yours?' She'd only met him a few times but somehow couldn't like him.

Nora shrugged. She wasn't going to discuss her friends with her cousin—not after this humiliating defeat. 'He's all right,' she said.

To her surprise, Gaby smiled. 'Don't sulk, Nora,' she teased, 'now you hair's cropped away from your face, you have to be careful what expression you wear.'

Nora almost laughed, she was so taken by surprise by the quip. Instead she turned to her breakfast again.

But as Gaby reached the door of the dining-room she paused. 'I have your word, Nora? No dangerous riding?'

'You have my word.' And the laughter had vanished as quickly as it had come, quenched by resentment that her cousin should doubt her.

She was still angry when she joined Buddy Garrenstein an hour later on the wide horse ride in the Bois. 'You're late,' he complained.

'I was delayed.'

'Well, last one to the oak tree is a cissy!' He dug his heels in and rode away at his strange, rolling gallop. He always looked a mess to European eyes, having learned to ride among cowboys on his father's lands in Omaha or Ohio or some such place. But he was bold and somewhat ruthless when it came to racing—he often won.

This time Nora didn't even compete. When he reached the oaks, he drew up, looking back for her.

'What's got into you?' he demanded as she came up at a respectable lady's-canter. 'Dipped your boots in molasses?'

She came alongside. 'I promised I wouldn't ride dangerously.'

'You did? What in the world made you do that, honey?' He was genuinely surprised. He had seen how she loved the reckless pursuit across rough ground, the quick reading of the land for a route to give some slight advantage, the risky leap over a wall or a fallen tree.

'I don't want to talk about it. I had to promise, that's all.'

'Huh . . .' He rode alongside for a few minutes in silence. Then he said, 'You don't have to keep your promise, though. Who's around to see what you do?'

They were speaking English, because his French was often inadequate. She wasn't quite sure she'd understood him. 'You mean break my word?' she asked, raising her eyebrows.

'Well, sure—why not?'

'I can't do that, Buddy.'

'Don't see why not. It was a dumb thing to promise, if you want my opinion.'

'I agree with you. But that's how it is. I gave my word. I have to keep it.'

He turned his head to study her face. She was riding bare-headed in the cold December weather, colour in her cheeks, a sparkle in her browny-grey eyes.

After a moment he said: 'What you gonna do for thrills, then?'

'I don't know, Buddy,' she said with a faint smile.

They rode on a few paces in silence.

'We'll think of something,' he said, putting plenty of innuendo into his voice.

FIVE

Buddy Garrenstein had had Elinore Tramont in his sights for quite a while. He enjoyed considerable success with the French girls because he was an American, and at the moment all things American were the rage. America was where jazz came from, America was the home of

Hollywood and the great film stars like Valentino and Clara Bow, America had thrilling gangsters, extravagant millionaires, and skyscrapers. Buddy was an American, therefore he was wonderful.

He was also the son of the American ambassador to France, which couldn't hurt. His people were New-York-State German, engineers who had done well with armaments during the war. The fact that he had flunked out of college was unknown to his girlish admirers, as was also his history of slight brushes with the law, carefully hushed up by his family.

He had been brought to Paris by his parents to get him away from 'bad influences' at home. They were aware that he was racketing around Paris instead of attending the language school where he was supposed to be studying, but what could you do? If they stopped his allowance he borrowed from undesirable sources, or forged his father's name to cheques.

The social set in which he moved were willing to forgive Buddy his faults because he made them all seem such fun. If he walked out of a restaurant without paying the bill, so what? Restaurants were coining money anyhow, in these post-war days of dizzy enjoyment. If he drank too much, what was unusual in that? And besides, when he had had a drink or two, he thought up wonderful stunts to enliven the scene—climbing the church tower in Clichy to hang Lucille's evening bag on the clock hands, a midnight race on the Seine with borrowed rowboats . . .

His pursuit of Nora didn't go as well as most of his plans. He could see she liked him, but there was something that always seemed to hold her back.

Which was strange, for she sure was a good-looking kid and almost avid to try anything new.

It had something to do with the pair she referred to as the Relatives—her guardians, he supposed. He'd met them, and to him they seemed harmless enough, certainly not severe or authoritarian. But she seemed unable to shake off their influence.

Like this business over horse-racing. She proved to be quite serious in not taking part any more. But the alternative thrill that Buddy had in mind seemed not to attract her.

'You're moving much too fast,' she told him, not teasingly but with complete frankness. 'I've seen what happens to other girls who fall into your arms, my friend.'

'But you're different, Nora—'

'Oh yes? Because I say no, you mean.'

'No, you're different. I really care about you, Nora.'

She laughed. It lit up her quiet features in a way he found irresistible.

'Oh, come on, baby, you know you like me! Why don't you give in to it? We could have such good times together—'

'But we have good times now, Buddy.'

'Oh, sure.' Sure—dancing cheek to cheek to a smoochy band, necking in the back of his old Peugeot. But it didn't get him where he wanted to go.

There was no help for it. He'd have to go along on the old footing for a while longer.

Nora only half-understood his plan. She had looked about her and seen many of the girls in her social set making relationships with men which would have horrified their parents, and she had been half-tempted herself. And yet . . .

Her own background acted as a brake on her. She couldn't rid herself of the feeling that she couldn't pair off with just anyone, just to be in the fashion. She measured the young men around her against an unconscious standard. Some were nice enough, and some—like Buddy—had the added attraction of being rather wild, rather careless.

If she ever took a lover, it might very well be Buddy. He was good-looking in a foreign kind of way—tall and loose-limbed and tanned, something like the stars of the cowboy films. She admired him for his physical courage, which he never seemed to think unusual. When he rode, he took the most awful risks without hesitation.

It was the same when she went driving with him. He had rescued a car from a garage where it had been abandoned by an irate tourist. With his own hands Buddy had repaired it and tuned the engine—souped it up, was the expression he used.

The result was that though the Peugeot-Bébé looked decrepit, it could pass almost anything on the road. He loved to take the car out on the fine new routes built with the war-reparations, 'open her up' as he phrased it, and go like the wind while the struts holding on the canvas roof vibrated with the speed and the folding cover over the bonnet shuddered and jerked as if it would fly open.

It was even better when she let him drive her little English sports car, a Sunbeam. She would sit beside him in the open bucket seat watching the fields and the houses flash by. His hands on the wheel were sure and confident. She admired him then more than anyone she knew, for the simple audacity of fearlessness. One mistake, and they might both be dead—but he never even seemed to think of that.

He saw that she loved speed. He felt it was a chink in her cool armour. He offered to teach her to drive as he drove, like a racing driver. She couldn't resist.

'No, don't brake . . . change down, drift into the corner. Now, foot down, change up . . . That's it, but don't jerk at it . . .'

They were out on the flat stretches of road to the north of the Seine. It was just after dawn in March, no one about. The sun was up but shining through clouds which cast a pearl-grey light over everything. Rain from those selfsame clouds had coated the road with a slick surface.

Nora had trouble controlling the Sunbeam at the bends. 'You're too rigid,' Buddy explained. 'You're expecting trouble and steering too far out. Pull up and I'll show you.'

They changed places. She watched intently as he drove them surging forward on the rural route, her eyes on his hands and feet rather than the road ahead.

So she never saw the farm wagon backing out of the gate until they were upon it.

She screamed a warning. Buddy was already jamming on the brakes. On the slippery surface the tyres failed to hold. The car skidded sideways and forward. There was a jarring and crunching as they hit the side of the wagon. It toppled away from the car, wavered. Its tarpaulin tore adrift. Nora heard a shout of terror, and neighing of horses.

Then the tarpaulin was engulfing her like the wings of some great bat. The Sunbeam was coming to a halt. There was a noise of tearing and rending, then a rattle of things falling all around like hail—root vegetables, the wagon's load. The sports car was heaved to and fro. The wooden framework of the old wagon fell upon her. Dimly, distant, she could hear the clatter of heavy hooves as the horses dragged at their harness, trying to get away from this terrible monster behind them.

It seemed like hours before she fought herself free from the wreckage. But it could only have been seconds, because sacks of potatoes were still slithering from the overturned wagon. And it was still shuddering and jolting as the carthorses tried to run away.

Nora staggered to the side of the wagon, where she held herself up for a moment, aware of the world spinning around her. Then she ran to the other side of the Sunbeam, which was half buried under shards of wood and the flapping tarpaulin.

'Buddy! Buddy!'

No reply.

She seized hold of the heavy canvas folds and tried to pull it away. But it was ungainly and heavy, trapped up at the front by heavy sacks and by being wedged as the sports car had dragged it inward in its crash.

'Buddy!' She was wailing now, desperate in case he were killed.

But to her relief a muffled voice replied. 'You okay, Nora?'

'I'm all right. How about you?'

'Get this damned tent off me.'

'I'm trying, I'm trying! Can you move?'

'Dunno. Wait. Yeah, I can move my arms, but I'm trapped by the legs. Wait a jiff.'

She stood helpless for a moment, then saw a bulging of the tarpaulin—Buddy was pushing it away from him with his hands. She took hold of a point and heaved with all her might, breaking

132

her nails. But it moved, it came towards her, and after a moment Buddy's head appeared.

'Goddammit!' he said. 'I nearly smothered—'

'Your legs, Buddy—'

'It's okay, the bonnet held up all right—it's these damned sacks of whatever—' He shoved and pushed and scrambled, eventually levering himself up out of the wreckage.

Seeing he was at least able to take care of himself, she left him. Always, dragging at her attention, had been the sound of the horses out of sight in the field, pulling in terror at their harness. She edged between the tilted wheel of the wagon and the gatepost. Two heavy horses were bucking and jerking, their big hooves striking against the crushed stone put down at the entrance to keep it from becoming too muddy.

She seized the halter of the nearest, holding him steady, speaking soothing words. 'Quiet, old fellow, it's all right, it's all over, nothing's going to hurt you. Now, now . . .' As he stopped jerking his head, she put her other hand on his nose and stroked him. He blew through his nostrils, nodded hard a time or two, and settled down.

She went round to the other side to speak to his partner. She had just begun to stroke his nose when her eye was caught by a bundle lying under his flank. A sack—one of the sacks of potatoes from the cart—

No. A man's body, with an empty sack half thrown over it.

Horror seized her. The driver of the cart—the man who had shouted at the moment of impact—how could she have forgotten all about him?

Buddy came round to join her, rubbing the small of his back and looking rueful. 'Felled by a load of murphies!' he groaned. Then his glance followed hers.

'Jesus,' he whispered.

Nora knelt down by the crumpled figure. The unnatural angle of his head and the crooked sprawl of his limbs told their story. But she drew aside the sack he'd been wearing to protect his shoulders against the rain, and listened for a heartbeat.

She looked up, shaking her head.

'We killed him,' she said.

'What? Oh, say—Nora—'

'It's our fault!'

'You can't say that! He shouldn't have been backing out on to a traffic route—'

'We shouldn't have been using the route for a racing circuit!'

He seemed about to argue, but closed his lips on the words. His angular, open-air face was pale. 'We've got to tell somebody,' he said after a moment. 'The authorities—the local gendarme . . .'

'One of us must stay with him.'

'Yeah.' He gave her a long, assessing glance. 'I'll go,' he said. 'You don't mind staying beside him?'

She swallowed hard, but shook her head. 'I'll be all right.'

After he left she knelt in a long silence, then got up to soothe the horses, who though no longer panicky were alarmed and restless at having to stay tethered to this vehicle that suddenly seemed tilted all wrong. She stood at their heads, talking quietly, but after a moment she leaned her cheek against a great shoulder and let the tears come.

Afterwards there were long sessions with the examining magistrate. She could never understand exactly what Buddy had said when he first took the news to the authorities, but somehow it appeared that the farmer had contributed to his own death by negligence. He should have had a companion to guide him out on to the road as he backed his horses. He would have had one, his son, only the youngster had talked himself out of the chore so that he could visit his girlfriend.

The sports car had not hit him. He had fallen from the driving seat, thereupon receiving injuries that caused his death. The driving seat was found to have no protection, no guard to which he could have clung—it was simply a board held high by two iron stanchions. The cart certainly didn't comply with regulations for safety in use.

Buddy didn't have diplomatic immunity, but he was who he was, the son of an important man, and must be given the benefit of every doubt. It was Mademoiselle Tramont's car, but he claimed he had been driving—well, that was what a gentleman would say to shield a lady from accusation.

The case was regarded as an accident with blame on both sides. Buddy was reprimanded. A large sum of money was provided as compensation to the farmer's family who received it with grim politeness. The case was closed.

Not for Nora. She couldn't banish from her mind the picture of the farmer's body, sprawled under the heavy arch of the horse's body. He had smashed first against the stones of the field gatepost and then on the broken stone surface of the entry. The examining magistrate, seeing her distress on the first encounter, had told her with surprising kindness that the man had broken his neck at once and had not suffered. But that didn't exonerate her. She had caused his death.

The Relatives were very gentle with her. They uttered no word of blame. But she knew they must think her silly and feckless. They had asked her to give up one hazardous sport so to spite them she had taken up another—and it had ended not in her own death, which they had so greatly feared, but in that of an innocent bystander.

She dropped out of her usual round of activity. But she didn't stop seeing Buddy, because she didn't want him to think she blamed him for what happened. The damage had been done by *her* car, driven too fast on a road unsuitable for it and in poor conditions, because *she* wanted to learn to drive at speed.

'Honey, I wish you'd snap out of it,' he mourned. 'You're not really here half the time— you seem to be looking over my shoulder at ghosts or something.'

She smiled and gave a shrug that meant, Perhaps I am.

'You've got to put it behind you. I'm as sorry as you are for the poor old guy, but what's done is done and you've got to forget it.'

'I can't, Buddy. 'She shivered. 'I can't sleep— I'm afraid I'll see him again, lying there . . .'

'Baby, baby . . . What you need is sweet dreams, not nightmares.'

'Don't you have nightmares, Buddy?'

'You underestimate me, sugar. I know how to drive the blues away.'

'But how?' She was puzzled. She'd never thought he had any kind of philosophy, certainly not a religion, to buoy him up in time of trouble.

'When I feel low I just take a pinch of Paradise Powder. See?' He brought from his jacket pocket a little silver box like a snuff box, opened it, and showed her the contents. It was a white silvery powder, like glucose.

They were in the back seat of the old Peugeot, in a lane above Sacré Coeur. The April night was full of the scent of chestnut candles coming into flower. They could hear faint music in the Place du Tertre some distance away. There were lights in a large window at the top of the hill, an artist's studio, but otherwise the only illumination were the flickering gas lamps spaced at long intervals in the alley.

Buddy put a pinch of the powder on the crook of his thumb and forefinger, like snuff. He put it to his nostrils and sniffed. 'Sweet sugar!' he murmured. 'Bucks you up quicker than your old champagne.'

'But what is it, Buddy?'

'Just a cute little old tonic, kitten, one of those things they use in South America—like quinine only this is more fun. Want to try?'

He was laughing, his eyes sparkling in the dim light. She sensed a heightened gaiety in him, as if the smallest joke would have sent him into peals of laughter.

His mood was infectious. She found herself laughing with him.

'Come on, Nora—look how good it makes me feel! It's like going up on a cloud and seeing the world through a pink mist—everything's good, everything's easy.'

She put out a finger, hesitating, dubious.

'Not like that, dumbbell—like this.' He turned her hand, put her forefinger and thumb together, and with a deft movement sprinkled powder in the crook.' There you go,' he urged. 'Try it.'

She put her hand up to her nostrils and sniffed, as she'd seen him do. The powder went up her nose and for a moment she thought she was going to sneeze. Then a momentary numbness followed. She rubbed the end of her nose with her knuckle.

'Give it a second,' he said. 'Almost-instant miracles!'

'Nothing's happening.'

'That's too bad! I thought I was going to give you a big thrill. Seems a shame you can't fly with me, baby.'

She giggled. 'You were just playing a trick on me! What a thing to do, Buddy!'

He put his arm round her. 'You've found me out—I'm a real fraud. Mr Mischief, that's me.'

What a good joke! She laughed, her heart suddenly light, her mind full of a golden mist. 'You know, I think I do feel something,' she said. 'Perhaps you aren't such a fraud after all. But you promised me an instant miracle, and this took a lo-ong time.'

'Better late than never.'

'That's right.' She found this old quotation tremendously apt. 'Better late than never! And the thing is, now we've had the miracle, what are we going to do next? Just sit there in this old car and watch the stars twinkle?'

'We could go to my place, baby—'

'Listen, there's music in the square—let's go down and dance, Buddy.'

'Why don't we go to my flat and dance there—play the phonograph and—'

'No, no, I want to dance now! There's the

139

music—it's got louder, hasn't it? They must have a bigger band than usual. Come on, it's a lovely night, let's dance in the open air in the square.'

She dragged him out of the car. He went with her, chuckling at her sudden energy and not unwilling.

The rest of that evening was a pleasant blur. She had a great time, everybody she spoke to seemed witty and friendly, the music was full of charm, the rough wine in the Montmartre café was sheer nectar. Every taste seemed heightened, every sense seemed keener, every moment seemed crammed with sensation and enjoyment.

When she woke next morning she was bewildered. The ceiling above her wasn't the pale cream of her room in the Rue Berger. It was blue, with cut-out stars pasted on it.

She raised herself on one elbow. The sheet slipped back. She was naked.

Something like a thunderbolt seemed to strike her. She sat up, dragging the sheet up in front of her. She shuddered, staring about her in consternation.

She was in a strange room, one she'd never seen before. It was well-furnished in a heavy, mannish style. Clothes, her own and a man's, lay in a tangle over chairs and carpet.

She put up a hand to her head. It felt odd— not exactly a headache, but as if it didn't quite belong to her. Her sense of balance was a little off. When she tried to swing her legs round to get out of bed, the room swam for a moment.

A door opened behind her. She twisted about.

Buddy had come into the room, a damp towel about his waist, another in his hands as he dried his hair.

'So you're awake at last, sleepyhead,' he said. He draped the towel over his shoulders, grinning at her. He looked tall, angular, quite at ease.

'Buddy . . .'

He padded across the room, to sit beside her on the bed. 'Honey, I just want to tell you—you were great!'

SIX

Before she could make a fool of herself and gasp, 'What are you talking about?', his arms were around her and he was kissing her.

Memory began to function. His body against hers, his mouth too, a whirling surge like being on a carousel going too fast, rhythms in her pulses she'd never known before, a piercing pain that made her for a moment come to awareness, made her almost cry out, 'What's happening to me?' But then a high tide of fervour catching her up in its force, drowning every other thought.

Buddy was kissing her shoulders, her breasts, murmuring against her skin. 'Oh, honey, lover-baby, oh, what a girl, you're so great . . .'

She tried to push him away. She had to think.

But he didn't want to give her time. His hands were seeking out the responsive curves of her body, so that something stirred in her blood. She found her arms tightening about him, and she was pulling him down to her.

This time she knew what was happening. One part of her mind was saying, 'I can't, I mustn't!' but the protest was blotted out by the needs roused in her by Buddy's caresses. She gave herself up to it, in wonder at her own abandonment—she who couldn't be close to anyone, she who had always been afraid to love.

When they were lying afterwards in a tangle of exhausted passion she thought to herself, 'It seems I've taken a lover.' Or was it the other way around? Had he taken her? She tried to recall how they had changed so startlingly to this new rooting, whether she'd encouraged him more than she meant to—for she'd never intended to go to bed with Buddy.

Yet she must love him. Otherwise what was she doing here, in his arms, in his bed?

Presently he crawled out from among the rumpled sheets, 'I'll ring down for coffee—'

'No! Buddy!' She clutched the bedclothes to her.

'Relax, relax, the guy from the café has to knock to be let in. You can go in the bathroom. And hey, honey . . . I still think you're great!'

They sat down to breakfast later, she in her

evening clothes, he in a Japanese dressing-gown. He murmured, 'Say, listen, do you have to do any explaining?'

'How do you mean?'

'To the Relatives. You've been out all night, kiddo.'

'Oh. Oh, I see. No, they're in Calmady.' Thank God, she said inwardly. She couldn't have faced them today. It would take hours for her to get over what she'd done. She knew it must be in her face if anyone looked at her.

Why should she take it so much to heart? Some of her friends had lovers, it wasn't anything new. Yet for her it was new. And the Relatives would be shocked, disappointed. They expected better of her. 'Better' . . . Why should it be better or worse to belong to Buddy?

But they didn't like Buddy—she knew that. It was unexpressed but present in their attitude. A total lack of enthusiasm whenever she mentioned him, a disinclination to include him in any invitations to their apartment or the Villa Tramont.

So be it. For many reasons, she would keep her secret. For the time being she had enough to wrestle with—the fact that her body was no longer her own entirely, that Buddy had claims on it and that he was necessary to her in a way she had never known before.

There were no obstacles in the way of their love affair. He had his little pied-à-terre in the Latin Quarter, and the Relatives were in

Calmady dealing with the wine business so that she could have him to the apartment often. The servants were given plenty of time off; if they guessed the reason, they knew better than to remark upon it.

Buddy seemed to have access to good supplies of his 'Paradise Powder', or as he sometimes called it, happy dust or snow. It seemed you could go into clubs in Pigalle and buy it, though supplies tended to be variable and you had to know 'the right guys'. The musicians in the jazz bands seemed to be the right guys.

Nora had taken it twice more before she put two and two together and understood that it was cocaine. For a moment, when the realization seized her, she was horrified. She'd heard Marc and Gaby criticizing the people who used drugs—'endangering their health, becoming addicts' . . .

'Yeah, yeah, that's the kind of thing they say,' Buddy shrugged, 'but you and I know different, don't we, sweetheart? Do you think you're endangering your health when you get up on Cloud Nine? It's great, you feel twice as alive— how can that be bad?'

He was right, of course. He knew so much more than she did, about everything—about love and life and how to live it. He was five years her senior, had seen a lot more of the world. Besides, he was an American. Americans were from the New World, eager for all that was modern and exciting. Old fuddy-duddies in the Old World were just behind the times, that was all.

He came to the Rue Berger one late afternoon. He was alight with pleasure. 'I've got the stuff, Nora—I was lucky, I walked in when Joey was there and he'd just got supplies. We're going to fly tonight, honey—really fly.'

They had until eleven that evening, when the servants would be back. They settled down in Nora's room, with wine and the precious happy dust in its little silver box.

Buddy was right. It was like flying. Everything in the world lay beneath them, until it merged into a golden glow where reality slipped away entirely. Even the intermittent ringing of the telephone seemed like the distant peal of angel bells.

Whether they made love Nora wasn't sure. But a beautiful languor engulfed her afterwards. Buddy was less affected—it was always so, he was more accustomed to the powder. As eleven o'clock drew near he struggled into alertness, dressed, and gave her a final hug.

'See you tomorrow, babe. You go to sleep now, dream of me.'

She didn't fall asleep. She got up, pulled on a dressing-gown, and wandered to the kitchen for a drink of water. She took the glass back to her bedroom, where she sat sipping it as she heard the sounds of the servants returning. She nodded sagely to herself. Buddy's timing had been good. But then Buddy was good at everything.

She was sitting at the dressing-table brushing her hair with lethargic strokes when she heard the sound of someone coming in. She heard voices in the hall. Buddy had come back? She got up and began to waver towards the door of her room.

There was a knock upon it. She opened it.

And there stood her Cousin Marc.

'Nora!' he said. 'Are you all right?'

She blinked. 'Perfectly all right.'

He was staring at her. 'Where have you been?'

'I . . . I've been here. Yes, I've been here.'

'Then why didn't you answer the phone?'

'The phone?'

'I've been ringing all evening. Where have you been?'

'I was here . . . I told you . . .'

'Why didn't you answer?'

'I think . . . I don't know . . .'

'Are you ill?' he said, stepping into the room and taking her by the arm.

'No, I'm fine. I feel fine.'

But his movement had made her sway. He caught her by the shoulders.

'You're drunk!'

'No I'm not.'

His gaze went past her to the rumpled bed, the bottle of wine on the bedside table, the two glasses.

'How much have you drunk?'

'Why are you speaking to me like that?' she said, summoning her dignity. 'You've no right to speak to me like that.'

'Damn it, Nora—what's been going on?'

She pulled free to sit unsteadily on the stool in front of her dressing-table. The lamp on the table reflected light onto her features from the mirror. Her cousin stooped to stare into her eyes.

She saw understanding dawn on his narrow, angry face. An expression of disbelief flashed across it, banished at once by horror.

'What have you been taking?' he demanded.

'None of your business!'

'Nora!' He shook her. 'What have you been taking? Tell me!'

'No I won't! You just don't want me to enjoy myself, that's all—you're always telling me not to do this and not to do that—'

'Nora!' He shook her so hard her words were jolted to silence. He slapped her on one cheek, a harsh blow. Her head turned sharply to one side under its impetus. Tears welled up. She began to sob like a child, stricken, shattered.

He dragged her to her feet, pulled her across her room, and thrust her under the shower in the bathroom. She fell limply against the tiled wall. He shoved her upright, turned on the shower full force, cold as the waters of the Arctic.

She stood there, the robe moulding itself to her body under the icy rain of water. Marc marched out, slamming the door behind him. She heard him stalk across her bedroom but after that the sounds of his passage were lost.

She stood there under the shower, crying, her tears mingling with the spray, broken-hearted at having displeased him, at having been found out in something that he disapproved of. She dared not move: he had placed her here, she must wait until he released her. She was being punished. She deserved it.

When the bathroom door opened again it was the maid, Lucie. She turned off the shower, helped Nora out, peeled off the wet silk peignoir, directed her arms into a warm towelling robe. Then she dried her feet and legs, put her feet into slippers, led her into the bedroom.

The empty wine bottle and glasses had gone, the bed had been whisked into decency. A coffee pot stood on the writing table. Lucie guided Nora into the chair by the desk, then went out. Not a word had been said.

Nora sat by the desk, her head supported on her hand. Her world seemed to be in ruins all about her.

Marc came in. He said, 'How are you feeling now?'

It was a great effort to raise her head. 'I feel woozy.'

'Exactly. Coffee is the cure for that.' He poured it, black and steaming hot. He offered her the cup. 'Drink it.'

But her hands trembled so much she couldn't hold it. He took it from her, held it to her lips. She sipped. It scalded her. She jerked her lips away.

He set the cup down, fetched a chair, sat beside her. He held the coffee to her lips again. 'Drink it, Nora.'

She tried again, and managed to swallow a mouthful. He stayed beside her, helping her to drink the bitter brew, then refilled the cup.

How much time went by she couldn't tell. She heard his voice, peremptory at first, but gentler as she shuddered and coughed and tried to obey.

'Come on now, darling—another mouthful—that's it, swallow it down. Now another. It's good for you, drink it down.'

The coffee pot was empty. She thought she was reprieved, but soon Lucie appeared with a replacement. The torment began again. She swallowed the coffee, went to the bathroom to be sick, drank more coffee.

There came a moment when the room came into focus. She saw her cousin's profile as he turned slightly from her to put down the coffee cup.

'Marc!'

He looked round. He met her gaze, and his frowning face lightened.

'Are you feeling better?'

'What are you doing here?' she cried. 'What's been happening?'

'Never mind. Go to bed now.'

'Marc—'

'Go to bed. We'll talk in the morning.'

'But I'm not sleepy—Marc—what's the matter?'

'You may not be sleepy but I am. I'm going to bed. We'll talk in the morning.'

He got up, walked out. A moment later Lucie came in. The maid treated her as if she were an invalid. She helped her into a night-dress, supervised as she got between the sheets.

'What time is it, Lucie?' she asked as she lay down.

'Nearly two-thirty, Mademoiselle.'

'So late?' She tried to catch at her wits. 'Why are you still up at this hour?'

'Never mind, Mademoiselle. Goodnight.'

She went out.

Nora lay for a long time trying to piece together the events of the evening, but it was like a kaleidoscope, shifting and changing.

At last, although she'd been certain she couldn't sleep, her eyes closed.

She was wakened by Lucie coming into her room and opening the shutters. The bright May sunshine told her that it was at least mid-morning. The maid waited until she had struggled to a sitting position then put a tray across her knees.

'Monsieur Tramont said to tell you that he

would like to see you in the drawing-room when you're ready, Mademoiselle.'

'Really?' Her mind was still in the mists of sleep. Then realization rushed over her. 'Oh!' She felt herself go cold then hot with dismay and embarrassment. 'Yes . . . of course . . . please tell him I'll be with him as soon as I can—'

'He said there was no need to hurry, Mademoiselle. Just when you're ready.'

As she bathed and dressed, Nora wondered whether she ever would be ready for the interview that was to come. Dreadful hints and half-memories flitted through her mind. It seemed to her that Marc had been here late at night, talking to her . . . and the shower had been beating down up on her . . . and Buddy had been there too . . .

No, that was impossible. Yet she recalled enough to know that Marc had seen her when she was out of control, drifting and lethargic from Buddy's 'snow'. She felt a deep, harrowing shame at the thought. She had never wanted Marc to see her at less than her best.

Then, if she was less than herself when she took Buddy's cocaine, why did she take it? What good was it doing her? Buddy could say it made you feel great, but that was such a passing thing. Afterwards she always felt strange—weak and listless, her eyes blinking, unable to focus.

When she had brushed her short hair into its little forward quiff and touched her lids with eye-shadow, she drew a deep breath then went to the drawing-room. Her cousin was sitting in a corner of the Louis Quinze sofa, a pile of documents on the cushion next to him. He glanced up at her entrance.

'Come and sit here,' he said, clearing the space.

She did so. She dared not look up at him.

'Now,' he said, taking one of her hands in both of his, 'I'm not going to have a long review of what happened last night. All I want is the answer to one question. Have you done that kind of thing often?'

She shook her head.

'How often?'

She shrugged.

'Nora, I need to know. You were clearly under the influence of some drug or other, I could tell that from your eyes. I have to know whether you've made a practice of it.'

'No!' She looked up and away again. 'No,' she said with more calmness, 'that was the fourth time—perhaps the fifth.'

'In how long?'

'Three weeks.'

'Ah.' There was relief in his voice. 'In that case, I think we can take it you're not addicted—'

'Addicted! What d'you mean, Marc!' she cried. 'It's a harmless—'

'It is *not* harmless! It can have terrible effects. Good God, Nora, didn't you even know . . .?'

She had stared up at him as she cried out. Now they sat gazing at each other.

He gave a faint smile. 'Well, things haven't got out of hand, I can see that. My dear, I don't know how you came to be mixed up in this kind of thing and I don't want to. I only thank God that I came home—'

'How did that come about?' she asked, thinking that if he had not come she would have been spared the humiliation of having been seen by him in such a disgusting state.

'You've forgotten, clearly,' he sighed. 'Last night you were supposed to be at a birthday dinner for Elvi Hermilot in Rheims. When you didn't come, I telephoned, but there was no reply. It was terribly unlike you not even to bother to let us know you couldn't come. I got so worried that in the end I left the party and caught a fast train. And walked in on you . . .' He left the sentence unfinished, for which she was grateful.

There was a little pause. Then she said, 'It's all over, that kind of thing. I don't believe I ever really . . . It never lived up to its promise, except the first time. Even if you hadn't turned up to shake me out of it, I believe I'd have given it up.'

'You won't let yourself be persuaded into it again? I believe it's a fashionable thing among the young set . . .'

She shook her head. 'No, that's over. It just doesn't appeal to me.'

'Good.' He rose, taking her with him. He dropped a kiss on the top of her cropped head. 'I must go. I have business waiting for me in Calmady.'

'You're just going to . . . leave me to myself?'

'Why not?'

'I mean . . . you . . . trust me?'

Again he said, 'Why not?' With a smile he gathered up his papers and began putting them in a document case.

She stood beside him, so grateful and beholden to him for everything—for rescuing her from her silliness, for believing in her—that she wanted to throw her arms round him.

But those days were over. She wasn't a child any more. The time was long gone by when she could throw herself at Marc as if it meant nothing.

When Buddy rang around lunchtime she avoided making a date with him.

'What's up? You sound funny,' he said.

'I had a bad night.'

'Oh, I've got the cure for that! Why don't we get together at my place and settle down for a snootful—'

'Buddy!'

'What's the matter?'

'Don't—it sounds so ugly—I don't want to do that any more.'

'Oh?' There was a faint anxiety in his voice. 'What's eating you, hon? You got an attack of the morals?'

'I don't want to do it, Buddy. I don't like what it does to me.'

'Aw, that's because you only do it on an amateur basis. What you want, baby, is to take a snort on both barrels—then you'd really—'

'No, Buddy, I don't want to be boring, but I just think it's wrong.'

She could hear him making little sounds of disagreement, but he let it go. 'So okay, we don't go for a sleigh-ride on snow any more. But we can still have fun together, can't we? You're still my girl?'

'Yes, of course, but I don't feel like seeing anybody today. I just don't feel well, Buddy.'

'Tomorrow, then?'

'I don't know,' she said doubtfully. 'I ought to go down to Calmady—'

He persuaded her she ought to stay in Paris to be with him. There was a party they could go to—it ought to be fun.

When he called for her, he seemed very bright and lively. Knowing him as she did now, she had to think he'd already taken something to buoy him up for the evening. She said, worrying for him, 'You oughtn't to use that stuff so often, Buddy. I've heard you can become—'

'Oh, for God's sake!' He stamped on his brakes as they came to a road junction, causing

155

the little Peugeot to rock about on its springs. 'Don't you start on me too!'

'I'm not . . .' But she decided not to have an argument. Later, as they were heading out towards Ivry, she said, 'What did you mean, "too"? Who's been criticizing you?'

He groaned. 'Gee, my family are dumping on me! You just don't know—your Relatives are so decent to you but mine are a bunch of Puritans!'

She linked an arm through his. 'Never mind, Buddy,' she said. 'It's just that they worry about you, I suppose.'

'They don't worry! They hand out orders. You don't know what it's like—and they're so damn close with money you'd think they wore it next the skin. I tell you, sometimes I . . . I . . .' His let the sentence die away. Then he said, 'I wasn't going to tell you, but the fact is, I've been canned.'

'Canned?' Her grasp of American idiom failed her.

'I'm being sent home. They just won't listen to what I . . .'

She couldn't understand what he meant. 'Sent home? But surely you don't have to go, if you don't want to, Buddy?'

'Are you kidding? What would I use for money if I stayed? They're going to cut off the blood supply, baby, so I've got to go along with what they say. I'm heading home soon's they can arrange a berth.'

156

'No!'

'Oh, yes, Nora.' He took the turning for the house where the party was being held, drew into the side of the road; and stopped. 'I wasn't going to tell you until after the party—didn't want to spoil it for you. But I've had a hell of a day. Mom and Dad have been on and on at me since breakfast.'

'But why, Buddy? I don't understand!'

Why? He couldn't tell her. The truth was that he'd been found out in a theft. To pay for supplies from one of his jazz-playing friends, he'd taken from his mother's jewelbox a ring she hardly ever wore. He thought it would be weeks before she noticed its absence and then might think she'd mislaid it.

How was he to know she often took it out and looked at it? It was the first ring her husband had ever given her, when he still hadn't made all his millions. She noticed its absence at once and caused a fuss. The servants were the first suspects but the butler had been indignant: 'Send for the police if you believe we have done something criminal, Madame!'

Mention of police had alarmed Buddy. He knew a detective would soon find out where the ring had been sold. He hadn't even bothered to go far afield to find a jeweller. So he'd thought it best to confess, pleading a sudden financial crisis.

But his parents were past the stage where they

would accept easy excuses from him. Why had he needed the money? Where had his quarterly allowance gone? And so on and so on until his father, with a grim face, had demanded the key of his little flat in the Latin Quarter.

What he'd found there had shocked Edgar Garrenstein. It seemed they had made a mistake in bringing him to Paris to get him away from bad influences in New York. His parents had talked together earnestly while he waited like a schoolboy outside the headmaster's study. There was much to consider, Buddy himself and his problems, the embarrassment he might cause to Garrenstein's career and to the American government.

'We've decided you'd better go home, son,' Garrenstein told him. 'You just don't seem to be mature enough to handle your life on your own, and God knows I don't have the time to help you, with all I've got on my plate here. So you'd better go home to your mother's folk for a while, straighten you out, put you on a new track. See what I mean?'

His father hoped the boy would view it as a new start. But Buddy saw it as paternal tyranny, which he was unable to withstand because the old man held the purse-strings.

He didn't explain any of that to Nora. He simply said his parents were old-fashioned, didn't approve of his Parisian circle, and had ordered him home.

Nora couldn't take it in. What would she do without Buddy? He was the man in her life, someone who had stepped in to fill the terrible gap left when she realized she must not think about Marc.

All through the party they kept returning to the topic during lulls in the gaiety. They agreed they couldn't bear to be parted. Yet Buddy seemed unable to think of defying his parents. 'They've got the bank balance, honey.' When she suggested a job, he laughed: 'Doing what?' And it was true—he had no training for gainful employment.

Once she hinted they might get married. The Relatives wouldn't approve of her choice but if they were presented with a *fait accompli* they would try to live with it. Buddy would be given something to do in the House of Tramont. But Buddy didn't want to be a married man. 'You know I love you, baby, but . . . gee . . . marriage . . .'

The party was being held in a big empty mansion in the absence of the young host's parents. It disintegrated into couples seeking bedrooms where they could end the night in private enjoyment.

As dawn broke, Nora lay beside Buddy in the pretty room that belonged to a daughter of the house. She had Buddy's head on her breast, one of his arms tucked under her shoulder-blades.

His body was familiar, it seemed somehow to have become a necessity to her.

Was it love? She hardly knew. She was only aware that her life would be empty again if she lost him.

That was when she decided—if Buddy couldn't stay in Paris, somehow she would get to America.

SEVEN

The Relatives were utterly taken aback at her announcement.

'New York? Why on earth should you want to go to New York?'

'Why not?' Nora returned. 'It's a lot more interesting than going to the Riviera for the hundredth time.'

Gaby was trying to recover from the surprise, trying to sound out what was really behind this. 'Oh, if you're bored with Cannes, we could certainly go elsewhere. Italy . . .'

'I'd rather go to New York.'

'But New York is no place to be in summer,' Marc said. He knew—business had taken him there once or twice.

'Then if we go now, we can miss the discomfort. And I daresay there are beach resorts— they say Long Island is very pleasant.'

'But what's put this notion into your head all of a sudden?'

Nora hesitated. 'I'm bored,' she said.

Bored . . . It was the last thing they ever expected to hear from her. Her metamorphosis into a social butterfly had been so comparatively recent that they'd thought she still had a lot to enjoy.

'Well, if the season isn't as much fun as you expected, there's always London—'

'I'd rather go to New York.'

That was the refrain. To all their objections and proposals, she said, 'I'd rather go to New York.'

'What can be behind it?' Marc said to his wife late that night when they were preparing for bed.

'Who knows? It may be just a whim. Everything American is all the rage with her set—the jazz, the cinema, all that sort of thing.'

'Well, she can't go, and that's that.'

'How do you propose to stop her?' Gaby enquired, pausing in the task of arranging her pillow to a pleasing hollow for her head.

'Well . . . we'll tell her she can't.'

'She's very determined.'

He sighed. He hadn't told his wife about the scene at the Paris apartment a few nights ago. He'd said their young cousin had had a bad headache. Now he wondered if he should confide the real facts. But no . . . There had been a tacit understanding between him and Nora on that point: she'd known he wouldn't tell Gaby.

'Everything's been changing too fast for her,' he said. 'She just doesn't know her own mind.'

Gaby said nothing. She felt Nora knew her own mind well enough. What bothered her was—why?

Two days later she heard some gossip that seemed to point towards an explanation. 'I was told today that the Garrenstein boy is being shipped home, Marc.'

'So-o?' he said, turning from the decanters to meet her eye.

She nodded. 'That may be why Nora wants to go to the States.'

He poured drinks—a whisky for himself, Campari for Gaby. He brought it to her, then sat across from her in a tapestry covered armchair. Outside the french windows, the May light was still shining kindly over the shrubs that bordered the courtyard. Beyond lay the winefields with their rows of flowering vines, the buildings where the wine was pressed and tested and blended. People were still about in the estate: it was necessary to work while the light held good.

'Are they lovers, do you think?' he asked.

She shrugged. He took it to mean that she didn't know. But Gaby was fairly certain Nora had been to bed with Buddy Garrenstein. There had been a change in her—not a surface difference like the one wrought by the clothes of Coco Chanel, but a deeper change that had to do with learning, with perhaps maturity.

162

Gaby still recalled her young days of love, her desperate need to be with the man who had been her first lover. She was sure that if Nora felt anything like that for Buddy, she would go to New York, no matter what anyone else said.

'Well, it makes no difference, I'm against her going to New York on her own,' Marc said. He swallowed some Scotch. Wonderful, comforting drink—why had the French allowed someone else to invent it?

'Quite so,' said Gaby. 'Therefore I think I ought to go with her.'

'What?' Marc actually started, so that whisky swilled out onto his knuckles.

'It makes sense, Marc. You know we're still haggling for that money owed to us there. Either we get paid in full, or we're going to have to tell them we won't ship out any more wine.'

The United States had been living through what cynics called The Age of Pain for nine years. In 1920, on a wave of idealism after the war, the government had passed the 18th Amendment to the Constitution. It was against the law to sell alcohol in any form.

As a result, an industry called bootlegging had grown up. This consisted of either making or importing liquor to sell illegally. It was an interesting statistic that exports of wine from Europe to the American continent had actually increased greatly since 1920, but of course the labels on the crates stated they were destined for Montreal

163

or Mexico. It was the business of the bootleggers to transport the wine and spirits across the borders of the United States.

This they did by ferrying cargoes across Lake Michigan or down the long coastlines to some quiet creek. They also ran trucks through forest trail.' into Maine and any other state with a border against Canada, or took it across the Rio Grande.

Vast fortunes were made. Unfortunately the money due to the European exporters wasn't so readily forthcoming. It wasn't that the boot-leggers didn't want to pay, it was simply that their bookkeeping was chaotic and their atten-tion elsewhere—on avoiding the Customs men or their own machine-gun-toting rivals.

The people with whom the House of Tramont had dealings didn't, of course, tote machine-guns. The correspondence was with lawyers and accountants. Marc had been to the States more than once to round up recalcitrant accounts, with Gaby along for the pleasure of the trip. All had been politeness and lavish entertainment.

But he didn't like the idea of her going to deal with these people on her own. 'It'd be better if I went, Gaby—'

'Come now, darling, the whole idea is to be a chaperon to Nora. How could you—'

'I could escort her wherever she wants to go—'

'Really? You'd go to fashion shows and tea

parties with her? Now, be sensible. It's far better if I do it.'

They had a friendly wrangle all evening but it was a foregone conclusion that Gaby would win. It did in fact make more sense that she should go—she could stay close to Nora far more easily than Marc. Besides, there was a series of meetings coming up in Epernay about the definition of the Champagne area, which Marc as a lawyer was more able to deal with.

And lastly there was the uneasy suspicion that there was an emotional crisis waiting to be dealt with between Nora and the Garrenstein boy. Marc was well aware Gaby was better equipped to handle this than he. He disliked Buddy Garrenstein: he was likely to be unfair in dealing with him. He was relatively sure that Buddy had supplied whatever it was that Nora had been taking, and he couldn't help despising him for it. It might be fashionable, 'all the rage', but it was wrong, and a man didn't treat a girl he loved like that.

But someone must accompany Nora. Someone must if possible guide her away from deeper involvement with Buddy. And Gaby could do it much better than Marc.

Neither said aloud what each privately acknowledged: that Nora had won. By sheer quiet stubbornness she'd made them fall in with her wishes. It was a staggering thought—that the shy, quiet little cousin could have so much steel in her nature. Yet they shouldn't have been surprised. She was, after all, a Tramont.

Her campaign, if it could be called that, had taken a week. Buddy was due to sail next day. She went back to Paris to meet him at a café on the Boulevard St Germain, where the café tables were crowded with students. Buddy, however, was at a table in the dim interior.

Their time together had been limited by the need for her to be in Calmady, persuading the Relatives to agree to the American trip. She would have gone without their agreement but she was glad to have that, if not their approval. And to tell the truth, she was relieved to have Cousin Gaby going with her. To be alone in a strange, fast-moving city, where they spoke a language that was only somewhat like the English she'd learned from tutors, wasn't a pleasant prospect.

She could tell that Buddy was depressed at the idea of their parting. His normally athletic body slumped. Yet he would shrug and move restlessly. The healthy outdoor skin had taken on a pallor that didn't suit him. He seemed to be in a state of nerves—in fact, sometimes when he spoke of going home he sounded downright scared.

'To hear you talk,' she teased, 'you'd think they were going to clap you in irons the moment you step off the boat!'

'You think you're kidding? Dad's detailed

166

some junior stiff from the Embassy to ride herd on me. I had to duck out a side door to come and see you.'

She was perplexed. 'But surely your father couldn't object to your coming to meet me?'

'Oh . . . Well . . .' Buddy was brought up short. 'Well, you wouldn't want a guy sitting at the next table, listening to all we said, would you?'

The fact was, Buddy was desperately trying to make contact with a supplier who would give him enough Paradise Powder to see him through the voyage home. Five days lay ahead of him, five days in the company of his anxious mother, with bridge parties laid on by the purser and evenings spent foxtrotting to the ship's band. The only way he was going to get through it was if he had laid in enough to last till New York.

In New York it would be no problem. He had connections there. But he had only a few hours left in Paris before they headed for Cherbourg and the ocean liner. Between now and eight o'clock tomorrow he had to have the precious snuffbox filled and another little box stashed away among his clothes.

'Once we're in New York, everything will be all right,' Nora said, as if echoing his thoughts.

'What d'you mean?' he said, startled.

'There'll be no Embassy types there to bother us. We can see each other any time we like.'

'Oh, sure. Sure. It'll be great.' He looked at

her, and through the pall of anxiety about his
drug supplier he saw her the way she always
seemed to him, young and cute and affectionate.
'You really are going to come, Nora?'

'Of course. It's all agreed. Cousin Gaby is
coming along too but that's no problem—she'll
have business appointments and dull friends to
visit.'

'That's great.' But he was looking at his watch.
'I've got to go, babe. There's a guy I have to
meet—'

Her face clouded. She'd thought they would
spend this last night together in his little apartment, a long, loving and perhaps even romantic
farewell. 'Oh, Buddy . . . But tomorrow you'll
be gone!'

'I know, I know. It's tough, but I have to go.
It's important. There's a guy I have to find.'

'Couldn't we meet—after you find him?'

'The thing of it is, I don't know how long it'll
take.' The vocalist of the Rhythm Ragmen had
given him a name and a place—a dive in a side
street off Pigalle. He had to go there and wait.
That was all he knew.

'But we can't just say goodbye here,
Buddy . . .'

'Well, any case, we couldn't go to my place.
Dad cancelled it out—took away the keys and
told the manager to rent it to somebody else.'
Seeing Nora's look of amazement he dashed into
an easy explanation. 'Well, I wasn't going to

168

need it much longer, was I—and the manager knew somebody who wanted to take it on.'

From all she could gather, Buddy's father was an ogre. This was strange, because when you met him at a gathering he seemed a very nice man. But then diplomats have to be nice in public.

So there was nowhere to go, and Buddy seemed on tenterhooks to meet this man. He was glancing at his wristwatch again. It was only nine o'clock yet he looked round for the waiter to pay the bill.

'So . . . this is . . . this is goodbye, Buddy?' she faltered.

The waiter was chinking coins from the pouch under his apron. Buddy was busy accepting change and giving a tip. He took her elbow and led her outside. The faithful Peugeot-Bébé was parked at the kerb. She thought, 'He'll drive us out to some pretty spot and we'll be in each other's arms at least for a few minutes.'

He said, 'I've got to rush, Nora. You see, this guy that's acting jailer will have missed me by now and if I don't get back pretty soon my Dad's going to raise Cain.'

It was his father's fault. She was angry, confused, anxious.

He saw the tears sparkling on her lashes in the Paris dusk. He remembered that he loved her, that she was his girl, the prettiest girl he'd ever met and the nicest. He put his arms around her and kissed her hungrily. 'That's to last until we meet in New York,' he said when he let her go, breathless and half-laughing at the ferocity of it.

'It won't be long, Buddy. We're sailing on the Mauretania.'

He glanced about, saw a cruising taxi, and hailed it for her. As he handed her in he dropped a kiss on her cheek. 'Be seeing you, honey.'

'Buddy!' She prevented him from closing the taxi door.

'Yeah?'

'I don't have your address in New York!'

He was heading in haste for his Peugeot. 'We're in the phone-book, sweetheart!'

Next moment he was in the Peugeot and her taxi was moving off to take her to the Rue Berger.

This wasn't how she had imagined their parting. She was in emotional turmoil. She'd expected to be grieved as she left him but she hadn't expected this feeling that somehow . . . something was lacking.

The trip on the Mauretania was quite enjoyable. She entered into the easy round of shipboard activities, got friendly with the people at their table, flirted a little with the polite young men, and even began to talk with Cousin Gaby again in something like the old way.

Since she refused the engagement with Edmond du Ceddres there had been constraint between them. For Mora's part, she felt guilty.

170

She coveted her cousin's husband—it was as simple and as harsh as that.

But now she had Buddy, and Marc figured less in her dreams than hitherto. Besides, Gaby had been very understanding about the change in her lifestyle. She had accepted the new, modish Nora with far less reluctance than Marc.

They shared a stateroom. They went to the ship's hairdresser together, they discussed the clothes of the other women passengers, an air of relaxation developed.

They were due to enter New York Harbour on the following day when Gaby at last broached the subject she'd been avoiding.

'Is all of this so that you can be with Buddy Garrenstein?' she asked bluntly over breakfast in their room.

Nora started but nodded. She felt she owed frankness to her cousin. After all, she'd refrained from interfering until now.

'What's the relationship between you two? No,' she said, as Nora looked offended, 'I'm not asking about your sex life, I'm asking if you think it's a lasting thing? Is there a future in it?'

It was a good question. 'I don't know,' she said slowly. 'I think a lot of him—he's so different, so full of life—and he's afraid of nothing.'

'He's afraid of his father, I gather,' Gaby said with some dryness.

That was true. It hadn't occurred to Nora

before. 'It's because of the money situation, you see. Buddy has no money of his own.'

'That seems odd. He's . . . how old? Twenty-four?'

'Yes.'

'A man of that age generally has an income, or a career, or something.'

'Oh, well, naturally, Buddy has an allowance . . .'

'And if his father threatens to cut it off, Buddy has to knuckle under.'

'There's no need to put it like that! Families have different ways of dealing with problems—'

'And what was the problem that caused Monsieur Garrenstein to order Buddy home?'

Nora stopped to think. Had she had an explanation of that? Buddy had said that his father didn't approve of his Parisian friends, which hardly seemed enough for such Draconian measures.

The fact was that she'd been so busy consoling Buddy over the injustice that she'd never really found out the cause.

'I don't know,' she said at length. 'He's a very old-fashioned man, Buddy says. No sense of humour, no understanding of how young people think or feel—'

'How very sad,' murmured Gaby, musing that ambassadors generally had experience of life. 'You're going to see Buddy in New York?'

'Of course.' Nora frowned. 'You're not going to object!'

'Certainly not. I trust you to handle your own friendships. I only want to say this, Nora—I have things to do in New York, but I want to spend some time with you when I'm free. Please don't disappear from the apartment without leaving word where you'll be—it's a big city and you'll be a stranger in it.'

It was a reasonable request, even a touching one. Nora felt a rush of warmth towards her cousin. For the first time the resentment over Gaby's manner of dealing with the dangerous riding episode began to give way. The surface friendship of the voyage might be something more. Perhaps they were returning to something like their old footing, but with more equality between them.

Nora felt that she would like that. Though she had learned in the last year to make friendships, old friends were best.

New York greeted the Tramonts with open arms. Journalists came aboard before the passengers disembarked, to ask for interviews of the famous and to take pictures. Nora would never have thought of herself as 'famous', but the reporters seemed entranced by the two Tramont women.

The evening paper showed they had hit the headlines of the society page. 'Bubbles Queen and Princess Conquer Manhattan,' it cried.

173

Below was a photograph showing Gaby holding her hair close to her cheek as protection against the stiff harbour breeze, while Nora was trying to capture a flying silk scarf. 'The beautiful Madame Tramont and her equally beautiful daughter—'

'Daughter!' laughed Nora. 'Don't they ever listen to what people tell them?'

'Never mind.' Gaby dropped a kiss on her cheek. 'I feel as if you're my daughter.'

Nora hugged her. It was the first spontaneous embrace since the quarrel.

As soon as they had seen their belongings unpacked and had a snack, Nora made for the telephone. She said, on the basis of this easy relationship, 'I'm just going to ring Buddy.'

'Very well, dear. I'm going to take a rest. We have a dinner engagement this evening, don't forget.'

'All right, Gaby.'

She found the telephone number of the Garrensteins in the big Manhattan phone-book. The call was answered by a very English male voice—English butlers had been in fashion among the American rich since the turn of the century. 'The Garrensteins' residence.'

'May I speak to Mr Garrenstein, please?'

'Mr Garrenstein is in Paris, miss.'

'Oh, I'm sorry, I meant Buddy Garrenstein.'

'Mr Charles isn't here, I'm afraid.'

'Can I leave a message for when he comes in?'

174

'Excuse me, I expressed myself badly. Mr Charles isn't staying at the apartment.'

She frowned. 'Not staying . . .? But he arrived from France a few days ago.'

'That's correct, miss. He was taken straight from the ship to a hospital.'

'A hospital! What's wrong with him? Did he have an accident?'

'I'm not aware of the cause, miss. May I ask who's calling?'

'My name is Elinore Tramont, I'm a friend of Mr Garrenstein's from Paris. What hospital is he in?'

'I don't know which hospital, Miss Tramont, I'm sorry.'

She heard in her head all Buddy's fears about how he'd be treated when he got home. She'd thought they were nervy fantasies but—could he have been right? Surely the butler ought to know where Buddy was being treated, if he were really in hospital.

'Is Mrs Garrenstein staying in the apartment?'

'Yes, but she's not at home.'

'Not at home? Do you mean she's out, or not available?'

'She's out, miss. Can I take a message for her?'

Deeply worried although she couldn't really tell why, Nora left her name and telephone number, asking that Mrs Garrenstein should return her call as soon as she came in. The butler said repressively, 'I'll give her your message,

Miss Tramont, but she's very busy at the moment.'

Nora was on tenterhooks for the call for the remainder of the afternoon and as she dressed for dinner. But though the telephone rang often, the maid never came to say Nora was wanted. The calls were all from friends or business acquaintances of Gaby's.

'I can't go out,' Nora blurted to her cousin when the car was brought to the front of the building for them. 'I'm expecting a phone call—'

'But the maid can take a message, Nora.'

'No! I want to be here—it's important!'

'I can see it is,' Gaby said, studying her with shrewd dark eyes. 'But we really must go, dear. This invitation is from old friends—'

'You go, Gaby. Explain that I've been prevented.'

'No, Nora, you mustn't behave like this. It's about Buddy, I suppose?'

Out it all came—Buddy's sense of being in disgrace with a puritanical father, his fears that they might be severe with him when he reached the States, the consigning of him to hospital and the stonewalling of the butler about his whereabouts.

'It's all a lie, of course,' Nora said. 'He was afraid they'd treat him like this—'

'Nora, Nora! What on earth do you suppose they've done to him? Locked him in a cellar? Don't be silly, the Garrensteins are civilized

176

people, not Mexican bandits! Pull yourself together!'

The sharpness of her tone made Nora draw back. Then she felt anger flood through her. 'Oh, you'd take their side, of course—'

'Now look here, Nora. You keep saying you don't want to be treated like a child, so don't behave like one. Think about this in a purely adult manner. In the first place, it's probably quite easy to check whether Buddy was ill or had been injured on the ship. You saw how the reporters clambered all over us when we docked—it would probably have made a news item if the Ambassador's son was sick.'

'Oh . . . Yes . . . How would one find out?'

For answer Gaby picked up the evening paper, held it out so that Nora could see the telephone number. She sat down at the bureau, called the paper, asked for the social columnist, and after a few introductory pleasantries, enquired if Buddy Garrenstein had arrived last week.

'You and he tied in together somehow?' asked the alert woman reporter on the other end.

'Our families are friends, it's a simple matter of letting him know we've arrived if he's in New York.'

'Hold on.' After a moment the voice came back. 'Yeah, he was carried off the ship on a stretcher. Sudden collapse, the ship's doctor said.'

'Collapse?'

'Yeah,' said the reporter, listening with interest to the concern in her voice. 'Probably drunk—lotta folk pour it down the last day on board, they know it's gonna be difficult to get a drink here in the Land of the Free.'

'Oh. . . I see. . .'

'How about an interview with you tomorrow, Miss Tramont?' It was always wise to press an advantage.

'With me? What on earth for?'

'I'd like to talk about your friendship with Buddy Garrenstein—'

'I can't stop now, I'm late for a dinner engagement—'

'I could drop by any time you say. Eleven o'clock?'

'No, I'm sorry, I really don't—'

'See you then. Thanks for your call.'

Nora, who had no notion of the tenacity of the New York reporter, hung up the phone with the full intention of dodging her tomorrow.

Gaby was waiting in the hall with her coat on. The maid had Nora's wrap ready. 'Gaby, I don't really want to go—'

'My dear, Dorothy here will give Mrs Garrenstein the number at the Lasalles', she can ring you there.'

Thus coaxed and reassured, she went. But Mrs Garrenstein didn't return the call and all through the dinner Nora was inattentive to their hosts. When they got home her first question was, 'Did

178

Mrs Garrenstein ring?' But Dorothy shook her head. The only calls had been for Madame.

As soon as breakfast was over, Nora was on the telephone to the Garrensteins' apartment. The same English voice said that Mrs Garrenstein had been unable to return her call yesterday and was unable to come to the phone at the moment.

'It's very important that I speak to her,' Nora insisted. 'Please ask her.'

'I'm sorry, miss, Mrs Garrenstein isn't taking any telephone calls.'

'Will you ask her to ring me today?'

'I'll give her the message, miss, but I know she's going out later on.'

Nora was beside herself with anxiety by now. She understood perfectly well that Mrs Garrenstein was simply refusing to know her. What had she done to offend the woman? They had seldom had much conversation except at social events or when they had met in Cannes, but they had always been perfectly polite to each other. 'Don't you think it's all terribly strange?' she urged to Gaby. 'It verges on being rude!'

'You don't know what lies behind it, my dear. Perhaps Buddy is really ill—his mother may be worried out of her mind. In her place, would you want to be bothered with phone calls?'

'But why don't they leave some message with the butler for Buddy's friends?'

Gaby sighed. 'I don't know, Nora. And now I

must go. I have an appointment with Hughes about setting up a meeting with Ducchese's people—I mustn't be late.' She was picking up a document case and her handbag as she spoke. 'What are your plans for this morning, dear?'

Nora made up her mind all of a sudden. 'I'm going to the Garrensteins' apartment.'

'Nora!'

'Well, I'm not being told the truth. I'm going there and I'm going to ask what they've done with Buddy.'

'Nora, you'll do no such thing!'

'I certainly will! I didn't cross the Atlantic to be treated like a doormat. I'm going this very moment—'

'No, no, you mustn't! Nora, take a hold on yourself! You can't go barging—'

'I don't want to. If they would speak to me in a civilized way I shouldn't have to do this. But I'm going to the apartment and I shall camp on the doorstep until they give me an explanation of the way they're behaving.'

Gaby argued but Nora was already going into her bedroom for her hat and gloves. They blocked each other in the doorway of the room as Nora attempted to come out.

'All right,' said her cousin in defeat. 'If you must go, I'll go with you.'

'Gaby, would you? It would be such a help!'

Yes, and less likely to end in a heated exchange

of accusations. 'Just give me a moment to put off my appointment—'

'Gaby darling, I know it's very inconvenient to you to do that, but—'

'Never mind, never mind.' Gaby was looking up the number in her pocket notebook. She postponed her meeting, then hurried after Nora.

They used the car which should have taken Gaby to her business friends. The address, which Nora had got from the phone-book, was on Park Avenue. They went up to the penthouse floor in a lift with a bellboy who looked at them with admiration.

At the Garrensteins' the door was opened by a portly gentleman who looked like a bishop. 'Good morning,' he said, identifying himself as the owner of the English voice.

Gaby sent in her card with a note scribbled on the back. The butler asked them to wait in the library. A long delay ensued. In the end the butler reappeared. 'Please come this way.'

The drawing-room was very modern, all angular smoked glass and chromium. Nora thought it much more interesting than the tapestry and spindly gilt chairs of Parisian drawing rooms, and certainly the soft satin sofas were more comfortable.

Mrs Garrenstein rose to meet them. She was a plumply handsome woman, her grey hair worn full and softly waved, her dress of muted pale blue crepe styled by a rising American designer.

'Please sit down,' she said. She gave a glance of apology at Nora. 'I believe you've called two or three times.'

'Yes, and I can't understand why you don't—'

'Mrs Garrenstein,' put in Gaby quickly, 'my young cousin is very worried about Buddy. As you may perhaps know, they were close friends in Paris.'

'They were? I didn't know that.'

Nora coloured. That hurt. 'Didn't Buddy—'

'He tells us very little of his concerns, Miss Tramont. Of course I knew you were in his set.'

'Nora would like to speak to him, if that's possible, Mrs Garrenstein.'

'I'm sorry, I'm afraid it isn't.'

'Now look here—'

'Excuse me, Mrs Garrenstein,' Gaby intervened once more, 'I do really think it would save a lot of upset if you could just let the two young people have a word. Nora feels very keenly about it.'

The other woman paused, looking down at her hands, as they fidgeted with a lace-edged handkerchief. Then she said, 'My son is in hospital.'

'He'd had an accident?'

'No, he collapsed on board ship from . . . from a sudden illness.'

'Oh, I don't believe *that!*' cried Nora. 'Buddy is as strong as a horse—'

'Young lady,' said Mrs Garrenstein in a voice

of stifled anger, 'I'm not accustomed to being called a liar. Buddy is in hospital.'

'Nora, be quiet,' Gaby urged, putting a hand on her arm. 'May we know the nature of his illness, Mrs Garrenstein?'

'He's still undergoing tests. We don't know exactly.'

'Huh!' snorted Nora. 'It's just as he told me—you're keeping him from seeing his friends as a punishment—'

Mrs Garrenstein's face seemed to crumple. 'Oh, what's he been saying to you?' she gasped. 'He's so . . . so . . .'

'He told me he was being sent home in disgrace and that you would be hard on him! I thought he was just being silly but now I see—'

'Yes? Yes, what do you see?' challenged his mother, clenching her hands and making herself speak firmly. 'Do I look like a dragon? I'm out of my mind with worry about him, and now you come here with silly tales he's told—'

'Mrs Garrenstein, please—we didn't mean to distress you.' Gaby frowned fiercely at Nora who, truth to tell, felt ashamed as she watched their hostess fight back her tears.

'I'm sorry,' Nora said. 'Perhaps . . . perhaps I got carried away. It's just that I'm worried too. He was so depressed just before he left Paris, and so much on edge. Sometimes I thought he was genuinely afraid of something. The idea of the voyage home seemed to fill him with dread.'

'And shall I tell you why?' his mother burst out. 'Because he thought he wouldn't get enough cocaine to see him through those five days! But he did, and he took it, and God knows what was in it but he collapsed—he was so ill—or perhaps it was just an overdose—I don't know, the ship's doctor didn't have much experience of that kind of thing. But at least he didn't die, and now he's . . . he's . . .'

She broke off. Nora and Gaby sat looking at her in horror.

'And now?' Gaby repeated with gentleness. 'I think you have to tell Nora.'

Mrs Garrenstein stifled her sobs. 'This could be the end of my husband's career if it gets out. I must ask you—you must promise, no one must know.'

'Of course.'

'Buddy is in a private clinic for the treatment of drug addiction.'

Gaby was waiting to help Nora through the shock of this revelation, ready with words of comfort. But to her surprise Nora sat silent. Then she whispered, 'Oh, poor Buddy . . .'

'It doesn't surprise you, dear?'

'No, Gaby. I knew he . . . he . . . But I didn't think it was so serious.'

'It's serious,' sighed Buddy's mother. 'He got into the habit here in New York—it was thought to be a "smart" thing to do—and it led to problems in other ways so we brought him out to

184

Paris. Not that Buddy hasn't always been a difficult boy . . . But we hoped he'd settle down—young men do, you know.'

'I'm so sorry,' Gaby said. It seemed a totally inadequate remark.

'Thank you. The doctors tell us the treatment may be lengthy, and they say he should go into psychoanalysis. I don't know . . .'

'If there's anything I could do to help—!' Nora cried.

'I don't think so, my dear. You're very sweet to think of it but . . . to tell the truth . . . Buddy's never so much as mentioned you. I'm surprised to find that you feel you . . . Forgive me . . .'

'What you mean,' Nora took it up, with a surprising lack of bitterness, 'is that I don't figure largely in his life and I might as well understand that.'

'He's not a *bad* boy,' his mother faltered. 'It's just . . . he's always been rather self-centred.'

'I think we've trespassed on your hospitality long enough,' Gaby asked, rising. 'Is there any point in sending flowers or cards to Buddy?'

'I believe not. He's in the hands of the doctors now and we must accept their advice. They tell me Buddy will be best if he's kept somewhat isolated—to tell the truth the director of the clinic—well, he says the patients use friends to smuggle in drugs and so . . .'

She was pink with shame. Gaby held out her hand and shook Mrs Garrenstein's. 'We'll go. I regret, Madame, that we've embarrassed you in this way.'

'Yes, indeed,' Nora said, hoping that her sincerity made up for the blunder she'd committed. 'I hope things go well. If Buddy ever mentions me, tell him he has my best wishes.'

She was silent on the short ride back to the Tramonts' apartment. Gaby didn't intrude on her thoughts, but dropped her under the scalloped canopy with a kiss and a pat on the shoulder.

In the vestibule, Nora was greeted by the porter. 'Say, I'm sorry, Miss Tramont, I tell her you're out but she won't give up!'

'What?'

A young woman in a mannish suit came forward. 'We had a date, Miss Tramont—you promised me an interview.'

'I did nothing of the sort,' Nora replied. She walked past on her way to the lift, busy with her own thoughts.

'Come on, Miss Tramont, one good turn deserves another. I helped you with information last night—and by the way, what gives between you and Buddy Garrenstein?'

Alarm bells rang in Nora's head. She knew the power of the Press from having been watched all last year by Parisian reporters.

'Who?' she said in a perplexed tone. 'Oh, the Garrensteins—they're friends of ours from Paris.'

'Then how come you didn't know if he'd arrived or not?' the woman persisted, accompanying her into the lift.

'Oh, that was just a mix-up, Miss—'

'Auber, Jennie Auber.'

'Well, look, Miss Auber, I'm sorry I wasn't here—I was out with my cousin—'

'Your cousin?'

'Madame Auduron-Tramont.'

'But I thought she was your mother?'

'No, no. I've got some spare time now—if you like I'll explain our family to you and perhaps you'd like to see my Chanel dresses?'

'Chanel? Is she a friend of yours?'

'I should say so. She's an amazing woman— you know she has an English duke backing her firm these days?'

Thus the reporter was led away from dangerous questions about the Garrensteins, and the promise to keep their secret was fulfilled.

After the reporter was gone, well satisfied with a minute examination of Nora's wardrobe and two cups of coffee made in the French style, Nora sat down to think.

Shorn of all romantic trappings, she had to admit that her affair with Buddy had been rather gimcrack. The fact was, she couldn't really remember ever deciding she loved him enough to go to bed with him. That had happened when she had been lost in some narcotic haze. Afterwards she'd wanted to persuade herself that love was involved but really . . . had she loved him? Had he loved her?

It seemed doubtful on both counts. Buddy hadn't asked for her, hadn't even mentioned her name to his family. She remembered now that as they parted in the Boulevard St Germain she'd had to call him back and remind him she didn't know his Manhattan address. There had been a certain lack of urgency in his need of her, to say the least. 'He's always been rather self-centred . . .'

As to whether she'd loved him, the answer might very well be no. But if that was uncertain, at least one thing was clear. It was all over.

But, she said to herself as she looked out of the window at the skyscraper peaks of Manhattan, here I am in the most exciting city in the world. Perhaps for all the wrong reasons, but I'm here.

So why not enjoy it?

EIGHT

The party at the Bensons' was one of those great come-and-go affairs trying to imply the hosts knew everybody worth knowing. Perhaps it was true, for Nora had met Helen Treubel the opera star, Paul Whiteman the jazzband leader, and at least two modernist painters who implied that they were famous.

Outside, the June heat wave pressed down on the city. Here in this huge apartment overlooking Central Park, the air conditioning was wafting cool air over the buffet table with its display of quail in aspic, oyster patties, devilled steak, gaspacho, and any flavour of ice cream you could imagine. A black pianist was dispensing sweet sounds from a white grand piano: the tune at the moment was 'Stardust'.

Nora was fending off the attentions of two eager young men. She was explaining that she didn't want anything to eat and that she would rather not dance just for the moment. The truth was, she was tired. New York in a heat wave was all that Cousin Marc had threatened. Tomorrow she was going to spend a week or so with friends at their Long Island home, where cool Atlantic breezes would temper the sunshine and the ocean would provide plenty of good swimming. She could hardly wait to get there.

Her suitors, understanding at last that she really wanted to sit quietly for a while, found her a corner of a big settee upholstered in soft pink leather, put cushions at her back and under her feet, and prepared to sit alongside to entertain her with their sparkling conversation. She let her mind drift away from the chatter.

They had come to this party because Gaby said she might meet there a certain Edward Cianelli. So far he hadn't showed up. 'Why do we want to meet him?' Nora had asked.

'That's a good question. All I know is that people say he has "pull"—it seems he could arrange a meeting for me with these tedious people who won't pay us for our champagne.'

'A financier? A politician?'

Gaby smiled. 'My darling, don't ask! People here in New York are very strange. The best title I can think of for Monsieur Cianelli is "entrepreneur"—but exactly what his business is, I'd rather not know.'

'You're not saying he's a gangster?' cried Nora, intrigued.

'He may very well be. It's surprising how many people *are*.'

'But he wouldn't be at a party given by a respectable family like the Bensons?'

'My dear, I'm told it's very likely, and that's why we've accepted the invitation.'

Invitations arrived in plenty. Everyone, it seemed, wanted to offer hospitality to the "Tramont Beauties", as the gossip columnists had named them. The item in the papers about Nora's friendship with Coco Chanel had had great influence. 'If you'd said you were a friend of Emile Chartier, they wouldn't have been interested. But Chanel—ah!' laughed Gaby as the cards and phone calls poured in.

Here they were, then, in this huge and impressive apartment, with a horde of people who seemed to have nothing in common except that they were in some way 'famous'. Of the two young men now paying her attention, one was a successful racing yachtsman and the other was a radio commentator. Neither of them knew how to take no for an answer.

Deliverance came unexpectedly. There was a stir at the outer edges of the crowd as the hostess fluttered forward to greet a newcomer.

'Gee,' said the radio man, 'it's Cianelli!'

'No kidding?' said the yachtsman, rising to stare over the heads. 'So it is—and he's brought Betsy with him!'

'Who is Betsy?' Nora said, roused out of her lethargy by the advent of the man Gaby wanted to meet.

'You don't know about Betsy Garforth? She's the girl Eddy's going to make a star.'

Nora rose also, to see these two 'famous' people. The young men drifted away from her, drawn by the attraction of the influential man and his beautiful protégée. Relieved, Nora quietly made her way to the buffet in search of a cool drink. She had the beginnings of a headache.

She was standing there watching the party re-group itself around the newcomers, when a voice spoke at her elbow.

'Excuse me.'

She glanced round.

'You're going to think this is some stupid new line to get to know you but . . . I think you and I are related.'

Nora raised her eyebrows. She was being

addressed by a tallish, dark-featured young man in black tie and dinner jacket. He had an angular face, not handsome but interesting. His dark eyes were studying her with approval.

'Related?' Nora echoed. 'In what way? Are we uncle and aunt?'

'No, seriously.' He seemed to mean it. 'My great-grand-father was a guy called Jean-Baptiste Labaud—'

She shook her head. 'I don't think there's anyone called Labaud in the Tramont family—'

'Well, it may be one of those old family stories. But when the old guy died—this was out in California, a wine estate called Bracante Norte— they found a letter among his papers. It was from a man called Robert Fournier-Tramont claiming to be his son.'

Nora drew in her breath. Robert Fournier-Tramont? Uncle Robert! Cousin Gaby's father.

But it was easy to tell a tale like that. 'Who are you?' she asked coldly.

'The name's Norwood, Peter Norwood—you may have heard of me?' As she shrugged dismissively, he smiled with some wryness and went on, 'I didn't really think you would have. I'm a theatrical director—got one or two successes to my name.'

'Oh yes,' she said in a distant tone, 'everyone here has some claim to fame, I gather.'

'Gee, you must be from Nome!'

'Nome?'

'It's the capital of Alaska. Listen, I'm sorry if I offended you. I just thought you'd like to hear some news about your American relations.' He gave a little bow and turned as if to go.

'No, wait,' Nora said, touching his sleeve. 'I'm sorry. You took me by surprise. Are you really related to Robert Fournier-Tramont?'

The indignant frown melted at her apology. 'Sure am,' he said. 'At least, if that letter was telling the truth. And I reckon it was, because Mom tells me the story goes that this Fournier-Tramont guy came to visit Great-Grandpa and got a big hello. So it looks like we're second cousins by the back door, wouldn't you say?'

Nora laughed. 'It's certainly a new way of getting to know someone. But I don't think it can be right. Robert Fournier-Tramont was the son of a sister of Madame Tramont who founded the firm, and she was married to . . . let me see . . . Auguste Fournier. Their son Robert was my great-uncle.'

'Yeah,' said Peter Norwood, 'but you know—there's skeletons in family cupboards. It *might* be true.'

'Let's find my cousin Gaby and ask her.'

'Your cousin—that's the one they say is head of the champagne firm now—hold on there, you say she's Robert's daughter?'

'Yes.'

'Gee, then . . . d'you think it'd be a good thing to tell her about it? It's maybe not something

193

you want to hear about your father—that he was the son of some guy in California when all the time you'd been thinking he was—'

'Gaby won't mind,' Nora said. 'It's interesting. And anyhow, it's all in the past now, isn't it?' She glanced about for Gaby, but it seemed that she had achieved the object of the evening—she was engaged in conversation with Eddy Cianelli. 'Oh, she's busy for the moment.'

'So I see! She's made a hit. Any woman who can take Eddy's attention off Betsy for so much as five minutes must have the lure of Mata Hari.'

'You know him?'

'Yes, thank God. He's my angel.'

'Angel!'

'It doesn't mean I say my prayers to him— well, maybe I do! He's the guy putting up the money for the show I'm doing.'

'Oh,' said Nora with a little burst of laughter, 'are you helping to make Betsy a star?'

'You know a lot for a recent arrival on these shores! Yeah, I'm going to put Betsy's name up in lights.' He groaned. 'Dumb broad . . . But all she's got to do is walk on in costumes loaded down with sequins and stand still looking beautiful. And she can do *that*, at least.'

Nora eyed him with amusement. 'When you said you were a theatrical director, I thought you might be directing Ibsen or Eugene O'Neill.'

'Just give me the chance! I could have had a ball with *Strange Interlude*. But I've got a talent for musicals and they're the big scene at present. I know you're going to say they're corny—'

'I wasn't going to say anything of the sort. I haven't seen an American musical.'

'You haven't? Your education has been strangely neglected! Listen, Miss Tramont, would you like to see one? It would be an honour to show you this great American art form—more beautiful girls with less clothes on than on any stage in the world.'

'Oh, they couldn't possibly wear less than Josephine Baker. But I'd love to go. Unfortunately I'm going out of the city for a few days, to spend some time where it's cooler.'

'Oh? Where?'

'Some friends of my cousin's have a house on Long Island—'

'Oh, then that's no problem! I could drive out and fetch you—'

'But Mr Norwood, it's such a long way—'

'Would you call me Peter? Since we're cousins, and all?'

She laughed. 'But, Cousin Peter, it's still a long way to Quogue—'

'No it isn't. It can't be much more than a hundred miles.'

'That's too far to go for a theatre. Perhaps we could defer it until I get back to Manhattan.'

'When are you due back?'

'Who knows?'

'May I call and find out your plans?'

'If you like.'

She found him an amusing companion for the rest of the evening, which was just as well, for Cousin Gaby was busy with the important Mr Cianelli. When they got home at last, Nora mentioned her new acquaintance as the two women sat out on the balcony of the flat, breathing the cooler air of the night.

To her surprise, Gaby accepted it quite calmly.

'You mean it's true?'

'Oh yes.'

'Great-Uncle Robert was the son of this Californian wine-grower?'

'Yes.'

'But how could it be? A foreigner?'

'He wasn't a foreigner when it all happened.' Nora heard Gaby sigh in the darkness beside her. 'Since you know this much, I'll tell you the other thing. My father was the son of Nicole Tramont.'

'No, Gaby—excuse me—you've made a slip of the tongue Great-Uncle Robert was the son of Paulette—'

'No. My father was Nicole's son, by Jean-Baptiste Labaud. It's too long a story to go into now. Labaud left Calmady and Robert was brought up by Nicole's sister to avoid a scandal. So you see, you and I are more closely related than you thought.'

'You are a direct descendant of Old Madame . . . And so am I . . .'

'Indeed. And that's why, Nora, I've sometimes seemed . . .. perhaps a little demanding of you. I have you, but you have no one else to hand on to—not so far. That's why the marriage with Edmond seemed so important at the time.'

There was a silence. Then Nora said, 'I wonder what ever happened to Edmond?'

'Oh, he married Laurette Barquerot—it was in the newspapers.'

'I wish . . .'

'What? That you had married him?'

'Not exactly . . . Though he was nice enough . . . And if I had, I shouldn't be here in New York, should I?'

'You're enjoying it?'

'Oh, so much!'

'And tomorrow you'll see the pleasures of Long Island. It's not a bit like the Riviera, Nora. I hope you won't be disappointed.'

'I wish you were coming.'

'No, no. Now I've met the interesting Monsieur Cianelli I must follow it up. I'm seeing him in a few days time, to give him facts and figures.'

'Can he really help?'

'It seems he is what the Americans call a fixer. He has friends in high places, and in low places too, by all accounts.' Gaby laughed.

'Do be careful, Gaby. It doesn't sound at all like doing business in Épernay!'

'Perhaps not. Like you, I'm enjoying it!'

Quogue proved to be, as Cousin Gaby had

warned, nothing like the Riviera. It was a scatter of small houses made of wooden boards. The one used by the Laportes had been a fisherman's dwelling, and though it had been beautifully fitted out the life there was of the simplest, lived in old clothes or swimsuits, and centred on swimming and sailing.

Unfortunately after two days a heavy mist came down, the result—so her hosts mourned—of the heat wave. 'It's likely to last for days, Nora. It's too bad! We promised you sun and sea, and now there's no sun and you can't see the sea.'

They urged her to go back to the gaiety of the city though they themselves, keen yachtsmen, would stay on until the weather cleared. 'You can come out again when it's better.'

'But I should feel so bad, treating you like a hotel—'

'Not at all, not at all! We want you to have a good time, my dear.'

And so when Peter Norwood called, asking if the weather had changed her plans, she told him she'd be back in Manhattan that evening.

He took her to see *Broadway Follies*, a lavish spectacle. It seemed to consist of young black men doing incredible dancing feats—buck-and-wing, Peter called it—and tall statuesque girls wearing almost nothing but long trains of sparkling cloth and jewelled head-dresses. The best thing about it was the music, which was played with verve by a large orchestra consisting mostly of brass and saxophones.

'I think I like jazz,' Nora said as they discussed the show at an after-theatre supper.

'That wasn't jazz! That was showbiz. If you really want to hear jazz, you have to go to Harlem.'

'Oh, then I'll go there. I'd like to get to know—'

'You won't go to Harlem! At least not just like that. It's not safe.'

'Really? But my friends and I go to the night-club districts of Paris without—'

'Harlem is where the black folk live. Point is, you'd stand out there, being white and obviously rich. I'm not saying they're all thieves, but if you go to Harlem to visit the jazz clubs it's best to go in a group.'

'I see.' She waited, for he had carefully set up a case for being her escort.

'I'd like to take you, if you really want to go. I've got friends who know the dives.'

'Thank you. I'd enjoy that.'

So he took her with a group of friends to the Cotton Club on the next night, and then she went to see him working with his chorus for the show which was due to start its out-of-town try-out in Atlantic City in July.

The rehearsals were interesting and often very funny. Betsy Garforth was certainly very beauti-ful, but she insisted on turning up in very expensive clothes. Over these were strapped makeshift outlines of the costume she would wear on stage. Certainly it was difficult to look glamorous with cane paniers strapped to the waist and a head-dress of plain wire, but she didn't even try.

'Dumb broad,' groaned Peter.

Nora's cousin listened with amusement to her accounts of the rehearsals. 'It's more like drilling them than directing them,' she said. 'And some of them don't seem to know their left from their right!'

'They're chosen for their looks, I take it, not their intelligence. Nora,' said Gaby, 'you seem very taken with this young cousin of ours.'

'Well, he's fun.'

'I must meet him.'

'I've been waiting for a chance to introduce him. But,' Nora added with a tilt of her cropped head, 'is this sudden interest because he's a long-lost cousin, or because you think I'm getting too interested?'

'Oh, I've no fears of that. I think you'll be very fastidious, after . . .'

There was a pause. 'You were going to say, after Buddy,' Nora prompted.

'You never mention him these days.'

'Well,' was the wry answer, 'if you recall, "he never mentioned me".'

Gaby smiled. 'I'm glad you can repeat that without rancour. But I should really like to know—how do you feel about him?'

Nora took a long moment to consider. 'I feel,' she confessed, 'as if I never really knew him.'

'Ah . . . I'm afraid that's often the case when you're in love.'

'Is that from harsh experience?' teased Nora.

'Let's say I know what I'm talking about.'

'Did you have a *lot* of lovers, Gaby?' There was naïvety in the question, but Gaby didn't laugh.

'I had enough to know that Marc was the man for me,' she replied. 'And despite all that's happened I still hope you'll have the same luck. But you must have realized by now that you're a very attractive girl—'

'Not when I look at those gorgeous females on Peter's stage!'

'Oh, nonsense—they're nothing but animated dolls to parade about wearing feathers and glitter. You're a different thing altogether— you're what the Americans describe as "sensational" because you epitomize what today's world seems to want. All I was going to say was, now that the men are always crowding around you, try not to make the same mistake again as you made with Buddy.'

'You and Marc never liked him, did you?'

Gaby shrugged. 'We just felt he was . . . I don't know . . . inconsiderate is perhaps the word. If you had married him, I'm sure we could have got along with him for your sake. But I could never imagine him taking any useful part in running the business.'

'You mean that's a prerequisite for a husband?' Nora enquired, teasing.

But she knew it would be a great boon to Marc and Gaby if the man she eventually brought to them as her future husband showed an interest in champagne-making.

She certainly didn't think of Peter as a future husband. Nevertheless, to set Gaby's mind at rest, she brought them together and saw a casual friendship grow up between them.

'Gee, she's a beauty!' he said to Nora once after an evening event. 'If she were thirty years younger she'd be up there on that stage among those dolls, and she'd make them look like nothing.'

Nora agreed. 'All the Tramont women were beauties,' she said, 'until I came along and broke the tradition.'

'Don't you think you're beautiful, Nora?'

'Of course not!'

'You don't see yourself the way others do. You're so keen and alive and zippy—and you've got those weird eyes, like a sea gypsy.'

He blushed. He felt he was getting quite poetic, and poetry was anathema to him. 'Anyhow,' he concluded, 'I think you're the tops, and it builds up my ego no end that you've let me be friends with you. The other guys could kill me, they're so envious.'

Nora couldn't help liking him a lot. He had something of the eternal college boy about him— a continuing enthusiasm tinged with cynicism, an intriguing mixture of sophistication and eagerness. It was pleasant to turn to him after some of the more tedious of the business dinners Gaby was forced to give.

The matter of getting money out of the bootlegging bosses looked as if it were coming to fruition. 'Monsieur Cianelli says he has it almost "fixed", so I propose that in about a week you and I should go to some nice cool mountain resort to recover from all this hard work. Would you like that?'

'Couldn't we go to Atlantic City? That's where Peter's going to have his first try-out.'

'But Atlantic City isn't at all agreeable, Nora. At least, I didn't find it so the only time I was there.'

'It isn't? Oh, then, of course—we'll go wherever you choose.'

'I thought perhaps somewhere in the Adirondacks?'

'Could we go to Pittsburgh afterwards?'

'Pittsburgh!'

'Well, that's another of Peter's try-out towns.'

'To tell the truth, dear, I thought of going home after we have our holiday. You know, back home . . . Marc was telling me in his last letter that the grapes look good this year . . .'

'You're homesick,' Nora murmured, surprised.

'Of course! Aren't you?'

'We-ell, not often.'

'Peter perhaps compensates for—'

'No, no. He's not as important to me as that, Gaby. No, certainly, if you want to go home, we'll do so. As soon as Monsieur Cianelli brings off this settlement, if you like.'

'You wouldn't mind?'

'Not at all. We'll do whatever you like. After all, it was I who dragged you here. The least I can do is hurry you home when you've had enough.'

'You're so sweet,' Gaby said, hugging her. 'I'm seeing Monsieur Cianelli tomorrow evening—he's invited me to a sort of celebration dinner at a grand restaurant, so I take it that means the money is more or less in his hands.'

'How much does he get for all this?' Nora enquired, frowning.

'Ten per cent.'

'Ten per cent! For getting money that rightfully belongs to us?'

'Well, darling it's better to go home with ninety per cent than with nothing—and the way things were going, it looked as if those extraordinary men at the head of the business were simply not going to pay.'

'If you say so, Gaby. But I've never liked the look of Monsieur Cianelli, and from what Peter says he's pouring out money like water over this silly girl he adores. I do hope none of that is Tramont money!'

'Dear child, so do I,' Gaby said fervently.

On the morning of Gaby's dinner engagement with Eddy Cianelli, Nora returned to Long Island to avoid the brazen heat in the Manhattan canyons. She spent a long day swimming and lazing on the sand. Seabirds balanced on sickle-shaped wings on the heat currents rising from the land. The sky was a pale clear blue, like Chinese silk. There was only silence, solitude, peace.

'You've got quite a tan,' Mattie Laporte said admiringly. To have a good tan was all the rage this summer.

'Yes, but I think I'll cover up tomorrow. I don't want my skin to start peeling.'

'John and I thought we'd do some sailing tomorrow. Would you like to come?'

'That would be lovely.'

'More wine?'

'No, John, thank you very much, I'm sleepy enough already. I'll go to bed, if you don't mind.'

Drowsy with sun and food, she dropped asleep very early. Thus she woke at once when the phone downstairs in the hall began shrilling at just after midnight. She sat up, startled, and then as the Laportes made no sound she rose and padded down to answer it. Probably something to do with sailing—some friend rounding up a crew for tomorrow.

'The Laportes' house,' she said.

'May I speak to—Nora? Nora, is that you?'

'Peter!'

'Nora, can you jump in a car and get back to New York at once?'

'But what's wrong? What's happened?'

'It's your cousin—'

'Gaby!'

'Yes, listen, if you could hurry—'

'What is it, Peter? Tell me!'

'It's—gee, it's just so awful—Nora, that guy Cianelli—it was him they were after—'

'Who? What are you saying?' She was icy with fear now, all her apprehensions justified in these few stumbling words from Peter.

'They shot up the restaurant where they were having dinner. The police think the gunmen had orders to kill Eddy and his guest but I can't believe that—'

'Kill Gaby? Peter—she's not—'

'She's hurt bad, Nora. She's in hospital. If you could get here—'

'Yes, of course—I'll be there in two hours.'

'I'll see you at the hospital.' He gave her directions and rang off. Instantly she was upstairs, pulling on trousers and jersey, pushing her feet into sandals.

The Laportes, roused by her conversation on the telephone, had got up. In six words she explained why she must get to Bellevue. John Laporte volunteered to drive her—'I know the roads better than you.'

It was as well she accepted, because anxiety and tension had made her almost incapable of handling a car. By two o'clock they were drawing up in the hospital parking lot. Peter was waiting for them in the lobby.

'The cops got in touch with me because they're trying to find Betsy Garforth, to give her the news,' Peter explained as they went up in the lift. 'She seems to be staying out of sight, scared, I guess. The minute I heard they'd got Eddy, I asked about your cousin. I remembered you said they had a date.'

'Yes,' said Nora.

'I said I'd find you. I seemed to remember you saying you'd go to the beach. Nora, I'm terribly sorry about this.'

'Yes.' She wished he'd stop talking.

'What happened?' John Laporte asked.

'Four guys with guns rushed in, as far as I can gather. They sprayed the restaurant with bullets. Eddy was killed outright, one other guy, and I think three injured besides Gaby.'

'And Gaby?'

Peter hunched his shoulders. 'Critical. She's been in theatre since I rang you.'

They reached the floor where Gaby had been taken. The nurse at the reception desk saw them to a little area set out with chairs, a low table, and an evergreen pot-plant. A white-coated man came out of an office when summoned by the nurse. 'We're doing all we can,' he said.

'When can I see her?'

'Oh . . . She won't be out from theatre for a while and then you know—the anaesthetic—'

As he spoke, a figure in surgical green came along the wide passage to the reception area. The doctor said, 'This is the surgeon, Dr Bailey. Doctor, this is Miss Tramont.'

The surgeon halted, shaking his head.

'I'm sorry, Miss Tramont,' he said in a weary voice, 'your cousin just didn't make it.'

NINE

The consequences of Gabrielle Tramont's death were so grotesque that Nora found she had to put up a mental block against them.

Almost as soon as the surgeon had told her the news, the homicide detective in charge of the case wanted to speak to her. Peter at once told her to say nothing. That was quite easy, for she was so dazed with grief that she couldn't understand any of the questions she was being asked.

Next Peter insisted she hire a lawyer.

'But I don't need a lawyer—'

'You certainly do! Don't you realize that Gaby

was dickering with a gangster, for money not legally permissible?'

'Oh, it doesn't matter about the money—'

'But it does, Nora, it does! Gaby was trying to get payment for illegal liquor. In the eyes of the law . . .' His words tailed off.

'What?'

'Well, you may as well hear it from me as from the cops. It was a criminal act.'

'How dare you!' she cried. She almost flew at him with her fists. 'How dare you say that about Gaby—'

He caught her wrists, pulled her close, encircled her with his arms. 'Don't, Nora, don't. I'm your friend, remember?'

She wasn't weeping. She was too angry and bewildered for tears. She dragged herself free. 'Go on,' she said in a stony voice.

'Your cousin was associating with gangsters, knowingly, to get money owed to her for illegal imports of champagne. You *must* be careful what you say. You can't admit you knew. There's some legal term for that—complicity, I think. But I mean it, Nora—you have to have a lawyer.'

There was a man the House of Tramont had employed to try to extract the debt in the previous year. Loomis Dearborn was only too glad to be of service. He told Nora to say nothing unless he authorized it. He called in the aid of the French Ambassador in Washington, who was aghast when he learned that one of France's

209

leading citizens had been gunned down by hoodlums. An official protest was presented to the State Department.

A kindly but embarrassed and determined captain of detectives gave Nora a fuller view of 'the case' on the morning of the following day. He had had facts from under world informers.

'It seems the story goes like this. Joe Ducchese didn't want to pay out what he owed but Eddy Cianelli moved in on the act and persuaded him. He had his own reasons. He needed funds for this show he was putting on to get his girlfriend Betsy into the headlines. How much commission was he charging your cousin, Miss Tramont?'

'My client denies any knowledge of a business relationship between her cousin and Mr Cianelli,' said Dearborn quickly.

'Oh yeah? Then what was the briefcase full of money for?'

'I don't know anything about a briefcase,' Nora said, before Dearborn could stop her. But when he'd given the words a second's consideration, he nodded approval.

'Then you don't claim the briefcase we found in the restaurant?'

'Certainly not,' said Dearborn.

The detective stared at the ceiling of his office. 'That's just as well, because the District Attorney has confiscated it. To go on with my case— Mrs Tramont met Eddy by arrangement at the

Maestoso Restaurant. The Duke heard about it from a snitch—'

'Who?' Nora asked.

'Joe Ducchese—he's known as The Duke,' her lawyer whispered. He was pleased at her obvious and genuine ignorance of such points.

'Joe heard about it and was annoyed. Apparently it wasn't the first time Eddy'd let some of Joe's money stick to his fingers. So Joe sends four of his gunsels to take out Eddy.' Captain O'Reilly frowned and cleared his throat. 'Unfortunately, these stiffs didn't get their instructions right. They were told Eddy was meeting this Gaby Tramont, but they heard it as "Gabby"— like, a nickname for a talkative guy. So they rolled in there with their armament blazing and found they'd taken out a dame—pardon me, I mean a lady.'

Nora put her hands up to her face and covered her eyes for a long moment. It was too stupid, too absurd. It couldn't have happened.

'I'm sorry,' said Captain O'Reilly, and waited.

'Have you more questions for my client at this time, Captain?' Dearborn asked with a meaningful nod at Nora, who was slowly coming back to awareness of her surroundings.

'Hm . . . Well, we may as well get it over, it's not going to get any easier. Miss Tramont, what reason did your cousin give for meeting Eddy Cianelli?'

'My client has no information on that point.'

211

'Miss Tramont, do you deny that the money Eddy took to the restaurant was a payment to your wine firm?'

'My client has no information on that point.'

'Miss Tramont, do you make any claim on the money?'

'Since she has no knowledge of why it was there, naturally my client makes no claim on it.'

'Say, Dearborn, just shut the hell up, will you? Miss Tramont, I'm sure sorry about what happened but we've got to clear it up. Your cousin wasn't the only person killed, you know—a poor old guy sitting at the next table took two bullets through the chest.'

'I know,' gasped Nora. 'I know.'

'My client is in great distress, O'Reilly. We would like to conclude this interview.'

'You'll conclude when I tell you! Miss Tramont, why was your cousin in New York if it wasn't to get money owing to her from The Duke?'

'My client—'

'No, I can answer that,' Nora said. It had got through to her that she must say something to keep Gaby's name from being dragged through the mud in a court case. 'I wanted to come to New York to be with a friend—'

'Who was this friend?'

She glanced at Loomis Dearborn. 'Do I have to give his name? He's in hospital receiving treatment for an illness—it would upset him and his family if he were—'

O'Reilly looked sceptical. 'Are you saying the only reason Mrs Tramont was in New York was to keep an eye on you?'

'It was the main reason. Any other reasons were simply . . . a kind of excuse, a rationalization . . . If you imagine she came to New York to drag money out of a gang of criminals . . . We don't need that kind of money . . .'

'You see how absurd it all is,' Dearborn intervened sharply. 'Mrs Tramont came here simply to be with her young cousin who was, I believe I'm right in saying, a stranger to New York. She—'

'Don't you understand?' Nora burst out. 'She only came because I was determined to follow Buddy! And now she's—she's—'

O'Reilly studied her. The grief was genuine. He stared coldly at Dearborn. Dearborn put an arm protectively about Nora's shoulders and returned the stare.

'May we go, Captain? Have you inflicted enough misery?'

O'Reilly knew when he was beaten. He was perfectly sure Gabrielle Tramont had been about to receive payment for illegal shipments of French champagne brought in over a period of the past two years, but he was never going to prove it. And even if he did, what good would it do? The Frenchwoman was dead, Cianelli was

213

dead, so was poor old Herbert Lowes. Nobody was going into the witness box to give testimony against The Duke. The state had the money he had reluctantly confided to Cianelli to pay his debt. There were a lot of loose ends but in the tangle of the war against the bootleggers, what were a few more loose ends?

'Okay, you can go for now,' he sighed. But both he and the lawyer knew he wouldn't be asking Nora any more questions.

When she first left the hospital at two-thirty that dreadful morning, Nora had sent a cable to Marc. Before breakfast time a reply had come: 'Hoax cable arrived. Please confirm all well.' While she was still trying to word an answer to that, a second cable came, even briefer than the first: 'Sailing today.'

'He heard the story on a radio news bulletin or something,' Peter said.

'Oh, God, Peter—what must he be feeling?'

The Tramont apartment on 54th Street was besieged by newsmen. Peter smuggled her out of a basement door and took her to his place in Greenwich Village. No one thought of looking for the rich Mademoiselle Nora Tramont in a set of rooms above a furniture shop.

Marc's liner docked on the Friday. Peter warned that reporters would flock round them if they met in public. He suggested they should greet each other in Marc's stateroom and, for purposes of disguise, bought her a cheap loose summer raincoat and a pair of dark glasses. She shed them in the passage outside the door as the steward knocked before ushering her in.

Marc rose to meet her. She was shocked at his appearance. He, who had always been so tall and upright, was shoulder-bowed. There were lines in his face she had never seen before. He looked as if he had not slept any of the nights on board ship.

She hurried forward, expecting to be engulfed in his arms, so that she could sob out her grief and guilt and remorse on his shoulder.

But he leaned back a little when she drew near. The only embrace was a formal kiss on each cheek.

'Marc . . .' She was startled.

'How are you, Nora?' he said. 'You look thinner.'

'I'm . . . I'm . . . But how are *you*, Marc?'

'I should be well enough. A sea voyage is said to be good for the health.'

'Oh . . .' She heard it in his voice—the coldness, the bitterness. 'Marc,' she begged, 'please don't . . .'

'Don't what?'

'Don't blame me too much for what happened.'

'Who should I blame, then?' he enquired politely.

She was silenced. She understood that if he unbent, he would shatter in pieces. The icy calm

215

and the irony—they were his defence. She accepted that she mustn't beg for his forgiveness, not yet—it would cost him too much to give.

They were mobbed by reporters as they left the ship, but Marc dealt with it quite simply. He walked through them as if they didn't exist, uttering not one single word to the questions hurled at him.

Once at the apartment he refused to leave it for the refuge of Greenwich Village. 'I have no intention of running like a rat,' he said. And each time he went in or out, he was the same—utterly contemptuous of the newsmen, utterly silent.

By the end of the day they were losing interest. It was clear they'd get nothing out of him, and besides, the Cianelli murder was being moved to an inner page of the newspapers. It was just another gangland killing in which innocent bystanders had been involved. True, one of the innocents had been the glamorous Gabrielle Tramont, but so what? There were other glamorous women to whom they could turn for a new story.

Peter Norwood rang to ask how things were going.

'Pretty badly, Peter. Marc is so . . . I don't know how to describe it.'

'All broken up, is he?'

'No, quite the opposite—he's too self-disciplined, too silent. He scarcely says a word to me.'

216

'Would you like it if I were to come around, just for the company?'

'Oh, would you, Peter? It would be such a comfort.'

Marc accepted this young stranger as if he were part of the furnishings. He accepted without comment the fact that it was Peter who protected them from many of the small wounds of everyday life.

It was Peter who found them a mortician when the body of Gabrielle Auduron-Tramont was released for burial. It was Peter who arranged for a short press release announcing the family's intention to take the body home for interment in the family vault at the parish church of Calmady. It was Peter who answered telephone enquiries from friends.

It was also Peter who suggested a doctor should be called to take a look at Marc. 'He's going to crack up, Nora. It's not normal, the way he's going on.'

Nora shook her head. 'That would only make him more angry.'

'You've got a transatlantic crossing ahead of you—don't you think he should have a check-up before you sail?'

'No. Nothing will happen.'

'How can you be so certain?'

'Because he's taking his wife home to bury her. He'll see that through to the end because that's what must be done. After that . . . I don't know.' The thought of the future at Calmady without Gaby was so terrible that Nora could hardly envisage it.

'Nora, I wonder . . .'

'What?'

'How would it be if I sailed with the both of you to France?'

'You, Peter?' Nora exclaimed, startled.

'Well, you don't look like you're going to have much of a time on your own with your cousin.'

'But why should you, Peter. I mean, it's wonderfully kind of you but . . .'

'I liked Gaby a lot. I'd like to be at her funeral.'

'Oh, Peter!' Tears welled up in her eyes at the word, but she blinked them back. She collected her thoughts. 'But what about your show?'

'Oh, that. That's all washed up.'

'You didn't tell me that?'

'You had enough to think about. But you see, Cianelli was the money-bags, and with him gone— and besides, Betsy's lost the urge to be a star. She feels if she gets up on a stage and there's a lot of publicity on how she was Eddy's lady friend, somebody might send a few gunsels after her too.'

'But you could get some other backer and a new star—'

'No, I don't think so. Nobody wants to touch the show with a barge pole. And though something else will come along by and by, at the moment I'm what you call "resting". So I thought it would be a good time to offer myself as an escort.'

'It's so good of you . . .'

'You see,' he went on, colouring up under his olive skin, 'if all that was true, about Jean-Baptiste Labaud and all, Calmady is where my family originally came from. I'd kind of like to see it.'

The day the Tramonts left New York, one of its spectacular thunderstorms broke over the city. Rain came down in curtains of water. The sky was full of rolling grey and black clouds. Great cracklings of light shot across the tops of the skyscrapers.

Nora stood looking about at the apartment, emptied now of their belongings. Its panelled walls and thick grey carpet, the richly ornate drapes at the windows, the nearly-good old masters lit for display—they suddenly seemed comforting, familiar. She realized that she dreaded going home to Calmady. To Calmady, where Gabrielle Auduron-Tramont would no longer be the directing spirit.

She was so thankful that Peter was to be with them. To him she could turn, sometimes, when she needed a friend. Because it was hardly possible now to speak to Marc. He was taciturn, withdrawn. Sometimes she felt he actually hated her. It was good to remember that Peter would be there, to act as a buffer between herself and that cold contempt.

On board she found her stateroom full of flowers, of messages of kindness from the friends she was leaving. Marc went to his cabin at once, but she and Peter went on deck to see the departure. A moment before the gangplank was removed, a huge bouquet of flowers was brought to Nora.

She pulled aside the tissue to read the card. 'With sincerest condolences, Joseph Ducchese.'

She stared at the card. 'Who . . . .?'

Peter took it. He went red with anger. 'It's from him—Joe the Duke.'

She gave a gasp of fury. She walked to the rail, and as the great liner drew away from the dock she hurled the bouquet with all her might towards the land.

It fell in a swooping arc, was trapped by the pouring rain, and dropped like a multicoloured wounded bird into the oily waters between the quay and the shipside.

She hurried to her cabin, slammed the door, and stood leaning with her forehead against the porthole as the skyline of New York disappeared behind the curtain of rain.

She had a deep sense of loss—not only for Gaby, but for something in herself. She was leaving something behind her—her innocence, her girlhood perhaps. Losing Buddy had taught her that hopes and dreams could easily come to nothing. The change in Marc when she first saw him had shocked her into realizing that he was nothing. The change in Marc when she first saw him had shocked her into realizing that he was an old man, that though she had truly loved him it was all dead and done with.

The wheeling and dealing over the circumstances of Gaby's death had dismayed her. Perhaps she had been made more realistic in her expectations, had been forced to grow up at last. But she had also lost the sense of habitual optimism that had sustained her since she met Coco Chanel and entered into the world of Parisian society.

To be smart, fashionable, bright, eager—these weren't enough. You had to be strong, you had to be tough.

From now on, that was what she would be. That was how you faced the world when the people you loved died or turned away from you. You didn't let yourself feel lonely or rejected— you simply squared your shoulders and went on.

Peter Norwood fitted easily into the setting of Calmady. His French was atrocious, but he had enough to make himself understood and was useful in helping with minor matters. The household, of course, ran itself—the staff were well-trained, needed little direction. Madame Presle coped with the huge funeral party without fuss. Monsieur Coubet said he could run the estate until after the vintage without further instructions.

Only from time to time they would say to

There was no hope of that. Marc walked in the funeral cortège like a ghost, shook hands with whoever approached him, watched the iron gates of the vault close upon his wife's body and thereafter withdrew from almost any contact with the world. He didn't go into his study, he didn't visit the estate office, nor the laboratory, nor the cellars. He seldom appeared for meals. When he did, he was almost totally silent. Attempts by Nora and Peter to engage him in conversation were greeted with a few words or a faint shrug of indifference.

'You sure you oughtn't to get your doctor to look at him?' Peter urged. 'You know, there's a sickness called depression. He could go really deep into it.'

'No.'

'But Nora—he hardly says a word. He doesn't eat enough to keep a sparrow alive.'

'He still looks after his appearance. The day he comes to breakfast without shaving or brushing his hair, that's when I'll start to worry.'

'But he's in such bad shape, Nora—'

'Don't you understand?' she cried. 'He's grieving. He's lost the only woman in the world he really loved. He has to be left alone to mourn for her. One day . . . one day it will be enough, and he'll be the Cousin Marc I used to know.'

But that day seemed long delayed.

A crisis arose after the vintage—there had been a very good grape harvest with an excess

A crisis arose after the vintage—there had been a very good grape harvest with an excess of excellent juice. Storage became a problem. Nora tried to cope, but other champagne-makers were having the same trouble. She couldn't find any extra cellarage.

She took the news to Marc. He said, 'Just let it go.'

'Let it go? The new wine?'

'Yes, why not?'

'But it's a great harvest, Marc! It could give us a great vintage! You're not saying we should just pour it away?' He shrugged.

'Marc, this could be the basis of a great champagne. Are you going to let the House of Tramont be the only firm that doesn't produce enough for the future?'

'Oh, the future,' he said dismissively, and made as if to walk out of the drawing-room.

She caught his arm. 'Marc!'

He paused.

'Marc, don't do this to me! You know I can't handle the estate on my own. I don't know enough. Don't turn your back on me like this.'

He stood looking at her, silent, detached.

'You know this area better than anyone else on the estate. You've handled affairs for all the property owners in the district, in times past. You can help me now—please, Marc.'

After a long moment he said, 'It's your busi-

'Hadn't you thought of that?' He actually looked amused. 'I only interested myself in the business because it was Gaby's. Do you think I care whether we make wine for the future or not? The future—what is it to me?'

'But . . . But . . .' She sought about for arguments to refute him. She knew he was speaking only from grief and exhaustion. 'Marc, Gaby wouldn't want you to think like that. She wouldn't have wanted you to—'

'What do you know about it?' he flashed, suddenly alight with anger. He glared at her from his gaunt eyes. 'All of a sudden, you know what Gaby wanted. Did you ever trouble your head about it while she was alive?'

She drew back, scared at seeing him suddenly alive with emotion again. It was like seeing a ghost put on flesh.

'I'll tell you what Gaby wanted,' he ground out. 'She wanted to see you married to some decent, good man like Edmond du Ceddres. She wanted to see you settled with children about you. But no—you had to throw it all back in her face. You had to go haring off after silly clothes, getting yourself up to look a fright, more boy than girl! And then you had to throw yourself away on a waster like Buddy Garrenstein—good God, couldn't you see he was as empty as a shell? No, no, you had to rush after him wherever he went—'

'Marc—'

'And you took my wife with you! Do you think we really cared about the money they owed us? That was only an excuse to be with you, to try to protect you from your own silliness —and she died, she was killed . . .'

The spate of words died away. He lowered his gaze, his body slackened.

Nora let a moment go by. She sat down on the sofa, for she had been wounded by his swift anger. But at least the armour of isolation had shown an opening. For the first time since he came to New York to reclaim Gaby's body, he had shown an uncontrolled reaction. She must pursue that advantage, force the opening to allow him to struggle free if he could.

'You can't make me any reproach I haven't made to myself,' she said. 'Don't you think those very thoughts have haunted me day and night since she was killed? And if it's any comfort to you, I know they'll haunt me till the day I die.'

He gave a little undetermined shake of the head, as if trying to refute the confession that she knew she was guilty.

'But even after all that has been said and admitted,' she went on, keeping her voice from shaking, 'it's still true that Gaby wouldn't have wanted us to let the estate go to pieces.'

'But what does it *matter!*'

'It mattered to her.' She sought about for words that would convey how deeply she felt it. 'Why did she fight all through the war? She and Great-Uncle Robert—making a little wine, creeping about the vine rows under shellfire— are you saying we should do what the German army could not, wreck the House of Tramont?'

'You know nothing about it! You never knew what she really was!'

'That's true. All I can tell you is that I feel she would have expected more from us . . . from you.'

He strode out of the room, not even sparing her a last glance as he slammed the door behind him. She sat alone, trembling at having brought him at last to speak of how he felt. She understood how deep his grief had gone. But she had to make him let it go at last, to return to the cares of ordinary life.

It wasn't just for the House of Tramont. It was for himself. He must make an effort or Peter's predictions might come true—he might make himself seriously ill.

He avoided her all that day. On the next morning, when she came down to breakfast, there was no sign of him. Nor of Peter, but that was quite normal, for he was a late riser. As usual she said to the maid, 'Is Monsieur Auduron-Tramont taking breakfast?'

'He took his coffee a little while ago, Mademoiselle. He told me to say he could be found at the stables.'

Nora's heart gave a tremendous leap. 'The stables?'

She drank a scalding cup of coffee and almost ran to the stables. It had always been the family habit to take a ride around the estate in the early morning. Since she came back from New York she had been alone on that little journey.

Today she found Marc standing by the head of the bay gelding he generally rode. Her own mare, Lulu, was held by a groom. When the man had helped her mount and moved away, Marc spoke.

'I thought over what you said. I decided you were right. You need help to manage the estate. I've come to the conclusion I must give you that help.'

'Thank you,' she said.

He swung into the saddle. 'In future I'll go round with you in the mornings. By mid-morning we ought to be in the office dealing with what Coubet wants done. The office routine is the most boring part. You'll have to learn how to look at the ledgers, how to deal with the accountants. I'll teach you.'

'Yes, thank you.'

'You have to be serious about it. You appealed to our loyalty to Gaby—you must mean what you say, you must work hard.'

'I'll work, Marc.'

'It will take some time. Dealing with the small *négociants* is difficult—Gaby had an instinct for it, perhaps you'll develop it too.'

'I'll try.'

'It'll take me a day or two to catch up. I've . . . I've lost track. But once we get back into it, we must become a proper team. Gaby and I . . .' He faltered. 'Gaby and I divided the chores between us. We'll see how it falls now that you're taking over. But one thing I must warn you— you won't have time for racing round Paris with the smart set.'

'I understand that, Marc.'

'Very well.' He tapped his heels against the gelding's flanks and they set forward through the stable gate. 'As to the storage of the surplus *cuvée*—is it in cask already?'

The fact that he had to ask the question showed how far he had let control slip from his hands. The grapes had been going through the press for days now, the whole of the estate working like a chain-gang, red-eyed with fatigue but determined to struggle on until the whole of this bountiful and exceptionally fine harvest was pressed.

The grape juice—the 'must'—had been pouring from the press through pipes into the fermentation vessels. Normally there was ample room for what flowed from the grapes. This year there were more grapes than usual, and more juice in the bunches. So there was more to be received for fermentation. In fact it was the result of all the work to defeat the phylloxera insect: for the first time since the war Champagne had grapes up to and even beyond the standard of pre-phylloxera days.

This year extra casks had been brought into use at Champagne Tramont. But they couldn't just be left standing, as they were at the moment, in corridors and equipment stores. The temperature for the wine to ferment was critical. Since all the firms in the Champagne region were that year producing more must than usual, storage was at bursting point. No one had much space to let, and even where space was available it might not meet the specific requirements of the great wine-makers.

Rapidly Nora gave her cousin a break-down of the problem—so many two-hundred litre casks already accommodated in good though unusual cellars, so many already left for twelve dangerous hours in places where they might take harm.

'It's quite easy,' Marc said when he had heard her out. 'We'll put it in the old Still Wine Shed. It will have to go overground to that point, because to get to it through the passages is impossible—there are staircases and difficult turns in the tunnels beyond the cellars we use.'

The ground under Calmady was a labyrinth of tunnels dug by the Romans when they first quarried chalk in the Champagne region. Nora knew the usual complex of cellars well. But what Marc said was news to her.

'I've never even heard of the Still Wine Shed!' He sighed. 'We used it—Gaby and I—during the war—it was an escape route . . . Well, never mind.'

He fell silent then, but when they reached the estate offices he dismounted to give orders for the re-opening of the old oaken gates with iron locks guarding the ancient cave where once, generations ago, still champagne wine had been stored for sale. Champagne Tramont no longer sold still wine, so the warehouse had long been disused. It caused some ironical amusement to Nora to hear some of the older employees say at once they knew where it was. How perverse they were! Couldn't they have told her that when the problem of the surplus must first became apparent?

She told Peter about it when they went for a walk after lunch. He grinned. 'It's always the way—the oldest inhabitant always knew it all along. But say, it's good news about your cousin. I thought he seemed different at lunch.'

'Yes, he didn't speak much, but he did seem to be paying attention to what we said.'

'Thing is now, Nora, to keep him from slipping back again.'

'Since I'm going to be his pupil, I'll see to it that he has a lot to keep him busy.' She hugged Peter's arm in her relief. 'It's wonderful to have him back to something like his old self.'

'Yeah,' Peter said. He was thinking that once he was sure Marc Auduron-Tramont was safe on the road to recovery, it would be tactful to remove himself to Paris. House guests who stayed for ever were a pain in the neck, even houseguests who were distant cousins.

He had been offered work in Paris by a theatrical management. They were putting on an all-black show, partly dance and drumming from the French Congo, partly sophisticated American jazz. He was qualified by his experience with spectacular revue and by the mere fact of being an American able to speak reasonable French. The black jazz players and tap dancers couldn't speak a word.

Strange to say, Nora scarcely missed him at first. She was so busy learning the business of running a wine house that she had little time for anything else. But Peter came to visit from time to time, and she went to Paris for the first night of the big show. It was a sensation. Peter was at once in demand to do another modern revue.

Six months went by in which they saw each other fairly regularly. They were good friends, affectionate companions. Marc, who at first had rather despised the career of theatre director, began to thaw towards Peter.

So it was without any misgiving that Nora came to him with a serious question in the June of the following year.

'May I ask you something, Marc?'

He was in the rose garden attending to the dead-heading. Recently he'd begun to take an interest in gardening: 'For my retirement,' he would say with a smile, though Nora protested that was years away as yet.

He put aside his secateurs. 'What is it, my dear?'

'Peter and I have been talking about getting married.'

He was so startled that, instead of putting the secateurs in his pocket, he dropped them. He stooped to pick them up. As he straightened he said slowly, 'You mean he's proposed to you?'

She shrugged. 'Not exactly. It's just sort of become a prospect for us.'

'Hmm . . .' He played with the secateurs, opening and closing them unthinkingly. 'Are you in love with him?'

She had known he would ask this question and had given it a lot of thought. 'No,' she said with complete honesty, 'but I'm tremendously fond of him.'

'And he? He feels fondness? Or love?'

'I think he feels the same.'

'Is there any particular reason why you should marry? I mean . . .' He went faintly red and looked away. 'If you and he have been . . . if there was a child coming . . .'

'Nothing like that,' she said. 'We've never even made love so far.'

'Then why?' He sounded baffled.

'I thought you and Gaby always wanted me to marry and settle down?'

232

'Ye-es . . . But, a foreigner? I certainly don't want to see you settled in the United States.

'There's no fear of that. Peter is finding an enjoyable career in Paris—'

'But what if he gets an offer from New York?'

'Oh, Marc, think of the situation there! They hardly seem to have a cent to buy an apple.'

It was true. Almost immediately after the Tramonts left New York, the stock market was seized with a convulsion that engulfed fortunes in seconds. Desperate measures to shore it up had failed utterly. American business was going into a tremendous depression which was closing down whole industries. Unemployment was growing, money had become as scarce as snow in the desert.

'Peter hears from friends, of course. There are no funds to put on the kind of show he's known for. Besides, he wants eventually to get away from that. Cocteau is suggesting—'

'Oh, that fool!'

'Marc, you may not approve of Jean Cocteau but he's very influential in the theatre. And he was so stunned by the all-black revue Peter put on that he's suggesting an all-black version of *Phaedre*.'

'He would,' growled her cousin. 'Why can't he leave the classics alone?'

'He's talking about putting Peter in charge. It would be a great step forward for him—Peter, I mean. And other things are being murmured. So the idea of his returning to America is somewhat remote.'

'Humph,' said Marc. He wandered to a marble bench and sat down. He stretched out his long legs. Nora followed him, smoothing her short linen dress over her knees.

'How should you like having a husband who was famous for doing peculiar things in the theatre?' Marc enquired.

She laughed. 'If I remember the stories aright, Old Madame's first husband wrote for the theatre.'

'But he didn't direct naked young women!'

'Are you asking me if I should be jealous?'

'I'm asking you if you wouldn't feel absurd.'

'No,' she said, taking it in total seriousness, 'I don't think so.'

'You don't think he might start asking you for money to finance some mad theatrical enterprise?'

'Oh . . .' She looked reproachful. 'Peter isn't a money grabber, Marc. And he's not like Buddy—he's not self centred.'

'No, he isn't.'

'You do like him?'

'I suppose I do.'

'I thought you'd be in favour.'

'I'm not against it. I'm just . . . surprised. When you refused Edmond du Ceddres, there was all that outcry about not being in love with him. I thought you'd want to be in love with the man you married.'

'I thought so too,' she acknowledged. 'But being so closely involved in running the business, I see the responsibility it entails. I understand now that marriage is almost a necessary step for the good of the family. And after all, time is going by.'

'Oh!' He laughed, and put an arm about her shoulders to give her a fatherly hug. 'I can see the wrinkles forming already!'

'Well, you can laugh, but I'll be twenty-one next birthday. And almost all the girls I was at school with are married—some of them with more than one baby.'

Her cousin studied the toes of his shoes. Was that what was at the bottom of it—the natural longing to have a baby? He remembered how Gaby had longed to bear his child. It seemed that Nature insisted that at some stage of her life a woman should fall victim to the urge to be a mother.

But on the other hand, Nora was vastly different from Gaby, who had been desperately in love with the man who would have been the father of the baby. Nora was viewing the whole thing in a way that surprised him. Except that, since Gaby's death, she had become suddenly much more sedate—as if the role of inheritor of the House of Tramont had sobered her beyond her years.

'If we're speaking only of the benefits to the Tramonts,' he began, choosing his words with care, 'what we want is a happy, stable union that will lead to children. Am I right?'

'Certainly.'

'Do you think you'd be happy with Peter?'

'Yes, I do.' She almost added, Happy enough. For one of the reasons that was urging her towards marriage was a sense of loneliness. Long hours spent in handling business, in being a hostess on behalf of the House of Tramont, in concentrating on the well-being not only of her own firm but of the whole region—these had brought home to her how small her circle was.

There was Marc, of course, whom she loved as a father.

There was Jean Coubet, the estate manager, brisk and good natured. There was Erneste Puchet, the chief of cellar, a somewhat morose man who nevertheless would smile for her. There was Madame Presle the housekeeper.

These were the people she saw every day. Beyond them were the estate workers, the law firm who handled the Tramont legal affairs, the other wine-makers, the wives of the wine-makers, the young matrons who had been her schoolfellows. Beyond them again there were the friends in Paris—Coco Chanel, impulsive and changeable, and the members of Chanel's circle, and some theatrical acquaintances brought to her through Peter.

There was almost no one to whom she could confide her deeper feelings. A longing had grown in her for someone to whom she could stretch out a hand in the night, who would speak to her in words only they could understand.

Peter was the only man she felt she could share her life with. There were others who flattered and courted, but she and Peter had shared experiences which put him on a different footing from everyone else. The notion of getting married was a point to which they returned more often as the weeks went by. It seemed the next logical step in their friendship.

'Is it part of your plan that Peter should play any role in running the business?' Marc asked.

'Not immediately. A lot depends on whether he goes on with theatrical work. It's a chancy business, as I'm sure you know.'

'In other words, Champagne Tramont would be a second-best job for him.'

'Oh, now! I didn't say that. There are a lot of gaps between productions—Peter would be here at Calmady, he'd be bound to pick up something of how we manage matters. And we don't actually need him to play a large role. That is,' she added, giving her cousin a playful pat on the arm, 'unless you're serious about retiring.'

'No, no, I'm willing to go on working as long as you want me to.' He hesitated. 'It's not the same now Gaby's gone, I can't deny that. But there are things I can do that need doing, and besides you need someone who can look back and quote from experience.'

'And I still haven't by any means learned all I need to know.'

'You're doing well. That's why I wonder if now is the right time to distract yourself with a wedding and all that kind of thing—'

'Oh, it would be a quiet affair. By the time we got through the arrangements, only just a year would have gone by since Gaby died. No one would expect a big affair—and besides, I shouldn't want it.'

'But you want children?'

'Oh, yes, I want *those!*' she agreed, laughing.

'But—forgive me, Nora—that's not the only reason? I mean, marrying just to provide an heir . . .'

'No, Marc dear. I'm genuinely very fond of Peter, and I feel we would be a happy partnership.'

'Then I have nothing against it.'

She took one of his hands. 'Couldn't you be a little more enthusiastic than that? I'd like your approval, not just a lack of criticism.'

He saw something in the smiling appeal—something forlorn and lonely. Good God, why was he being so churlish? She was a young pretty girl, who needed someone to love her.

He leaned over to kiss her on the cheek.

'My dear child,' he said, 'you have my blessing.'

TEN

It might be said that Marc Auduron-Tramont stood in the role of father-in-law to Peter Norwood. Like most fathers-in-law, he was inwardly convinced that the man wasn't good enough for his little girl.

There were many things about Peter that irritated Marc. His casual American manners—why, the man seemed continually surprised at being expected to shake hands with friends on meeting! And those awful clothes he thought suitable for country wear—more fitting on the trainer of a prize-fighter, shawl-collared sweaters and loose flannel trousers. And he never got up until late in the morning.

On the other hand, his late rising meant that Marc could breakfast alone with Nora, which pleased him. And once Peter was up, he was full of New World energy. He played a good game of tennis, giving Nora all the competion she could handle. He rode well, was a fair shot—which endeared him to the neighbours when they took out the boar-hounds in the thickets to the northeast of Calmady. He liked to swim, and was even now interesting himself in the construction of a swimming pool at the Villa Tramont—though what the good of that was, Marc couldn't see, because it would freeze almost solid in winter.

Best of all, the man took quite a lot of interest in the business—but that was only to be expected, since the blood of wine-makers ran in his veins.

Nora's happiness was the touchstone. If Peter was making her happy, that was enough. Well, she seemed happy. Not exactly the radiant young bride, but pleased with life.

This was a topic of enquiry with Nora's old school friend Émilie, now Madame Georgiot and mother of two children. The years had added plumpness to Émilie's already rounded contours, but that didn't prevent her from ordering creamy desserts when she and Nora met for lunch on Nora's business trips to Paris.

'I see you're wearing your skirt past the knee,' she remarked as Nora pushed her chair back a little, to relax with her coffee. 'Is that Chanel's new line?'

'She says clothes are going to be longer. Something about a Depression always bringing in longer clothes. But there's no Depression in France.'

'Not yet! Alphonse says the Exchange is very jumpy.'

'He's not worried, though?'

'I suppose not,' Émilie said, delving into her *charlotte aux marrons*. 'He doesn't talk to me about business.'

'Doesn't he?' Nora was surprised. 'What do you talk about then?'

'Good lord . . . I don't know . . . the children, the house . . .' She licked her spoon without shame. 'Oh, that was gorgeous! And what, might I ask, do you and your American husband talk about?'

'About the wine, and the estate, and the new swimming pool, and the show he's producing—'

'That production of *Phaedre* was a real flop, wasn't it?' Émilie said with some satisfaction. 'Such a peculiar idea . . .'

'The idea was Cocteau's, not Peter's. He only went along with it for the experience.'

Émilie beckoned to the waiter for her coffee. She waited until it had been poured, with plenty of cream, and helped herself to sugar. 'What's the new show?'

'Oh, it's a translation from the English—a long and complex thing by an American called Thornton Wilder. Peter's very keen.'

'Don't you find it wearisome, being parted from him for long spells while you're in Calmady and he's in Paris?'

Nora had asked herself that question too in the six or seven months since the wedding, and the honest answer was no. She was always much too busy to miss Peter. Sometimes it worried her. She'd hoped that they would grow more in love as the months went by, but they were still almost the same as before—good friends, affectionate companions, responsive lovers. But not closer, not more necessary to each other.

'I suppose we make up for it when we're together,' she hazarded.

'You're not afraid he's going to meet some glamorous actress and fall head over heels for her?'

'No,' said Nora with conviction, 'I'm not.'

'How strange you are, Nora! You've changed so much! When I think how you used to agonize over being pretty enough to attract a man . . . And now look at you, the absolute epitome of all that's attractive and smart . . . I don't know how you keep so slim! Every mouthful I eat goes straight on my hips!'

'Well, I've a lot more to do than you have,' soothed Nora. It was no use suggesting Émilie gave up rich food.

'More than I have! Just you wait till you've got children! *Then* you'll find out what it's like to be busy! And speaking of that—any signs so far?'

Nora shook her head.

'Oh, well, early days yet. Although, mind you, I conceived Juliette on our honeymoon. And that was so odd of you, Nora, going to Berlin for your honeymoon—!'

'Well, I had business there.'

'And Peter? What did Peter do while you were out talking business?'

'He went to the theatre, of course. He was tremendously struck by German drama—he's thinking of—'

'Oh, never mind the German drama, tell me the really important things! Is he good in bed?'

'Émilie!'

'Well, it's more to the point than the Berlin State Theatre. I'm always thankful that for all his faults—and heaven knows he has plenty, he's so boring about politics sometimes I could scream!—but for all that, Alphonse is a wonderful lover! I sometimes wonder where he learnt it all, but I've too much sense to ask, of course.'

'I'm happy for you,' Nora said, laughing. 'And I thank you for your kind interest in my love life and assure you it's quite satisfactory.'

'I've always thought that Americans are probably a bit naïve in that way. Are they?'

'Good gracious, Émilie, I haven't been to bed with the whole American population!'

'But you've been to bed with two. Oh, don't deny it! I always felt sure you and that awful Buddy Garrenstein were a torrid pair.'

'Torrid!' Nora was amused at the word. She had been too bewildered and innocent to become 'torrid' with Buddy.

'Funny you seem so attracted to Americans. I could see the point of Buddy—he was so reckless and original, and of course his father being an Ambassador . . . By the way, did you see in the papers last month that Monsieur Garrenstein had lost all his money in that terrible stock market crash? So it's a good thing you never thought of marrying Buddy. But Peter is a nobody, comparatively speaking. I mean, who are his family? You never say.'

'I'm quite satisfied about his ancestry, Émilie,' she teased. 'There aren't any armorial bearings and certainly not so much money as the Garrensteins, but Peter's family back ground suited the Tramonts very well.'

'Did his relatives come to the wedding?'

'No, you know it was a very small affair.'

'Absurd,' pouted Émilie. 'I'd got Alphonse to agree I could have a new frock and shoes—and then we never got an invitation. I wonder you even allowed the press photographers.'

'It's very difficult to stop press photographers.'

Émilie frowned. Press photographers were in general not the least interested in her.

'That dress Chanel made you was rather clever. Not many wedding dresses you could wear afterwards without alteration.'

'Now, Émilie, don't be catty. I told you at the time—I didn't want a big fuss.'

'No, but all the same—it all looked terribly casual! I wonder you bothered to go to church.'

'The village wanted that,' Nora said, smiling at the recollection. 'In the last hundred years, almost all the Tramont women have been married in the parish church. Luckily Peter had no objections.'

'No objections? You're not saying he's an atheist!' Émilie said, shocked.

'No, I told you—his family background is in

all ways perfectly suitable. He was brought up a Catholic. But like a lot of us in the aftermath of the Great War, he's not much interested in religion.'

'But you wouldn't have married him if he hadn't been a Catholic?' Émilie insisted. 'I mean, think about the children—how ever would you bring them up?'

'Luckily that didn't arise. Peter was able to satisfy Father Letillac that he was properly baptized and all that sort of thing.' She grinned to herself at the recollection. Father Letillac had been so earnest, and Peter had thought him so absurd. But when it came to repeating the Catechism and other tests the curé had put him through, he had apparently come through with flying colours.

Émilie went on with her little pricks, like a bandillero trying to enrage a bull. She was envious of Nora, and couldn't understand how it came about that the plain little girl of her schooldays should now seem so much more endowed with desirable gifts than herself: But Nora refused to be perturbed. She was accustomed to Émilie's probings. Sometimes, indeed, she felt sorry for Émilie.

'Watch out for all those beautiful actresses!' was her friend's parting shot outside the restaurant as she stepped into a cab.

'I refuse to worry about other women,' Nora called after her, laughing.

Which only proved how wrong she could be.

It was a day of sunshine and showers in April. Marc was at a trade fair in Lyons to inspect new wine-making equipment. Peter was in Paris rehearsing his cast in *The Bridge of San Luis Rey*, Nora was in the estate office in the newly-built block near the old aviary. She was busy reading a report by her accountants on the benefits to be paid to the workers under a new health insurance scheme.

Her secretary, Charles Nouet, came in looking faintly perturbed.

'Madame, there's a lady to see you.'

'Have I an appointment at the moment, Charles?'

'No, Madame.'

'Who is she?'

'She . . . er . . . refuses to give a name, Madame.'

Nora raised her eyebrows.

'Tell the lady it's not convenient. I'm busy.'

'The lady says . . . excuse me, Madame, perhaps she's a little eccentric. She says she's a relation.'

Nora sat back in her leather chair. 'Of mine?'

'I suppose so. She just said . . . When I told her you were unlikely to see her without an appointment she said, "Tell Mrs Norwood-Tramont that I'm a relation."' He hesitated then added, 'She speaks very poor French.'

'She's a foreigner?'

'American, I should think, Madame.'

'Oh, perhaps she's a relation of my husband's—I see. Er . . . what does she look like? I mean, is she young, old, presentable, or what?'

'Young, Madame, rather chic but her clothes aren't new.'

'Sounds all right. Perhaps some relative of Monsieur Norwood's who's come to study or something of that kind. Show her in, Charles. And . . . Charles . . . after about ten minutes, remind me I have an urgent appointment.'

'Quite, Madame.' He went out, his pale face creased in perplexity. Something about the visitor's manner, which he'd failed to convey, had worried him.

Nora rose as she was shown in, ready to extend her hand if she liked the look of the newcomer. The young woman who faced her was most definitely American, her clothes showing the almost aggressive colour of last year's New York fashion—petrol blue with lemon yellow trim. Her hair beneath her pull-on velour was a pretty copper but badly cut. She wore too much make-up, was clearly nervous, but put up a brave front. A glance at her ungloved hands showed she was married.

'Good morning, Madame—?' Nora said in English, her voice asking a question.

'Good morning, Madame Norwood.'

'The name is Norwood-Tramont,' Nora said. 'The Tramonts keep the name after marriage.'

'Yeah, I saw that in the magazine. Peter's called Norwood-Tramont too?'

'Legally, yes. Professionally he prefers to keep his own name. May I ask—?'

'Professionally,' repeated the visitor. 'He's still into theatrical stuff then?'

Nora smiled politely. 'It's kind of you to call and enquire after him. You told my secretary you're a relation?'

'You could say so,' said the young woman, sitting uninvited on one of the chairs facing Nora's desk. 'I'm his wife.'

Nora felt her breath leave her body in a gasp of astonishment. She knew colour had drained away from her face. She was almost at once icy cold.

Shock, she said inwardly. I've had a shock.

Yet even then, she never doubted what the young woman said.

Nevertheless, she had to summon her wits and put up a fight. 'You must be out of your mind,' she said. 'Peter is married to me.'

'You may think so. But he isn't.'

'How dare you say that—'

'Listen, Mrs Tramont or whatever, I don't want to make this worse than I have to. My name is Lily Norwood—Lily Solosky as was. Peter and I were married in New York four years ago.'

'I don't believe you—'

248

'Listen! Hear what I'm trying to tell you. I don't mean you any harm, I'm just trying to clear this up so as to benefit all of us—'

'Benefit? Ah!' Nora exclaimed. 'Is that what this is? A scheme to get money?'

'We-ell . . . Yeah . . . I wouldn't have come here just to be a nuisance, you can believe that, Mrs Tramont. I need money, and when I read in this magazine how you're the owner of this big wine firm that's famous all over the world, I knew I could make a buck or two. But I don't want to cause trouble. It can all be decently settled, no sweat.'

'If you imagine,' said Nora, drawing herself up, 'that I will pay one penny to anyone coming here with this nonsensical story—'

'He never told you about me, huh?' Lily Norwood said. 'Well, I don't blame him. It wasn't what you'd call a long and successful marriage, and I'm not saying I'd have told a guy who proposed to me that I was still tied up. After all, Peter and me were in different countries—different continents, even. It's not as if we were likely to run across each other.'

No, thought Nora, not unless you came on purpose to meet him. But what was she thinking! This mad young woman could come here and tell any tale she liked.

'Have you any proof that you even knew Peter?' she demanded in a hard voice.

'Sure have.' Lily delved in her handbag, to

produce an envelope. She handed it across the desk.

Nora sat down. With a trembling hand she opened the envelope. She took out a folded sheet of paper.

A marriage certificate. A certificate of marriage before a judge of the New York Court, on the 8th June 1927. Signed by all the parties concerned: Peter Norwood, Lily Solosky, witnessed by Hans Brebner and Joseph Martindale, Judge Herbert Bymel officiating.

'It's genuine,' Lily said in her flat little voice. 'You can write to the office if you like, but it's genuine, I guarantee.' She paused, looking wary. 'I'd like it back, please.'

Nora returned the paper and envelope. She heard them rustle, knew her hand was shaking.

'Are you saying that Peter married me . . . bigamously?'

'Say, I don't want to make you take this any harder than I have to. I'm kind of surprised he never told you about me at all, but I thought he'd have said he was married and divorced. He thought he was divorced—yeah, no kidding, I went to Reno, he gave me the dough. But, see, I never went through with it.'

There was no way Nora could have produced a sound, a question. She simply sat staring at the girl who was her husband's wife.

'Too bad for him, huh? I just didn't bother. I never thought I'd be going back to New York and never thought I'd ever see or hear of him again. Seemed a waste to spend the money on a divorce. I used it to stake me to some really nice new clothes and landed a good job—there's some big shows in Reno, a girl with looks can make out all right.'

'You're . . . you're an actress?'

'Dancer,' said Lily. 'Pretty good, too. My stage name's Leta Lolita—classy, huh? But I was in an automobile accident—nothing much, but I was in plaster six weeks, lost my job. You know how it is, you have good luck and bad luck and that was my spell of bad luck. And things just didn't pick up, and I need the dough, so that's why I'm here. No hard feelings, I hope?'

Nora looked at her. She tried to think straight. 'But the divorce,' she said. 'The divorce—surely Peter expected to hear from you—receive a formal announcement, a document?'

'Yeah, prob'ly. But he was moving around some at the time. He was assistant director on a musical—it went on try-out, I think Boston and Hartington and like that. He prob'ly thought the papers never caught up with him, if he thought of it at all.'

'But he must have thought of it—!'

'Nah, you know what he's like easygoing. Pete's quite glad to let things go along how they like, if it's no trouble. It wasn't as if he wanted to get in a double act with anyone else. He was busy just then, his career was picking up.'

As Lily stopped speaking, the two women sat looking at each other. Nora's mind was in a whirl.

'Hell of a note, isn't it?' Lily said with what appeared to be quite genuine sympathy.

'I . . . I don't understand you. You don't seem to want Peter, you don't seem to bear him any ill will—you've just come for money?'

'For a bankroll, yeah. See, Mrs Tramont, I broke my leg in that accident. It hasn't healed well. I don't think I'm going to get anywhere as a dancer from now on. And you can't imagine how hard things are now in the States.'

'How big a bankroll?'

'Well, it's gonna have to last me a long time, till things get better. Then I thought I'd like to open a little hotel in Reno—there'll always be gamblers coming to Reno, no matter how hard times are. But I don't want a flophouse—I want a respectable place, I wouldn't mind meeting some respectable guy and hitching up again so you see I need to have a nice place.'

'And if you get this money, what then?'

'I go back to Reno, I get the divorce, and everything's legal.' She smiled, the scarlet mouth moving attractively. 'I'm no shark, Mrs Tramont. Give me enough to live for a year and buy a decent piece of property, and you won't hear from me again, ever. You can do it all legal—call in your lawyers, I'm willing to sign a contract, and send you the divorce papers as soon as I get them, and all that.'

Nora drew a breath. 'What sort of sum do you have in mind?'

'I had a look around as the taxi brought me,' said Lily after a hesitation. 'This is a big place. And before I got on the boat I asked around—Champagne Tramont is worth a fortune. So I thought . . . a hundred thousand dollars.'

The French franc was a healthy currency at the moment compared with the vulnerable dollar. All the same, translated into francs, a hundred thousand dollars was a very large sum.

But of course Peter's first wife didn't expect to get that. It was the opening gambit in the bargaining.

'That's far too much. The business couldn't stand it.'

'I'm sure you could manage, Mrs Tramont. If you can't take it out of the business, I hear you got paintings and antiques in your house worth a lot more than that.'

'You're very well informed.'

'I asked around. I'm no dope, Mrs Tramont.' She opened her handbag to search about for a cigarette. As she lit it, Nora could see her hand was trembling. Lily Norwood wasn't as confident as she made out.

All the same, she had made a plan and she had that stubborn courage that would make her stick to it. Nora's mind flickered over what must come next. It was impossible to raise a large sum—even if less than a hundred thousand dollars—without having to explain it to the accountants. It would also take time.

There was no way she could keep the news from Marc. It would have to be discussed.

And as for Peter . . .

'What are your plans now?' she asked.

Lily raised pencilled eyebrows. 'Meaning what? I'm going to stay here until I get the money—'

'You won't get anything until I get a legal divorce document.'

'Okay, okay, I understand—I'm willing to take a down payment and get the rest when I send you the stuff.' She drew on her cigarette. 'But I want a contract. I talked to a lawyer before I left Reno—'

'You haven't discussed this with other people!'

'Sure I have! What d'you think—I'd come here with no idea of what to ask for? Oh, relax, relax, I didn't name any names, I just asked this guy for his advice and wrote down what he told me.'

'And did he tell you it was legal to extort money?' Nora asked angrily.

'He told me I could ask for compensation for the injury done to me, if you want to know,' Lily replied, shrugging and stiffening. 'And he told me to hire a good French lawyer, to make sure you didn't use some trick I couldn't foresee—'

'Mrs Norwood,' Nora said, rising, 'I think

we've said enough to each other for the time being—'

'Listen, don't get sore, I don't mean to annoy you. I just want you to *see*—'

'I do see, believe me. But I can't go on with this conversation. It's too . . . too . . .'

'Humiliating?' Lily suggested. There was no malice in her tone. 'Yeah, I guess it's a big shock. I'm really sorry. But a girl in my position, she hasn't got too many things going for her and everything's so bad all around, I would have been a dope to pass up a gravy train like this.'

'Let's break this off for the moment, Mrs Norwood. I can't go any further until I've spoken to Peter, and my business partner—'

'Sure, sure, discuss it, speak to your lawyers. I'm in no hurry—I don't mind spending a coupla weeks—'

'Where can I get in touch with you?'

'Well, I came straight here from the station. I haven't found a hotel so far. I thought of asking for a room at that place I passed, I guess you'd call it an inn—'

'No, no!' The idea of having her stay in Calmady was intolerable. 'How did you actually get here?'

'I took a cab from the station.'

'I'll have our car brought round to take you to Rheims. There's a very good hotel there—I'll get my secretary to reserve a room. Please, Mrs Norwood, be discreet.'

Lily smiled. 'It would be rotten, wouldn't it, to have everybody talking about you and laughing behind your back? Sure, I don't want to do that to you.' She paused. 'It would help me a lot if you'd take care of the hotel bill.'

'Certainly.' Nora pressed the button on her desk. Charles came in, looking inquisitive. 'Charles, arrange for the car to take Mrs Norwood to the Hotel de la Place in Rheims.'

'Mrs Norwood?' Charles said, with a quick glance at the visitor.

Nora ignored the implied question. 'When you've done that, ring the hotel and book a room.'

'Certainly, Madame. For how long?'

'That . . . is undecided as yet. Mrs Norwood is here on an indeterminate visit.'

'I see.' He went out, looking injured. He had expected Madame to give him some sort of introduction, or at least some slight explanation. But she had been so pale and tight-lipped he hadn't dared say any more.

When the door closed behind him, Lily grinned. 'His curiosity is gonna kill him.'

'He's just the first of many,' Nora returned. 'God knows what people are going to think.'

'Look, it's not so bad. Nobody's gonna know anything from me. I can say I'm Pete's sister-in-law—married to his brother.'

'But then people will wonder why I don't have you as a house guest—'

'Tell 'em I wanted to be free to go around, back and forth to Paris. That's where Pete is, isn't it? I went up to the house first and asked, and the butler said he was in Paris.'

Oh God—the servants! 'What did you say? What did you tell him?'

'I didn't tell him anything,' Lily said, rather indignant. 'I told you—I don't want to make it tough on you. I just asked if I could speak to Mrs Tramont and he said you were at the estate office and the taxi driver said he knew where it was and dropped me off outside the door.' She looked uncomfortable for a moment. 'I really wanted to speak to Pete first. I felt I owed it to him to explain about the divorce and all. But I didn't want to go back to Paris and look for him—the butler didn't say where in Paris and I don't speak French too good. In fact, I learned the questions I had to ask by heart, from a girl I know who speaks the lingo.'

There was a tap at the door. 'The car is here,' he announced.

'Thank you, Charles.' His head disappeared. Nora said to Lily, 'It's not far to Rheims. You'll be there in time for lunch. In the meantime I'll telephone to Peter—'

'Tell Pete I was asking for him,' Lily said. She rose, straightened the skirt of the blue flannel suit, and turned to go. At the door she stopped. 'You'll be in touch?'

'Of course.'

'You're not what I expected,' she said. 'I thought you'd be a high-powered business-woman.'

Nora gazed at her, once more put at a loss by this strange young woman.

'It woulda been easier if you had. I didn't think you'd be just another girl like me.'

'And I didn't even know you existed.'

'Yeah. Tough, huh?' She opened the door and went out.

ELEVEN

Nora had her secretary put through a call to Paris to find Peter. As she expected at this time of day, he was at the theatre. The assistant director was on the line when Charles put the call through to her desk.

'Would you please tell Monsieur Norwood I want to speak to him.'

'I'm afraid it isn't convenient—'

'This is his wife speaking. Please ask him to come to the phone.'

'Oh! Oh, one moment, Madame.' There was a long pause, during which various noises could be heard a long way off in the background, echoing sounds as if in an empty hall. Presumably they came from the stage.

The assistant director came back. 'Madame, Peter says can he call you back later? He's in the midst of something difficult. Or I could take a message . . .'

'Very well,' Nora said with some grimness. 'Tell him I should like him to come home as soon as possible. Tell him Lily is here.'

'I beg your pardon? What name was that?'

'Lily.' She spelt it for him. 'Tell him she arrived at my office half an hour ago. I need him here.'

'Very well, Madame, but I really should tell you it's unlikely he'll be able to leave the theatre for some time—'

'Monsieur,' Nora said, her voice hard and flat, 'tell my husband what I said.'

After she had put the receiver back on the hook she debated with herself whether to try to contact Marc in Lyons. But it seemed a waste of time to do that. Marc would be home the day after tomorrow. Meanwhile she could have further talks with Lily Norwood during which she'd try to reduce her demands to something more reasonable, and have enquiries made through business agents in the States to see if there really had been no divorce.

But she had few hopes on that score. Lily had clearly used up almost all her savings on this trip to France. The sort of girl who would save money by not getting a divorce was unlikely to waste money on a trip to Calmady without being sure she'd recoup her expenses.

Peter arrived soon after lunch, looking tired and rather querulous.

'What's all this nonsense?' he demanded as he shed his raincoat in the hall. 'I was in the middle of a big scene with the leading actor—'

'Please come into the drawing-room,' Nora said.

He looked at her sharply. Her voice had betrayed something to him. Nora was seldom angry. But there was anger in the way she led him into the spacious, elegant room and carefully closed the door.

'Well? Did Theo get the message right—Lily's here?'

'Your first wife. I was taken aback. If you remember, you'd never mentioned her to me. I've put her into a hotel in Rheims.'

'She just turned up here?' he said, avoiding the challenge.

'Yes.'

'What the hell for?' He was bewildered. 'I haven't seen her in over four years.'

'She came,' Nora replied on a note that cut like a knife, 'to tell me that you and I are bigamously married.'

When he first came in Peter had been ready to have a fight over being dragged away from his important affairs. As the situation gradually unfolded he'd begun to take up a position of defensive annoyance. Now all the aggression drained out of him. He stared at Nora in disbelief.

'You're kidding!'

'Not at all. She was shown into my office about ten-thirty and explained the situation with great frankness. She never got a divorce when she went to Reno.'

'But . . . But . . .'

'You're going to say you gave her the money for expenses. She used it to finance a new outfit so that she could get a job. She never bothered with the divorce.'

Peter's olive skin flushed up. 'That can't be true! Good God, she wouldn't pull a stroke like that!'

'You know her better than I do, I suppose, but I found her completely convincing.

'I can't believe it!'

'I'll have enquiries made, of course. I could have put that in hand already but I needed to check with you first. Did you really receive no papers from her after she went to Reno?'

He sat down on a gilt-legged chair, as if his legs had given way beneath him.

'No, I didn't get anything from her . . .'

'You didn't think that strange?'

'Good God, Nora, I was on the move from city to city at the time. We had a show, *The Girl in the Gift Shop*—we were in Baltimore, Cincinnati—'

'Don't let's have a travelogue. You supposed the documents never caught up with you?'

He gave a little frown. 'Don't take that tone,

Nora. I took it for granted the divorce went through.'

'But it seems it did not.'

'I can't believe it—'

'You have no legal proof that you were divorced?'

'No, but I took it for *granted*—'

'Then I must send a cable to Loomis Dearborn to have enquiries made. It must be done discreetly, of course.'

'But I don't understand . . . What's the point of Lily turning up here to tell this story—'

'The point,' Nora burst out, 'is to get money! What did you think she wanted? To claim you back?'

He flinched. His dark face went darker. 'Say, that's no way to speak—'

'Don't dare to tell me what way to speak! A complete stranger walks in, tells me she's married to the man I thought was my husband—'

'Thought was your husband? But, Nora—I *am*—'

'You're not! How can you be my husband when you're already married—'

'But I'm not married to her! It's all nonsense! She's just—'

'What? Attempting a fraud? Do you really think she'd come all the way to Calmady unless she was sure of the facts? Don't be naïve, Peter. I only met the girl a few hours ago but one thing I'm sure of—she knows the value of money, she invested all she had to get here so she knows she's going to do well out of it.'

Peter put his head in his hands. 'Oh God,' he groaned. Nora stood looking down at him. After a moment she said, 'It seems strange to hear you call on God. You told so many lies before Him.'

'Lies?' He looked up at her. 'I never lied—'

'You didn't? When Father Letillac talked with you didn't you tell him there was no reason why we shouldn't be married? That you were a Catholic in good standing? You produced a baptizmal certificate—shouldn't you have produced a marriage and a divorce certificate too? And if you had, what do you think Father Letillac would have said? A divorce?'

'But that wasn't anything, Nora! I never even thought of it. Lily and I were only married for a few weeks. And it was so long ago—I tell you, I'd forgotten about it! It just wasn't important, didn't matter!'

Nora turned away in bitter anger. 'Didn't matter! You never told me a word about it. You kept it from me.'

'I didn't, Nora. I just never thought of it.'

'How can you say that? We confessed our past relationships —at least, I thought we did. I told you about Buddy—'

'I never felt any of that was important—'

'When I asked if you'd had other girls, you just said, nobody ever mattered to you—'

'And that was true, Nora!'

263

She made a gesture of dismissal as she swung round on him. 'Nobody ever mattered? Not even a girl you loved enough to marry?'

'You've got to understand. The marriage didn't really mean anything—'

'Ours, too? Is it a meaningless ceremony to you, is that it?'

'Come on now, Nora—don't pretend you care all that much about ceremony! You—'

'What are you talking about? When have I ever said I didn't think the marriage ceremony was important?'

'Well, you didn't want a big fuss when we got married—'

'But that was because it was so soon after Gaby's death! Surely you understood that? You *must* have known it was serious to me, Peter! Why else were we married in church?' She drew in a gasping breath. 'Don't you understand what you've done? We're religiously married—in front of a priest—and you went through with it although you knew it was wrong!'

'Don't be ridiculous! As far as I knew I was legally divorced—'

'Good God, don't you even understand what you've done? The Catholic Church doesn't recognize divorce. You would never have been allowed to go through the service if Father Letillac had known you were a divorced man—'

'Are you going to claim you're deeply religious

now? Is that it? What rubbish! You believe all that stuff as little as I do!'

'I believe it enough not to lie in church!' she cried. 'I believe it enough not to keep things hidden when I go to confession! I simply . . . I simply can't understand how you can excuse yourself in this way—you don't even seem to understand what you've done'

'Sure I understand,' he said in a hard voice. 'I didn't tell you about a six weeks' marriage that I'd almost forgotten about and that I thought was legally over. Now it's all come out and you're sore because you feel a fool—'

'Don't speak about it in that tone! Don't dare belittle what you've done!' She was trembling with rage at his uncaring response. 'You haven't even said you're sorry! Not once!'

He flushed. 'I don't see I've much to be sorry for. I never thought Lily was important and I never thought you'd behave like a vixen when you found out about her—'

'Damn you!' she almost shouted. 'I don't care about Lily! I don't care if you went to bed with a hundred girls or even if you married them! What I can't stand is that you must have known that to go through a church ceremony with me was wrong—*wrong*, Peter, a sin if you believe Father Letillac!'

'But I don't believe Father Letillac. That's the point. And neither do you, if you're honest.'

'Don't you understand?' she insisted. 'We're

265

not married—neither in the civil nor the religious sense! You were a married man, and that invalidates the civil ceremony. And you concealed the fact you were a divorced man, which invalidates the religious ceremony.'

'Gee,' he sneered, 'I see you've worked out all the finer points!'

She drew back from him. 'I've had several painful hours in which to do so,' she said. She was suddenly calm again. 'I think you'd better go, Peter. Perhaps when you think this over, you'll realize it can't just be shrugged off.'

He frowned, looked uncertain. 'What are you saying? You want me out of the house?'

'Perhaps you'd better go back to Paris.'

'Now look here, Nora! I'm not going to be dragged here and then sent away—'

'I apologize. I imagined you would want to be called home to discuss what to do about the unexpected arrival of your legal wife.'

'No, no—now, wait, Nora—I didn't mean it that way. Listen, all I meant was—damn it—your attitude has taken me aback. I don't feel I've done anything wrong but you're accusing me of all kinds of things. Be honest—you *know* I thought I was free to marry you. As for deceiving that old fool of a priest—if Lily hadn't turned up here you'd never have known a word about it.'

'And that would have made it all right?'

'Well, wouldn't it? I'm prepared to take my chances on going to hell for keeping my private affairs to myself. If you don't tell Father Letillac, what's the harm?'

'Honesty . . . integrity . . . those things don't mean anything?'

'Honey, I'm as honest as the next guy, you know that. But you've got to have a sense of proportion about it. You can't live nowadays by a set of rules invented hundreds of years ago.'

'You mean being honest has gone out of date?'

'Sarcasm isn't going to help. See here, Nora—your cousin Gaby came over to New York and was dickering with a guy to help her get money for illegally imported champagne. You saying that was a completely honest transaction?'

Nora felt herself shiver with distaste. 'Gaby is dead,' she said. 'Don't drag her into this. And besides, Gaby was honest with me, and with her husband. Between people, Peter—between people who are supposed to love each other—how can there be confidence if there are lies or hidden things?'

'That's a bit holier-than-thou, coming from you, isn't it?'

'I don't understand what you mean.'

'You've always been completely honest with me, is that what you're saying?'

'Certainly.'

'What about those parties you used to go to with Garrenstein—what about the men you slept around with then?'

She stood looking at him in amazement. 'What?' she whispered.

'Don't think I didn't hear about them! Jazzmen like to gossip, you know. When I was rehearsing that show, I heard about the kind of thing you got up to with Garrenstein and his pals. But, see, I didn't make a big thing of it. If you wanted to keep it a secret—'

'Be quiet.'

Startled at the steely interruption, he gaped at her.

'I'll reply to what you've just said. It hardly matters, but I think I owe it to myself.' She waited a moment to choose her words. 'I never had any other lover except Buddy Garrenstein. I told you that before we got married. Did you think I was lying?'

'What does it matter? Live and let live, that's my—'

'Do you think I'm lying now?'

'Listen, when a party gets out of hand, anybody can do anything—'

'You don't believe me.' She said it with quiet surprise. 'You really don't believe people can be honest with each other.'

'I certainly don't think it's anything to get in such a state about—'

'How much is there about yourself that you haven't told me, Peter?'

He laughed, angry and indignant. 'You want a list? You want a written confession? See here,

Nora, we got married because we felt we could be a good partnership. You wanted a husband and a family for the sake of the business, I wanted a wife and a settled home. Let's not pretend we were heart-to-heart over every slightest thing.'

'Please go.'

'Don't act the hurt innocent. We had a friendly business arrangement—it didn't include soul-searching and breast-baring!'

'Peter, the more you say, the less I like you. Please go. Please!'

He shook his head. 'No, there are things to settle. What's to happen about Lily?'

'Nothing, perhaps,' she said bitterly. 'She's your problem, after all. Perhaps you're the one who should deal with it.'

'But she's asking for money. You're the one who holds the purse strings.'

'How true that is. I'm asking myself whether it's worth paying out money for you.'

'Nora!'

But even before he exclaimed in outrage, she'd heard the cruelty of her own words. She went scarlet. 'I'm sorry. That was a rotten thing to say.' She tried to pull herself together. 'We've both said things in the past few minutes that we're going to regret. But I've insisted I want honesty between us, and so I'll say this too. I found out this morning that we're not really married, Peter. And now I'm wondering if I want to change that.'

269

'Don't be absurd! You've got to do something about it! If you don't, Lily's going to give the story to the newspapers. How would you like that?'

'Not much.' She shook her head to herself. 'I'll get in touch with her, see how much she'll take to keep quiet.'

'Look Nora, you've got to do more than that! She's got to go back to the States and get a real divorce.'

'No.'

'You mean you won't ante up for that?'

'No.'

'Damn it all, Nora! Are you saying you don't care about our marriage?'

'What marriage?' she asked, too weary to argue or accuse any more. 'What marriage, Peter?'

TWELVE

By the time Cousin Marc came home two days later, matters had gone from bad to worse—in fact, to disastrous.

Peter, angry and resentful, had gone back to Paris. There his rehearsals had been wrecked by his own bad temper causing a crisis between himself and his leading actor. The actor stalked out, the actor's wife who was also in the cast followed him, the play was therefore left without star names to attract the public, and the backer became restive. He told Peter he must apologize and get Cesar Ralli back. Peter refused, and was fired.

When Nora rang him at the Paris apartment to ask if he would come to a three-way meeting between himself, Lily and Nora in Rheims, he hit out at her. 'What's the point of a meeting? I thought you agreed you and I were through.'

Nora was hurt. She had intended to apologize for all the things she'd said on the previous day. Instead she told him she would speak to Lily alone, if he preferred that.

'No,' he said, '*I'll* speak to Lily alone. How do I know what you've been saying to each other? It's time I got the story straight from her.'

What happened between them Nora never actually learned. Lily rang in some alarm, to say Peter had told her he didn't care whether she got a divorce or not since he was all washed up with Nora.

Nora tried to ring Peter but couldn't get hold of him. The fact was, he was out on a spectacular drinking bout. So still in total confusion about what she wanted, she sent a cable to Loomis Dearborn asking for verification of the facts she'd already been told. This was the state of play when Marc came in, demanding a cold drink because the April sky was suddenly full of very hot sunshine and the train had been suffocating.

'I have something to tell you,' Nora said as she watched him sip the ice-cold Belgian beer.

He glanced at her over the glass 'Something serious, I can see.' He thought perhaps it might be that she was expecting a baby. She didn't look well, and in the early stages of pregnancy some women tended to look pale and fatigued.

'It's something very serious, and very unexpected. I don't know what you're going to say . . .'

She told him the story as briefly as possible: Lily's unexpected arrival, the neglected divorce, the bigamy of her own marriage, Lily's suggested solution.

She watched Marc's fair-featured face lengthen in utter incredulity. He set down his glass with care on the silver tray. He picked it up and set it down again.

'My God.' It was hardly above a whisper.

'I've spoken to Peter about it,' Nora said, soldiering on under a burden she felt would crush and kill her. 'He feels he's innocent of any wrong-doing because he genuinely believed—'

'Innocent?' Marc burst out. 'What the hell does he mean by that? Had you ever heard a word of his having already been married?'

'No.'

'No! And on the marriage certificate he's described as "bachelor".'

'He says he was married to this girl for such a short time that—'

'Damn him!' shouted Marc, leaping to his feet and striding to the door as if he would find Peter there, waiting in the hall. 'How dare he! How dare he do a thing like this! I always knew he wasn't good enough for you—'

'Marc . . . please . . . Marc . . . we must be discreet. Please don't make a fuss—'

'Make a fuss? I'll make a damned earthquake! When I get my hands on that boy I'll thrash him to within an inch of—'

'Marc, what good would that do? We've got to think. I've been over and over it and I don't know what's best—'

'What's best is to get shot of him and never see him again! He's a bloody scoundrel, and— Where is he, if it comes to that? Is he in the house?'

'No, he's in Paris—'

'Just as well for him!' Her cousin was trembling with fury. His broad hands were clenching and unclenching as if he had Peter's bones in them. 'The bastard! The low-down, rotten—' He broke off. He had been about to say some even worse things, and it was his habit never to use bad language in front of women. He drew a deep breath, walked to a chintz armchair, and threw himself into it. Then he leapt up again and began pacing about.

'Where is this young woman?'

'In the Hotel de la Place in Rheims.'

'Who else knows about it?'

'Here in France? Only you and I, Peter and Lily. I cabled to Monsieur Dearborn to make sure of the facts she'd given me, so he's the only other person involved from my side. Who she might have spoken to before leaving the States, I don't know. She said she consulted a lawyer, without giving names.'

'Did you believe her?'

Nora nodded. 'She struck me as a very straightforward person. She doesn't want to harm me, it's just that times are hard in America and she needs money.'

'Oh, really? She doesn't want to harm you. No no, she just comes barging into your life and tells you you aren't legally married. Nothing much, just a little part-time job to earn some cash.'

He was much more angry on her behalf than she had been for herself. If he had liked Peter better in the first place he might have been trying to find mitigations, but he had always simply put up with Peter because Nora liked him. So instead of trying to help patch up the marriage, he gave rein to his anger. His little girl had been tricked and insulted—he hated Peter for that, and could never imagine himself speaking to the man in future.

'What ought we to do, Marc?'

Nora's question brought him to his senses. He stopped pacing up and down. He went to the table, picked up his beer, and swallowed some to ease a throat now parched and dry not only from the heat, but from anger. Then he said, 'What do you want to do?'

'I . . . I can't make up my mind.'

'Oh?' He studied her. She was very pale, there were dark shadows under her grey-brown eyes, she looked even thinner than her usual slender self. Poor little girl! If only Gaby were here, Gaby with her womanly intuition, his darling, quick-witted Gaby . . . she would know what to do for this poor waif.

But, lacking womanly intuition, it still seemed to him that Nora wasn't leaping to save her marriage. She didn't reply to his question with, 'We must pay off this girl and go back to how it was before', or 'I want it all settled, Peter is more important to me than anything on earth.'

That pallor, that weariness—perhaps they came from facing the fact that she had married a man she didn't love enough. If everything went well between them, it was an enjoyable relationship. Peter was different enough from the run of Frenchmen to make him interesting, he was good-natured and easygoing. But there was no passion to weld them together when things went wrong.

'Tell me truly, Nora,' he said. 'Do you love Peter enough to forgive him for all this?'

'I do . . . I thought I did . . . I do, really, only you see—he won't see that he's done anything particularly wrong.'

'But good heavens, Nora—apart from never

telling you about this girl . . . there's the matter of concealing the divorce from Father Letillac.'

'He thinks it's old-fashioned and silly to care about that. He doesn't take religion seriously. And, to tell the truth, neither did I, Marc. Only now . . . it somehow seems such a terrible thing to have done.'

'You're damned right,' grunted Marc. 'It's shameful. There's got to be *something* in life that you hold sacred, surely? And even putting that aside, Nora—he should have respect for your beliefs.' He paused. 'Did he marry this other girl in church?'

'No.'

'You see,' he said, his quick lawyer's mind working, 'that could have meant that you and he were still religiously married because the church would disregard a prior ceremony in a town hall. But the fact that he's lied—I mean, Nora, he went to confession with old Letillac—what in God's name could he have told him?'

'He doesn't see it that way. It's no use expecting him to care about it from that point of view—'

'I don't give a damn what he "cares" about. It's you I'm thinking of. Do you really want to go on being married to this man?'

This was the kind of question that expects the answer no. And that was what Marc got. After a long hesitation, Nora shook her head.

'I think it's all over,' she said in a tone of

desolation. 'I simply can't picture myself ever sitting down across a breakfast table with him, let alone . . .'

Let alone going to bed with him, she'd been going to say. But she was too fastidious to discuss such a thing with Marc. He, however, caught the hint. He was grieved beyond words for her. Poor child . . . She kept giving her heart to quite the wrong men.

'Do you want me to take things over?' he asked.

'As far as possible. I suppose I'd have to . . . I'd have to see our lawyers and tell them . . .'

'I think you'll need an ecclesiastical lawyer as well. Let me talk to Jean Sellier. He'll know whom to approach. And how about . . .' He hesitated. 'And Peter? Do you want me to handle him?'

She longed to say, Yes, I never want to see him again. She had been bruised enough in spirit to want to shrink away from any further encounters, to say only, Let me go back to the time before I ever met him. But that was impossible. Besides, there had been some truth in the accusation he had hurled at her. She had married him so that she could have a father for children yet to be—she hadn't really wanted him for himself.

'I ought to see him again to give him a chance to speak sensibly. We were too angry the other day to talk sense.'

'I don't quite know what *he's* got to be angry about,' Marc grunted.

'I'll go up to Paris on Monday to see him. Meanwhile, I must talk to Lily again—'

'I'm coming with you.'

'No, that might scare her—'

'A young woman who makes a trip across the Atlantic to wreck another woman's marriage doesn't scare easily!'

'Perhaps it was an easy marriage to wreck,' Nora said on a note of mourning for something broken beyond repair.

Next day was Sunday. It had always been the family custom to go about once a month to the service in Rheims Cathedral. This they did, having arranged to meet Lily after lunch.

After the service Nora was seized by an impulse to hear an impartial voice. She asked Marc to go ahead to the restaurant where they were to eat, while she herself went into a confessional.

'Bless me, father, for I have sinned.'

'Tell me your sins, my daughter. Are they of the mind or the flesh?'

Haltingly she explained her dilemma. 'I feel the marriage is over—'

'It never existed, my child. I am not skilled in Catholic law, but I am sure a divorced man cannot be validly married in church—and your husband believed himself to be a *divorcé*.'

278

'And yet the marriage did exist, father. For over eight months we have been man and wife.'

'Tell me, my daughter, is there . . . are you expecting a child?'

'No, father.'

'Perhaps we should be grateful for that. It would have made matters very distressing.'

'What I came to ask, father, is this—when he obtains a divorce from his first wife, is it my duty to marry him again—I mean, legally marry?'

'You certainly couldn't be married in church and in our eyes it would be no marriage at all. I couldn't encourage you to do that, my daughter.' His tone was perplexed. 'It needs a deeper mind than mine to resolve the problem. But to me, it is clear that you have never been married to this man and never can be in the eyes of the church.'

'Is it your opinion . . . do you tell me that I need feel no guilt for wanting the marriage to end?'

'What guilt do you bear? You told me you knew nothing of his past—that was true?'

'Oh yes! It was a great shock to me to learn the truth.'

'Then I cannot see that you have any reason to feel guilty. Perhaps God sent the first wife to speak to you so that you could help him to turn away from his sin—because he committed a sin in what he did.'

'But he doesn't believe that! That's what

makes me so uncertain. He thinks it's all nonsense.'

There was a pause. Then the unseen priest said, 'My child, you know it is my duty to keep husband and wife together, for marriage is sacred. But you are describing to me a man who sees nothing sacred in it. You should not allow his wrong thinking to make you feel guilty. I cannot tell you whether you should remarry in a civil ceremony and continue to live together in the eyes of the world as man and wife. If you love him greatly, perhaps that would be best. But if you decide to live without him, you are behaving according to the laws of your church. That is commendable.'

He went on to ask if she had any personal sins to confess, she told him she'd been very angry and resentful and full of hate, he gave her a penance and sent her away.

For the first time since Lily had walked into her office, she felt something like normal. The confessor's words had heartened her. A dreadful sense of guilt had been gripping her, telling her she was in the wrong to feel she should seize the chance to be free again.

She ate a respectable meal, talked with some vitality to friends at a nearby table. Though she was dreading the coming interview with Lily, she went to the Hotel de la Place with her confidence at a better level.

Lily was introduced to Marc, who bowed

frigidly. She had had coffee brought up, which she offered. They explained they had just finished lunch. They sat looking at each other, not knowing how to begin.

Marc decided to take the plunge. 'My cousin has told me how things stand. I believe you've seen Peter?'

'Yes.' She frowned. 'He kind of implied that none of this mattered a heck of a lot, since he and Nora were on the rocks anyhow.'

'Did you get the impression he was firm on that?'

'He was as wild as a goose with no feathers,' Lily reported. 'I thought he was going to hit me, he was so mad. But when I calmed him down and got him to talk about financial matters he said . . . er . . .'

'That no money might be forthcoming, eh?'

Lily looked away. After a moment she employed herself in pouring coffee, into which she busily stirred sugar.

'Look, I think I deserve *something* for coming here and putting things straight!' she blurted.

'Do you really? That's like a car driver saying he thinks his accident victim owes him something for having a nice broken leg.'

'But I spent out every cent I had to come here!'

'That was a risk you took.'

'I'm going to get something out of it,' she insisted, drawing her thin brows together in anger. 'If you won't cough up I'll give the story to the newspapers—they'll pay me for a gossip item like this!'

'Ah, now we come to the point.' Marc smiled with contentment. 'I knew it would come to this in the end. It's arrived at common blackmail. As you can imagine, we are on much better terms with the local police than a complete stranger would be, and a foreigner at that. How would you enjoy facing a court case under a foreign jurisdiction and in a language you don't understand?'

The bluster of anger disappeared at once. 'Say, don't get sore! I only meant—listen, I've got to get money somehow. I can't stay here for ever, I wouldn't want to anyhow. If you'll just stake me to my fare home, and a little for living expenses—'

Marc glanced at Nora. She nodded.

'That makes sense. We would agree to that. In fact, we would even be fairly generous in those circumstances. We wouldn't want you to go away with any sense of grievance, Mrs Norwood. What do you say to ten thousand dollars?'

It was clearly more than she had expected. She looked so thankful that Marc felt sorry for her. She was no businesswoman, that was clear, and thank heavens she was no crook.

'Very well. I'll bring the money to you tomorrow. In the meantime we'll arrange a passage home for you, and of course your bill here will be taken care of. I hope you'll be ready to sail by mid-week?'

'Yes, sure—why not—anything you say.'

'Then that's settled.'

Nora hadn't spoken a word so far. Now she said, 'You don't seem to care at all about what you've done.'

'Huh? What've I done? Listen, in Reno folk are breaking up all the time—it's no big deal, unless somebody's heart gets broken. And if you want to know what I think, there's no broken hearts lying around here.'

'How can you possibly know—'

'I had Peter's side of things in the uncensored version—if you think he's wasting away from grief, forget it! He told me he found the whole ball game hereabouts a hell of a bore. And he didn't take too kindly to things that were said about some show he put on—said the audience were a bunch of narrow-minded snobs.'

'But that's only on the surface—'

'Think so? He didn't give me any bedroom details but I didn't get the impression his love life was all that great. And as for you, sister, all you've got is hurt pride. I don't blame you,' Lily Norwood added. 'I'd be mad as hell if this had happened to me. But don't try to make me feel bad by saying I've broken anybody's heart because it simply ain't so.'

Next day Nora drove up to Paris to attend to some business at the offices of Champagne

Tramont and to see Peter. She telephoned to make sure he was at home before she turned up at the apartment at the Rue St Honoré. The new maid looked inquisitive and apprehensive as she opened the door to her.

'Monsieur said to say he would be in the study, Madame.'

'Thank you, Susanne. We don't want to be disturbed.'

'Very well, Madame.'

She went into the study to find Peter waiting with a letter held out. 'Was there any need for this?'

It had been arranged that a block of the personal shares in the company should be made over to Peter so that he could feel more involved in the firm. The papers should have been sent to him at about this time. Instead, at Marc's behest, the lawyers had written to say that the matter had been deferred indefinitely.

'What's the idea? Afraid I'll run off home with some of your precious shares?'

'I'm sorry, Peter—that was just an unhappy coincidence—'

'Oh, sure! Just one more way to make me feel I don't measure up to the high standards you expect! Well, okay! I never wanted any part of your high-and-mighty firm anyway, and if you think I enjoyed the role of Prince Consort to the Queen of the Champagne Country, you're crazy!'

The outburst came to an end. She felt beaten about by the rush of words.

'Well?' he challenged.

'I came to give us a chance to talk sensibly—'

'What about? About how you'll be big-hearted and forgive me for what I've done, and how I have to reconcile myself to being in the wrong for the rest of my life? Forget it! If you want to know, I've already booked my passage. I'm going home.'

'But what will you do, Peter? Times are so bad—'

'Not everywhere, don't you worry about that. For instance, Reno's still in business. They put on shows in Reno. Maybe Lily and I will get together again—'

'Peter!'

He could see it hurt her, so he went on with it although it was quite untrue. 'Yeah, I think that's what I'll do. I'll get Lily to introduce me to some of the showbiz folk she knows back there, and you can bet it'll be a whole lot easier than trying to live up to the rules set by other people. I might not even bother to have Lily go through with the divorce. What the hell! At least she isn't a nag.'

Nora couldn't bear to hear any more. She had to settle only two important points, and then they could say goodbye for ever. 'I'd better go. But first I need to know—will you go to the lawyers who will contact you today or tomorrow, and sign a statement about your first marriage?'

'So that you can get it all legally shut down, huh? Sure, why not.'

'And will you let them have an address through which you can be contacted? There will be business matters to settle.'

'Anything you say. What we want is a clean break.'

'Yes.'

He had calmed down enough now to see that she was deeply hurt by what had just been said. He stifled a sigh. 'Look here, Nora, don't take it too much to heart. We've got to accept that we'd never get over this, so it's better to split up and put an end to it. I'll co-operate in any divorce proceedings or whatever. Then we can both start over, with no hard feelings. What do you say?'

'That's best,' she agreed.

When she turned to go, he held out his hand. She took it. They shook hands and parted like polite strangers.

THIRTEEN

For a long time it passed unnoticed in Paris society that the Norwood-Tramonts had separated. Peter Norwood had gone back to New York, probably to do some show or other after the failure of his latest Parisian venture—well and good. The season took up attention, the usual balls and parties and engagements and marryings. Autumn came. Peter Norwood was still in America. How odd—but Americans were strange, everyone always agreed on that, and nowhere stranger than in their marriages, which they treated very casually.

The legal ending of the bigamous marriage through the civil courts was quietly and easily arranged. The annulment of the church wedding was much more difficult. In the first place the Vatican had to be convinced that it wasn't just another ploy—becoming more and more common in these immoral times—to get a divorce. Through the autumn, into the winter, on into 1932 . . .

Nora didn't stay at home moping while this went on. There was enough to engage her attention elsewhere. The Depression had at last come to France, not in such a severe form at first as in the United States or Germany, but enough to make it appreciably harder to sell expensive wine. So Nora went on sales drives in the places where there was still money or an influential ruling class who wanted to show off.

Spain was a good market. She spent some time in Madrid, more in Rome where the friends of the dictator, Mussolini, seemed to have formed a new aristocracy within the old families. From there, with recommendations to Herr Hugenberg, the commercial magnate who had given financial backing to Adolf Hitler, she went to Berlin.

It couldn't be said she liked these people. But they had power, they had money, and they wanted to adopt what they thought was the appropriate lifestyle. This meant having champagne at every big event. So Nora Tramont helped her agents in Germany to take orders for champagne.

She was in Berlin during the elections of July. A stalemate was produced—Hitler's party gained half the seats in the Reichstag but the parties making up the other half would not let them take power.

'The atmosphere was really frightening,' she told Cousin Marc when she got home. 'Troopers in brown shirts marched about, ordering passers-by to form "spontaneous" demonstrations in their favour. I was really thankful to get away.'

'We're no better off here,' he replied dourly. 'Another uproar! That fool Herriot is trying to control a cabinet who don't agree with a word he says.'

'What's the argument now?'

'Oh, he says we ought to accept that Germany can only pay a smaller sum in reparation. I hear there was some talk of handing back some bit of the Congo to them, or something. Paris is full of colonial civil servants giving reports to senior officials about which bits we can give away!'

Nora laughed, glad to be back in the easy atmosphere of Calmady—easy, that was, until the tests began for the new vintage and nerves became strained. It was three years since a really great vintage had been made, in 1929. This year, it was hoped, something special would emerge from the blend. But no, it was a good wine, a 'good average', as Puchet remarked.

There was better news for Nora at the lawyers' office. She was invited to Paris to receive a large document covered with ecclesiastical seals. The Vatican legal department had accepted her plea. Her marriage to Peter Norwood was declared null and void.

A quiet announcement was placed in the respectable newspapers. It was picked up by the gossip press so that she immediately became a target for speculation. She told her secretary and her house staff to say she was out to all telephone callers except known friends. She answered no written requests for an 'exclusive'. When she was accosted by reporters outside her Paris apartment she simply remained totally silent in face of all their questions.

So the interest died down in about a month. Not entirely, of course. One or two of her friends had the hardihood to ask point-blank.

'What happened?' Émilie demanded. 'I thought you and he were such a contented pair?'

'I told you, Émilie, I don't want to discuss it.'

'He was running after those gorgeous actresses, I suppose?' She waited for Nora to agree or disagree, and when she did neither went on, 'No, it couldn't be that. You don't get a dispensation from the Pope for that. Is it on grounds of desertion? For of course he's been gone ages and ages.'

'Émilie, what does it matter? It's over, that's what counts.'

'You don't really seem to have much luck with men, do you? I mean, first of all there was Edmond and you—by the way, I saw him recently.'

'Who?' asked Nora, who had switched off as she sat, a captive, in Émilie's elegant little sitting-room.

'I don't believe you're listening to a word I say! I'm telling you I saw Edmond du Ceddres the other day. I must say, you made a mistake there. What a stunner he's turned out to be!'

'That's good. And how is François?' François was Émilie's younger son, who had a hearing defect and was undergoing treatment.

'Oh, François can hear perfectly well when he wants to!' retorted Émilie. 'But I'll tell you what—the specialist who's treating him is rather good-looking. And he gives me the most mean-ing looks sometimes, Nora! It quite makes my heart flutter.'

Nora chuckled. 'You're incurable, Émilie. You're always on the verge of some great affair. Yet you have everything, really—why can't you just be happy?'

'Listen to who's talking! *You* have every-thing—fashion-plate appearance, money for

clothes and travel and enjoyment—and freedom—oh, God, Nora, if you know how bored I
am with being tied down to a husband and
family.' She paused, light dawning in her eyes.
'That was it, wasn't it! That was the reason you
got an annulment!'

'Now what?' Nora sighed.

'You couldn't have children with Peter! I knew
I should find it out in the end! What was it—
he was impotent? You never consummated the
marriage?'

'Émilie darling, do stop snooping around in
my private life. I have no intention of discussing
the reasons with you.'

So she might say, but Émilie was certain she'd
discovered the truth. She said so to all the friends
she had in common with Nora and quite a few
who weren't in the least interested. But it had
one good result. The story was widely believed
and everyone stopped wondering about it. Moreover, they felt kindly disposed to Nora because
of it. Poor girl—married to one of those strange
Americans who turned out to be even stranger
than most.

Nora and Marc went to the Paris première
of the American film *Grand Hotel*. Afterwards
there was a party given by the Department of
Trade. It was a grand affair, the women in their
jewels and the men in their medals and ribbons.
Nora was looking sensational in a black backless
evening dress that fell to her ankles in a long

swathe of shimmering satin. She wore no jewellery except a small diamond brooch on her shoulder strap.

The wife of the Minister, anxious to ensure that Madame Tramont enjoyed herself, kept bringing suitable young men to join the group around her.

'Have you met Monsieur du Ceddres?' she inquired as she led forward a tall, very tanned newcomer in a finely tailored tail suit.

'Oh!' Nora felt herself colour up with embarrassment.

Edmond du Ceddress bowed. 'Madame Tramont and I met some years ago,' he said. 'But she's probably forgotten by now.'

'Oh, then I'm renewing an old acquaintance—how nice! How long ago since you knew each other?'

'I think perhaps . . . six years?'

'Six years! My goodness—Madame Tramont, I'll leave Monsieur du Ceddres with you to talk over old times.' Smiling she went away.

'No talking over old times!' protested Alain Bouvier, elbowing Edmond aside. 'That gives you an unfair advantage.'

'I leave it to Madame to lead the conversation,' Edmond said.

Since Nora most decidedly didn't want to talk about old times, she mentioned the film she had just come from. 'Did any of you read the book?'

'Who's it by—?'

'It's one of those great thick novels—'

'Vicki Baum—she writes very well—'

The conversation became an argument over the merits of the film version as against the book. Nora let the talk flow on, now and again finding Edmond's eye resting on her with perplexed interest.

She had changed, of course. Since they knew each other, she had changed dramatically. Her looks were now an asset to her, her face and figure the height of fashion, dressed to perfection by Chanel. Moreover, she had learned a lot, seen a lot, since she made a hysterical refusal to Edmond's offer of an engagement ring.

But she wasn't like Émilie. She wasn't looking for romantic relationships with every man who smiled at her.

Although . . . if one were thinking of taking a lover, Edmond du Ceddres might not be a bad choice. As Émilie had said, he had changed greatly. The tall trim figure was now very spare and rangy, as if he had lived a very active outdoor life. The suntan seemed deeply ingrained, not just the result of a summer on the Riviera. His voice had deepened and gained resonance, so that when he spoke his words were attended to. Besides, he had authority in his manner.

And with reason, she gathered, as the talk became more general. Edmond had spent three years in the Colonial Civil Service, working in the French Congo. 'It's a tradition in my family,

293

to give some time to government service,' he explained. 'I chose the Colonial Service because I wanted to take a good look at overseas investment.'

'Are you here to help Herriot hand some of it over to the Boches?' Bouvier enquired.

'I'm here to give a report and answer any questions. But I've no wish to help dispose of the Congo. It's a very lucrative area—the mineral deposits are enormous. However, you don't want a lecture on copper layers at the moment, I imagine.'

'It's a dangerous place, surely?' Galliard Rosel put in. 'Wild animals and jungle fever and all that, eh?'

'Oh, well, you have to suffer to be profitable,' Edmond said, paraphrasing the proverb, 'You have to suffer to be beautiful'.

Nora laughed. Edmond glanced at her and laughed too. They shared a moment of enjoyment. Then Nora remembered that this was a married man, and turned away.

As the party broke up, he sought her out. Her cousin Marc had gone to fetch her wrap.

'Excuse me, Nora . . . We both of course recall what happened in the past but . . . I wonder if you would object if I were to call one day?'

She was surprised. She was about to say, 'Ought not your wife to do that for you?' but Marc appeared with her cloak. She smiled meaninglessly, saying to her cousin, 'You remember Edmond du Ceddres?'

'Good lord yes! How are you, my boy?'

'Quite well, sir, thank you. And you?'

Marc was shaking hands with cordiality and a complete absence of embarrassment. 'Oh, not bad, not bad—this cold November is playing havoc with my sinuses but I can't complain. I thought you were out in Africa?'

'No, I've been back about a month.'

The butler came to say their car had drawn up for them outside, and held Nora's cloak for her. She made her way without haste but with determination to the porch. Marc joined her there.

'Nice to see the boy again. I wonder how the world's treating him these days?'

She murmured that she hoped Edmond was doing well. The talk turned to other matters as they rolled towards the Rue St Honoré.

Nora was surprised when she got home next evening to find Edmond's card on the salver in the hall of the apartment. The maid reported that Monsieur du Ceddres had called about half-past eleven. 'I told him you were at the office, Madame. He said to say he was sorry to have missed you.'

Well, I'm not, thought Nora. She sensed it would really be too dangerous to resume an acquaintanceship with Edmond.

She saw him several times at gatherings. Then came a Christmas concert at the beginning of

December. He was in a box across the concert hall. He rose to bow towards her. She acknowledged it with a slight inclination of her head. She hoped the distant response would be enough to tell him to stay away but no, at the interval he came to her box to pay his respects, leaving the lady in dark green satin—presumably his wife—to her own devices.

'I've been hoping to hear from you,' he said as he stooped over her.

'I've been very busy,' she said, wondering why she didn't just simply say, 'It would be very inappropriate for me to contact you.'

'May I fetch you some refreshment? An ice? Some wine?'

'No, thank you.'

'Martino is singing very well, don't you think?'

'Very well.'

The other members of her party had drifted out of the box. He took a seat on the spindly gilt chair beside her, 'Why are you so evasive when I talk to you?' he asked. 'If you're still embarrassed about what happened in the past, I've forgotten all about it.'

'That's very generous of you, considering how badly I treated you.'

'Not at all. You were too young to be tied down in an engagement—I see that now. But things are different now.'

'They certainly are!' she said with indignation. 'You, for instance, are a married man.'

'What?' He looked at her with genuine bewilderment.

'You married within the year after our supposed engagement came to nothing.'

'Yes.' He looked away. 'You hadn't heard?'

Now it was her turn to be bewildered. 'I've heard nothing about you—except that a friend told me you'd married.'

'My wife was killed four years ago in a skiing accident near our home.'

She gasped. She tried to express her regret.

'It's all right. It's a long time ago now. It's the reason I chose to enter the Colonial Service—I wanted to get away, to think things over.'

'After a tragedy like that,' she murmured. 'Of course . . .'

'No.' He shook his head and gave a little smile. 'You don't understand. I had to come to terms with the fact that I felt no deep grief. Ours had been an arranged marriage, you know. I realized some months after her death that my wife and I had never progressed further than a friendly acceptance of each other.'

She went through a series of emotions—pleasure that he would confide something so personal, relief that he had felt no great sense of loss, dismay at her own selfishness. She'd never been good at hiding her feelings. When she recovered her composure it was to find Edmond watching her with interest.

'I . . . I hadn't heard of your loss. I'm sorry I

297

was curt with you.' She blushed. 'But who is the lady in your box?'

'The wife of Henri Despins, a former colleague of mine. He is supposed to be joining us, but he's missed almost half the concert by now.' He gave a little enquiring tilt of the head. 'And now that you know she has no claim on me, may I hope we can be friends?'

'If you like.'

'You must know I would "like"!' he exclaimed on a laugh. 'I've been trying to get to see you again ever since we ran across each other at that party at the minister's!'

'That's very flattering.'

'Don't pretend it surprises you. I saw it in your eyes that first evening—you knew very well I was more than just interested.'

'Yes but then I still thought—'

'Oh, so you admit you were aware of it! That can only mean . . .' He leaned towards her in the dimness of the concert hall box and, picking up her hand from her lap, imprinted a kiss on the palm. 'Nora . . .' he whispered. 'Nora . . .'

She let her hand lie in his for a moment. Then, without haste, she withdrew it. 'People will see,' she murmured.

'No, they're all too busy chattering. Nora, when can we meet? Somewhere where we can be alone? There's so much I want to explain to you.'

She gave a little shiver. His voice was so urgent and intense, so full of meaning.

'We . . . we could . . . I don't know . . . Perhaps you could come to call at the apartment some evening.'

'Will your cousin Marc be there?'

'He's generally in Calmady. He doesn't come to Paris very often.'

'When? Tomorrow?'

'No, I have an evening engagement—'

'Afterwards?'

'That would be late. I . . . I don't think so, Edmond.'

'The day after tomorrow, then. Shall I come?'

She relented. His eyes were fixed on her with an eagerness she could almost feel burning into her skin. 'Come to dinner. We can talk afterwards.'

'Thank you. Until then, Nora.'

'Until then.'

Next morning a bouquet of roses was delivered to her apartment. There was no note, no message. But she knew it was from Edmond. On the following day there was a little silver brooch in the shape of a heart—but still no word, no message. She pinned it to her dress with trembling fingers. And when she changed for the evening she took the brooch from her business dress to transfer it to the shoulder of her evening gown.

These tokens from Edmond meant more than

words. She knew the coming meeting between them would be fateful. She gave the servants the evening off, so that when he came she was alone and almost breathless in the big apartment.

She opened the door to him. He stepped inside. His eyes examined her face with fervent keenness. He saw the little brooch on her gown. One finger touched it gently. 'Do you like it?' he asked.

She laughed, light-headed. He shrugged off his coat, threw it with his hat into a chair. Then turning, he took her at once into his arms.

'Nora . . . I've thought of nothing else but you since the night of the concert.'

They kissed with a consuming avidity. It was as if they had been in love since that day years ago when she refused him, and all their physical passion had been stored up until now. She went with him to her bedroom, they undressed heedlessly and then, clasped in each others arms, fell on the bed.

They made love at first quickly, momentarily sating their hunger. But then they caressed and kissed and embraced, exploring each other, whispering, teasing, learning each other through and through during the long hours until midnight. If Nora had sometimes felt she had missed the grand heights of physical passion with the men she had known, now she was compensated as Edmond lifted her on the crest of the great wave of fulfilment.

The little boudoir clock roused them with its soft chimes. 'The servants will soon be back,' she whispered as they lay with his cheek pillowed on her arm.

'Oh, Nora . . .. Think of the years we've wasted.' Reluctantly he freed himself from her clasp.

'Tonight has made it all worth while, my darling.'

When she opened the outer door to say good-bye to him, they clung for a long time. 'Tomorrow?' he whispered, and felt her nod against his shoulder. 'I'll ring you.'

When he had run down the great stone staircase to the entrance hall, she wandered back to her room, suddenly lost and lonely without him. She lay down in the rumpled bed, the scent of his body still caught in the folds of the sheets. She was sure she was too happy, too enraptured to sleep. But the languor of love crept over her, and her eyes closed softly, When her maid brought in the morning tray, she woke already half-knowing that something wonderful had happened.

'Good morning, Madame. It's a poor day, I'm afraid.'

She sat up, watched with drowsy lids as her coffee was poured.

'You didn't eat the meal Yvette prepared for you last night. She's anxious to know if there was anything wrong, Madame?'

'No,' said Nora. 'No, nothing wrong, nothing at all'—and was glad that the light was not shining full on her face as she felt herself blush in a mixture of delight and embarrassment.

Within a week or so their relationship was no secret. They were so blatantly in love that it shone out of them each time they met. Marc enquired, 'I suppose you two are going to get married?' and was answered with, 'Oh yes, of course, in a week or two.'

'When, for instance? I don't want to act the stern father-figure but there seems no reason to delay.' He chuckled. 'There's been a long enough delay, in all conscience!'

'Isn't it strange, Marc, how it's come about? I reproach myself . . . What a fool I was to send him away at first!'

'No, my dear, Gaby and I were wrong to try to arrange your life for you. Oh, not to want to see you happily married,' he corrected himself, 'that was our duty. But I realize now that you were far too young, younger than your years.' He gave a half sigh, half laugh. 'And who was that mysterious married man you loved so much, eh?'

Nora looked knowing. 'That's a secret I'll never tell anyone,' she said, as if it were a joke. But she spoke truth. It could only harm the relationship between herself and Marc if he ever learned that he had been the one she loved so dearly seven years ago. Nor would it be something to confide to Edmond, although in every other respect she intended to be totally open and honest.

What did it matter? Everything was different now. The mistakes of the past would be the basis for this new, all-embracing love. Her marriage to Edmond would be something quite different from the halting relationship between herself and Peter.

Her marriage to Edmond . . . That brought her back to her cousin's question. 'I'll speak to Edmond about it,' she said. 'It just never seems important when we're together. But perhaps . . .' She thought about it. Christmas was upon them, with the round of engagements which included a party for the children of the estate at Calmady and then of course they were in the midst of testing for the new champagne blend. And for Edmond, too, there were business ties. The skiing season was in full swing: he was sometimes called to Grenoble to deal with local problems although the resort was managed by a competent team.

'Let's plan for something in the spring,' she suggested.

'It's up to you, my love. Edmond doesn't have to consult anyone, after all.' His parents were dead now, his father carried off by pneumonia in the cold winter of two years ago and his mother by a lack of desire to live without him. An elder brother had been lost in the war. Edmond, like Nora, was the last representative of his line.

They were walking in the grounds of the Calmady estate when Nora at length brought up the subject. 'My cousin wants to know when you're going to make an honest woman of me, Edmond.'

'Good gracious, that's a thought! My angel, would you love me as much if you were an honest woman?'

'I certainly couldn't love you more.'

It was a cold January day. She was wrapped in furs and wore a great fur beret which almost engulfed her. Out of this mass of wrappings only her nose, pink-tipped with the raw wind, could be seen. Edmond planted a kiss on it. 'Who is this strange creature in wolf's clothing who wants to trap me into matrimony?'

'It is I, Red Riding Hood.'

'Who wishes to become Mrs Red Riding Hood. Very well. In fact, Nora, the decision is yours—we can go in front of the magistrate any time you like.'

She spoke of her idea for a spring wedding. 'Nothing elaborate,' she added hastily. 'In our situation it would hardly be right. But the blending will have been finished and I'd be more—'

'Oh, I see! I'm to take second place to the wine! What kind of a life am I to lead, I ask myself? Perhaps it would be better to keep you as a mistress, in a Paris apartment draped in satin and lace and no nonsense about running Champagne Tramont to distract you from loving me.'

'Very well,' she said. 'But I warn you, I have very expensive tastes. I'll expect emerald necklaces and a castle in Spain.'

'But you'd be worth it.' He drew her close, slipped his hands under the great shaggy fur coat, and pulled her against him so that their bodies touched.

'No, don't,' she whispered, half in delight and half unwilling. 'One of the workers might come by.'

'And what would they see? Madame Tramont and her fiancé making love—just what they would expect.'

'Oh, Edmond—don't—' But they were wrapped in each others' arms, kissing passionately among the birch trees, when in fact a vineyard assistant plodded by on his way home.

They decided to have an Easter wedding and to go to Spain for the honeymoon. Then everything was thrown into chaos by a crisis in Edmond's wider business affairs. Something had gone wrong at the copper mine in the French Congo, a cave-in or some kind of landslide. The workers refused to go back in, the manager cabled that a legend was building up about a juju, production was at a standstill, what should he do?

'Fool!' grunted Edmond. 'The directors

appointed him against my advice. Now I shall have to go out there and sort things out.'

'No, Edmond—no!'

'But yes, darling. I've got to go. No one else on the board of directors has any experience of the region—in fact, of Africa and its problems. After all, I served three years in the Colonial Service there—it was at my recommendations we bought into the copper mines. I *have* to go.'

'There must be someone else they could send, darling! I refuse to believe you're the only man that could deal with the matter!'

'Tichenbourg, perhaps—but he's in South America. I can't think of anyone else.'

'But isn't there anyone there—some other European with experience of mining problems? Edmond, please don't let yourself be pushed into taking this on at such a time!'

By dint of arguing strongly she convinced him that he wasn't indispensable except to Nora herself. They parted that evening with the matter settled—he would make sure someone else handled the Jimbando mess.

But when they met for lunch next day, it was to say he now felt he really must go to the Congo. 'The only European in the area who could deal with it is a manager for a rival company, Nora. You can't reasonably expect our board of directors to feel any confidence in him. We had a long session this morning and it's quite clear I must go.'

'Very well,' she sighed, seeing she must give in. 'But not until after the wedding.'

'Then the wedding must be brought forward, because I must go within a week—'

'But that's impossible, Edmond!'

'It's impossible to wait. Each day's delay allows the witch doctor to build up this story about juju in the mine. As it is, by the time I get there it may be damned difficult to make him back-track—'

She threw up her hands. 'I never heard of such a thing! What are you expected to do—hold an exorcism? It's a priest they need, not a company director—'

'Darling, it's no big thing. All I have to do is bribe the witch doctor—'

'Good God, can't the existing manager do that, if it's only a matter of money?'

'No, it's not money—at least, not entirely. There's no way of knowing what he wants until I actually speak to the man. But you can be sure, the witch doctor wants something and for some reason he absolutely refuses to tell Lombard. So I must get there as quickly as possible, find out what he's after, and satisfy him.' He took both her hands, kissing them one by one. 'It won't take so very long, dearest. Two weeks or so to get to Senegal, another week for the train journey to Jimbando, two weeks there to bargain with the juju man, and another three weeks to get back to France. Two months in all.'

'Two months!' she wailed.

'It just means putting off the wedding from April to June. Surely you don't have anything against being a June bride?' He was teasing and coaxing her now.

'Yes, I have! It means you think business is more important than me!' she accused, using the same tone.

'Oh, and who was it who said Easter would be a good time for the wedding because the blending of the champagne would be done by then?'

She had the grace to blush at that, and then she began to laugh, and the matter was settled in laughter and kisses. Edmond must go to French Equatorial Africa, she must use the interval in making new arrangements and having a new dress designed, and in June he would be back to walk down the aisle with her.

She went with him to Cherbourg the night before he had to embark. They chose a quiet hotel in the old part of town. Outside a fresh sea breeze was making a whining in the cracks of the shutters. She blotted out the sound by burying her head against Edmond's chest. They made love with a fierce passion that they knew had to last them through the parting of months.

She didn't go to the quayside to watch the steamer move out. She didn't want to disgrace herself by weeping and clinging to Edmond, begging him not to go. On the train back to Paris she sat alone in her carriage, looking out of the window at the landscape dashing by but unseeing, uncaring.

Her cousin was very gentle with her. For days he didn't chide her for being withdrawn and taciturn. Then, when a week had gone by, he ventured to remark that Edmond wouldn't have wanted her to pine away to nothing in his absence.

A cable came, saying the ship had passed the Canary Islands. He was more than half-way there. 'Come, my dear—you see? It won't be long before he's back with us again.'

'It's another six weeks at least, Marc . . .' She felt as if a part of her body had been hacked away. It was impossible not to ache with longing, with the pain of being apart.

Then one morning she came to breakfast radiant. Marc was startled and delighted at the change in her. True, it was a beautiful day outside, April at its loveliest, a china blue sky with a silver-gold sun reigning in it. Spring, he said to himself, spring is good for everybody.

If he had but known it, spring had nothing to do with her happiness. She had found out for certain that morning that she was going to have Edmond's child.

FOURTEEN

Nora hugged her secret to herself. She would share it with no one else until she could tell it to the man who would be happiest to hear it, the baby's father. She pictured to herself how Edmond's face would crinkle with delight, the white smile lines around his eyes disappearing into the tan of his skin.

She could have sent the news by wireless telegraph, through either Dakar or Libreville, to be sent on by train to Jimbando. But she couldn't bear the thought of other eyes seeing it before Edmond did. And though it was possible to send letters, by ship and then by a light plane service run by the French government to Libreville, it hardly seemed worth it—by the time the letter reached Libreville Edmond might already be on his way home.

She visited a specialist in Paris, who confirmed her pregnancy and said she was a little overstrained. He advised her to slow down, to rest more. But she was busy. It wasn't a time when she could easily sit back and think only of herself.

Events in Europe were moving with an ominous marching tread. The strange, mad dictator in Germany, Adolf Hitler, had declared a national boycott of Jewish businesses and suppressed the trade unions. These actions had repercussions in

310

neighbouring countries. There were plenty of people who actually thought such things should be done in France.

Nora found herself involved in stupid arguments with her fellow wine-makers. Some were emphatically in favour of Hitler and made no secret of it. 'We've plenty of communistic workers in France—Hitler's showing us how to deal with them,' they growled.

Negotiations were going on to form a permanent and official committee to settle grape prices. The small vinegrowers, the worker-owners, were determined to have their say in its formation. Some of the more hard-faced estate owners pointed to Germany—'That's how to deal with 'em!'

'But that's nonsense,' Nora urged. 'These men aren't communist trade unionists—they're owners like ourselves, only on a smaller scale—'

'Yes? And do you remember 1911, when they tried to burn us down?'

Nora of course didn't remember 1911, and found it hard to argue against the older owners with grudges to back up their opposition to the new committee.

Then there were the transients, the people who came in each August and September to pick the grapes. They were part of a growing body of workers in France who were faring very badly as the world-wide economic depression took hold. They looked with longing towards America, where President Roosevelt had just announced the Tennessee Valley Authority with powers to revitalize the wrecked agricultural economy and give a Fair Deal to the workers. Why couldn't the French government do something idealistic and noble like that?

'Just let them try,' grunted Marc when he heard reports of the unrest. 'Any government that tried Roosevelt's ideas would be out on its ear in minutes.'

Yet nothing could really depress Nora's spirits. She spent time arguing, dictating letters, serving on committees, discussing, negotiating, all in a rising atmosphere of political anxiety. But she was happy. She was carrying Edmond's child. No woman could feel anything but blessed who had that to sustain her.

At last she heard from him, a cable from Dakar. He had settled the problem at Jimbando, would board ship the following day, sent his love, and ended by suggesting she book the same hotel room as a welcome home.

She coloured up as she read it. She passed it to Marc, who perused it and innocently said, 'What hotel room is that?'

'Never mind,' she replied with a stifled laugh.

And Marc, looking up at her from the cable, grinned inwardly.

She sent a reply assuring him that she would book the hotel room. She kept an anxious eye on the shipping news, to make sure the *Aigle*

Français kept to its timetable. Every few days there it was—passing the Cape Verde Islands, the Canaries, docking at Lisbon.

She expected a long-distance telephone call from Edmond when he reached Lisbon. But it didn't come. Worried, she rang the shipping line. 'Yes, Madame, the *Aigle* touched Lisbon according to schedule. No, no trouble of any kind. A passenger called Edmond du Ceddres? One moment, Madame.'

After something more than one moment, the clerk came back on the line. 'Monsieur du Ceddres left the ship at Lisbon, Madame.'

'Left the ship?' At first she was astonished, but then she understood. He was going to come home by train, arrive a few days earlier than she expected, take her by surprise!

'Thank you,' she said in delight to the clerk, and hung up. At once she asked the operator to connect her with the hotel Maire de la Roche at Cherbourg. 'That room I reserved for the 2nd June,' she said. 'Will you please bring that forward?'

'To what date, Madame?' enquired the receptionist politely.

'To . . . I don't know . . . from tomorrow, please.'

'Tomorrow, certainly. Until when, Madame?'

'Until I get there.'

'Which will be when, Madame?'

313

'I'm not sure. Just keep the room in my name—is that understood?'

'Very well, Madame,' said the receptionist, not understanding in the least and privately quite convinced the client was mad.

The *Aigle Français* had reached Lisbon yesterday. Allowing Edmond a night in Lisbon to recover his land legs, he would be on the train today. Lisbon to Paris was—what? Some eight hundred miles. He would take the express train, via Madrid and Toulouse. He would reach Paris probably by Thursday.

She was so excited at the thought that she felt really giddy—she had to lean forward to let the blood come back to her head. Steady, steady— she mustn't get into a state, it was bad for the baby. But, oh, he would be here soon, and it was almost too much to bear.

She got out her prettiest dress, a little anxious in case it was too tight for her now. Soon her boyish figure would be gone. But for the moment all was well, the grey-blue crêpe slid over her hips and stomach, she tied the white bow at the neck, stood back, surveyed herself. Not bad for an expectant mother . . . But she must have her hair done, the new short waved style would be just right for the dress. And she must cancel all her appointments for Thursday.

She went up to Paris in a glow of happy excitement. The city always looked its best in May, but as she stepped out of the railway station on that last beautiful week of May weather she thought it a dream city—all colour and gaiety and light.

At the apartment there were no flowers in the vases. She felt it almost as a personal affront. She sent out at once for roses and lilies from Grasse, anemones from Normandy, vast bundles of greenery from the banks of the Seine, and supervised while the housekeeper and the maid did arrangements for every room. The place must be full of welcome when Edmond came.

She scarcely slept that night, she was so excited. Next day she had her hairdressing appointment, and went also to see Coco Chanel, about her wedding dress.

'Ah,' said the little dress designer, surveying her at arm's length. 'A new lover, eh?'

'No, Coco darling, the old one is coming back. I want to be sure the dress is going to be ready. We settled on June 10th before he left but he'll probably be back on Thursday and there seems no reason to wait another week . . .'

'And the wedding guests? Can you let them know in time? I don't want to waste this dress on a congregation of ten.'

'We'll manage. I told you it was going to be a small affair.'

'La, la,' said Madame Chanel, watching as the *vendeuse* slipped the dress over Nora's head. 'You've put on weight.'

'No I haven't, Coco.'

'No? Well, it looks a little snug to me.'

Nora emerged from the silk folds to find the dressmaker studying her with shrewd dark eyes. She felt herself colouring up.

'Aha,' murmured Chanel.

Nora glanced at the assistant. Chanel nodded to her to leave the fitting room.

'Please don't tell, Coco.'

'No one else knows?'

'No, and I want Edmond to be the first I tell. Please, Coco.'

'Oh, of course, understood. I wish you well, my dear. It's wonderful to see you so happy. When I think of the poor little subdued moth I used to know . . .' She sighed. 'Eh, well, he's a lucky man.'

'Oh, no, Coco, I'm the lucky one. To think I once said no to him . . .! But I was only seventeen at the time.'

'Well, I'll let out the seams of the dress just a fraction, so that no one will notice.' She laughed. 'But don't delay longer than the 10th June otherwise I'll have to make the dress a size larger. I'll have it delivered to your apartment the day after tomorrow, so that you'll be ready for whatever day you choose.'

Nora slept well that night, catching up on the sleep she'd lost. On Wednesday she went to the office in the Rue Lelong, where by arrangement she met Marc to brief him on the various things she was going to commit to his care while she was in Cherbourg.

'You're sure he's going to turn up tomorrow?' Marc ventured.

'Oh, absolutely.'

'I think he should have telephoned through from Lisbon. What's the point of not telling you?'

'But then it wouldn't have been a surprise.'

'I'm getting too old to like surprises,' he complained. Nora smiled to herself, thinking that the surprise had not been intended for Cousin Marc. 'Besides,' he went on, 'what if he's missed any of his connections?'

'Not he,' she said stoutly.

Everything was ready next day. She had the cook prepare tempting little snacks to go with the celebratory champagne—Tramont Baptiste 1911, one of the very finest vintages. She put on the pretty dress, studied the new hairstyle, was on the whole pleased with herself though her verdict, as always, was that she would never win any beauty prizes.

It was of course useless to expect Edmond in the early morning. He would want to go to his bachelor flat to shave and change and make himself presentable. But if he had been on the train arriving at about nine he would be with her by eleven at the latest.

At a quarter to eleven she found herself drifting into the kitchen to make sure the champagne was on ice. 'Of course, Madame,' Cook said in an offended tone. 'And the canapés . . . they're in the larder.'

Nora drifted out again.

By noon she was growing impatient. What was he doing? Even if he stopped *en route* to buy flowers, he ought to have been here by now.

Unless, of course, he was on the southern express which would arrive about midday.

Well then, he would be here by about two. She rang for the maid, to say with her compliments to Cook that the champagne should be removed from the ice bucket for half an hour otherwise it would be too cold for perfection. And also that the canapés would probably not be required now, and could preparations be started for the luncheon she had suggested?

Cook, having been given this message; smiled and grumbled. 'Does she think I don't remember her instructions? Prepared for every eventuality, we are. Eh, well, I was young once myself, I know what it's like to wait for a sweetheart.'

She had prepared the soup overnight. She now began on the veal Marengo. She was perfectly certain that almost none of this food would be eaten because the two young people would be too busy kissing and talking. But then you never knew—a man who'd been abroad for two months would perhaps want a good sample of French cooking when he got home.

Two hours later the food was consigned to the rubbish bin. 'Monsieur hasn't arrived?'

murmured Cook, though she knew perfectly well Lucie hadn't answered a summons to the door.

'He's been delayed, I suppose. Madame is telephoning the railway information office.'

The information office said there was yet another international express train today arriving at nine-thirty.

'Thank you,' Nora said, and went to her bedroom. It was time to change into an afternoon dress. As she put it on she felt a shiver of apprehension. What if she had got it all wrong? What if he wasn't coming to 'surprise' her today?

Nonsense. He had left the ship at Lisbon. It could only have been in order to take the overland route back to Paris. Allowing him leeway for this and that, he ought to be here by this evening. He would send a message if anything unforeseen had held him up.

She had eaten nothing all day. Cook sent in a tray with soup and a sandwich à l'Anglaise, but she could take nothing. She drank coffee, however, and was revived by the caffeine so that her depression lifted. He would be here soon. He'd been on one of the earlier trains, had gone first to report at the headquarters of his mining group. Of course, how silly she was, that was what he had done.

Although it seemed strange . . . If she had been coming home after a parting of eight weeks, she would have been at the door as soon as a taxi could bring her from the station.

Marc came home at seven, enquiring softly in the hall if Monsieur du Ceddres was still here.

'He hasn't come yet, M'sieu,' Lucie said, taking his hat and coat.

Marc frowned. 'But . . .'

Lucie nodded towards the drawing-room. 'Madame is still waiting.'

Marc was disconcerted. He'd let Nora's certainty carry him along to the extent that he had expected to find them sitting hand in hand on the sofa. But as he quickly reviewed the situation he could see now that there had never been any real reason to predict that Edmond would arrive by the southern express. For all they knew, he had taken a detour to his home in the Southern Alps. Or he had hired a car and was driving back—which would certainly be slower than the express.

He nerved himself to face his young cousin. She looked up as he came in, but not with expectation because she knew that if he had been Edmond, Lucie would have shown him in with a beaming face.

'Well, dear . . . It seems you were a little too optimistic in your ideas . . .'

'No, no,' she said, springing up from her chair. 'He'll be here. There's another train tonight. I rang the station.'

'But Nora . . .'

'He's coming,' she said. 'I feel it.'

It was so unlike her to claim fey intuitions that he was startled. He looked at her with new intentness. She was strung up, her strange grey-brown eyes alight with an eagerness that worried him.

'Darling,' he said soothingly, 'don't build on it. We don't really know—'

'*I* know. I know he's coming.'

'Of course he is. But not perhaps tonight.'

'Yes, he'll be here.'

He saw it was useless to argue further. Instead he contented himself with pouring drinks for both of them. Brandy, it was a time when brandy was called for. But Nora didn't even sip hers, simply sat with it in her hand.

At his reminder, she went to change for dinner. They sat down to eat at eight. Despite his gentle urging, she ate none of the excellent sole or rosemaried lamb. When they left the dining-room at nine, she went to the window of the drawing-room to look down into the street.

The June evening was still bright with lingering sunlight. Cars came and went below, taxis, an occasional delivery boy on a tricycle. But no taxi drew up outside the big entrance door.

At midnight Marc, exhausted, said he thought they ought to go to bed. 'No, I'll wait up. He'll be here soon.'

'Nora, my dear, he won't come now. If your idea of giving you a surprise is right, he wouldn't come barging in in the middle of the night. He'd wait till morning.'

'No, he'll come, I'm sure of it.'

'I think you should go to bed,' he said, using the tone he'd used when she was a child and was being given instructions.

She looked up at him. There were rings of darkness under her eyes. 'I'll wait.'

He gave up. At about two in the morning, roused by some sound, he sat up in bed thinking. 'He's here!' He got up, pulled on a dressing-gown, went to listen at his door. But nothing else happened, no ring at the doorbell, no sleepy maid hurrying down the hall.

Quietly he left his room. The light was still on in the drawing-room. He opened the door with caution, put his head in.

Nora had fallen asleep in her armchair. Trying to get comfortable in a half wakeful state, she had hit with her arm, and toppled over, a lamp on the table next the chair. It was this sound which had wakened Marc.

He went in, intending to rouse her and get her to bed. But when he looked down at that sleeping face, he drew back his hand. He went to his own room, fetched a blanket, and draped it over her without waking her. As he went out again, he switched off the lights.

My poor little girl, he thought, his heart aching for her.

He rose as usual. Nora didn't appear at breakfast. The maid said she was in the bath. He had to leave for an early business appointment, so he left a message: Ring me if there's any news. He didn't want to come home again expecting a happy couple and finding only a desperately lonely girl.

Nora steeled herself for the day. She selected a frock and dressed with the same care, she even made herself eat something, because she knew it would be bad for the baby if she didn't. But it was no good, she was sick almost immediately afterwards.

As the hours progressed a haze seemed to fall over her. Everything seemed to be happening at a distance, through glasses which didn't quite focus. Edmond didn't come. There was no message. She didn't need to ring the information office, she knew the train times, and each time it seemed reasonable to expect him she went to the window to watch for his taxi. But the day passed, by the afternoon he still had not come.

She rang his apartment. It was in a block over by the Bois, with service available for single gentlemen and a riding stables nearby. The porter said Monsieur du Ceddres had not returned from abroad and was not expected yet.

'Have you a date when he is due to arrive?'

'As far as I recall, Madame, Monsieur is on one of the French-Africa steamers, I believe due on June 6th.'

'But he left—' She'd been about to say, he left the ship at Lisbon. But it was not the porter's business. 'Thank you,' she said.

She rang the shipping office again. Would they

check that Monsieur du Ceddres was a passenger on board the *Aigle Français* due at Cherbourg on the 6th June?

'Ah, we had a previous enquiry about Monsieur du Ceddres,' replied the obliging clerk. 'He left the ship at Lisbon.'

'Are you *sure?*'

'One moment, Madame, I'll check.' After a pause he came back. 'Yes, absolutely, Madame, Monsieur du Ceddres decided to leave the ship rather unexpectedly. Four other passengers disembarked but they had only booked to Lisbon. The purser's list is up to date on all points.'

Where would he be? Where would he have gone, if not home to Paris, home to Nora?

To his home near Digne, perhaps.

She asked the operator to find the number and put her through. After a long delay the phone rang, and the operator said, 'I have your number in Digne, Madame. You're through.'

A surprised voice on the other end said, 'Yes?'

'Who am I speaking to?'

'Er . . . This is Pierre Crispon, the caretaker. Can I do anything for you, Madame?'

'Is Monsieur du Ceddres there?'

'Monsieur du Ceddres?' The caretaker was clearly astounded. 'Good gracious no, Madame, the house is closed up, has been for months.'

'Do you expect him?'

'Not at all, Madame. I don't know if you're aware—Monsieur du Ceddres is abroad—'

'But he's on his way back—'

'Oh, yes, Madame, I believe so, but he's going straight to Paris. Monsieur is to be married, you know.'

'I . . . Yes . . . Thank you.' She had a second thought before she disconnected. 'If Monsieur du Ceddres gets in touch with you, will you let me know?' She gave her Paris number. She could hear the man repeating it as he carefully wrote it down. 'You won't forget to let me know?'

'Of course not, Madame. But Monsieur isn't coming here at all—we've no instructions to open up the house.'

There was only one other place to try. She rang the office of the Compagnie des Mines Explorateurs and asked for Edmond's secretary. A creaky male voice replied.

'This is Madame Tramont,' she said. 'Have you had any word from Monsieur du Ceddres?'

'Oh yes, Madame—'

'You have?' Oh, thank God!

'Yes, a very good report on the mine at Jimbando, sent via the wireless telegraph at Dakar, and then a much fuller document sent by mail from Lisbon. The managing director—'

'You've received a package from Lisbon?'

'Yes, Madame. The *Aigle Français* touches Lisbon on her way home—'

'Is there a note with the report? Any message about his intentions?'

She could hear the perplexity in the secretary's

voice. 'There was no need for any note, Madame. His intentions were always known to us—we expect him on the *Aigle* on the 6th—'

'But he left the ship at Lisbon!'

A pause. 'Did he? Well . . . Even so, there would be no reason to let us know. He isn't expected in the office, you know, because of . . . because of his marriage . . . Madame, I don't quite understand. Are you sure Monsieur du Ceddres landed at Lisbon?'

'Yes.'

'He got in touch with you? You have some message for us?'

'No. I am asking *you* whether Monsieur du Ceddres has been in touch.'

'I just explained . . . we got his report . . . From Lisbon, yes, but I assumed he had put it in the post during a few hours ashore . . . You say he didn't re-embark?'

'No. I took it for granted he was coming home by rail.'

'By rail. Yes, that seems logical. But if the *Aigle* touched Lisbon according to schedule, Monsieur du Ceddres ought to be here if he came by train.'

'I thought so. But I've had no word. I wondered if you . . . if he had telephoned . . .'

'No, Madame. Not a word. I'm at a loss.'

She could think of no one else to ask. She waited all that day, hoping for a telegram, a letter, a telephone call. Nothing came.

326

And the next day was the same. Marc, by this time terribly worried not only for Nora but for Edmond, went through the same routine of enquiry that she had tried. But the answers were always the same. Edmond had not been in touch with anyone.

The *Aigle Français* docked at Cherbourg. Marc went to meet the ship. He spoke in person to the purser. 'But I assure you, sir—Monsieur du Ceddres paid his bar bill and so forth, had his luggage taken ashore, and left us at Lisbon.'

'But why? Did he explain why?'

'No, sir,' said the purser, looking as if he thought it odd that passengers had to explain their actions.

'How did he seem?'

'I beg your pardon?'

'Did he seem well? Did he seem worried? Anything you remember about his manner?'

'Nothing, sir. In fact, he seemed very quiet and thoughtful, if anything. Perfectly normal, if that's what you mean.'

It was inexplicable.

Nora heard his report with a calmness that frightened him more than hysterics. 'There's an explanation,' she said. 'He'll tell us when he comes.'

'But Nora—'

'He has a reason for what he's done. I know him, Marc.'

'But Nora, why hasn't he written, or tele-phoned—'

'I don't know. But it'll be all right. We're to be married on the 10th. He'll be here by then.'

'My dear, I don't think—'

'He'll be here.'

He sent for their Paris doctor, a young man with a shrewd brain. Nora refused his help. 'There's nothing wrong with me, thanks.'

'You're under a strain, Madame,' he said, eyeing her and making a guess of his own. 'Your cousin told me—'

'Everything will be all right when my fiancé arrives.'

'If you would just let me prescribe a seda-tive—'

'No thank you. I'm perfectly all right.'

Anyone could see she wasn't all right. And she herself was becoming alarmed by her own physical state. She felt weak and shaky. Her head swam. She couldn't eat. If she forced herself to swallow something, she was sick. If she lay down to rest, her mind was full of dreadful images. If she tried to sleep, her dreams were a miasma of shapes and sounds, with Edmond's face and voice drifting among them.

On the morning of the 10th June she woke from a restless, unhealing sleep. She dragged herself out of bed. It was too early yet for the maid to bring her coffee. She stood uncertain in the middle of the room, shivering despite the warm June weather.

She went to the wardrobe, slid open the door, and saw the wedding dress hanging in its wrappings of muslin. She took it down from its hanger, unpinned the muslin, laid the dress across her bed.

It was of champagne-coloured silk crêpe, mid-calf length as Chanel was now designing. It had a fluted hem, a soft edge to the neck. With it she was to wear a little hat of the same material, with a gardenia tucked in among the champagne-coloured veiling.

For a long moment she stood staring down at it. Then her knees gave way. She fell to the floor beside the bed, her upper body across the dress, her hands crumpling the soft folds. Her desperate, silent tears fell on it.

That was how the maid found her when she brought in her coffee.

FIFTEEN

Edmond Renaud du Ceddres seemed to have vanished from the face of the earth.

The odd thing was, no one but the Tramonts seemed particularly perturbed. His business colleagues hadn't expected to see him in person until the next board meeting, the household staff in the Basses Alpes had no instructions to open

329

the house, and the porter and valet at the apartment block were sure Monsieur du Ceddres would arrive when he was ready.

Marc took the necessary steps to prevent vulgar gossip. The few guests invited to the wedding were quite ready to accept there had been yet another delay due to business problems. The newspapers had no reason to question his request that the wedding announcement should be held over for a while.

Only to that old family friend, Elvire Hermilot, did Marc voice his fears. 'Something must have happened to the boy,' he said. 'He would be here, or he would have sent a message . . .'

'Perhaps you should go to the police?'

He sighed. 'Don't tell Nora, but I tried that. They say that as there has been no crime committed, they have no reason to interfere.'

'But didn't you explain that he was coming home to be married?'

'Exactly. Until that moment the inspector was looking vaguely concerned, but that was the point at which he gave me a knowing smile, Elvi. He said bridegrooms are always disappearing, and they generally turn up in their own good time.'

'But that's nonsense—'

'Apparently not. They say unbalanced or unwilling bridegrooms are high on the list of missing persons.'

'Edmond isn't unbalanced or unwilling!'

'You know that and I know that, but I couldn't convince the police. And the way they reacted . . . Well, I wouldn't want Nora to hear of it.'

'I don't like the thought of her alone in that Paris apartment, Marc.' The two of them were in the handsome drawing-room at Calmady, trying to think of some other avenue to explore.

'She's not alone, the servants—'

'That's not the same. Would she like it if I went there to be with her?'

'No, Elvi dear, she wouldn't. She's so certain he's going to walk in any minute that she regards anyone else as an intrusion.'

'How is she?'

'Getting thinner every day and looking like a ghost. In a way, if I knew and could convince her that Edmond had changed his mind about marrying her—if there were any certainty, even of the worst kind—'

'Marc!' Mademoiselle Hemrilot stared at him through her fashionable spectacles. 'You're not thinking he's . . . he's dead?'

'I don't know. I don't know. I got a wine-making acquaintance of mine in Lisbon to talk to the police. They would know, of course, if a man holding a French passport had stayed in any of the hotels.'

'And?'

'Nothing. Nor was there any report of an accident or a sudden illness that fitted Edmond. He seems to have left the *Aigle* and disappeared, utterly disappeared.'

The butler came to announce lunch. They sat down to it. Mademoiselle Hermilot was about to finish her consommé when suddenly she laid aside her spoon.

'Marc . . . Are the marriage settlements still being discussed?'

'Yes, of course.'

'You're in touch with his lawyers?'

'We-ell . . . Actually I haven't heard from Debusson in a couple of weeks. But yes . . . everything's still going forward.'

'I wonder . . . shouldn't you speak to them?'

He sat back in his chair. He frowned. 'I suppose . . . Why not?' He got up, throwing down his napkin. 'Forgive me if I do it at once, Elvi.'

'Certainly.'

Monsieur Debusson was of course at lunch. His secretary promised that when he came in he should be given the message to telephone Monsieur Auduron-Tramont urgently.

Marc and Elvi had finished lunch and were in his study looking at the correspondence with the law firm when the telephone rang.

'Ah, Monsieur Debusson. Thank you for returning my call. You and I haven't been in touch for some time, I see by looking at the papers. Three weeks since you sent me a draft—' He broke off. 'Yes. No, nothing. We haven't heard from him. No.' He raised his eyebrows at Mademoiselle Hermilot. 'Can you tell me what it's about?'

Elvi rose and came to his side, trying to hear what was being said on the other end. The voice came to her faintly. '—Something to convey to you that cannot really be dealt with over the telephone.'

'You want me to come and see you?'

'If you would be so good.'

'When?'

'Whenever it suits you, Monsieur Auduron-Tramont.'

'Tomorrow?'

'Very well. At what time?'

'Eleven o'clock.'

'That will suit. Thank you, Monsieur.'

'Thank you, Monsieur Debusson.'

As he was replacing the receiver Elvi cried, 'He knows something!'

'Yes, I think so . . .'

'Telephone Nora and—'

'No.'

'But Marc—'

'No. I feel it in my bones. It isn't good news.'

That feeling stayed with him next morning as he set out for Paris. Mademoiselle Hermilot went with him, to visit Nora. It was a pretext. They both felt someone should be with her when Marc returned from the lawyers, although neither could say why.

Monsieur Debusson's secretary was on the alert for Marc when he arrived promptly at eleven. He was shown straight in. They shook hands.

'Monsieur, please take a seat.'

'Thank you.'

'You are here over the marriage settlement between Madame Tramont and Monsieur du Ceddres.'

'Yes.'

The other man coughed, shielding his face for a moment. It seemed to Marc he was very embarrassed. His face under its silver hair was flushed, his eyes would not quite meet Marc's.

'I have to tell you, Monsieur, that the matter is not to be taken any further.'

Marc sat staring at him.

'You understand what I am saying? There are to be no further discussions of the marriage settlement. There will be no marriage.'

Marc was so dumbfounded that he actually stammered. 'What d.did you s.say?'

'Everything is to be broken off.'

'You—you've had instructions? From Edmond —Monsieur du Ceddres?'

'That is so.'

'Instructions to break of the discussions?'

'Yes, Monsieur.'

'He told you in so many words that the wedding was off?'

'Yes, Monsieur.'

'When was this?'

'Two weeks ago.'

'Two *weeks* ago? But why didn't you get in touch?'

'I had no such instructions.'

'Good God, man,' cried Marc, leaping up and leaning over him as if he would pull him out of his leather chair, 'you can't just sit there and say you had no instructions, as if it didn't matter!'

'Sir! Sir!' Debusson shrank back. 'Monsieur Auduron Tramont, please be calm!'

'Calm! I'll knock your head off—'

'I understand your feelings, sir, but please understand *my* duty is to my client—'

Marc took his hands off the desk, straightened, and drew one or two steadying breaths. 'I'm sorry,' he said, 'but I can't understand how you could take such orders.'

'I was most unwilling, Monsieur, I assure you. Please sit down again.'

When he had done so, Debusson resumed. 'I received a letter stating Monsieur du Ceddres' intentions. It was undoubtedly his handwriting—'

'You didn't accept such a thing without verifying—'

'No, no, of course not. I replied at once, saying I could hardly believe what I had read and asking for verification. But he was adamant. He told me in a tone I had never heard from him before that I was to do as I was told.'

'You mean he sat there in this very office—perhaps in this very chair—and told you to break my cousin's heart, and you *let* him?'

'He didn't come in person. He telephoned. I said I wished to see him and he said he had no intentions of coming. I told him I could not in conscience accept such instructions and he replied that he could soon find a lawyer who would do as he was told.' A quaver came into Debusson's voice. 'I have known Edmond du Ceddres since he was a boy, and I have never known him speak so.'

'You should have told him to go to the devil!'

'Monsieur, I have been handling the affairs of the du Ceddres since his father's time. And it seemed to me . . . Edmond was so unlike himself. I felt this wasn't the moment to desert him. So I agreed to act. He then replied very curtly that he wasn't asking me to act—quite the reverse. I was to wait until your law firm contacted me and then simply inform them that he had withdrawn.'

'Without any explanation?'

'Exactly.' Debusson sighed deeply. 'I said that you would be totally justified in bringing a suit for damages. He laughed at that—'

'Laughed?'

'With no amusement. He said that if I thought the Tramonts would bring a suit, I didn't know them. But if they did, I had his authority to settle for any sum they cared to ask for.'

'This is unspeakable!'

'Yes,' Debusson said, his voice sad. 'I told him so. I told him he was behaving in a very ungentlemanly way but he simply put the phone down.'

A little silence fell. 'Very well,' said Marc. 'Give me his whereabouts. I'll see the scoundrel and break his neck.'

The older man shook his head. 'I am expressly forbidden to give you his address.'

'What?'

'He said he couldn't foresee anything but trouble in having the Tramonts in touch with him. He wants it clearly understood that he wishes to have nothing to do . . . nothing to do with the Tramonts.'

Marc stared at him, speechless.

'I don't pretend to understand him, Monsieur. I may say I have been dreading this interview. Of course I expected your law firm to be the first to query the delay. I thought I would be telling all this to Messrs Tebloc et Lellenier. I don't know whether that would have been better or worse.'

There was a pause. 'But it's . . . it's insane,' Marc said at length. 'It's almost as if he's . . . punishing Nora. Punishing her? For what?'

'I don't see it that way, sir. It seemed to me he was in the grip of some obsession—'

'You mean he was out of his mind?'

'I can only tell you he was quite unlike himself.

But I don't mean by this that he was hysterical or strange. He was totally in command of himself. He knew what he wanted and he was determined to have it. I asked him, before the conversation ended, what he thought his friends would say to this behaviour, what the world would say. He said it didn't bother him in the slightest.' He ran a hand through his immaculate silvery hair. 'I was at a loss. But my respect for his father's memory forbade me to wash my hands of him. I can only hope that by and by he'll come to his senses.'

'Oh yes,' Marc said bitterly, 'by and by he'll wake up to the enormity of what he's done. By which time my little cousin will have thrown herself in the Seine.' He hesitated. 'Look here, Debusson, you've got to tell me where I can find him.'

'No, Monsieur, I'm sorry.'

'I've *got* to talk to him.'

'What good would that do? You wish to compel him to go on with the marriage? What basis is that for a happy life? For some reason he wants to escape from his bargain—a man compelled against his will doesn't make a good husband.'

'But Nora has done nothing, absolutely nothing, to deserve this! If he's under some misapprehension—been told some lie against her—'

'I asked him what he had against the young

lady, Monsieur Auduron-Tramont. He said it was nothing to do with her.'

'Don't be ridiculous—nothing to do with her!'

'He meant, his reason had nothing to do with her. He said he had changed his mind, that's all.'

'Oh, dear God in heaven!' Marc spent a moment grappling with it. Then he looked at the other man. 'Monsieur Debusson, you've spent your whole life dealing with people. What's your conclusion?'

'I have to tell you that in the two weeks since I spoke to Monsieur du Ceddres I have been quite unable to make any sense of it. But I do assure you, the boy means what he says. You must accept that.'

When Marc got home to the apartment he was met in the hall by Elvi Hermilot. She looked at him anxiously. 'What did you learn?'

'Nothing good. I must tell the news to Nora first. How is she?'

'She hardly seems to notice I'm here. She looked up when she heard your taxi below but lost interest again when I said you had got out.'

'I must speak to her at once. Elvi, the number of our doctor is in the notebook by the telephone. Please ring him, ask him to come.'

She studied him for a moment, then went to the library without further instruction.

When he came into the drawing-room Nora was sitting in an armchair with a book in her hands. She produced a shadow of her usual smile. 'I didn't know you were coming to town today?'

'I came with Elvi, I dropped her off here before I went on to Monsieur Debusson.'

The name caught her attention. 'Debusson?'

'Yes.'

She stiffened. 'There is news?'

'Yes.'

Her whole face came alive. 'Oh, thank God! Thank God!'

'Wait, Nora—'

She leapt up. The brightness wavered. 'There's something wrong? Oh Marc—he's not—not—'

'So far as I know he's alive and well, Nora. But he has been in touch with his lawyers.'

'Why with them? I don't understand! Why hasn't he been in touch with me?'

'Sit down again, Nora. I have bad news.'

Pale as ivory after the rush of colour to her cheeks, she obeyed. He sat on the low table in front of the armchair, took her hands.

'Edmond has called the marriage off.'

She said nothing.

'Do you understand, my dear? There is to be no wedding.'

'No,' she said, averting her head.

'His lawyer has been told to cancel the negotiations for the settlements. Edmond has withdrawn.'

'Don't be silly.'

'Nora, I mean it. It's all off.'

'No, you've got it all wrong. 'She turned to look at him, hard-eyed and earnest. 'You men—you get hold of the wrong end of the stick—'

'His lawyer had it in writing, Nora. It's true.'

'No, it's a lie!' Suddenly her voice soared. 'Why are you telling me silly lies? Edmond would never do such a thing!'

'Nora, Nora—'

She wrenched her hands away and jumped up. 'You must be mad to come to me with a story like this! Not a word of it is true! Edmond loves me. If he's alive and in this world, he'll come to me and we'll be married.'

'No, dearest. It's not so.'

She flung herself at him in fury. Her fists beat at him. 'How dare you say such things! I hate you! You're trying to prevent me from marrying Edmond—but nothing could stop us—you don't know what we mean to each other—'

He captured the flailing fists, pulled her close, held her hard against his shoulder. The wild words died away. She was wracked with dry sobs. When at last she seemed calmer he let her go. She stepped back a pace or two. He was surprised to see there were no tears. Her eyes were clear and alert as she searched his face.

'It's true?'

He nodded. He took her elbow, put her back into her chair. He knelt beside her. 'Nora, Monsieur Debusson hated every moment of our conversation, but I've no doubt he was telling the absolute truth. Edmond wrote to him cancelling everything. Debusson thought it was a mistake so replied asking for an explanation. Edmond phoned him. There was no mistake.'

After a moment she said, 'Where is he?'

'I don't know. Monsieur Debusson wouldn't say.'

'But he's got to tell me—'

'No, dear. Edmond has forbidden it.'

'Forbidden?'

'He wants no contact with us.'

'No. That can't be right.'

'You must accept it, Nora. He doesn't want to see you.'

'I refuse to accept it! I . . ., I refuse . . .' Her voice trailed off. She sat staring into the emptiness of her life. Then she said, 'No, Marc, I won't accept it.'

'There's nothing else you can do.'

Yes there is, she cried within herself. I have to do something. I have to think of my baby.

'I want to see Monsieur Debusson.'

'Good God, no!'

'I must see him, Marc.'

'You'll only be hurt—'

'Shall I?' she countered, with a laugh that seemed to come from some bitter wound in her breast. 'Dear me, how terrible that would be!'

'Nora—'

'I refuse to believe any of this unless I hear it

342

from Edmond himself. I want to see Debusson, to learn where I can find Edmond.'

'He won't tell you, Nora,' Marc said, shaking his head. He knew more about the confidentiality between lawyer and client than she.

'He'll tell me. Take me to see him.'

'Nora, I don't think—'

'If you won't go with me, I'll go alone.'

He was astonished at her hardihood. He'd expected a collapse, emotional and physical. Instead there was this strange, steely determination. He got to his feet, stiffly, thinking that if he were younger he could deal with this better. 'Let me ring him. I'll make an appointment—'

'An appointment?' she flashed. 'Are we going to discuss my investments? *Tell* him I am coming to see him.'

With a deep unwillingness he went to the study. Mademoiselle Hermilot was there, pacing up and down. 'I haven't been able to contact your doctor, he's out on a call—'

'It doesn't matter, Elvi. I don't think we need him. To my astonishment Nora isn't prostrated by my news.'

'What on God's earth is it? You look as if the world is coming to an end.'

He told her briefly, as he waited for the operator to connect him with the lawyer's office. Monsieur Debusson, of course, had gone to lunch, would be back at two. He told the receptionist that he and Madame Tramont would be

343

there at that hour. 'I'm afraid Monsieur Debusson has an appointment then,' she said.

'Tell him we're coming. And cancel the other appointment.'

'Oh, I couldn't do that—'

'Do it, girl!' Marc said, and rang off.

Nora accepted the information with a slight nod of the head. She went to her room to change into a street dress. She felt perfectly calm. Her greatest fear—that Edmond was dead—had been set at rest. As to Marc's news, she would soon put it all in order. She had only to see Edmond and everything would be all right.

A meal was served but no one ate much. Nora didn't even see what was set before her. She watched the clock, for the moment when they could set out to the lawyer's.

They were shown in at once. Debusson came to greet her, with a kindness that almost unnerved her. She wanted to be cold and businesslike.

'My cousin has told me of his interview with you. I want you to say it all again to me.'

'Madame!'

'You see, I'm sure there's a mistake somewhere. You must have misunderstood—'

'Madame, I have it in writing—'

'Yes, but he meant only a delay. Some other date is to be—'

'No, Madame, the marriage is entirely out of the question.'

'Tell me what he said to you on the telephone.'
She was very controlled. It was as if she was held together by wires as strong as those on aeroplane wings.

Debusson cast a glance of agony at Marc. He was scarlet with distress and embarrassment. Nevertheless he went through what he had been told, softening it as much as he could. Nora listened, feeling herself wither a little more at every word.

'You see, Madame—there can be no mistake.'

She said nothing.

'Come, Nora, let's go,' Marc said, half rising.

'No. Wait. Give me Edmond's address, Monsieur Debusson. I must see him myself.'

The old lawyer shook his head. 'I'm afraid that's impossible.'

'But I *must* see him.'

'That is exactly what Monsieur du Ceddres wishes to avoid.'

'The man's a coward!' Marc snarled.

'I agree with you. Nevertheless, those are his wishes and I must carry them out.'

'How can you abet him—!'

'Monsieur, there is nothing illegal in being a coward,' Debusson said in a sad voice. 'If Monsieur du Ceddres wished me to do anything outside the law I should of course utterly refuse. But he is perfectly within his rights to withdraw from a mistaken marriage and to refuse to see the fiancée—'

Nora heard the little argument going on as if from a far distance. She pulled herself together. 'You have an address at which he can be reached?'

'Yes.'

Marc gave the other man a hard look. Had Debusson been younger, he might have suggested he call for the du Ceddres papers, go out of the room on some pretext, and leave Marc to find what they needed in the files. But Debusson was too old and set in his ways to fall in with such a notion.

'Give me the address, Monsieur Debusson,' said Nora.

'I am desolate, Madame, but I absolutely cannot.'

'You don't understand!' Her voice rose, against her will. She didn't want to sound emotional, hysterical. 'I must speak to him. It's essential. There's something I must tell him.'

'Tell it to me, Madame. I will write him—'

'It's something I can say only to Edmond. But it's some thing he *must* hear.'

Debusson shook his head.

'At least you could write to him and beg him to see me,' she said. 'You could do that.'

'It would be useless, Madame. I wish you would under stand that it would be less painful to yourself if you—'

She unpinned a little silver brooch Marc had often seen her wear these days, a tiny thing in the shape of a heart. It was on the collar of her dark blue linen dress. She laid it on the leather blotter in front of Debusson.

'Send that in the letter,' she said. 'Say to him that I'm not simply being importunate. There is a reason I must speak to him. Tell him that if he ever meant anything when he gave me that brooch, he must believe I need to speak to him—to him, and to him alone.'

Debusson watched her face, moved beyond words by her earnestness. He took the tiny brooch between thumb and forefinger, drew it towards him, nodding.

'You'll write today?'

'Immediately.'

'When . . . when will he receive it?'

He understood she was trying to find out whether Edmond was in the city. He sighed. 'Not today, nor tomorrow—next day perhaps.'

'He's a long way off, then?'

He made no reply. She looked at him, her strange eyes dark with anxiety. 'Tell him it . . . it's a matter of life and death.'

'Madame . . .'

'Tell him.'

'Very well.'

In the taxi going home she sat with Marc's arm about her shoulder. She was scarcely aware of his presence. All her consciousness was projected forward, to that moment a few days distant when Monsieur Debusson would let her know she could meet Edmond, tell him the important news that would change everything.

Friday came, then Saturday, and Sunday on which of course nothing could happen because the lawyer's office was closed. Monday, the letter might have reached Edmond. He might actually be sitting down to write a reply. Nora's heart beat heavily every time she thought of that. She couldn't believe he would fail to respond. He *must* respond—or her life was meaningless.

The maid came into the drawing-room where she was sitting alone. Elvi Hermilot, who had at Marc's invitation stayed on for a few days, had gone out for what she called a constitutional. Marc was at the Rue Lelong.

'A telephone call for you, Madame.'

'Take a message, Lucie. I don't want to—'

'Madame—it's Monsieur du Ceddres.'

A red haze rose in front of her eyes. Her head swam. She got up. Then she thought of the telephones in the apartment—one in the hall, too public. One in the study. 'I'll take it in the study, Lucie,' she said in a voice scarcely above a whisper.

She picked up the receiver. She heard Lucie replace the one in the hall. 'Hello?' she said huskily.

'Nora? This is Edmond.'

'Yes.'

How absurd. How pitiful. She could think of nothing to say. Her mind had gone completely blank, like a cinema screen when the projector is turned off.

Edmond said, 'I got your message. A matter of life and death, you said.'

'Yes.'

'What does that mean?'

'Edmond, where are you? Edmond!'

'What is it that's so important?'

'Don't. Edmond, don't speak to me like that—'

His voice was flat, distant. It was almost as if he were a million miles away, on some other planet.

She heard him draw a long breath. 'If you only wanted to speak to me to tell me I'm a cad, I know that—'

'No, no! Edmond, listen—no, it's important— I can't seem to—'

'If you want me to apologize, I do. But I can't change my mind.'

'You must, Edmond.' All at once the words began to surge to her lips. 'You must change your mind. We must be married. You see, I'm expecting a baby.'

There was a long silence. She didn't break it. She knew he was still there—the communication between them, so fragile, hadn't been broken.

'When did you discover this?'

'While you were still in Jimbando. I didn't write—I wanted to tell you, to see your face . . .' She let the sentence die away. She didn't want

349

to reproach him by any hint. She wanted to be clear and plain with him.

'We must be married,' she took it up again. 'Your baby can't be brought up without his father.'

Still he said nothing.

'Edmond, I don't care what you feel about me. I understand something's changed you—I can't imagine what it is but you must have some feeling for the baby. He must have your name. You can't let your baby be born a bastard.'

Her voice began to quaver. She despised herself for her weakness. She remained silent, waiting for him to reply, steeling herself to speak again if he did not.

'Edmond, it will be a boy. I know it. This is your son we're speaking of.'

She heard him make a sound, as if he were clearing his throat. He said, 'When?'

'December.'

She was tense with expectancy. His voice when he said that one word told her the news had been like a thunderbolt to him.

There was a faint, metallic click.

He had hung up.

She sat in Marc's leather deskchair with the silent receiver in her hand. It was finished. She had told him the most important thing in the world and it had failed to move him. There was nothing left, nothing.

Seconds ticked by. She replaced the instrument. She sat for a long time staring before her—at the neat papers on Marc's desk, at the tray with its handsome fountain pen of gold and ivory, at the little silver-framed photograph of her Cousin Gaby.

Presently she rose. As she went out of the room she found the maid hovering in the hall, her face alight with enquiry. One glance at Nora caused the girl to turn and hurry away.

She went into her bedroom. She sat in the pretty little armchair in front of her bureau.

Life was over if Edmond didn't care about the child. So she might as well end it. What future was there for her or the baby, without Edmond?

She had a sudden recollection of the car crash with Buddy Garrenstein. It was so easy to meet Death—one had only to set out towards him. But her car was at Calmady. Tomorrow she would go to Calmady and next day she would go for a drive, a long drive, along the straight fast roads of the Marne, and somewhere she would find release from this meaningless existence.

It appeared that the maid told Elvi Hermilot and Marc about the phone call. Neither questioned her but she could feel their anxious gaze upon her. They could tell there had been no help for her in speaking to the man she loved. She couldn't bring herself to tell them, to say, 'He broke the connection.'

She slept well that night, to her own surprise. And in the morning when she awoke, the morning on which she had decided to set out for Calmady, she had changed her mind. She would live. She would bring the baby into the world. She would raise him, care for him. No matter how Edmond had changed, this baby would have something of him, and she would bring him up to be like the Edmond she had known.

For the first time in days she went out for a walk. A short distance tired her. She realized how weak she had let herself become. Never mind, from now on she would start to take care of herself. She must be strong and healthy, to bear a fine healthy baby.

There was a message for her on the telephone pad when she came in. 'Please ring Monsieur Debusson at once.' Frowning, and trembling with the surprise of it, she did so. 'Madame Tramont? Is it convenient for you to come and see me at once?'

'What about?'

'It isn't proper to discuss it on the telephone. Can you come?'

'You've heard from Edmond?'

'Yes.'

'I'm on my way,' she said, and darted out again.

She was lucky enough to hail a taxi at once. She ran into the offices of the lawyer, hardly checking to be recognized by the secretary.

Monsieur Debusson met her at his office door. 'My dear lady, please—please—be calm. I have something very important to say to you. But also very . . . very strange.'

'What is it? Edmond has been in touch with me—that was yesterday morning—'

'I know. He telephoned me last evening and then again early this morning.'

Debusson had put her into a chair. He now stood leaning back against his own desk, looking down at her. 'Madame, Monsieur du Ceddres has asked me to say that if you wish to be married he agrees to that—'

'What!'

'He told me the news you gave him. I see now . . . I understand why you were so insistent . . . Madame, I give you my deepest sympathies . . .'

'I don't need sympathy!' she cried, clasping her hands. 'Don't you understand? When Edmond and I see each other everything will be all right. That's all that's needed—just to see him—'

'No.'

'But yes. You don't really know him. What-ever made him act so strangely, it'll all die away when he sees me.'

'No, Madame. Monsieur du Ceddres will not be at the ceremony.'

· He was looking down at her with concern. She saw his faded blue eyes glisten with the beginnings of tears. She thought, He can't be weeping for *me*? And then she thought, He's not even talking sense.

'What on earth do you mean, Monsieur Debusson?'

'Monsieur du Ceddres agrees to a wedding. But he refuses to come to the ceremony. The marriage must be by proxy.'

SIXTEEN

Marc was so enraged that he looked as if he might suffocate before he got the words out.

'Impossible!' he shouted. 'Out of the question! How dare he!'

'Marc, I've already agreed—'

'Agreed? Are you mad?'

'You don't know everything. I had to—'

'Don't talk nonsense! Are you afraid of appearing before the world as a jilted woman? Who the hell would care for more than a week! It doesn't matter. After this you break off every contact with him—'

'No, Marc. No, I can't do that. I'm expecting his baby.'

They were in the office at the top of the fine old building in the Rue Lelong. Recent modernization had improved the facilities but the office of the *patron* still retained its old panelling, its segmented windows with their heavy shutters. They were partly closed now to keep out the direct sunlight of the very hot day of late June. There was an air of calm and composure entirely at variance with the tone Marc had just used.

But now he sat back into the chair from which he had risen. All the red of anger left his face. He half-reached out a hand towards her, then let it fall to the desk.

'Oh, Nora.'

'I'm sorry, I should have told you before. But you see, I wanted Edmond to be the first to know.'

She was alarmed at how much the news wounded him. She thought to herself, I shouldn't be inflicting this on him. He's not a young man any more.

But he had to be told. He was her only relative, the man who had been a father to her ever since the day he and Cousin Gaby had come to take her home from Tours.

She had come straight to the head office of Champagne Tramont when she left Monsieur Debusson. She had been shaking and upset when she got into the taxi, but had made herself seem self-controlled as she walked through the outer office to the lift.

Her first reaction to Monsieur Debusson's news had been much like Marc's. Indignation, incredulity, a desire to hit back at someone, anyone, for this insult . . .

'Madame, once again it's no wish of mine

to tell you this. But I have had two telephone conversations with Monsieur du Ceddres. He understands he has responsibilities towards the child which he doesn't wish to shirk—the child must have his name if you still wish it under the circumstances. He therefore agrees to a wedding ceremony. He asked me to say, Madame, that it must be a civil ceremony only. He says that it may well be you could wish to have your freedom in a year or two, in which case a civil marriage would make it much easier.'

Her first anger had died. She was almost listless. 'What does it mean?' she begged. 'Why won't he . . . even see me? What have I done?'

Debusson shook his head. 'I have no idea. All I can tell you is that he is determined, utterly determined, to have no actual contact with the Tramont family. I tried to get an explanation from him but he would only say that his decision was final on that point.'

'Is it . . . I mean, I never heard of such a thing . . . Is it even legal?'

'Oh yes. If you remember, Napoleon Bonaparte married Marie Louise in just those circumstances—a proxy wedding.'

'But that was a hundred years ago.'

'The law has not been changed. Signatures are required to various documents of verification, of course, but there is absolutely nothing against a marriage of this kind, and in fact it can occasionally be convenient. In these difficult times I have

356

heard of cases where one or other of the parties is kept from appearing because of passport difficulties.'

She heard the reassuring words rolling from his tongue and half took them in. But already she was thinking ahead. To be Edmond's legal wife must give her some advantage. She might be able to enlist Debusson's help in her cause. What he wouldn't tell a pleading fiancée he might well divulge to a legal wife. Moreover, the fact that Edmond agreed to the marriage, if only for the baby's sake, showed that he wasn't entirely unapproachable. She thought now that perhaps he had put the phone down on her yesterday because he was too moved to say any more. Perhaps. Perhaps it wasn't all entirely hopeless, after all.

She didn't say any of this to her cousin. She let him talk out his indignation and then, when he fell silent, she said, 'I've agreed to it, Marc. It's got to be.'

'Nora, where's your pride?'

She smiled. 'This isn't a time for being proud. This is the time for ensuring my baby has a name.'

Debusson had said he would be in touch within a week. Everything, he had assured her, could be done with the utmost discretion. There would have to be a special licence and four witnesses to the ceremony—she could bring her cousin and perhaps one other? She thought of Elvi Hermilot and nodded.

'I myself will be the third witness and my secretary will be the fourth.'

'And the . . . the groom?'

'Ah.' He blushed with embarrassment. 'I have a confidential clerk—very reliable, not a youngster but on the other hand not aged like myself. I thought to ask him. He . . . he would be tactful, Madame Tramont. Unless you have anyone else you could ask?'

'No!' She put up her hands to hide her face for a moment. She couldn't prevent the grimace of distaste that had passed across it. But she steadied herself. She rose. 'I leave it to you, then, Monsieur Debusson. You will let me know the place and time?'

'Very well, Madame.' He hesitated. 'I wonder . . .'

'Yes?'

She could see a great conflict of emotions within him. Then he said, 'I wonder if you are wise to agree?'

She stared at him. 'I must, Monsieur Debusson.'

'But it strikes me that . . . I wonder if my client is perhaps . . . unbalanced at present?'

It was a new thought. She stood with head bent, considering it. 'You mean he may be mentally ill?'

'It had occurred to me.'

358

'Oh then . . .' She smiled. 'All the more, I must go through with this. If he's ill, he can be cured. And then everything will be all right.'

'Oh, Madame . . . It's a great risk.'

'But how? If he stays as he is now, we never meet and so there is no risk. If he recovers, we're man and wife, as we were meant to be.'

He came to escort her to the outer door. 'What faith,' he murmured. 'I don't know whether to admire you or be afraid for you.'

She nodded as she shook hands. 'I am afraid,' she admitted. 'But I hope. So long as he's not totally indifferent, I feel I can hope.'

This was the face she showed to all Marc's angry argument. So long as Edmond cared enough to go through with even a form of marriage, she would hope.

'God damn it!' Marc cried. 'How can you even want him now? He's a selfish, arrogant sadist—'

'No.'

'How else can he inflict this insult on you?'

'I don't understand it any more than you do, Marc dear. I only know that I have to go one step at a time. And the step now is to go through with the marriage.'

Elvi Hermilot, to her surprise, supported her. 'His behaviour does have a mixture of the rational and the irrational that suggests mental illness—'

'I don't believe that for a moment,' Marc interrupted. 'There never was a saner, more sensible man then Edmond du Ceddres—'

'But that was before he went to Africa in March. Who knows what may have happened there?'

'You'll be suggesting next that this witch doctor at the mines put a spell on him!'

'Marc, don't keep on feeding your anger against him. We don't know what happened. But as Nora says, he feels concern for the baby. That must point to something—'

'To what? To me it just seems to give him another opportunity to humiliate her—'

'Try to see it as an attempt on his part to repair at least some of the damage. It must mean he feels something—'

'Oh, wonderful! How good and generous of him! It's his baby, he damn well knows it, and he graciously condescends to marry Nora at second-hand so as to make sure he has a legal claim on it—'

'That's not how he's thinking,' Nora said.

'I can't imagine how you think you know what he's thinking!'

But as that first day ended and other days succeeded, Marc's outrage died. He saw that to his young cousin something like hope had been given. He thought it mistaken but he was glad at least that she had it. He had been truly afraid she might make away with herself at first.

The wedding day was fixed for a week later.

Debusson saw to all the details, pulled a few strings so that the *officier de l'état civil* came to his office instead of carrying out the ceremony at a local town hall.

He was a friendly little man, rather like a Parisian sparrow, but he soon saw that his usual kind jocularity would be misplaced here. He read out the usual warnings about lets and hindrances, looked through his heavy spectacles at the group around him, and sighed. Weddings should be happy occasions, he always felt. But not this time.

Marc took Nora aside for one last moment. 'You don't have to go through with this parody,' he whispered. 'Please, Nora. We'll raise the child at Calmady—what does it matter if you aren't married!'

She smiled and shook her head. 'It's Edmond's baby,' she said. 'It must have Edmond's name.'

She stood before the *officier* with the law clerk at her side. He was a quiet looking man of about thirty-five, and apart from one long glance when she first came into the office he had avoided meeting her eyes. They went through the questions and answers, he placed the ring on her finger, the ring brought by Monsieur Debusson that morning in an unfashionable district.

'By the authority of the state of the Republic of France, I pronounce Edmond Renaud du Ceddres and Elinore Nicole Norwood-Tramont to be man and wife. My felicitations.' He stopped abruptly. He had been about to say, as usual, 'You may kiss the bride, Monsieur.'

There was an awkward pause. Then Marc took his cousin in his arms to kiss her and wish her luck. He was still certain she had made a bad mistake, but he could honestly say he wished her all the luck in the world. Everyone else shook hands, the little pile of documents was signed by everyone present and the stamps were placed on them.

It was done. She was Edmond's wife. With a hand that trembled she set her signature to the last of the papers. She looked up with blurred vision when Marc touched her elbow.

'What would you like to do now, my dear?'

'I want to go home, Marc.'

'To the apartment?'

'To Calmady.'

The relentless routine of the vines saved her reason in the weeks that immediately followed. A bad reaction set in; she felt weak, lost, afraid at what she had done. For a while she was in dread that some message would come from Edmond after he received his copies of the marriage documents, but there was nothing but silence, and somehow that seemed worse.

But the vines were tended, the bunches of grapes hung on the twigs, harvest came and the pressing was done. A good harvest—a good omen, the country folk said, for a healthy baby.

Monsieur Debusson telephoned. He reported

that he had had an acknowledgement of the safe receipt of the legal papers. 'Monsieur du Ceddres says he feels there is no need for any further communication.'

'But the baby—'

'He will see the announcement of the birth in the usual newspapers.'

'Surely he'll want to see him?'

'No, Madame.'

'My God, Monsieur Debusson, I was sure he—'

'No.'

'Give me his address, Monsieur Debusson. I beg you!'

'No, Madame. Better not. To tell the truth, I have some apprehension about what might happen if I did. I feel more and more certain that my client is not perhaps in full control of his faculties.'

'But you said at the outset that he seemed perfectly sensible—'

'Yes, and still seems so. But these are not sensible attitudes.'

She thought about Edmond's life before all this had happened. 'What about the business side, Monsieur Debusson?'

'He has given me power of attorney to deal with most matters. There are good managers at the ski resort and on the estate. As for the boards of the various companies on which he served, he has resigned his directorships.'

She shivered. 'That sounds almost as if he were . . .'

'What?'

'I don't know. Turning into a recluse?'

'It may be, it may be. I don't understand it. But one other thing I was to tell you, Madame. If ever you need funds, I am empowered to provide them.'

'Thank you, it is very unlikely I shall ever ask for Edmond's money.'

'Yes, I understand.'

The estate workers at Calmady were pleased to have her among them. They smiled as she walked among the vine rows, or stopped to talk with the chief of cellar. They could see her figure becoming heavier. They didn't know when the child was due but looked forward to its coming. As to the non-appearance of the young Monsieur, well . . . he had his own affairs to attend to, he had this big business somewhere in the mountains, and he travelled abroad to wild places too. So long as young Madame stayed at Calmady, they were content. It was a long time since there had been a baby at the Villa Tramont.

The baby boy came on the day of St Francis Xavier, the 3rd December, a Monday. All the estate people gathered round the entrance to the great cellars to drink champagne in honour of the heir—François Edmond du Ceddres.

It was the first time in generations that there had been a male child. In a way it caused consternation. 'But the head of the firm has always been a woman! The luck of the firm lies with that!'

'Nonsense,' said the younger folk. 'And anyhow, he'll be a Tramont. They'll change his name by and by.'

But Nora had already told Marc she wouldn't do so. 'He's Edmond's son. He must bear Edmond's name.'

'Well, until he's grown up, at least,' Marc said easily. 'When he's a man he may decide to change it himself. It's an advantage to have the Tramont name. I know from experience.'

But she shook her head.

The baby was christened soon after Christmas. She had photographs taken, sent them with a letter to Edmond through the office of the lawyer. The baby was shown sleeping blissfully in the midst of his lace frills and finely made shawls.

In her heart Nora expected a reply from Edmond. She felt no one could resist wanting to hear more of such a fine boy. But days went by and there was no response.

She had to go to Paris on business, so she took the opportunity to visit Monsieur Debusson. 'Did you send my letter and photographs to my husband?' she enquired.

'Of course, Madame.'

'Has he replied?'

'He telephoned to let us know he had received them.'

'I should like him to . . . Ask him to let me know what he thinks about the boy. Just a few lines, Monsieur Debusson.'

'Monsieur du Ceddres dislikes writing letters.'

'Then ask him to telephone. I want to know how he feels about the baby.'

Debusson smiled, sighed and nodded. He could see she had hoped that the baby's birth would change everything. But the more he had to deal with Edmond du Ceddres the more he was convinced that the man was trying by every means to cut himself off from the world. What his motives were, Debusson had no idea. But he knew Nora's hopes of some future reunion were totally vain.

Three days later a call came through to Calmady. It happened that Nora was out in the laboratory sampling the various blends from last year's pressing, and was out of reach of a receiver. By the time she was found, the call had been closed down.

The butler had written down a message. 'He would not say who he was, Madame. He said you would know,' and he gave a frown of incomprehension. 'He said that he had liked the photographs but you need not trouble to send any more. He is glad everything is going well.'

'And what else?'

'Nothing else, Madame.'

That evening Nora went to bed with a bad headache. She knew it was reaction to the cruelty of the message. She slept badly, but woke with a determination to do something she had thought of more than once.

She went up to Paris by train without telling Marc what she intended. She was back in time for dinner. After they had begun the first course and the servants had gone out, she said, 'I have something to tell you, Marc. I don't know whether you'll approve.'

'What is it, my pet?'

'I've hired a private detective to find Edmond.'

SEVENTEEN

The detective, Joseph Allegri, was efficient and workmanlike, not exactly cynical but certainly disillusioned. His brief from Madame du Ceddres-Tramont was to find her missing husband, without letting anyone know he was looking for him. Good enough. It wasn't easy for a man to disappear in France: papers were demanded of almost anyone from time to time. And from what he was told about the replies to letters and so on, it was fairly certain Monsieur du Ceddres was somewhere in France.

He expected to come back with a favourable report in a week or two. In fact, it took him the whole of February and the first week of March.

He then telephoned Madame Tramont with some pride to say he had the information she wanted.

'It's a village called Chervais, Madame. In the Alpes Maritimes. Monsieur du Ceddres owns a house a mile or so outside it and he's living there.'

'Living there . . .' It had an odd sound. 'With a woman?'

Ah, so that was what she feared? Only natural. 'No, Madame, as far as I can ascertain he is alone except for a servant.'

'Alone . . .'

'I wonder, Madame, if he has had a . . . a religious experience? His way of life, from all I could gather, seems almost monastic.'

'What do you mean?'

'It seems he never goes out. The villagers have never even seen him. And as far as they know anything about it, the house is rented to a Monsieur Paradou—which is in fact the name of the servant, I believe.'

'Then how can you be sure Monsieur du Ceddres really is there?'

'I'm sure, Madame.' He had had a photograph to show to people, but it had been useless when he got to Chervais because, so it appeared, the owner of La Grange had driven in by night and had never stepped outside since. But the car in which he had come —that was the same car he had traced all the way from Lisbon—at its last daylight sighting had had the man in the photograph in the back seat.

The servant had been driving. The servant had been added to the trail in Paris in early June. He had no photograph of him but the description was unmistakable—a tall middle-aged man with grey hair and moustache.

The servant Paradou was rarely seen by the villagers, although from time to time he drove out in the big Packard car. But he had only once stopped in the village, to use the telephone at the tabac. 'That was to report the telephone at La Grange out of order,' Allegri explained.

'As to the rest, they have their provisions delivered to the house. It's a grim little place, more like a . . . a prison, I was going to say. That's what made me wonder . . . You couldn't imagine anyone wanting to live there unless he was . . . if you know what I mean . . . undergoing expiation or something.' The more especially if he had a smart, attractive young wife like Madame Tramont. It would have to be something very powerful to make him choose that retreat—but if it were religious, why didn't he enter a monastery?

'How do I get there?' Nora asked, picking up a pen to make notes.

'To Chervais? Ah . . . it's a bit of a backwater. Farming mostly, though they take summer visitors—climbers and walkers, you know the kind of thing. First you have to get to Barcelonnette and then you turn east.' He read out the instructions: shorter than the report of his own long, tedious journey—many stops and starts along the route, tracking the Packard bought by Monsieur du Ceddres in Lisbon the day he first set foot again in Europe.

Nora thanked him, assured him a cheque for his services would be in the post to him at once, and hung up. She found to her own amazement that she was quite calm. She had waited for this moment, planning ahead to what she would do.

She rang for her maid, told her to pack some clothes. 'Warm clothes, for the mountains. And tell Nurse to get herself and François ready.'

'You're going away, Madame?'

'Yes, to the Alps.'

'But—Madame—it's so unexpected—'

'Be quick,' Nora said, ignoring the faltering protest. She waved her out of the room, then sat down to attend to the business side. She wrote the cheque for Allegri, gave instructions to the chief of cellar at Calmady and to the sales manager in Paris. Then she telephoned Marc, who was in London on a business trip.

'I'm going at once to see him,' she said when she'd told him Allegri's news. 'I've given instructions for everything here but perhaps you'd better get back as soon as you can—'

'Nora, don't go!'

'But I must, Marc. That's why I hired Allegri—'

'You don't know what you may find there! He sounds so strange—'

'I've got to see him. Surely you understand that?' 'Wait, then—wait till I get back and I'll go with you—'

'Wait?' The mere tone of her voice told him how impossible that was. 'No, I'm going now. I hope to get there by the day after tomorrow at latest.'

'You're driving?'

'That seems best—it's easier with the baby—'

'Good God, Nora! You're not taking François?'

She stifled a sigh of impatience. Of course she was taking François. It was time for Edmond to meet his son.

It was early spring on the lower slopes of the alpine valleys east of Barcelonnette. New grass was springing with, here and there, the yellow of primrose and the white of meadow saxifrage. There was a warm sun reflecting off the snow higher up on the approach to the Col de Lar.

Nora drove with concentration but without strain. They had stopped overnight, first in Varennes and then in Romans. They had had a break in Barcelonnette for lunch and now, as the afternoon wore away, they were approaching the village of Chervais at last.

She was less unnerved than she had expected by her nearness to Edmond. It was because she had the baby and his nurse to think about.

iette was a devoted young woman, well-trained but rather limited: her first reaction to the proposed trip had been disapproval, and then alarm. She had never been to the Alps, she expected they would get lost in snowdrifts, were there savage eagles that might attack a baby?

The gradual approach through perfectly normal towns had soothed her. She had begun to enjoy herself. The baby was no problem—a sturdy little thing of four months, he slept in his comfortable padded basket, took his feeds with eagerness, and kicked his wool-clad legs.

'Where shall we be staying in Chervais, Madame?' Mariette enquired as they slowed at the wooden crucifix in its shelter on the sloping entry road.

'I don't know, at the inn, probably.' She had a sudden tremor. Was there an inn? She hadn't even asked Allegri that. But yes, as they rolled quietly down the main street, there was the inn, stone and wooden beams, a sign swinging in the sun: Auberge de la Croix.

The proprietor hurried out as the big Citroën came to a halt outside. 'Madame?' he enquired, leaning down to the driving door, thinking she would ask for instruction on how to get back to the main road.

'Have you accommodation? A couple of decent rooms?'

'Accommodation—certainly—this way, Madame oh, a baby, my goodness—my wife will be so pleased—a moment, Madame!' He scurried ahead. He could tell they were going to earn money. Nora's car, her sable jacket, her gold wrist watch, the neat uniform coat of the woman who got out with the child in the Moses basket—it all meant money.

Madame Grest came at her husband's call. Astonished at visitors so early in the season, she nevertheless showed Nora upstairs to a handsome little room warmed by the stove in the main lounge below. Across the passage was another room, almost identical, for the nurse and baby. The bathroom, rather primitive but perfectly clean, was at the end of the corridor.

'How long will you be staying, Madame?'

'That depends. I can't be certain. Why?' Nora asked with wry humour. 'Are you expecting others to need the rooms?'

'No, no—not at this time of year—by Easter, of course, but that's not till late this year. Now, what can I bring you, Madame? Coffee? A glass of wine? Something stronger—cognac?'

'Coffee, please, with plenty of milk. Mariette!' The nurse came across the passage. 'Do you need anything to eat?'

'No, Madame, I'm still full up with lunch. You should eat something, though.' Nora was breastfeeding the baby, a fact which Mariette kept well in mind at all times.

The coffee was quickly brought, hot and very strong. Nora ate a piece of home-made bread with butter, to please Mariette. Then she said, 'Which road do I take for La Grange?'

'La Grange? You're not going there, Madame?'

'Yes, I am. Can you direct me, please?'

'Madame, I wouldn't go there if I were you. That's a very funny set-up up there.'

'In what way?' Nora asked, hiding her keen interest.

'Well, they never come out! The manservant goes past now and then in the car, but as for the other—! People round here don't like it, I can tell you! They think he's up to no good.'

'What does that mean? You think he's a criminal?'

'Well, Madame, I ask you . . . Never shows himself, never sets foot outside—I tell you what we think. We think he's one of those gangsters from Marseilles, hiding out after some big gang fight. You know they're always up to something bad, down south in the city.'

'Dear me,' Nora said. 'Well, for all that, I need to know how to get there.'

'Do you know Monsieur Paradou, then?'

'Who? Oh, I see. No, I have never met Monsieur Paradou.'

The landlady was dying to ask why she was going to La Grange in that case but didn't quite dare. There was something about this lady that let you know you had to mind your manners.

She gave directions, watching with disapproval

as Nora went out to get into the car once more. Mariette came out also, a little anxious at being left alone with the baby at the back of beyond.

'I'll be back in an hour, Mariette,' Nora soothed, 'in plenty of time for six o'clock. You settle in and unpack. Order what you like for dinner—we'll eat at eight o'clock.'

Thus reduced to the mundane, the surroundings didn't seem so strange. Mariette nodded and turned back to the inn. Nora drove away.

La Grange proved to be something like a small fortress—an old square stone building surrounded by a courtyard and a wall. It had clearly been a watch tower in days gone by.

Nora imagined that it had always belonged to the du Ceddres. The family name came from the Piedmontese for 'cedar tree', and was a relic of Crusading times when some forebear had brought back saplings from the Holy Land. The Piedmontese had been the rulers here in these mountains for generations until the boundaries had changed to give this terrain at last to France. The square tower was a relic of fortifications in the days of the old clan wars.

There was an oaken door in the eight-foot-high wall, reached by a rocky path from the narrow mountain road. Beside it a bell chain hung with an iron loop for the hand. She seized the loop and pulled it, hard. The bell clanged inside. She waited. No one came. She pulled it again, two or three times. The clamour rang out but there was no stirring from within the square building. Again and again she rang the bell, but no one came to the thick oak door. Could the place be empty? But the villagers said Edmond never left it. He must be there. Why didn't he answer?

At length she went slowly down the path to the car. She drove further up the mountain road, trying to get a viewpoint from which she could see into the courtyard, perhaps get a glimpse of the door or the windows of the house. But the turns in the road were such that La Grange was soon out of sight.

Night was beginning to come in the narrow valley, the sun sinking behind the peak. She must go back to Chervais, to her baby.

Chilled and scared at the memory of that threatening house, she drove carefully back to the inn.

Madame Grest could hardly wait to find out what had happened. She brought clean towels to Nora's room on purpose to ask how she had fared.

'It seemed no one was at home,' Nora said. 'Are you sure Monsieur Paradou never goes out?'

'Oh, absolutely certain, Madame! No one has ever seen him go out.'

'But no one answered when I rang.'

'They never do,' the landlady told her with

some triumph. 'I tell you, they're expecting the police—or rival gangsters from La Cannebière!'

Nora shook her head. 'That can't be right. And in any case, I hear they have their food delivered. They have to open the door to take it in, surely?'

'Oh, that—yes—that's true, they do. The man-servant opens the door in the wall at eight o'clock when the postman calls, and at three in the afternoon when the grocer's van arrives from Barcelonnette, every day or so.'

Nora could understand why the villagers thought there was something sinister about the people at La Grange. To tell the truth, the more she heard, the more she became frightened her-self. There was something so obsessive, so mad-seeming about the whole thing. Why in God's name was Edmond living like this? What could it mean?

Sharing the evening meal with Mariette did nothing to help her frame of mind. Mariette was feeling threatened again as the night closed down on the valley. She didn't like the mountains frowning all around, she didn't like the way the wind whined in the shutters. Her nervousness affected little François. He grizzled and com-plained instead of settling down to sleep as he usually did after hi feed.

But at length everything was calm. Nora went to bed exhausted. She asked the landlady to call her, however, at seven in the morning.

'You're going out so early?' Madame Grest asked, surprised.

'I'm going to deliver the mail to La Grange.'

'But there seldom is any mail.'

'There will be some tomorrow,' Nora said.

A little before eight she was on the road up to the tower. It was a cloudy day, windy, with rain blowing in gusts along the valley. The building, as she glimpsed it first, seemed more forbidding than ever, its slate roof gleaming a steely grey, its shuttered upper windows like blind eyes.

She drew up in the road. For a moment she sat breathing in shallow, brief gasps. She was frightened, she didn't deny it. Her heart was hammering against her ribs. Yet what was she afraid of? She was only going to ring a bell and speak to a servant.

A grilled wicket in the heavy door swung open when she had waited a few minutes after tugging the bell-pull. Somehow she expected a great creaking of rusty hinges, but in fact it swung open so silently that it took her by surprise.

The man who stood behind the ornamental wrought iron fretwork was clearly Jean Paradou—tall, grey-haired and moustached. He wore a proofed canvas coat over what looked like a white jacket.

He gaped at her. 'Where's the postman?' he asked.

'There's no post this morning. Tell Monsieur du Ceddres his wife is here.'

He gave an audible gasp. She waited. 'Well?' she demanded.

'I . . . I'm sorry, Madame, that's impossible. Monsieur never sees anyone.'

'But I'm Madame du Ceddres!'

'I can see that,' he agreed, still off balance. 'Nevertheless, my instructions are to let no one in.'

To her own dismay and anger, she burst into tears. 'I must see him, speak to him! Tell him I'm here!'

'It would do no good, Madame—'

'Don't dare tell me what good it would do! Go and tell him—I've brought his son—he *must*—'

The words were swept into incoherence as sobs choked her. She threw her hands up to her face, ready to claw at her own cheeks for her weakness, but instead leant against the stone doorframe, while the tears trickled through her fingers.

When at last she recovered enough to look up, she found that Jean Paradou was watching her. The expression on his face, to her consternation, was pity.

'Wait,' he said.

He closed the upper door. She heard his footsteps on a paved path or court. There was a long interval during which nothing happened. Nervously she wiped her tears away, pushed the handkerchief into the pocket of her fur jacket, clenched and unclenched her fists.

At length she heard returning footsteps behind the door. She waited for the servant to re-open the wicket, but for a moment nothing happened.

'Nora?'

It was Edmond's voice. Her head began to swim. She steadied herself against the stones.

'Nora? Is that you?'

Sudden fury seized her. She beat against the door with her fists. 'Open the door and you'll see who it is! Open the door, Edmond!'

She could hear nothing for a moment. Then he said, 'Go away.'

'No! I won't go! It's taken me months to find out where—'

'You've wasted your time. Go away.'

'Not without an explanation! I want to know what I've done to deserve—'

'You've done nothing. Just go.'

'But I've brought François to see you—he's here in the village—'

'Nora, in God's name, go back, take him home—'

'Home? We have no home without you, Edmond! You must explain, I can't go on without knowing why—'

'There's no need for explanations. You must accept it. We can never have a life together.'

'But we're man and wife! We have a little boy.' She hit the door with clenched fists. 'I'll bring him here, and then you'll open the door. You'll open the door to see your son, Edmond!'

Although the thick door stood between them, she knew the thrust had reached him. There was a long silence. Then he spoke.

'Don't bring him, Nora. I can never see him, and he can never see me.'

'But why, Edmond? Why? I don't understand.'

'Don't ask any more. Just believe me—I can never see you or the baby.'

'I refuse to believe you can cut yourself off from us—'

'But I must, Nora!' There was desperation in the words. 'I must, for your sake and his.'

'That's nonsense. What we need most in the world is to have you with us. Darling, don't you realize what it's been like without you? I can't go on like this. Open the door, my darling, please, please—open the door.'

'No.'

'Edmond—'

'Nora, listen to me. I can't see you. I'm a leper.'

She thought he meant in some moral sense. She rushed into speech. 'Oh, it doesn't matter what you've done. Your sense of honour is too—'

'Darling, *listen!* I mean what I say, literally. I can never have any contact with you or our son.'

He spaced out the words so that she could not possibly misunderstand.

'I've contracted leprosy.'

EIGHTEEN

Nora never forgave herself for the instinct of revulsion at the words. She actually took half a step back from the closed door. Terrible images flooded through her mind—Ramon Navarro in the film *Ben Hur* meeting his mother and sister in the Valley of the Lepers, blacks glimpsed in travel documentaries limping away on crippled limbs . . .

But this was Edmond. Edmond couldn't be a bundle of filthy rags that one must never touch. Edmond couldn't be a hunched figure with mutilated fingers and toes.

She came back to touch the rough surface of the door with the palm of her hand.

'It's a mistake,' she gasped.

'No mistake. I went straight from the boat to a friend of my university days. He's a research scientist at the Institute of Tropical Diseases. He recognized the signs the moment I—'

'But you had no signs, Edmond!' How well she knew it. That tall lithe body in her arms, explored by her lips and searched by her eyes—there had been no sores, no lesions.

'Yes,' he said. 'Not noticeable. One doesn't imagine . . . I may have had it for three of four years, Nora. Since I was working for the Civil Administration in Africa.'

'But there would have been symptoms—'

'Yes, two or three little white spots on my skin. One on my back, one on my instep, one between the fingers of my left hand. And who do you think recognized them?' He laughed. The bitterness was harsh. 'The witch doctor at Jimbando.'

'Oh, it's all untrue, darling! He only said it to scare you because you and he were on opposite sides—'

'No. He had no reason to scare me then. We'd agreed a settlement, he'd got what he wanted—it was easy, he wanted some special cattle from another region, I simply had them brought by train . . . And then, as we were drinking native beer by the boma, watching the cows settle down in their new home, he said to me . . . he said to me . . .'

'He was lying, Edmond!'

'Jussot says not. And in any case . . . I've seen it in others . . . I know it's true.'

She summoned her powers of argument. 'We can't just accept the word of some stupid African and one doctor! We must get another opinion—'

'Nora, for God's sake!' It was a groan of horror. 'Do you know what you're saying? If you start dragging in other people, I'll be sent away—to a quarantine hospital, shut up like a convict! Don't you understand? Leprosy is a notifiable disease, and there's no treatment except isolation, strict isolation.'

'What else are you enduring now?' she cried, pushing at the door helplessly. 'I can't even *see* you, Edmond! Edmond, open the door and let me see you!'

There was no reply. She understood, as if he had thrust the words into her with a blade, that he would never open the door to her.

But she couldn't give up. 'Listen, my darling, this isn't just your problem, it's mine too. I'm your wife. It's my right to be with you—'

'No.'

'You can't lock me out for ever, Edmond! I want to be with you—!'

'And the baby?' he interrupted. 'You'd be prepared to leave him, never see him again?'

'No, that wouldn't be—'

'Wouldn't be right, wouldn't be possible—of course not! What do you want, to expose our son to the infection? Because Jussot says some people are more apt to be infected than others and François may have inherited the trait from me.'

'No, Edmond—listen—'

'Jussot says I'm one of the unlucky ones— something about my system not having the right kind of defence against the bacteria. Thank God, he says you're almost certainly not endangered— but who knows, Nora? Who knows, if you were to live with me? And besides . . .'

'We'll get advice—'

'Besides,' he went on inexorably, 'there's no

cure, it can only get worse. Should you like that, Nora? Living with a man whose hands and feet become paralysed, who can't feel pain so that he injures himself, cuts off his own fingers, becomes ugly, perhaps blind—'

'No! No, darling, no! It won't happen—'

'You think it will be different because I'm the man you love? You think love can turn back the disease?'

'There must be some way—'

'There's no way. It's a life sentence. And you see, so long as I'm not shut up in an institution, I can choose how long that life will be—'

'Edmond, don't even think of that—'

'Go away, Nora. Go away and forget you ever knew me.'

'You know I can't.' She began to weep, senselessly, helplessly. 'I love you. I could never forget you. You're mine, you always will be'

'Don't waste your life on me. I tried—oh, God, how I tried—I wanted you to hate me, to turn your back and start again—'

'Edmond, my darling, Edmond, don't even think of a thing like that. There could never be anyone else.'

'But there must be,' he said, hurriedly, trying to convince her. 'You and I can never see each other. It's pointless to keep me in your mind. Go away, find someone else, be happy—'

'I won't go, I'll never go. I'll stay here forever, Edmond, even if I never see you—'

'Oh, that will be wonderful,' he said. She could hear the scornful rejection in the words. 'A prolonged torture for both of us. And François? What will you do? Bring him here to this mountain village, bring him up like a hermit? Don't be silly, Nora! If you come here to live, you'll be noticed—Madame du Ceddres-Tramont and her son, why is she here? Is that what you want? To attract attention, to have me dragged off to an institution in Marseilles or Algiers?'

'Oh, no . . .'

'Because that's what will happen.'

'No.'

'Nora, don't cry.' His voice had come nearer, as if he were leaning close to the crack of the door. 'Dear heart, don't cry. Tears don't help. Our world's come to an end but we must just . . . accept. Go away, I beg you. Go away. Take François, go back to the real world.'

'But I want to help you, Edmond—'

'You can help me by going away. It's less hard to bear if you . . . if you . . .'

'Edmond!'

'I'll think of you all the time. I'll remember how you wouldn't give up, how you came, how you wanted to share . . . But it's easier if you go away. A little easier, my love . . . Please go.'

She was beyond words, beyond tears. She stood with her body pressed against the oak door, desperate to feel some contact with him.

'Goodbye, Nora.'

'No, no—'

'Goodbye, my darling. Kiss François for me.'

'Edmond—'

But she could hear his footsteps going away on the stones.

How she got back to the village she never remembered, but she must have driven quite well because she pulled up outside without attracting any attention. It was still only about nine in the morning. The inn was quiet. She climbed the wooden staircase to her room as if her legs had iron shackles on them.

Across the passage, the door of the room stood open. Mariette was bathing François. He was kicking and splashing in the big enamel bowl, crowing with pleasure.

Nora went, picked him up, wrapped him in a towel, and hurried with him into her room. There, she threw herself into a chair. She held the baby against her breast, rocking back and forth in a voiceless misery that could have no end.

After a few minutes Mariette came tapping timidly at her door. 'Madame, Madame! Is anything wrong?'

Nora could as yet make no reply. The baby, at first startled by her sudden actions, had by now snuggled against the soft fur of the sable jacket and was looking up at her with his blue stare, pleased with this new, enjoyable experience in the arms of someone he instinctively loved. She bent her head, taking comfort from the velvety fuzz of his hair against her cheek.

'Madame, may I come in?'

Nora sighed. 'Yes, come in.'

'Are you all right, Madame?' Mariette asked with veiled anxiety as she slipped in and closed the door. She knew too many stories of mothers suffering from post-natal depression. True, Madame Tramont always seemed so brisk and self-controlled. Yet what had caused this wild-goose chase across country? And this strange morning excursion into the mountains and now this eruption into the calm of the nursery?

When she met Madame's grey-brown eyes, however, her fears were set at rest. There was grief there, but no madness.

'It's time for the ten o'clock feed, Madame,' she offered. 'I didn't know if you'd be back so I prepared—'

'No, no. Everything is as usual. Go away, Mariette. Come back in half an hour.'

There was comfort in the age old ritual of feeding the baby. The selfish eagerness of the child, his concentration, taught her to think more clearly. And when at last she handed him back to the nurse her mind was able to work again.

All day she let her thoughts dwell on her predicament, even while she went through some-thing like the usual routine of the baby's world. The weather, after a dark and cloudy start, had turned sunny. She and Mariette took the baby

388

for a walk to the end of the village street and back again. They had lunch in a corner of the main downstairs room, with village men coming in for a drink and glancing at them with curiosity.

While François took his afternoon nap Nora lay on her bed, half-drowsing, half-thinking. Then at last, as dusk was falling, she came to a conclusion.

First of all, Edmond would never come back to the oak door to speak to her. She knew this without having to think twice. If she were to return he would refuse to respond, and if she continued to try to see him he would run away. He had set himself up one sanctuary, he could do it again.

She alone was an insufficient army. She had to call on resources. She needed to know more, to find out what might be possible for them. She couldn't entirely banish hope, although that was what Edmond wanted. She would go to Paris to see the doctor . . . his name was Jussot, she recalled . . . she would speak to him and find out the facts.

She didn't feel capable of driving her car at present. She asked for and was found a man who would drive them to Lyons next day—for what he considered a sizeable fee because the villagers were busy moving their livestock up to the spring pasture. She told Mariette to pack and to be ready to leave immediately after breakfast. She paid her bill, adding a large tip so that the innkeeper and his wife would remember her with friendship. She wanted no adverse gossip when she left: she didn't want to endanger Edmond in any way.

At Lyons she was driven to the Hotel du Savoyard where the firm had a suite on call for their managers and shipping agents. She had her car put into the garage to be collected some time in the future. She asked the receptionist to book two overnight sleepers on the Paris express, then sat down in her room to write to Edmond. It would reach him, she told herself with a sudden stab of pain, by the postman tomorrow at eight.

'My darling husband, I'm on my way to Paris to see Dr Jussot. Don't blame me for wanting to know more and trying to find some way for us to have a life together. François sends you his love, and I send mine. Nora.'

She went out herself to post it. She didn't want it to lie uncollected for a day or so in the hotel postbox.

Then she put through a call to Calmady. Yes, her cousin had come home, rather unexpectedly, he was here or at least, madame, he had gone out to talk to a grower who was threatening to pull up all his vines this spring and plant herbs instead, did you ever hear of such a thing, madame!

'Give Monsieur Auduron-Tramont a message. Please write it down, Madame Presle, it's very important. Tell him to meet me tomorrow at the Paris apartment. I'm on my way there now.'

'I thought that was where you were speaking from, Madame—'

'No, I'm in Lyons.'

'Lyons!'

'But I'll be in Paris by morning. Have you written down the message?' For Madame Presle, who had been housekeeper since her childhood, was growing old and forgetful now.

'Yes, Madame, and I'll put it on the hall table so he'll see it the moment he comes in.'

The journey to Paris was uneventful. Young François took it all in his stride—this strange rocking room with a machine making a snorting noise somewhere outside, unusual but, in the end, soothing.

Marc himself opened the door of the apartment to her when she stepped out of the lift. 'Nora—my dear girl—what happened—how are you—'

Questions tumbled out. His pale-skinned face was drawn with anxiety. Nora said, 'A moment,' and turned her attention to putting Mariette and the baby in their familiar rooms before she came back to Marc.

He had ordered coffee and croissants in the dining-room. She sat down to drink thirstily and, to her surprise, to eat. For the first time in three days, she was hungry.

'I found him,' she said.' The place is like a

391

miniature prison. He won't open the door to me.'

'Did you find out—I mean, is he—is he unhinged?'

'There's nothing wrong with his mind,' she said with a great, weary sadness. She looked at her cousin. 'Marc,' she begged, 'don't shudder at what I'm going to tell you.'

'Shudder? What on earth—? Don't be silly!'

'He has leprosy.'

To his eternal credit, Marc Auduron-Tramont took the blow without flinching. He sat across the table staring at his young cousin. He closed his eyes for a long moment and then reopened them. Then he said, his voice somehow steady though husky, 'When did it happen?'

'I'm not quite sure. That's why I have to see the doctor. His name is Jussot, he works at the Institute for Tropical Diseases. As soon as I've finished this—' she gestured at her plate—'I'm going to ring him—'

'He won't be there, darling. It's not nine o'clock yet.'

'Well, then, at nine-fifteen. I must see him. It's the first step.'

'The fist step to what, Nora?' Marc asked. Because he had lived longer, he had heard more of leprosy than Nora. It was a living death.

When she was put through to Dr Albert Jussot, she announced herself at once.

'Ah,' he said.

'You expected to hear from me?'

'Not expected. But I'm not surprised.'

'I must see you.'

'Yes, of course.'

'May I come at once?'

'Not here,' he said. 'That would be imprudent. Come to my private address.'

'Let me have it.' She wrote at his dictation. 'What time?'

'This evening—'

'This evening? But I want to speak to you *now*—'

'I understand, Madame, but I have cases here and some cultures to see to. I can't be free until about five o'clock.'

'Five o'clock . . . .'

'I'm sorry, I can't make it any earlier.' He heard the anguish in her voice. He felt pity for her—he had pity for many he had seen in the course of his work. 'Five o'clock at the Rue Colbert. If I'm not there the concierge will let you in.'

'Thank you.'

If it had not been for baby François, the interval might have driven her out of her mind. But the baby made his demands and she devoted herself to him. The weather outside had turned wintry—sleet blew past the windows, the afternoon darkened early to evening.

She changed for her meeting with Dr Jussot as if it were a business appointment. She didn't want to meet him as a distraught wife but as a sensible woman seeking a solution to a problem. She put on a well-cut dress of fawn wool and a necklace of pearls which had belonged to her Cousin Gaby.

She and Marc were driven to the Rue Colbert almost in silence. He had spent the intervening hours dealing with one or two business matters and then looking up the disease in the encyclopaedia in the library at his club. What he had read gave him no pleasure.

'Leprosy runs a long course though death may occur through other infections entering the weakened body. Persons suffering from leprosy should be segregated and children particularly should not be allowed to remain with leprous patients. Oil from the seeds of the chaulmoogra tree (East Indies, genus Hydnocarpus) is the usual treatment although its use is largely for alleviation. No cure is known in the present state of medical knowledge.'

Dr Jussot had made a special effort to be there before them. He came at once to the door, a small, plump man of about thirty with hair already thinning and a piercing gaze behind gold-rimmed glasses.

'Come in. It would be wrong to greet you with "I'm pleased to see you". Please, take a chair. I've made some tea—I find it refreshing at this hour. Will you have some?'

He fussed about to fill in the awkwardness of

meeting. Both his guests accepted tea. He sat down in a battered chair by his equally battered desk, but sat facing them.

'Now,' he said. 'What do you want to know?'

'Tell me how Edmond came to you in the first place.'

'Yes. Well, he came to me at the beginning of June last year. He told me that while he was in . . . the name eludes me . . .'

'Jimbando.'

'Yes. One of the natives had taunted him with having the "great sickness". Do you know what I'm talking about?'

'Yes, I do.'

'At first Edmond thought nothing of it but on board ship he had time to look closely at his skin and saw that two or three small areas of coloration had spread. He kept to his cabin throughout the voyage, avoided contact with everyone except the purser and even to him, he tells me, he spoke with a silk scarf over his mouth. He bought a car in Lisbon and drove to Paris by easy stages, sleeping in the car and keeping away from everyone. He already suspected, you understand, that what the man had said to him was true.'

He paused. 'Go on,' said Nora.

'He and I know each other from a long way back. He came straight to me, asked me to examine him. I had no doubt the moment I looked at the patches. Besides, he was already suffering from hyperaesthesia of the finger nerves—he picked up a glass of Scotch in his left hand and dropped it, he couldn't feel it properly, you see.'

He picked up his cup and put it down. 'I was very shocked, of course. So was he, but he'd had some weeks to get used to the idea. He'd already faced the possibility, made some plans. You do understand, Madame du Ceddres-Tramont, that leprosy is a notifiable disease? I should have informed the authorities straight away. But he begged me not to do that. He said he would live in seclusion somewhere, totally isolated.'

'And that's what he's done.'

'No, it's not quite as total as he intended. I persuaded him to take a servant with him—I knew of a man, an ex soldier, formerly an orderly in the Medical Corps, who had taken up the role of male nurse.'

'Jean Paradou?'

'Ah, I see you've learned part of the story. Paradou was willing to live with Edmond at—' He broke off.

'It's all right, I've been to Chervais, I know where it is. Go on, Dr Jussot.'

'What possible inducement could make Paradou take up a job like that?' Marc said, wondering.

'Oh, well, he's being paid very handsomely, and he has a widowed sister to whom he's devoted—his salary is paid to her. And you know, leprosy isn't nearly as infectious as people imagine. Missionary doctors can spend their entire lives in leper colonies and never catch the disease—'

'And others can contract it after a short visit,' Marc said, having heard of such a case.

'Well, that's true. It seems to have something to do with the body's defences. You know how some people never catch so much as a cold—'

'This is different from the common cold, doctor,' Marc said. 'This is likely to last Edmond's entire life.'

Jussot nodded, looking sadly at his teacup. 'Unless the case burns itself out—it does that sometimes, and if the patient is declared free from infection then he can go back into society.'

'How long?' Nora asked, her face lighting up. 'What sort of time?'

'Who knows? Eight years, ten, twelve?'

'Eight *years!*'

'It's seldom less. I'm very sorry, Madame, but I have to be honest. You understand that even if he were to make a spontaneous recovery, he would be disfigured—the disease leaves marks, nerves are destroyed, he could go deaf or blind because of the inroads of the disease.'

Marc made an angry gesture, as if to silence him. But Nora caught his hand. 'No, Marc, I came here to be told the truth. Dr Jussot, is there any way in which Edmond and I can be in contact?'

'That is up to you. And to him, of course. I should think he would never permit it.'

'But I want him to see his son—'

'His son! My God, you have a child?'

'Yes, François, four months old—'

'Madame, on no account must you bring the child in contact with the father. Leprosy is particularly dangerous to children, and to male children at that. And you see, the fact that Edmond contracted the disease leads one to think he may be particularly susceptible, and the child may have inherited that susceptibility.'

'But . . . he's never seen the baby . . . it seems so cruel . . .'

'Yes, Madame,' Jussot agreed. 'It is one of the cruellest diseases in the world. It has been in existence since the time of the Pharaohs. And here we are, one-third of the way into the twentieth century, and still we do not know how to cure it.'

'There must be some line of enquiry,' Marc suggested. 'Research must be leading somewhere.'

Jussot shook his head. 'These are hard times, Monsieur. Money is very scarce for medical research. And since such funds as are available are dispensed by white men, they go to research on diseases that attack white men. Who cares that poor people in tropical countries live in misery from a disease that cuts them off from everything they hold dear? No, no, it will be a long time before leprosy is conquered.'

'But François will never see his father!' Nora cried. Her voice seared like a burning brand.

Jussot could find nothing to say.

'Doctor,' said Marc, 'I have in the past visited friends in an isolation hospital. I had a friend who had TB after the war . . . Wouldn't it be possible to let Edmond see the child—from a window, say?'

Jussot nodded and shrugged. 'It's possible, certainly. But surely you know Edmond! He won't allow it.'

'But—'

'You see, he'll feel it only makes things worse.'

'I could persuade him,' Marc said, nodding with determination. 'If I could just talk to him—'

'He won't come to the gate,' said Nora. 'I think he hated himself for coming that once.'

There was a pause.

'I have the telephone number of La Grange,' Jussot ventured in a troubled voice.

'The telephone! Of course! He rang me—'

'Yes, I insisted, when he told me his plan, that he must install a telephone before he went and cut himself off from the world. I couldn't have forgiven myself if there had been some emergency.'

They sat looking at each other. Then Jussot pulled towards him a tattered notebook. He turned the pages, held it out.

Marc dialled. It took an interminable time for the connection to be made on the old-fashioned, cumbersome French network. But at length Nora could hear a faint voice on the other end.

'Is that Paradou speaking? This is Marc Auduron-Tramont. Tell Monsieur du Ceddres that I need to speak to him.' A pause. 'I'm aware of that. Tell him that I'm with Dr Jussot, who himself gave me the number. Please ask him to come to the phone.'

A long pause. Then Marc nodded at Nora.

'Edmond?' he said into the receiver. 'This is Marc here. I want to come and see you.'

NINETEEN

The arguments Marc used with Edmond weren't successful at the first attempt. Three long telephone conversations took place, over four days.

In the end he prevailed. 'Damn it, boy, I'm nearly sixty years old,' he said. 'What does it matter if I'm exposed to infection? I'm prepared to take the risk, which Jussot in any case says isn't very great at my age. And we have to talk, face to face.'

'We can say all we have to say on the telephone, Marc.'

'Are you determined to be a martyr? Is that it? Because if—'

'That's a rotten thing to say,' Edmond said.

'Well, what possible reason can you have for not seeing me in person? You've seen Jussot, I hear—'

'Yes, twice—once when he let me stay with him in Paris, and once when he came to look me over. But Jussot's a doctor—'

'And I'm a lawyer. What difference does the profession make? We're both men, we're both vulnerable or not, as fate chooses.'

'But why take the risk, Marc? Why don't we—'

Marc didn't say, because I want to see if you're disfigured, I want to know if it would wound Nora to see you, I want to find out what the place is like so I can arrange *something*—so that you can see each other, so that you can look at your son.

Aloud he said, 'Are you afraid I'll reel back in horror? Is that it?'

And at that Edmond had given in.

Marc drove the big limousine with Nora and the baby in the back. This time she didn't bring Mariette along; the fewer people involved the better. They stopped in a larger village further down the valley, at a decent little hotel called La Fleche. They took a night's rest, although Nora was too tense to sleep and, to tell the truth, Marc had a restless night too.

When Marc rang the bell at La Grange about ten the next morning, he was admitted at once by the manservant.

'Good morning, sir. Did you have a good journey?'

'Not bad. You've had more snow up here than we saw on the road.'

'Yes, sir, the wind piles it up in the shadow of the slopes. Well, now . . . May I say a few things before I show you into the house?'

'Please. I'd value any advice.'

'Monsieur is not as yet greatly marked by the disease, but you'll see a noticeable patch now on his right cheek, and he's lost the sense of touch in most of the fingers of his left hand.'

'Does that mean that the illness is gaining a lot of ground?'

'It's not good, sir. However, Monsieur fights back. He has applications of medical oils which are supposed to help check the spread in time. He takes a lot of exercise, gardens, goes for walks—'

'Walks? I understood my cousin was told Monsieur du Ceddres never went out?'

'Well, that's what the villagers think. But in fact he walks up in the mountains. He's been out quite a few times in the winter, avoiding the footpaths of course. But as summer comes on and the climbers arrive, he'll stay inside the grounds except perhaps at night. There's a paved court all round the house with some plants and trees in little beds—you'll see, sir—if he wants exercise he can walk or run around those and cover quite a distance.'

'What does he do for entertainment?' asked Marc, thinking it sounded very drear.

'He listens to the radio, puts music on the gramophone. He's taught me chess—I don't play well but he says I'm improving.'

'And how is he? In spirits, I mean?'

'Er . . . That was really what I wanted to say to you, Monsieur Auduron-Tramont. He's . . . he's very unsettled by these recent events. He had resigned himself very well to never seeing anyone —in the first six months here, he was very equal in temper, never a cross word from him. But after Madame came . . .'

'Yes . . . Well . . . She was in the dark, you see. If she'd known, she might have handled it differently. It was a mistake not to tell her in the first place.'

'No, sir.'

'I beg your pardon?' Marc said, unaccustomed to be flatly contradicted by a servant.

'Excuse me for being blunt, sir. When I first came into the job I saw Madame's photograph on his bedside table and when I asked, he said it was the girl he'd been going to marry. He half-explained . . . that he'd cut himself off from her in the most callous way he could find, so that she'd be angry and hate him. Monsieur, I've served overseas, I've seen leprosy. I wouldn't want to condemn any woman I loved to being tied to a leper.'

'But the baby—'

'He didn't know about that at first, of course. I can tell you, sir, when he made that telephone call and she told him . . . Well, I thought he would lose his mind. He didn't talk to me—we didn't know each other well enough then, I'd only been with him a couple of weeks. He rang up his lawyers, and then he spent all night thinking about it, and next morning he telephoned again. He didn't tell me about the marriage for a long time. But of course, the minute I saw Madame at the grille, I knew who she was. And I knew it meant trouble.'

'Trouble,' repeated Marc, with some bitterness. 'Whichever way we go, there's going to be trouble. Madame isn't going to give up, you know.'

'She must, she really must, sir. You think they can look at each other from a distance and be satisfied with that? Well, it won't work. That's what I wanted to say, sir. Please believe me. The stress it would put on both of them—especially him, sir—and then you've got to understand that the patch on his face is going to get worse. Do you think he wants to subject her to that?'

Marc realized that they were like advocates arguing a case for a client except that they were far more personally involved than any advocate would ever allow himself to be. He stifled a sigh. Poor lad, to have no one to fight for him except a servant of a few months' standing.

'We'd better go in,' he said. 'He'll be wondering what we're doing.'

Foolishly, Marc had expected the interior to be as gloomy as the outside of the building. But Edmond had had the place painted in pale colours. On the stone floor of the entrance there were rush matting and a cheerful pottery vase for umbrellas and walking sticks . . . Past that, a narrow staircase went up, with doors beyond.

Edmond came to one of the doors, silhouetted against the light from within the room. 'Come in,' he said,

Marc obeyed, holding his breath for his first sight of him. Edmond went to a chair by the big log fire. When he turned, his face was clearly visible. He had a patch of white skin going from his cheek-bone to the chin on the right side. Yet he was still the same man—still very upright, spare, the dark brown hair well barbered, the eyes direct and keen.

Marc steeled himself. He went forward, holding out his hand.

'Oh come, don't be absurd,' Edmond said, waving him to a chair the far side of the hearthrug. He himself sat turned half away from him so that the white patch wasn't noticeable.

The room was comfortable after the manner of a bachelor establishment. On the pale green walls, landscapes were hung—they looked like Hobbema. The furniture was comfortable, made for use, leather armchairs and solid tables. On one table a chess game was laid out, half-played.

'Well,' Edmond remarked after he'd given Marc a moment for inspection, 'did you have a good chat with Jean about all my difficulties?'

Marc was taken aback. 'Well . . . he . . . I . . .'

'Jean's getting very protective. It's good of him, but I'm not incapable yet.'

'He says you're losing the sense of feeling in your left hand,' Marc said, deciding to plunge right in.

'Yes, worse luck. I hoped it might hold off a while yet. I try exercising it—I've taken up carpentry—but it's not like arthritis, you can't improve it by using the muscles.' He paused. 'If I can convince you of that, your visit will have been worth while. It's important to understand, Marc—no one knows how to prevent the inroads of this disease. It has to run its course, however long it takes. And I want you to know that things are going to get worse before they get better.'

'I understand that, my dear boy. I've had a long talk with Jussot—'

'God knows why I let his name slip out when I talked to Nora.' He stopped abruptly. Then, after a moment, he went on. 'How is Nora?'

'Fundamentally, she's well. She was determined to have a fine healthy baby so she took good care of herself—all that new-fangled nonsense about vitamins and so on, she paid heed to all that. But of course she's . . .'

'Unhappy.'

'That's putting it mildly.'

'I know how she feels,' Edmond said. His voice was the slightest bit unsteady.

'And the baby, he's—'

'Don't talk to me about the baby,' he interrupted. 'I don't want to hear it.'

'But Edmond! It's your own son—'

'Don't you understand? I'm trying not to care! If once I let him become a person to me, I'll never be able to . . . to . . . put him out of my life.'

'Edmond,' Marc said gently, 'why do you have to be so hard on yourself? You don't have to cut yourself off so completely. You could be in touch—we could send photographs—and there's the telephone, he could ring you up when he learns to talk—'

'For God's sake! And say what?' Edmond cried. 'Talk to a man he never sees, knows nothing about? What would we talk about? What happens here that I could report to him? I played chess with Jean, the leaves have come out on the birch tree in the courtyard, my left hand has completely ceased to function—is that it?'

'But you look on the dark side all the time, Edmond. You can recover—'

'Oh yes. In about ten years, perhaps.'

'Well, even if it's a long time. François ought to know his father in the meantime, be ready to meet him when he's able to rejoin—'

'Are you mad? Picture it—the great reunion! I clasp my son in my arms and what does this ten-year-old boy see? A total stranger with his face disfigured and some of his fingers missing!' Edmond jumped up, paced to the tall narrow window. The light fell on him. 'Look, Marc. This has happened in six months.'

The scar of the advancing disease was plain to see. He held out his left hand. There was a limpness about the three main fingers, which were marked with a shiny pinkish skin now.

'Think what may happen in ten years,' he said. 'Think what a nightmare I may be, and stop talking foolishness.'

Shock held Marc silent for a moment. He had told himself that he understood what was happening to Edmond, but the reality—and the possibilities of the future—were frightening.

Yet he had to remember Nora—Nora and her determination to do something for her husband. 'All right,' he agreed, 'the outlook's bad. But the boy is your son, yours and Nora's, and she wants him to know his father. Even in some slight degree, Edmond. You could let her write to you, and telephone from time to time.'

'I don't see the point. What would you tell the kid? This man—his father—is shut up in a building at the end of nowhere. He can't come out because he's dangerous to the rest of the world.'

'We'd tell him you're an invalid. That would be enough.'

'You think so? When he gets to school, and the other boys hear it—"your father's an invalid"—but you visit invalids, you take them flowers and grapes—how are you going to account for his never seeing me?'

'We'd think of something, man. Give us time—it's all new to us—'

'Well, it isn't new to me,' Edmond said without bitterness, 'and I know how it should be handled. Nora should divorce me as soon as it's legally possible. She can do it on grounds of desertion. Then she should marry some nice fellow who'll be a father to François, and forget all about me.'

'No!'

'It would be best, Marc. It's what I want her to do.'

'She never will. She loves you, Edmond.'

'Don't you think I know that?' The words flared out like a darting flame. But in a moment he had himself in hand again. 'It's because she loves me that she's in danger. She wants to see me—I know that, because it's what I'd want in her place. But it would be wrong. It would only make things worse.'

'She wants that, yes. But she also wants you to see the baby. I think she feels . . . I'm guessing but I think she feels it would give you something to live for.'

The words hung in the air between them.

Neither needed to say that Edmond had a choice—to live through whatever kind of life he might have before him, or to take his own way out.

Marc went on, 'She's very frightened. I don't blame her. She thinks the boy is your link with the future. If she can only get you to take an interest in him, you'll want to go on.'

'A child is open to infection, Marc—'

'Not if there's a lot of empty air between you. I drove around a little before I came here, my boy. There's a pretty substantial little stream runs down the mountain about half a mile up the road—if you were on one side of it and Nora with the baby on the other, I don't think any harm could possibly come to them.'

He could see Edmond was considering it.

'What's the stream called?' he asked, to prevent the other man from thinking of objections.

'The Marget. I often walk by it—how did you know?'

'I'd no idea. I just saw it and I thought . . . It's a natural barricade.'

Edmond was shaking his head. 'I don't think so. It's setting a precedent.'

'That's true. But you could go on seeing him—as long as you think it's right, as long as you think it wouldn't . . . wouldn't . . .'

'Frighten him out of his wits?'

'Edmond, there's a long way to go before that's

in question. Don't rush to meet sorrow. If in the end you have to cut yourself off entirely—'

'You ought to say "when", not "if"—'

'All right, all right. But in the meantime, give yourself some happiness. It would make you happy, don't deny it—to see the boy?'

'Oh yes.' There was a wealth of longing, impossible to conceal, in the words.

'Very well then. Shall I ring Nora and tell her?'

'Ring her?'

'She's sitting in the hotel, waiting.'

'You mean you told her you were going to try this on?'

'No, no. I didn't want to raise any hopes. But she's there, hoping and praying for something. Let me telephone her.'

Edmond shook his head. 'The telephone, I should think, is a very infectious point in the house. No. I'll ring her.'

Marc smiled to himself. Edmond stood staring at him in indecision but then suddenly gave in.

He went out. After a moment Paradou came in. 'He looks almost happy,' he said. 'What have you done, sir?'

'He's going to see his son.'

'Ah.' Paradou shrugged and smiled. 'You must be a very clever man, Monsieur.'

By and by Edmond and Marc went out together, Edmond leading the way and keeping a good space between himself and Marc. He still had plenty of strength. He led on up the steep

411

slope at a pace that kept Marc almost breathless behind him.

The air was very cold after the bad weather. Snow lay uneven underfoot. There was a path walked into it, where apparently Edmond had been out two or three times in the past few days. It led up a shoulder of the valley, over it and then back round a shallow depression. From its rim one could see the little river tumbling down in tumultuous young energy, refreshed by snows that had melted in the earlier spell of fine weather.

They came out on an uneven cliff overlooking the stream. Below, it rushed away in a spate of cold grey water over and around grey boulders. A snow bunting flew up as they took up a position on the rocks.

They waited.

By and by the sound of a car could be heard. Nora had hired it at the hotel in a flurry of impatience after Edmond's phone call. She took the mountain road with tremendous care, in reaction to an elation that tempted her to be careless. She was going to see Edmond!

The baby clad in layers of wool, slept in the Moses basket to which he'd become quite accustomed. The dull daylight shone on his rosy face Already she could picture herself holding him up to Edmond could imagine the smile of delight that would light up his father's face.

It would make all the difference. It would be

a link with life. So long as he could sometimes see the child, Edmond would try to go on living.

She saw the two figures on the bluff. She slowed, guided the car into the side of the road, and put on the brake. Then she got out, fastened her suede coat against the keen wind, and picked up François.

When he felt the cold air on his cheeks he woke, blinking. Then he gave a little whimper of annoyance. She sheltered him against her shoulder.

'Shh . . . now François, be good. You're going to see your father.'

She walked up the slope to the side of the stream. It was about ten feet wide, deep and forceful. She picked her way with care. François went on voicing his disagreement with this form of entertainment.

She had some yards to go to be exactly opposite. Edmond moved suddenly, overcome with longing to see them. He strode forward on his side of the water. Marc, taken by surprise, made to follow him.

His feet went from him on the icy rocks. He felt himself go headlong, flung out a hand to save himself from crashing on his face, hit a rock with his arm and went over sideways into the stream.

Nora saw Edmond swing round. Marc was being carried away at once by the strength of the current, breathless with the fall and the iciness of the water. He couldn't even call for help.

Without a moment's hesitation Edmond jumped. 'Edmond!' Nora screamed, but it was far too late to stop him.

For a moment there was no way of distinguishing one man from the other. They were a thrashing pair in the midst of a torrent of water among the boulders. They went downstream together, passing the spot that Nora had reached on her side of the water.

There was no way she could help. The baby was in her arms, if she turned and ran she might slip with him and fall. She looked about for a second, wild to find a safe place to put him down. But there was only slippery snow and rock.

Marc and Edmond were far past her, downstream, always downstream, their heavy winter clothes saturated now with water, dragging them down. She saw a hand shoot out, grasp an overhang on the far side of the stream. For a moment the two struggling figures paused. Marc heaved himself up, or was helped up. He fell across the outcrop of rock, his upper body half-balancing the downward drag of his legs. He threw out his hands, grabbed at the roots of some mountain shrub. He heaved, strained, came further out of the water.

But Edmond could find nowhere to grasp—the only spot was where Marc was pulling himself out. He went on down the fast current, dashed against the rocks as he went.

'Edmond!' cried Nora. 'Edmond, hold on—'

She ran down the side of the brook, careless now whether she fell or not. She slipped, went sprawling. The baby, crashing to the ground, screamed in terror. She got to her knees, caught him safely to her. 'François . . .' But he was unharmed, the cocoon of shawls had saved him from injury. She laid him down again, in a cranny between two great boulders.

She sprang up, raced down the bank of the stream. She was just in time to see Edmond go over a waterfall about thirty yards ahead.

Gasping, weeping, calling his name, she scrambled down among the wilderness of boulders that led to the pool below.

Edmond was lying there, wedged among the rocks. He had dropped ten feet with great force. She threw herself into the calm pool, heedless of the icy grip of the water.

He was lying face down, head towards her. She got her arms under his shoulders and heaved with all her strength. She dragged him, pulled and tugged, and got him through the shallows of the pool to the bank.

She fell on the rocky edge, pulled Edmond's head into her lap. 'Edmond . . . Edmond . . .'

His eyes were closed. The white patch on his cheek was covered with the blood that had flowed from a great gash on his head.

He never heard her as she called to him to open his eyes, to speak to her. At last she laid him down. With a great, wearisome effort, she got to her feet. Almost at a shamble she went back up the side of the stream.

Her little son was lying in the cranny where she had left him. He had managed to get one fist free from the shawls and was waving it in the air, crying furiously at being left in this cold, unwelcoming spot.

She took him into her arms, held him close, stood shivering, murmuring to him. Sometimes she said his name, sometimes she said his father's.

That was how Marc and Jean Paradou found her when they got to her half an hour later.

TWENTY

Since Marc was too shaken and Nora too dazed, Jean paradou took charge for the time being. Before he even reported the accident, he did what he had always been told to do if anything went wrong at La Grange. He rang Dr Jussot in Paris.

Jussot arrived next morning. By that time the body had been taken to the mortuary of the little hospital down the valley, and Nora was beginning to get her wits back. Marc, however, was in bed suffering from the gashes and contusions and the effects of physical shock. A polite sergeant of police was waiting in the hotel lounge to interview Madame and Monsieur when they were ready.

'How much should I tell him, doctor?' Nora asked Jussot.

'Just answer his questions about the accident.'

'But there has to be a post mortem. The local police surgeon will see—'

'I'll try to deal with that. We don't want a fuss, Nora. It's the last thing Edmond would have wanted.'

'Yes.'

Jussot introduced himself to the police surgeon who, at first, was annoyed at interference from a Parisian know-all. But Jussot was so polite and so flattering that they collaborated on the post mortem. They easily agreed that death had been due to a 'pond' fracture of the parietal bone caused by a fall on to some hard matter, in this instance the rocks at the foot of the waterfall. Contributing factors were a compound fracture of the left tibia and many lesions and wounds to the face. As to any variations of skin colour, these were lost among the bruises and discolorations caused by the accident.

Without any hesitation the police surgeon signed the death certificate, shook hands warmly with Dr Jussot, and invited him home for a drink.

The police sergeant carried out his enquiries then forwarded his report to the inspector. The inspector summarized the statements before submitting them to the *sousprefêt*. He, an impatient man, skimmed through them.

Madame and Monsieur du Ccddrcs were walking with their baby and a cousin of Madame's, Monsieur Auduron-Tramont, by the River Marget, which was very high because of the recently melted snows. Monsieur Auduron-Tramont slipped and fell in, Monsieur du Ceddres leapt in and was able to help him to safety. (See Site A on attached plan.) He, however, was unable to find any other spot at which to get a handhold and was swept over the waterfall at Site B. Body recovered at Site C—Madame's deposition records that she tried to drag him out.

Conclusion: No suspicious circumstances. The *sous-prefêt* initialled it and added, 'Recommendation: No further proceedings.' The *juge d'instruction* concurred. The body was released for burial.

To the surprise of the village of Chervais, Madame decided to have her husband laid to rest in the local cemetery. Touched, they asked that representatives from the village should be allowed to attend the funeral. Marc, who was restored more or less to himself after one helpless day in bed, asked that only a senior member of the local parish council should come, since the funeral was to be private.

The news of the accident had of course reached Paris. But Paris was in an uproar over the repudiation of the disarmament clauses of the Versailles

Treaty by the Germans, and the Bourse was having hysterics over the devaluation of the Belgian franc. In other times they would have made a great story out of it: married only a little over a year, glamorous rich young widow, orphaned son of only four months now heir to the Tramont wine fortune and his father's considerable estates . . . But the funeral was to be very small-scale and so they deputed a young reporter from a news agency in Lyons.

It was the local custom for the women to remain at the church after the funeral mass and for only the men to go to the interment. Nora bowed to this tradition. And so Edmond Renaud du Ceddres was followed to the grave by the local curé and four men: Marc Auduron-Tramont, Dr Albert Jussot, Jean Paradou and Georges Manasse of Chervais.

Later, when the cemetery was empty, its headstones gleaming within the snug boundary wall on the mountain slope, Nora went alone with her arms full of spring flowers. She spread them on the newly turned earth. For a long time she stood there with head bent.

She wasn't praying—she didn't know who to pray to. She was waiting for Edmond to speak to her, to explain his death, to give it meaning.

It troubled her greatly. Even through the first haze of grief, doubts had gnawed at her. The routines of the police enquiry and the funeral deflected the first agony. Then there had been the need to dispose of the contents of La Grange without spreading any infection: Paradou and Jussot had dealt with that. Paradou had been given a hand some sum when his services were dispensed with.

There were many letters of condolence to answer. There was her son to care for, but the after-effects of Edmond's death made her unable to breast-feed any more. There had been some trouble in the ensuing change-over from mother's milk, but in the end he accepted the new regime. He was thriving, gaining weight as he should, looking every day more like the father he would never see.

Yet all the time the doubts in Nora's heart grew stronger. They were back at Calmady before she mentioned them to Marc.

He had taken charge of the matter of raising a headstone for Edmond. He had to discuss it with her.

'I should like to have an inscription on it, Nora. He saved my life. I should like to have the version of the lines from St John that are generally used, "Greater love hath no man, that he give up his life for his friend". Do you agree?'

She shook her head.

'Too fulsome? But it's true, Nora.'

'Is it?' Suddenly she was able to ask the question. 'Is that why he died, Marc? Just to save you? Or did he decide to take that way out?'

'Nora!'

'I saw him swept past by the current, you know. I *saw* him. He wasn't making any effort to save himself.'

'Dearest girl . . .' He rose, came to her, put his hands on her shoulders. He looked down at her gravely. 'Don't torment yourself with thoughts like that. I was with Edmond for more than an hour before he telephoned you that day. Ask Paradou if you like. He told me—for the first time in weeks Edmond looked happy. I assure you, Nora—he was looking forward to seeing you and François. I'd persuaded him that there could be months, years, before he had to accept total banishment. For that moment he was happy. He had something to live for.'

'But he saved *you*. Why didn't he save himself?'

'I walked both banks of that stream later, Nora. With the water so high, that spot where he heaved me out was the only handhold. And *I* was lying half-dead on it—he couldn't grab at anything except me, and probably drag me in again.'

'And yet—'

Marc led her to the sofa. There he pulled her down to sit beside him, but turned so that he could look her squarely in the face. He wanted her to know he was telling her what he utterly believed, what he felt was the absolute truth. 'You have no conception how cold it was, my dear. I couldn't feel what I was grabbing to pull myself out with, and I have two good hands. Marc had almost completely lost the use of his left hand—the nerves of the fingers had atrophied. His right hand was probably numb with the cold. And his clothes were saturated, dragging him down—I know, mine felt like a lead weight when I ran for help.'

There was a long pause. He could see shadows of fears and memories in Nora's strange, clear eyes. 'You see, I feel it was my fault,' she said in a low voice. 'I wanted so much to see him, to show François to him. I feel I forced the situation on him, and that it was perhaps too much . . . That he felt I would be too strong for him, that I'd force him to what he felt was dangerous.'

'You're wrong. He wanted to see the child. He wanted to live for him, and for you. His death was a tragic accident.'

He said it with all the sincerity he could put into his voice.

He could see how Nora's mind was working. She thought that Edmond had seen a door open for him, through which he could with honour leave a life that had become intolerable. By his death he would free his wife and son from a burden that could only grow greater as time went on. Once he had made certain Marc was safe, he might have let the water take him where it would—and it had taken him to a hard death among the rocks of a mountain pool.

But Edmond wouldn't have wanted Nora to

suffer remorse. Grief was enough for her to bear, to heap guilt and unending regret on her would be too much.

She must be convinced that her husband had died accidentally, through an act of courage for which he deserved the highest praise. It was what Marc knew to be true but he lacked the eloquence to make it clear to her.

He said simply: 'You should be proud when you think of Edmond. Most men can be brave when it comes to the point—if they're made angry enough, or if they stand to lose a lot. But Edmond had something more. He could face the knowledge of his illness, he could change his life so that as few people as possible were harmed. When he jumped in to save me, that was a different aspect of the same man, bravery in action. He was never a coward. And he wasn't the kind of man to leave you with a load of guilt—for that reason alone, he would never have just *let* himself die.'

'You really believe that?'

'I know it.'

She turned her head away, saying nothing. She got up, moved uncertainly about the room. When she looked back at him he saw that she had accepted what he said. Perhaps she didn't entirely believe it but it was a creed by which she could reshape her life. Edmond had wanted to live, but she knew he might have been glad to die in that moment, with his son held up for him to see in his mother's arms.

'As to the headstone,' she murmured, 'I should prefer something simple. His name and the date of his death. He wouldn't want any unnecessary tributes.'

'But I feel—'

'I know—we owe him more.' It was a simple statement of fact. They had learned in those last days how strong Edmond could be and they wanted to make a memorial for him, something worthy.

Years ago, the founder of the House of Tramont had named a great wine after the man she loved and lost. But that was not appropriate for Edmond. Wine had not been of importance in his life except that Nora reigned over a great wine estate. Otherwise, like most men, he regarded champagne as something to drink when there was a celebration.

It was true that a great wine was being made this year. A bitter vintage to Nora, for it would mark the year she was widowed. But she could hear in her mind Edmond's laughter if she suggested giving his name to it. 'Me? My name on a label? No, no —that doesn't sound like me, Nora.'

What else had she to offer? She had wine. She had money.

She said, 'Marc, I've been thinking of starting a fund to help research into leprosy.'

'Oh . . .' It was a note of caution. 'That would attract attention, don't you think? And gossip . . .'

'I don't see why—'

'Come now—your husband has just died soon after returning from Africa, suddenly you give money to a fund to investigate a cure for a terrible disease—'

'I could do it anonymously. Jussot would handle it for me.'

'But then, Nora . . . Edmond would never be connected with it. How would that be a memorial to him?'

'*We* would know. That's all that matters, surely. And Edmond . . .'

Marc smiled and sighed. 'You think Edmond would know? You believe that?'

She shook her head. 'Perhaps not. I went to the grave, you know, Marc. I stood there calling to him in my heart, asking him to speak to me so that I would understand what had happened to him. I couldn't . . . couldn't believe . . . that he had simply ceased to exist. But nothing happened. I didn't hear his voice, I didn't sense him near me.'

'My dearest girl . . .' He came to her, put an arm about her slender waist. 'He's here, always with us. He's here, in your thoughts of him, in my regard for him—in his son, who's going to be so like him.'

She leaned her head against his shoulder. He

had always been there, all her life. He offered her an affection pure and dependable.

'You'll help me to make a good job of bringing up François?' she murmured. 'You'll tell me if I'm getting too possessive?'

'But will you listen to me?'

They both smiled. It was the first tiny joke they had had between them since the awful news of Edmond's illness broke upon them.

'I'll always listen to you, Marc. You've always been the best friend I had in the world. And I know you'll be a friend to François too. I want you to help me make him into a man his father would have been proud of.'

Marc looked ahead into the future. He felt he had some ten good years ahead of him still, ten years in which to be a father still to Nora and beyond her to her son. He felt a surge of hope, of energy. He had something to live for—and that was strange, for when Gaby died he had been sure nothing would ever make his heart beat strongly again.

But for Nora, there would always be an emptiness. Edmond himself had told her she must remarry, but she knew she never would. Even if she were ever to feel something like love again for a man, marriage was out of the question.

In the House of Tramont, a young widow in black went once again to the desk in the office, to take up the duties of running the great wine house. Men come and go, but the land remains, the land and its fruits—the vines with their precious burden, the juice that flows into the vats, the sharp juice that makes the wine of celebration, kept for a generation perhaps in coolness and the dark. For although there is grief, there will be joy. To everything there is a season.

Work and time, time and work . . . out of those two ingredients a life can be made.

Nora du Ceddres-Tramont had more. She had a loving, steady friend to be with her through the years to come, the years already threatened by war clouds.

And she had a son to bring up to fill the place in the world that Edmond had left for him.

We very much hope you have enjoyed
this Large Print Book

If you would like to find out about
our range of other titles,
you can either enquire at your
local library or contact
the publishers by writing to us at:

Remploy Press
Lightowler Road
Hanson Lane
Halifax
HX1 5NB
or by telephone on 0422 350517

Our policy at Remploy Press is to
continually improve our product and
we would welcome any suggestion or
ideas of additional titles you may
have, from you . . . our valued readers